Discovering the World

Discovering the World

THIRTEEN STORIES

Thomas Jeffrey Vasseur

MERCER UNIVERSITY PRESS
MACON, GEORGIA
2001

ISBN 0-86554-718-1
MUP/H538

© 2001 Mercer University Press
6316 Peake Road
Macon, Georgia 31210-3960
All rights reserved

First Edition.

Book designed by Mary Frances Burt

∞The paper used in this publication meets the minimum
requirements of American National Standard for Information
Sciences—Permanence of Paper for Printed Library Materials,
ANSI Z39.48-1992.

Library of Congress Cataloging-in-Publication Data

Vasseur, Jeffrey Thomas.
Discovering the world : thirteen stories / Thomas Jeffrey Vasseur.
p. cm.
ISBN 0-86554-718-1
1. Southern States—Vietnam Literature—Social life and customs— Fiction.
I. Title.

PS3622.A85 D57 2001

813'6--dc21   2001018293

Contents

"Wherever you are, wherever you stay, wherever you stand motionless, the world is like the one you covet."

—Jean Giono

Noonan

The summer I was twelve, I would stand alongside Route 45 and watch a red Pitt Special do hammerhead stalls at dusk. It was a hot, thick-aired summer, reeking of honeysuckle and the diesel fuel on my father's work clothes, a time when time itself began to change for me and the world stopped being a child's. Because of some of the things that happened that year, I started realizing that the turquoise-colored globe sitting on our living room coffee table was really a gigantic place full of thousands and thousands of backyards, some like my own—huge famous rivers and colorful rectangles of land—an inexhaustible world by any boy's, girl's, or any one family's standards. I learned that if you couldn't imagine the world from another person's perspective—much less from, say, a thousand at once—then you should strive for a more complete view if at all possible or find a way to see the things that surrounded people's decisions, their habits and beliefs and their pasts. And even then you had only begun to understand them, who and why and what they were, because of the other people they lived with and among, people who necessarily influenced their compulsions, their talents, and limitations. This was the same stretch of time when I first learned how to listen and how to throw a curveball, when I heard my parents briefly hate each other and saw drunkenness for the first time. I don't think it would be an exaggeration to say that I stumbled across death too that year, discovered how you could become drawn-in, or invigorated just by the thought of it.

Noonan William's biplane appeared one day in the same area which Calvert City's smokestacks occupied along the horizon, burning invisibly during daylight, but always towering there off in the distance, marking the spot where my father and so many of my friends' fathers had worked, or still did—Union Carbide, Air Products, and B. F. Goodrich. The orange fires from the chemical plants seemed ages away to me back then, strange but beautiful, ironically remote, unconnected to the communities surrounding them. At night bright flames flickered steadily at the tips of these smokestacks and once, when I was even younger, three or perhaps four years old, I asked my father why the flames never burned the stacks themselves. He told me that they had been designed that way. "Because they're not supposed to," my father explained.

The air stunts began in the early spring and they lasted throughout all of the hottest and more humid months. At the first buzz of an engine, I used to run out the screen door and turn up the driveway where a persimmon tree had gnawed through the graveled surface. Standing before the highway, I would watch Noonan fly. For the longest time no one knew it was him up there, but everyone watched for the plane: farmers spraying soybeans, women hanging their wash, children riding their bicycles on the tar-gooey road up to J. R. Sullivan's for Fudgesicles or frozen banana twin-pops. Sometimes you could see a goggled speck and a tiny waving arm as the pilot flew low after doing some maneuvers, or perhaps you heard the engine at night, its pitch suddenly soft, then loud again, as the plane rose and dropped through the air.

By the time school let out and summer vacation had started, Noonan flew generally around sunset, about seven o'clock, then later and later as the days grew muggier and longer. In the beginning, all the people who knew him well had their suspicions about what he had been doing with his spare time, but no one knew it was actually Noonan—not for sure. By mid-June everyone began to expect the sound of the plane at dusk, and they looked forward to the air show that would follow. People started sitting around in lawn chairs until someone said "sssshhh," cupped a hand to their ear, then scanned the horizon. If it was a false call, they would tease the person who said he or she had heard something, then everyone would stand around and talk some more, drawing out their conversations between trimming their grass or watering the shrubbery. They remained talking and stayed outside, just in case the biplane would suddenly appear after all. People began waiting a little longer before they went indoors and turned on their television sets, chatting to one another about come what may, watching from their backyards or from their front porch swings.

I suppose it was at the picnic at Coach Burkeen's house that I first saw him in person. Noonan Williams was sponsoring our Little League baseball team that summer, and he had bought us new uniforms, red and white pinstriped ones with Williams Concrete printed over the player's number. Many of our fathers knew Noonan well and had known him for many years. Almost all of them had worked together in the chemical plants at some point and many were construction workers like my father, pipefitters, operators, or teamsters. Some of them had been on the same basketball team together in high school, then had joined the Marine Corps after graduation. Throughout the picnic at Coach Burkeen's the men stood around and growled out stories, laughing loud, deep, Parris Island laughs. We were expecting a championship season that year and there were two tables covered with food: barbecue, baked beans, potato salad, and watermelons sunk in troughs of ice water for dessert. All throughout the meal, a couple of our mothers took turns scurrying in a silent contest to see that glasses of lemon tea were brimming. Noonan and his wife arrived late. The men all shook hands with him, and they talked and joked with him for a while. They were nice enough to Mr. and Mrs. Williams, but they had acted strange somehow, quite different, just as soon as he arrived. It was as though they thought Noonan shouldn't have come to Coach Burkeen's along with all the rest of the families, and, after saying hello to them, Noonan spent most of the afternoon away from the men, sitting upright on the edge of a lawn chair, eating from a plate Mrs. Burkeen had made up for him and joking with all of their wives.

My teammates and I had so much in common at that age, in that time and place. Most of our fathers had tanned, rugged faces from working under the sun all day, but Noonan Williams had a face that was even darker, almost black, the color of the ice tea he was drinking without lemon. I remember him telling Mrs. Burkeen just to fill the glass full of ice, then to pour. Whenever he talked or laughed his teeth flashed brightly against his brown skin and the dark clothes he wore that day. He had on a navy-blue sports shirt, blue jeans, and wore sandals, I recall, because none of my father's friends wore sandals, or tennis shoes either for that matter. Hearing one of them say that Noonan was becoming a "real card," I glanced over and noticed that his hair was long for a man his age in 1973, long, at least, for the part of the world where we lived. Not shaggy, or over his shoulders, but considerably longer than that of the flat-topped men who remained standing, loosely in a group, huddled together over by the well-house.

Some of my friends were playing hotbox on the opposite side of the yard, but I quit the game to stand where the men were talking under their breaths. They began glancing around from time to time, looking over their shoulders, or from under a tilted Pepsi, to where Noonan sat talking with all the women.

"He used to be a go-getter, but he's a fat cat now," one man said.

"Letting his business go to the dogs," said another.

The first man explained that Noonan was letting someone else manage the company for him. He shook his head and cleared a kernel of corn from his front teeth, stared at this, then flipped his toothpick onto the lawn.

"I don't know about that," the other one said. "The old boy's making a mint pouring swimming pools. But that's all right," he said. "He'll find out. He'll discover what all of this pussyfooting around will do for him."

"The son of a bitch really soaks it up," said the second man. "Drinks like a fish whenever he takes a notion."

"Hell, so do we—that's not what I'm talking about," the first man said, and then everyone laughed.

When Noonan and his wife got up from their lawn chairs, he came over and chatted with all the men some more before leaving. Noonan explained that the uniforms were ordered, then asked if anyone had been up on the lake lately. He had recently heard Bob Vannerson say that the crappie were still spawning, and that was a lot later than usual wasn't it? Noonan talked about fishing with the men he knew who fished, then he shook everyone's hand for the second time and smiled awkwardly before moving away. After he started towards his car, something told me that my father and his friends thought differently of Noonan Williams than they had in the past. There was something between them that had changed. During the last couple of years his concrete company had become very profitable due to all of the subdividing going on and the new interstate coming through Western Kentucky. Because of all the septic tanks and swimming pools, all the culverts and cement he sold, Noonan Williams was starting to get wealthy, and now he had been "gallivanting" and "carrying on" some people said, living in a way which I heard more than one adult characterize as being selfish or ridiculous or wild.

"We'll see y'all at the game," Mrs. Williams yelled over her shoulder from their dark green Corvette. She was a pretty lady and had bleached blonde hair, Mrs. Burkeen explained later on, though I couldn't tell the difference and I didn't care.

Noonan appeared more serious now, focused, as he pulled down his sunglasses and started away. I liked the way he looked in those glasses, with his wife, driving that car.

At that point it was perhaps six o'clock. Maybe six-thirty. After the Williamses had left, most everyone else stayed to eat the watermelon, then we talked about the upcoming baseball season. The men discussed new highway jobs coming up, and someone mentioned taking our team to St. Louis so we could see the Cardinals. Of course, my friends and I were all wide-eyed, excited and fascinated by the idea of watching a professional baseball game. So Buddy Robinson, the third baseman's father, promised to see what he could do about rounding-up a bus for the trip to St. Louis. "The cat has burst out of the bag while it's still just a kitten," Mr. Robinson exclaimed, but he thought he could come up with something. A thin, busy man who sold insurance, he was also our first base coach. Whenever we went on road trips or to play in all-star tournaments in Illinois, Buddy Robinson usually chartered and drove the bus. He smoked cigars and talked endlessly while he drove, tallying up our mistakes during previous games and offering sprawling solutions, always inserting the phrase "on it" into his conversation whenever he was excited, nervous, or thinking about what he was going to say next. "If I were you, on it, I'd always take the first strike." Next, he would pause and struggle briefly, then begin again. "On it, so you can see what these new pitchers are going to throw at you." "You're still dropping your elbow, on it, and you've gotta learn from your mistakes. It's like Bill Christian, the man who lives down the street from me. One day he cut off the tip of his index finger clearing out the grass chute from his lawn mower while it was still running. Three weeks after they'd sewed it back on I stopped while he was out in the yard and asked him how did he do it. So Bill reached down to show me, on it, and he cut his index finger off again!"

It had been over an hour since Noonan had driven away in the green convertible Corvette with his pretty wife. My friends and I were excited about the road trip. We were playing a version of tag which involved throwing a wiffle ball at one another's bare legs when we first heard the biplane's engine, then we quickly headed for a clearing at the back of the two-acre lot. There was much pointing and a relative hush, all except for the distant motor, which sounded like a horsefly in a jar at first, then grew progressively louder as the plane came closer. "Whoever's in that thing must have a screw loose," Coach Burkeen said. But I noticed that he too wore an expression of muted excitement and fascination, adult envy, like he'd just witnessed a grand slam in Busch Stadium or had seen Lou Brock walking through the local supermarket. This was a look which showed how he was inwardly thrilled by such an occurrence, but determined to act calm as he stood up and clapped with all the other fans in the stands, or strolled over with his grocery cart to ask Lou for an autograph.

Most of our parents shook their heads and we all smiled reversed smiles, with our mouths open, as the pilot dipped down, turning the plane's wings over slowly, quite deliberately, like the hands of some special clock he was setting. I'll always remember how my mother put her hands on her hips and "aahhh-ed" as the scarlet biplane flipped over gradually, then roared upside down over the subdivision.

My friends and I went wild.

. . . .

That year I had a feud going with Greg Edgeman, the pitcher for Mullen Motors. He had a better fastball than me and could hit home runs at will, it seemed, but we got along fine off the field. I liked him because he was continually grinning, wearing some sort of stain—mustard or a grape Kool-Aid crescent usually—pasted on his round and beaming freckled face. The games between Williams Concrete and Mullen Motors were always drawn-out and dead-serious, especially for our mothers and fathers. We played them on the first game of the season that summer, and Noonan Williams sat on the top of the bleachers, cheering us all on, yelling "Fire 'em in, Hoss!" as I pitched, standing up and shouting at the occasionally blind umpires, until his wife wrapped her arms around him and locked her fingers together behind his neck. After the game Noonan bought the team hot dogs and snow cones at the concession stand, but we had lost on another home run by Greg Edgeman.

My father hadn't come to the game. For some reason, or perhaps several, he and my mother weren't getting along that year, or maybe I should say that their closeness would come and go. Sometimes they would try and do things together, like when they hired a babysitter and went to the picnic at Coach Burkeen's, but then things would get worse again and would stay that way for a while. I never knew what had happened between them exactly, but whatever had happened left a scar that took some time to heal. Their bitterness had its origins in something I can only vaguely account for even now, something which had to do with guilt, resentment, or maybe even money—the extra bills which started coming in after my baby brother was born. There was a subdued yet very tense atmosphere in our household, and all I can trace it to solidly, for sure, is the night when they began talking to one another angrily, using voices I had never heard from either of them. Not ever in our house. Not anywhere else. The words and names came out high-pitched and hateful sounding, violent and shrill as they drifted back to my bedroom.

I lay wide-awake staring at the walls. Something told me that I should stay put and keep out of this, so I kept perfectly still and just listened, asking myself what sort of horrible, irrevocable thing had happened. I wondered if my parents were discussing a fire, or a car wreck, and if things would ever be the same again—even in a million years. What happened next is muddled because of the passage of time and the inevitable distortions of maturity, but its outcome remains crystal clear and still seems awful. Many things were said that night which carried meanings I couldn't understand then, so I would never remember them precisely. But I definitely recall the yelling and some cursing and then my father saying: "Okay. That's it!" He said this quickly, in a somewhat quieter voice, but with a decisive tone which seemed to clarify something for them both.

Next, I heard him come thundering through the dining room, sounding bigger and heavier than I had ever thought of him as being, and then my mother behind him saying: *Don't go, don't go... I'm sorry... Don't leave tonight, please don't leave like this.* Next there was the sound of the aluminum screen door slamming and shattering glass, and then my mother's inscrutable pleading. Then silence. From my bedroom, I soon heard only the crick-crick of insects again, coming from behind the thin storm window at the head of my bed. But as I found out later and can imagine hearing now, with my mother's ears, and seeing in slow motion with her eyes, there was something else that occurred out of earshot, some comparatively undramatic sound which preceded another louder one and had followed my father's huge angry footsteps out the door and into the driveway—a sound which stopped him there. A sickening sound which forced him to turn and come back before he got into the car and left the house. From where I lay, the silence was suddenly pierced by my baby brother's screaming, then my mother's voice—a calmer, human voice I could recognize but which was nonetheless frightening: *Come back, oh my God, please come back... how... how... how could this have happened,* she began sobbing, the sound of my brother's wailing helpless now and knowing no boundaries, and my mother equally out of control.

Finally, my father came back inside. He asked me if I could be a big boy and go back to sleep for him while he drove my mother to the hospital. She had accidentally dropped Andy and they needed to go to the emergency room, he explained. My father was shaking too and that scared me more than anything else I had heard or had imagined so far. His face was the color of my sheets.

This happened shortly after my little brother's first birthday, the summer we won the Bantam league championship and the same year that Noonan Williams did something which made an indelible impression on hundreds of people besides myself. I should tell you that when my mother stumbled and lost her grip that night on the back porch, Andy flew from her shoulder face forward and landed with his chin just over the edge of a concrete step, which had fractured his collarbone but broken his fall. The injury could have been serious, much much worse, and I realized this from watching my parents, noticing how they treated each other and avoided the subject during all the weeks which followed. At first, I believed they would be kinder to one another after the accident, and in a way they were, but it took some time.

My father started working harder than ever, and he began building B. S. A. motorcycles with our neighbor Sonny Calhoun. Sonny was a boilermaker at one of the plants in Calvert City, and now he lived all alone. My mother disliked him. But I don't think her reasons had anything to do with Sonny's character or some of the rumors we had heard. All I'm sure of is that Sonny became tied-up with the complex things that were happening between her and my father and the financial problems they were having. She always complained about their new enterprise. They worked nights in the garage and the clanking and carrying-on kept her up, she said. But my father claimed we needed the extra money. Whenever she complained about Sonny as a choice for a business partner—he was a brute, an animal, she said—my father would defend him and say my mother would feel differently if she only knew Sonny's side of the story, or if she had seen the scratches on his face the day his wife Leslie left him for another man. No matter what he said, though, my mother was always ice-cold to Sonny. She hated those motorcycles with a passion, perhaps because my father always kept one around for himself to ride. He and Sonny would work sometimes past midnight, long after I heard my mother get up and shut off Johnny Carson. So this, too, was part of that summer. My father's new business-on-the-side and the different stories I heard about Leslie and Sonny. Who knows what actually happened between them? But she had slapped him, and he had slapped her, and once Leslie did walk around the grocery store with a black eye and her hair pulled tight in a ponytail.

The unassembled motorcycles arrived in huge wooden crates, and I was amazed that Sonny and my father could put all the parts together and make the motors run. There were huge hunks of metal in meaningless shapes: entire engines and pieces of frame, detached headlights and kickstands, and the tiny ball bearings which Sonny greased and placed inside the accelerator handles. I would help pack them in sometimes, and Sonny once said that if it wasn't for ball bearings then the world would be in bad shape indeed. Then he would rub his belly and grin. "Makes things smooth," he would say.

run outside, drawn like moths or catfish to lanterns. They saw something irreverent and foredoomed in what Noonan did. He would zoom over the land adjacent to subdivisions, glide over their remaining farmland, but always pull up in time. People felt sure that something would eventually go wrong—an error in judgment, a malfunction, the wind. And Noonan Williams was the kind of person who gave them the impression that something just might.

One evening he came to a baseball game and sat in the bleachers very quietly, something highly unusual for Noonan. He never made a complaint about any of the umpire's calls, then afterwards I heard Ernest Boyd's mother say that he had hardly spoken to anyone all night long, and that he'd been drunk as a skunk. "He's just got no business coming to the boys' game like that," she said.

A couple of days later, I was downtown buying a batting glove when Noonan walked in front of the sporting goods store. I ran outside and yelled, and he turned around suddenly, like a rabbit that has been flushed and frightened, and whose quick movements in turn frighten you.

"Are you coming to the tournament?" I asked him, a little confused by his reaction and by the strange way he looked.

Noonan's hair was blowing around and his suntanned face was even darker with stubble. He stared back at me blankly and didn't say a word, squinted his eyes and looked alternately into mine, then vaguely over them to a space above the top of my head. Then I smelled the sharp, sweetish smell, something I would know later as bourbon. And that's when I first suspected that Noonan Williams was drunk. Still drunk, or drunk again. When I showed him my new batting glove Noonan's expression changed, though. He became relaxed, affable, familiar.

"Why hello boy," he said clearly, without slurring.

It seemed as though my face had just slipped his memory. So I reminded him again about the upcoming baseball tournament.

"Sure, sure. I'll be there."

"My slider really works good now," I told him. "And you don't have to throw your arm half-off either, you know? It all depends on how you hold the seams."

"Same thing that makes an airplane fly," Noonan told me.

He nodded and appeared quite interested in what I'd just said, then, in a split-second, his eyes clouded over. He seemed far away once again.

"The coach told me not to throw the slider at all," I told him. "But me and the catcher think it might surprise some of the batters."

"Well," Noonan said. "You're awfully young to be throwing curveballs if you ask me. Just don't hurt yourself. Be careful with that arm. Listen here," he told me, quite out of the blue. "Have you ever been up in an airplane? You ever been flying?"

"No," I said. "I never have."

Noonan Williams laughed and mussed up my hair in a playful, respectful way which I still remember and at the time considered rare in many adults. "Well, I've got myself an airplane," he told me. "So I was wondering if you would like to go flying with me sometime? How about tomorrow morning?"

Of course, I wanted to say yes, right then and there, more than anything in the world, but I hesitated and thought through my options. I mumbled something about having to have the yard mowed by the time my father got home from work. "I promise to have you home in plenty of time for that," Noonan said. "I was lucky to have run into you today. Get permission from your folks, and I'll pass by around eight in the morning. That sound okay?"

It was as far as I was concerned. So that night I didn't tell my parents anything about having met Noonan Williams, and I didn't breathe one word about our plans. After my father had left for work the next morning, I told my mother I was going for a bike ride with a friend, then waited for Noonan at the end of the gravel driveway which led to our house. He smelled like aftershave and stale beer when he opened the door. Then we rode along without talking for the most part, my silence stemming from the fact that I was doing this behind my father's back, quite certain of what would happen should he find out about it. Mr. Williams seemed to be still waking up, though, and I remember wondering if he'd slept at all considering the way he looked. Not combing your hair and smelling like beer in the morning—wasn't that what people called gallivanting? Wasn't that perhaps what was wild about Noonan Williams?

We turned onto the road which led to the lakes, and he stopped at a bait shop built from concrete blocks where he bought us sausage and biscuit sandwiches wrapped in foil. Noonan seemed to be taking his time. While our sandwiches heated in the toaster oven, he drank some coffee, which livened him up some, and chatted with the lady behind the cash register about deer hunting. Then we drove on to Kentucky Dam Airport. Inside a small office built across from the hangar, Noonan had another cup of black coffee and talked with a man who wore a unicom headset and sat behind a desk covered with candy bar wrappers. Noonan told the man, who occasionally spoke into a microphone below his mouth, that I was one humdinger of a baseball player and that today he was giving me my very first flying lesson. On a cork noteboard there was a light-blue aviation map covered by dark green and magenta-colored lines. Noonan pointed out the airport and located the highway we had driven out on, then he showed me the place on the map where I lived. He pointed to the hunter-orange wind sock which fluttered out by the runway and said it showed pilots which direction to take-off and to land from. He talked patiently, effortlessly, seemed awake and at ease, so unlike how he'd been earlier in the car, or the day before on the sidewalk downtown.

"Come on," Noonan said. "Let's go see the plane."

It wasn't until I glimpsed the pair of wings and saw the red paint that it actually dawned on me I would be flying in this particular plane. The thought scared me, but it thrilled me too. Above all, I didn't want Mr. Williams to think I was nervous. On the way to the airport, he'd asked me if I had been given permission from my parents. So I had quickly lied. Told him "yes sir."

Walking toward the biplane, it now occurred to me that I really should be a little scared, perhaps more frightened than I was because I had lied to my parents. This important fact might bring bad luck, I readily convinced myself. Then I thought of what others—people who were older and surely knew more than me—had all been saying about the stunt plane and the madman who flew it.

"Well, what do you think?" Noonan asked, once we stood before his airplane.

"It's pretty."

That was all I could think of. Mr. Williams grinned and seemed to like it. He stooped underneath a bright lacquered wing, then untied a rope which held the plane in place.

"This thing's made out of aluminum, paint, and cloth, so you gotta moor her down tight," Noonan told me. "Undo the other side. I'll get the chain in the front."

I did what he'd asked.

Suddenly, Noonan was standing in front of the plane, smoothing his hand across the wooden propeller, looking on either side of it and under the cowling. "If you haven't flown in a few days, then you need to check up under here," he told me. "A robin red-breast could sure ruin your day." He smiled and explained that the birds would build their nests in the little crannies behind the prop, using twigs and string and grass. They loved the shadowed, tucked-away cavities, and their nests would clog up the passageway which allowed cool air to flow over the engine. Pointing to different parts of the airplane, Noonan explained how they all worked. He used his hands when he talked, moving them up, or slanting them at an angle, suddenly swooping them down toward one another to illustrate, for example, how wind hits an airfoil and makes it lift. Placing an arm across one of the wings, he told me that there was nothing magic about flying and that right here was the key to it all.

"It's really simple," Noonan said. "So simple that the man who thought of it must've had a little magic in him, I reckon. See how the top of this curves?"

I nodded.

"Well, what happens is that the wind moves faster here and tries to catch up with what's flowing beneath it. The air has to equal itself out and that causes the plane to go up. Makes it fly."

Noonan talked quickly but clearly, always using his hands, scrunching over and occasionally shifting his arms, adjusting his body to demonstrate something, to help me understand.

"The engine makes a lot of noise," he said. "But once you're moving fast enough, the airplane's just pulled into the sky. As long as you're moving fast enough, you're going to be just fine."

Mr. Williams mussed up my hair, just like he'd done the day before, then held me lightly by the back of the neck. For some reason he always called me Hoss.

"Come on now, Hoss," he said. "Let's go flying."

He handed me a pair of goggles, then I waited in the front seat while he walked around the plane, looking it over inch by inch. Peering around the side of the fuselage, I saw him check the oil and drain some sky-colored fuel out of a spigot into a little glass vial. Then he climbed into the seat behind me, put on a pair of aviator sunglasses, and began fiddling with some instruments on the dash. I saw different sections of the wings moving up and down, listened to the sound of pulleys and cables sliding smoothly beneath my seat. Noonan asked if I was ready, then he started the engine, letting it idle for a moment or two before raising its pitch and pulling away from the tie-downs. As we coasted along, still on the grassy area, he kept moving the controls. Then he said something indistinguishable into the radio, as we were moving off the grass and onto the runway, pulled along by the squalling motor, faster and faster, suddenly off the ground and into the hot summer air.

When I got back home that afternoon I tried to act very tired. Considering the length of my trumped-up bike ride, I decided to run around the house a few times to work up a sweat. As it turned out this further deception was uncalled for because my mother didn't suspect a thing. I could hear the fan running in the den where she was ironing some clothes, watching *Days of Our Lives* and *Another World*. So I went back to the kitchen and made lunch. While eating my sandwich, I thought about what it had been like to feel utterly light, and I remembered not so much what I had seen—the small boats in and around the lakes, the tiny people in the boats, the size of houses—but most of all what I had sensed. What it had felt like precisely, the very moment we left the ground.

While we were up, Noonan couldn't talk because of the engine's noise, but he would thump on the side of the plane to make me look at something, fly over places I knew, circling them, or tipping down a wing like an index finger in order to point these special places out to me. We passed over my grandfather's cattle farm, glided over the Cumberland, then down the Ohio River, soared above the downtown area where conveyor belts spat soybeans and corn onto barges hunkered low in the muddy water. Sitting at the kitchen table, I could remember all of this, but mostly I wondered about, and could still precisely feel, what it was like to leave the ground and not come down again for an extended period of time. Flying seemed inevitable and so effortless after the talk with Noonan that for some reason I didn't want anyone else to know about what I had just done. My parents never found out that I'd gone flying with Noonan Williams, and I never told a soul about sneaking up our driveway and waiting for him to pick me up that morning. I'd fessed up to my lie on the way home from the airport and asked Noonan not to let anything slip which might cause me to get in trouble with my father. Noonan said that we would "both be in the dog house," so we agreed never to breathe a word. A few days later I saw him at the baseball tournament, and he just smiled his white smile and winked.

Soon enough our team advanced toward the inevitable show-down with Mullen Motors. After the second game of the playoffs, Ernest Boyd's mother said Noonan Williams had been drunker than she had ever had the honor of seeing him. "Nine sheets to the wind this time," she said. "Just who does he think he's fooling?" I walked back to the parking lot with her and Ernest, and Mrs. Boyd told us that she'd actually smelled the whiskey on his breath.

"You wouldn't want to light a cigarette around that man," Mrs. Boyd warned both of us, although neither of us smoked.

"I just can't understand it," she said. "What would make a man want to do that to himself?"

Mrs. Boyd was putting her body-length lawn chair into the trunk, and I got in with my parents who had parked their car next to hers. She talked a while about how scandalous such drinking was if you asked her, and my father started our car, hoping that she would take the hint. But Mrs. Boyd kept on complaining about Noonan while grabbing for Ernest's two younger sisters. They were running around the car sucking on lollipops and waving around yard-long Pixie Stix, screaming with delight and effortlessly eluding their mother. Mrs. Boyd finally snagged one of the girls by the arm and slapped her hard with the back of her hand. She stopped talking about Noonan Williams long enough to scold the child for having gotten so dirty at the playground. "Just wait till your Daddy sees you, young lady," she said. "You look like you've been sucking a sow! Now give me that! You've got it all over you for crying out loud!"

Mrs. Boyd took the sucker away from her daughter, then put it into her own mouth while she cleaned the little girl's face.

"'Night Waldeen," my father said politely.

But after we pulled onto the street I noticed that he wasn't smiling, or rather, my father was trying not to smile. The same look was on my mother's face, too. It was hard to tell what they were thinking, but I was sure that neither of them approved of what they had just seen Mrs. Boyd do to her daughter.

"Goddamn!" my father said, his voice shaking with laughter or anger. Maybe a little of both. "Now I can sure understand why we don't see hide nor hair of Mr. Boyd. I can certainly sympathize with his wanting to stay away from that."

Then in a different tone. "What do you think son?" he asked me. "Which one would weigh the most? Mrs. Boyd or her car?"

What he said was a little mean. But as usual Mrs. Boyd had eaten a whole lot during the game, three hot dogs, two popcorns, a large Coke and one cherry snow cone, then sat in her lawn chair smiling sweetly.

I burst out laughing and leaned forward to get a look at my little brother who was grinning and yipping in his car seat, giggling as if he'd liked the joke as well. My mother laughed some, too. But she told my father that was no way to talk.

"Well, what a game! Good damn!" Daddy said, looking over at my mother. "Good damn ball game. Wouldn't everybody say that?"

Then we all laughed some more, and it was clear to me that he and my mother were getting along much better. Now my father had started coming to all of my baseball games. As a matter of fact, I can't remember him missing a single one after that night, throughout all the years I played.

We won the championship in the next few games against Mullen Motors, then I spent the rest of the summer mowing yards and loathing the thought of starting school. One night at the supper table, my father said some man had told him that Noonan Williams was in some kind of trouble. It wasn't hard to figure out why. Everyone knew it was him in the airplane by this point, and the impromptu stunt shows were not what they used to be, say back in May or early June. Anybody could tell that the pilot was in a different mood, but who could tell why this had happened? For the longest time Noonan had made us all look up, open our mouths and "aahhh" like my mother did that day at Coach Burkeen's, but now whatever he did looked crazy—more dangerous than beautiful.

One evening I stood out by the driveway and watched Noonan drawing attention to himself, spinning fiercely and flying wild. The red biplane jerked and flipped, spun suddenly into Dutch-rolls, then shot straight-up into the sky, smoking and sputtering until it dropped down violently. Watching it, you felt sick at times, like someone was behind you and squeezing hard on your stomach. I tried to picture what his face looked like up there and whenever I thought of the stunts he had gotten into trouble for I had no difficulty imagining the expression he might have worn when he'd done them. Before flying out of view that evening, Noonan Williams lowered the engine to a light hum. He leveled the wings and flew one last, lazy circle. It seemed like a joke, or an insult somehow, at least that's how it struck both my parents who had watched him, too, from our backyard.

Stories began to circulate that Noonan really was mentally disturbed. Eventually we found out exactly what he had done to get into trouble with the flight authorities. During the last few weeks of boating season, he had acquired the habit of buzzing pleasure craft on Kentucky and Barkley Lakes. They're on any map, in the far left corner of western Kentucky, two huge, man-made TVA lakes which stretch down into Tennessee. What Noonan would do was this. He would fly above the water-skiers and the bass fishermen and let them watch a few stunts, first gain a little altitude, then barrel right down at them—pulling up at the last minute, just as he'd done over the soybeans and corn. People ducked and tossed their rods and reels, slung their daiquiris and piña coladas overboard. They dove from the tops of their houseboats, then waited in the water until the madman had passed and left them alone.

Apart from his weekend descents upon the boaters, Noonan Williams is said to have zoomed over the fairways of Calvert City country club early one Sunday morning and to have caused a rich lady lining up a chip shot to pee in her shorts. Because Noonan didn't take any precautions whatsoever—didn't even cover the call numbers on his plane—the lady's enraged husband called the FAA with the information they needed to investigate the incident. A stiff fine was levied which Noonan laughed at and paid off in one dollar bills, people said. They claimed he drank more than ever now and that he seldom went home to Peggy. Noonan let his hair grow even longer and word had it that he even smoked marijuana, that he was shacking-up with some other woman, a waitress, a younger woman who was even wilder than he was.

One night my father took the family to the drive-in for corn dogs and milkshakes and who was there but old Mrs. Boyd. "D'ya hear about our fearless sponsor?" she asked with considerable pleasure. "Mr. Williams has been put in the loony bin. They've locked him up and they'll throw away the key," she told us all.

We didn't know what to think about what Mrs. Boyd had told us, but it was disproved only a couple of weeks later. Noonan made the Sunday papers after his scarlet-colored biplane was sighted once again flying under the bridge which spans the canal connecting Kentucky and Barkley lakes. A barge captain saw the pilot everyone knew to be Noonan Williams go through twice, the first time quick and close, his plane's right wing skirting just past one of the bridge's massive concrete pilings. Steel support cables cross under the lower arches of this bridge and the witness explained that the pilot flew a yard or two above the water to avoid these, but he appeared to get very close to one of those concrete pilings.

"It was like he was flirting with it," the boat captain said. "Trying to nick the base of that pillar with the right side of his airplane—to kiss it with the edge of one wing. He would dip down for a gander at that gap he'd been through, then roar up and circle around some more."

According to the barge captain, the red biplane's last stunt consisted of this. The pilot finally came down once again and flew straight as an arrow along the canal. Just inches above the water. He held a direct course and passed cleanly through the opening with room to spare, pulled up smoothly, then glided out of sight. Noonan disappeared the same day he did it. He never returned to the airport.

School was in full swing by the time we found out what really occurred, what had finally happened to Noonan Williams the summer he briefly disappeared. I got off the bus one day and my father was sitting in the backyard, carving a tremendous orange jack-o-lantern for me and my little brother. "Guess what," he said, perhaps remembering part of what I was remembering, standing there and watching the sky, the slow, steady sunset, the distant globe of reddish light dropping over the old horse barn and moving onward, toward I-24 and the lakes and the horizon's limit.

"Noonan Williams is back in town," my father told me. "He sold his airplane up in Ohio. Somewhere around Cleveland I believe they're saying."

The next summer Williams Concrete was our team's sponsor once more. Sometimes Noonan would come out to the practice field on weekends to pitch us batting practice, or use a fungo-bat to hit the outfielders fly balls. We started calling him Newt at his request, and whenever he was on the field with us I had a hard time thinking about baseball because of our secret, because of that smile of his which was as persistent and mysterious, as wide and white as it ever was. I kept looking at him whenever he wasn't looking at me, and laughing at least with his eyes. For some reason I wanted to play better whenever he came to our games, or to work harder whenever he gave me advice. I always wondered what all the things he had done really meant.

The Woman Who Sugared Strawberries

They met one day while Barbara was having lunch and waiting for her next class at Marais Dance Center where she had been given a scholarship for the summer. Didier worked in one of the law offices in the district and had noticed her before, sitting at one of the iron tables on the terrace, eating a salad and drinking a glass of grapefruit juice. She was quite tall and stylishly dressed, usually reading a book, he noticed, first *L'Assomoir*, then *Au Bonheur des Dames*.

"If I only ate lettuce and read Zola, I think I'd cut my throat," he said, once he had mustered the courage to talk to her.

"These days," she told him, "That's all I eat."

Barbara was five-foot-eight and had just turned twenty-two. She was a dancer from Houston who had trained since she was five to be a ballerina in a prestigious company. Far from being frail, or petite—the kind of woman a male lead could fling into the air like a child, or a sackful of oranges—she was muscular and sturdy, Texas-boned, she would say with a laugh. She was a very powerful person who trained with weights to strengthen her legs, and who could fill the rehearsal room with sighs by jumping higher than some of the men.

Classical dance became her focus, her passion. Her father was particularly proud, supportive of her artistic ambitions. He was a petroleum engineer who spoke Spanish, ran a research company, and owned a large chunk of land in West Texas where business partners raised livestock and grew sunflowers which they sold for their oil. When his daughter started ed dating her first boyfriend in high school, Barbara's father once took her out to lunch and found out delicately, but without fumbling his words, whether she and her boyfriend had slept together. How had he known, his daughter asked him in tears. At the time, she'd been only seventeen. They talked about how an unplanned pregnancy would ruin her dancing career, then agreed that an abortion would be a particularly traumatic thing to go through, especially at her age. Later that same day, Barbara's father made an appointment with a doctor and Barbara began taking the pill. He paid for a tutor to help her through the trigonometry and the French courses she necessarily missed while performing, or while attending workshops in San Francisco, Chicago, or New York.

When she was younger, only fourteen and fifteen years old, Barbara would pack a suitcase full of pointe shoes, leotards, and leg warmers. Then the next morning on his way to work, her father would drive her out to Intercontinental airport. She would fly to New York for week-long seminars with renowned teachers and other gifted young women, some of whom were flaky and frivolous, Barbara now thought. They would dance six hours a day, work very hard, then go out at night to watch European movies. Once another girl from Salt Lake City had rented a hotel room for the afternoon where they drank champagne and talked about their favorite instructors. They each bought and ate pint cartons of chocolate or coffee flavored Haagen-Dazs, then took turns going to the bathroom in groups of three. This strange ritual was something Barbara would never forget or repeat: her face in the mirror, looking oddly robust, healthy and flushed and smiling. She had held her long hair back with one hand, keeping the other free, then leaned over the sink and laughed wildly at the other girls, who were gagging themselves, vomiting and laughing too, poised over the toilet and the bathtub drain.

On that first day in the café Barbara had done most of the talking and Didier had mostly listened. He had studied literature to begin with, then switched over to law, Didier explained, when his turn came. He had switched because teaching literature in France's public schools was an abominable way to go through life. They ordered more coffee and talked about her ballet classes, about movies, about Paris. Her French was good, and Didier told her so. Before the afternoon was over, he had convinced her to see a film with him later that week.

Love, as all the poets—and even naturalists like Zola—were continually insisting, love was sublime, irrational, and overwhelming. But Didier certainly didn't have anything too lofty in mind when he asked Barbara to dinner the following weekend, then eventually back to his apartment for a drink. During the following weeks, though, love was precisely the word that came to mind whenever he so much as saw her for a few minutes. He spent his spare time thinking of things which might interest her and began devising ways of getting off work early, of leaving the law office where he clerked for the rest of the day. When she broke her ankle dancing at the Centre de la Danse one afternoon, Didier did everything he could to keep her from sinking further into one of the most resigned and most bitter depressions he'd ever witnessed—a real case of *les cafards*. He told her that in France, whenever you were depressed you had "the cockroaches," and the slang phrase had put a smile on her face.

Finally, he convinced her to share his apartment on Rue des Blancs Manteaux. Barbara had spoken with her father on the phone and arranged to stay in Paris for the time being. This decision made sense because she'd made so many contacts, she explained to him, and there was an orthopedic dance-specialist who practiced in Neuilly.

While Didier could only vaguely imagine what she was going through, part of him was almost grateful following the accident since it gave him more time with Barbara, made her more receptive, slowed her down some. Before that it was hard to have a whole weekend alone with her. She was always brimming with energy despite her workouts, wanting to stay out late with all the Vogue photographers and models she had met, eat small meals in fancy restaurants, or go out dancing at Les Bains-Douches, a discotheque near Pompidou built over the ruins of some Roman baths.

. . . .

When August came they left Paris in his family's Fiat, a little black car which sounded like a lawnmower and had a sunroof. "You know a little about the city now but not about France," Didier explained, as they were losing sight of the skyscrapers. He headed for the Atlantic coast, using the freeways to get to the ocean faster, then later on they would take only the smaller roads to avoid the traffic. Their first night, on L'Isle d'Oleron, they ordered platefuls of black mussels in garlic butter and drank two bottles of fantastic wine. Barbara was still getting over an emotional blow following her last visit to the doctor's office before leaving the city. While it was unrealistic at this point, she'd hoped to hear that the operation had been conclusive, an unquestionable success. Her right ankle had been fractured in two places and a shard of bone chipped off its lateral side. Now there were tension bands made of twisted wire, intricate sets of steel pins and screws in the joint—in Barbara's body. A long maroon scar shaped like an "L" ran along the side of her foot, then continued eight inches up her calf. She hadn't seen it until the doctor changed the cast.

Didier was playful and so sweet that first night. He handled her leg like it was something overly fragile, a small animal, or perhaps a dried flower. The next day he was equally adorable, hilarious, so full of life. He built her sandcastles on the beach with the well-tanned children from the island, then made fun of all the German tourists who sunbathed without their clothes "Why is it?" he asked her. "That the people who take their clothes off in public are the ones who never should and vice versa?"

"Don't look at me," Barbara told him.

"Come on. We'll never see these people again. Not if we're lucky." Didier joked with her. "I will if you will."

"No way, not me."

They tied a plastic bag around her fiberglass cast, and Barbara tried to swim, but came back after a couple of minutes. The water off the island was swarming with medusas, translucent globs of electrified jelly which you had to dodge once you got past the waves, then began floating in the calm troughs between them.

"What do you think of that?" Didier asked.

He pointed out one of the Germans playing paddleball.

Thirty meters or so from where they'd spread their beach towels, two men were playing the game on the wave-hardened sand near the ocean, huffing drunkenly and shouting, yelling to one another like overweight dragons. One of the men was red-faced as a result of his exertions and had allowed himself to become somewhat aroused, a fact which didn't seem to concern him in the least.

"Stop pointing you idiot. He'll see you."

"Well, I certainly see him," Didier said. "I guess one of the jellyfish got him."

They had three whole weeks together, pure vacation time without schedules and chock-full of sweet alternatives, before Didier had to be back in Paris and restart his law classes. So next, they went to the fort at La Rochelle, then headed south to visit some of the Bordeaux wineries. Afterwards they drove inland, following the rural roads colored mustard and off-white on their Michelin map, traveling back through the interior before heading to the Mediterranean and all the bigger summertime crowds.

At the end of the first week, they started out for the town where his father was born, a small village on a hill, a place called Viella in the département of Gers. Didier helped her find it on the map and said that this old village was something Barbara really had to see. Viella was only a hundred kilometers from the Atlantic Ocean, but ages away from the bustle in Biarritz—where there were larger, and louder, and even more naked Germans. His father's village was a century at least, he told her, from Saint Tropez and the crowded, blue coast.

From the moment they pulled into that driveway at his great-aunt's house, Barbara was surprised to discover such a place still existed. She had grown up in Houston during the seventies and early eighties, a stacked up, spread out, oil-boom world, full of shopping malls, fast food and freeways.

A woman was feeding chickens when they drove up. Slowly slinging out fistfuls of breadcrumbs from her upturned apron, to the left then the right, like she was scolding the birds—or conducting an orchestra.

Madame Deluc squinted and looked surprised when she saw the car. She smiled, but seemed not to recognize Didier until he told her who he was. Then she hugged him, brushed off both hands and shook Barbara's. She asked Didier if his friend spoke French, and Barbara, utterly fascinated by the woman's southern accent, said a few sentences to show she could manage quite well.

"Why, she speaks just like a Parisian," Madame Deluc said, still facing Didier. "I'm so glad you've stopped to say hello. Soon everyone will be back for lunch."

She took them into the house through the side door, past an entryway full of hat racks, dirt-covered boots and work clothes. Didier explained they had eaten croissants at the hotel before starting out, but Madame Deluc set out bread and bilberry preserves, then fed the fire with split logs next to the oven. Apart from those she had seen in westerns and frontier films, this was the first old cooking-stove Barbara had ever laid eyes on. She motioned toward it by tilting her head, then mouthed the sound *bois*, the word for wood. She intended it to be both a question and an exclamation of her interest. Didier held up his hands. He nodded silently as if to say: "Didn't I tell you? But just wait. The best is yet to come."

Madame Deluc looked perhaps fifty years old, clear-eyed and with mostly still dark hair. But somehow she seemed old already, weary looking, stooped a little at the shoulders. She began asking Barbara questions about their trip when an even older woman, Didier's Aunt Florence— his grandmother's sister who lived with her son's family—joined them in the kitchen. From the way they both looked at her, it seemed these two women were as intrigued by Barbara as she was with them and with their house. Barbara noticed how carefully they examined her clothes and wondered if she'd dressed improperly. She was wearing one of Didier's shirts, a lavender button-down which was too large but very comfortable. Also, a white pair of cotton stretch pants, which fit her legs snugly yet slid easily over the cast.

Both of the women seemed to think that she was ill, which was something different from being injured. They kept urging her to eat more, or to drink some more of the tea. Where had they gone on their trip so far? they asked. What did she like best about France? Barbara told them that she was just beginning to really see the country, and that she enjoyed being out of the city. She told them what Didier had said earlier, about how Paris was wonderful but that Paris wasn't France, and this seemed to go over well.

Suddenly, Aunt Florence wanted to change her dress.

Didier told her they would wait outside.

"They're wonderful aren't they?" he asked once he and Barbara had left the kitchen area.

"My aunt's husband must be dead by now," Didier explained. "One day he disappeared, and they never heard anything else from him. They don't know whether he wandered off into the woods, shot himself, or fell down a well. No one ever talks about it, but he used to hit her. My father said he was a real *conard*. A real bastard."

After a while, Aunt Florence came out wearing a blue dress with a metal zipper down the back and a hand-embroidered marguerite on the front pocket. She adjusted her hat to keep the sun off her face, then began the tour of the Deluc's farm by showing them her patch of baby's breath and azaleas, a vegetable garden, and the shed where the tractors were kept. A Portuguese family lived in the old house now. They tended the orchard, Aunt Florence explained. She pointed out the new fruit trees, then explained how they were trying to grow kiwis. The agricultural experts said the trees would do better in France if the farm were just a bit further south, or if the summers were longer and less dry. "But kiwis bring a high price," she said. "So it seems well worth a try."

Barbara guessed that Didier's aunt had to be seventy, sixty-five at the very least. She moved around quite nimbly though, stepping across ditches with a little bounce, slipping agilely through the strand of a barbed wire fence. As they continued up the hill, toward the village of Viella, they could make out a bright red tractor and the hay baler in one of the lower fields. It was hard to see clearly because of the hazy heat, but Aunt Florence explained this was where Monsieur Deluc, his son, and the Portuguese men were working in the hay.

"It's getting very, very hot," Aunt Florence said. "But it would be best if it didn't rain today."

Barbara noticed vague shapes of the distant farm workers heaving squat yellow squares onto the rear of a flatbed truck. A man dressed in blue clambered over a wall of hay, stacking bales as they came.

Once they had walked a little further up the hill, Viella's postman passed by on a bicycle with cracked leather side bags, one of which was closed and contained letters perhaps. The other was propped open by a long, brown baguette. Barbara glanced over at Didier to let him know how much she was enjoying herself, how she could hardly believe such a place still existed.

As they walked on, his aunt began to explain about her friend, Sophie Veuillot, the woman she was taking Barbara to meet. She and Sophie had grown up side-by-side and had done everything together like sisters, Aunt Florence told them. They had skipped rope and gone to Mass together, roamed all around the countryside after school, talking about the houses they would have someday and the beautiful families they would raise. But by the time Aunt Florence had married her husband, Sophie had gone away to Paris, then all of a sudden she left again for the United States where she had lived for over half of her life. Ten years ago, Sophie had come back to Viella when her brother started dying. Then after the funeral she'd decided to stay.

When they arrived at Sophie's house set into the hillside, a low building with a red tile roof and poured concrete walls, they could see her through the doorway, standing up at the sink and washing a glass. Sophie Veuillot had cotton-white hair and wore eyeglasses, Barbara noticed. No one else she had seen all day on this French farm wore eyeglasses, and this small detail was one of several which seemed to distinguish her. A slate-gray tomcat sat symmetrically on the threshold watching her rinse and dry the glass, his back turned parallel to the road.

"*Mon Dieu,*" Aunt Florence said, with sudden concern. She leaned over the concrete wall which partitioned-off Sophie's yard and kept stray animals away from her tomato plants.

"Sophie, what is this?" she called out. "Come and tell me. What has happened?"

The old woman dried her hands and came outside, moving from side to side without bending her knees, her legs somewhat stiff, but still solid and trustworthy. Sophie wore a very simple cotton dress and a blotched apron, perhaps stained by tea. She had a worried expression and seemed confused by the fact that her friend wasn't alone as usual.

But Aunt Florence offered no explanation. They both stared at the yard and the scorched wall of the house.

A couple of hours earlier, Sophie Veuillot told her, the grass in her yard had suddenly burst into flames. She had been reading the newspaper in the back room when she heard someone shouting. If it hadn't been for her neighbor, Monsieur Gazonnaud—the man who'd passed by and put out the fire—she didn't know what would have happened to her home. She wondered if the straw she used around the tomato plants had caught fire, if the sun had shone through one of the jars then started the blaze. She used canning jars to start some of her plants in and kept them on the ledge full of water. Maybe the hot sun had caused the fire. But Sophie said she wasn't so sure. There were a couple of children running around who were wilder than monkeys. Perhaps one of them had mischievously thrown a match over the garden wall.

"No, no. Absolutely not," Aunt Florence reassured her, seeing that she was getting rather upset. "Maybe that's what happened, you know. The sun, I mean. Everything is so dried out."

Sophie nodded and thought about it.

Didier's aunt moved the jars out of the sun, then stepped back to where Barbara was standing in the road.

"Speak some American with her," Aunt Florence said in French. Then she smiled coyly, like she was wearing a new dress, or a hat that she was unsure of but eager to show her good friend, something she hoped Sophie Veuillot of all people would approve of and admire.

"Hello," Barbara began, not really knowing what to say. "I'm really sorry about your yard."

The words in English seemed bland but substantial, like halved potatoes or pieces of dark bread. It had been weeks since Barbara had spoken much of her own language.

Sophie leaned forward, confused once more.

"*Comment?*" she said.

Clearly, she had not understood.

"I'm from the United States," Barbara told her, then she motioned over toward Didier. "We're here visiting his family."

"Oh, excuse me,..." Sophie began with genuine surprise. Then she laughed. "I've not spoken English in so long, you realize. Never mind about my yard—no one was hurt. What have you done to yourself?"

Barbara said she had broken her leg dancing. She briefly explained where she was from and what she was doing in France.

Sophie Veuillot nodded and said that she had heard of Texas. She told Barbara how much she had loved living in the United States. "New York, New Jersey, Massachusetts," she said. "I had so many friends over there."

Soon Aunt Florence explained that she and Didier were going to find the new priest. They were going to the cemetery so he could see his grandfather's grave, then they could all walk down to have lunch. The young girl was hurt and needed to rest. Aunt Florence turned toward

Didier, who looked at Barbara and shrugged, then they started off up the hill.

After they'd disappeared up the road, Sophie Veuillot opened the gate and Barbara passed into the yard. She balanced herself on one of her crutches, leaned over and tried to pet the cat, but he scampered away, staring at her with enraged yellow eyes.

"Frederick doesn't trust you yet," Sophie told her. "But he will, he will. Don't worry about him, okay?"

They passed through the kitchen and into a room sparsely furnished with a chifforobe covered with photographs, an overstuffed chair and a reading lamp, a set of hearth tools next to the fireplace. Over the mantel hung a framed lithograph of a Cunard ocean liner. There was a crowd of multicolored, variously dressed people squeezed together on its promenade deck, wearing straw hats and summer clothing, waving goodbye and throwing paper streamers. The picture made Barbara think of long ocean trips, about drinking gin-and-tonics and playing shuffleboard wearing white. A few weeks earlier, she had watched a TV documentary about underwater explorations of the Titanic. What it must have been like to climb into the lifeboats, then cast off into the icy darkness from the noise-filled sinking ship.

After a few minutes, Sophie returned, carrying a tray: a crystal bowl full of cashews, glasses of ice, and two cans of Coke.

"Do you like this?" she asked. "I mean, are ballet dancers allowed to drink this stuff?"

"I do now," Barbara told her laughing. "Fruit juice is much better for you. So I try to drink that. But this is fine."

"You know something? I always keep it," Sophie Veuillot told Barbara. "Once a week, the little girl across the street goes into town and does my shopping for me. She has to carry all those heavy Coke cans, the poor thing."

Then Sophie told Barbara part of her life story. She said she had first arrived in New York City on the 24th of August, 1930, and that she would never forget the date. She was supposed to have made the trip with a girlfriend, someone she had worked with as a secretary at the Bourse in Paris. Her friend had married at the last minute, though, and Sophie had decided to go on alone.

On the ship going over, there was a businessman who offered her a job, which amounted to meals and a small salary. It mostly involved cleaning his house, the man told her, going to market for him and his wife. "But they turned out to be very *special* people," Sophie Veuillot said laughing, remembering her first employers. "At any rate, this was my first job in America." Next, the old woman told her something, in such a way, that surprised Barbara. It made her immediately grasp how different Sophie's life had been, how dissimilar from that of Didier's relatives whom she had met earlier. After six months, Sophie said, she had been forced to quit the job and give up her room. The businessman had begun to sulk. He seemed to resent having to pay her small salary, because it allowed her to spend time away from the house. Gradually, he had become curiously attentive, bolder in his attentions, and to a certain extent the same could be said of the businessman's wife. She would fix Sophie tea and say how much like a family they had all become, offer to style her hair, or pamper her in other little ways. One night the three of them huddled over the radio as though it were an egg they were waiting to see hatch. Suddenly, the businessman slipped his arm around Sophie's waist, while his wife smiled carefully, then looked her straight in the eye.

"She didn't bat an eyelash," Sophie added.

"Well?" Barbara asked her. "What happened next?"

She had the impression she was talking to one of her friends back in Paris, like Anita, a contemporary dancer from Dayton, Ohio. Someone she knew very well. Someone much closer to her own age.

"What did you do?" Barbara asked.

"Why nothing at all," Sophie said. "What could one do? I didn't say anything. But I left the next day, though, then I got a job selling perfume. Because of my accent I suppose."

Sophie asked her if she had ever been to New York City. "It's not the same as Paris," she insisted. "It is the most lovely city in the world." Had she heard of the Saks department store?

"Of course," Barbara said. "Of course I have."

"Well, I worked there for twenty-four years," Sophie Veuillot told her. "But it never seemed like work, you know. There are no words I can use to describe it."

She had waited on the most elegant customers Barbara could imagine, Broadway theater stars, film actors and actresses. The most beautiful people in the world came into the shop, millionaires from Brazil and the gorgeous women with them, their wives or their girlfriends who had skin the color of chocolate, women who moved and dressed like rare, tropical birds. One afternoon, a man wearing a tuxedo came into Saks, then he started tap-dancing for all the girls who worked the perfume counter. Later on, he married one of Sophie's best friends. She had met so many interesting people. On another occasion she had spent an entire evening with Maurice Chevalier. He had come into the department store, talked to her a few minutes, then invited her out. "I wore blue, he wore blue, and the chauffeur wore blue as well. We all had dinner together, the three of us, then Monsieur Chevalier took me out dancing."

Barbara was amazed, half incredulous. She could sit there silently and listen for hours, but Sophie wanted her to talk too.

How did she hurt her leg exactly? And how did she meet Didier? Was she in love with him? Or did she know yet?

"Talk to me about everything," Sophie told her. "Start telling me all about yourself."

Barbara laughed and said yes. Yes, she believed that she was in love. Didier had been so good to her. After the injury he always brought her presents on the way home from work, sometimes just little things, Tintin comic books, *pain au chocolat* or *mille feuilles* from the bakery. She had broken her ankle after rehearsal one day, while dancing with another American girl, her friend Anita, a stunning black woman from

Ohio who specialized in contemporary dance. Before she'd met Didier, Barbara and her friend Anita would sometimes go out to The Locomotive or Les Bains-Douches, and one night the entire crowd had left the floor to give them room and watch them dance together. Afterwards, when all the young wolves came up to compliment them, or offer them free drinks, Anita playfully started kissing Barbara suddenly claiming that they were a couple.

On the day of the injury, Anita had brought in a cassette player and new tape from a band she'd just discovered. It was late and the studio was empty. Barbara had been passing through the hall. "What's this?" she stopped and asked. Soon Anita had turned up the volume, until the music filled the building's whole top floor. "You're going to love it," she promised. "Get out here girl." Anita closed her eyes and began circling around the room, plugging herself into the singer's low voice. She began swaying and rocking, then raising her legs slowly to the music. Her long hair was tied tightly into dozens of fine braids which she periodically flung over her shoulders. She bent over and danced with her head down a while, her hair spilling onto the floor, then drew her neck back swift-ly—so the first thing that showed in the studio mirror, after the glistening wing of her hair, was Anita's focused face, Anita's smiling opened mouth. She continued swinging her hair back and forth, round in circles, then in figure eights. It was obvious, Barbara thought watch-ing her, why all the *jeunes loups* in the Parisian discotheques had bothered them.

Finally, Barbara slipped off her pointe shoes and began to dance alongside her. She gracefully spun away from the wall's full length mir-ror, then moved out onto the floor. On her first day at the Marais dance school, the director had called Barbara into his office and asked, "What is the significance of dancing for you?" It had seemed strange, such a bullshit question, she'd thought. That was like asking a painter to explain the meaning of his or her work, but using words instead of acrylics, watercolors, or oils. "Why do I dance?" she replied. The direc-tor had nodded and started smiling. "Because that's what I'm good at," she told him. Then later on that very afternoon, Barbara had showed him that she was, indeed, very talented. Dancing was something which gave her life vigor. Some kind of focus. Some form. It was exhilarating and exquisite, the various things one's body could be *made* to do. Whenever other people watched her dance, or Barbara saw herself run full speed across a rehearsal room, then rise into the air—her back perfectly arched, her head straight, her legs parallel to the floor—that was precisely what dancing meant to her, that was what ballet signified.

While dancing with Anita, though, the ceaseless control of classical dance was no longer of such concern. Whenever Barbara moved her whole body like this, outside the mythic perfection of choreography, there was margin for wildness, sheer caprice, utter abandon. She shifted her weight from side to side, swung her own hair in circles to the music. Barbara jumped toward the front wall and reeled backwards away from it, leaping up in such a way that made her feel as if she might stay in the air, possibly hang there and never come down. So at first, when the singer's voice suddenly changed—became high pitched, grating and piercing—Barbara conflated the shrill sounds in her ears with the real pain. Her ankle. Her ankle hurt so bad. She collapsed onto the hardwood floor and was unable to move, or call out for help. Most of all, she wanted the music to stop. It was as though someone had stuck a scorching needle into the socket of her ankle, then filled it with a liquid which made her whole leg burn.

"Oh shit!" Anita screamed, when she noticed her. "What happened Barbara?" Then she asked more softly. "Babs, are you alright?"

Soon, the fire in her body became more general. That day Barbara had felt as though she might be sick, as if throwing-up might get rid of the flames. "Could you get someone please," she had asked. "I'll have to go to the hospital. It's broken. I know it. I just know it."

. . . .

When Didier and his aunt returned from the cemetery, Barbara and Sophie Veuillot were still sitting at the kitchen table.

Still talking and sharing stories.

"This new priest is retarded," Aunt Florence declared. "It took us an hour and a half to find the grave all by ourselves."

She seemed very pleased that Barbara and Sophie had found things to talk about and told Sophie they would wait for her to get dressed. She was coming to eat with them if she had to drag her personally.

"I could bring up the car," Didier offered.

But Sophie said this wouldn't be necessary. "Besides," she said smiling. "All this talk about the cemetery is depressing. I'm not ready to be eating daisies by the roots just yet."

Didier and Aunt Florence burst out laughing.

Then the four of them started slowly down the hill.

Madame Deluc seemed very pleased, but somewhat surprised, that Sophie Veuillot had agreed to come for lunch. They spoke to each other affectionately in quick, hard-to-follow regional French, then she had them all sit down and went to get glasses for Pernod, white wine, or whiskey. The dining room led into a larger room where Barbara saw an upright piano and a mahogany secretary, also a Sony television sitting on a stand with wheels. Soon Monsieur Deluc and his son arrived, and they too were taken off guard, somewhat baffled by their house brimming full of guests. While pouring everyone's second aperitif, Monsieur Deluc joked about the various advantages of having surprise visitors, especially when it was this hot during their hay season. Everyone's tone of voice and the formal deference they showed Sophie Veuillot made it quite clear to Barbara that she had now become the Deluc's principal guest.

Once everyone had taken a seat at the table, Didier's aunt served bowls full of fresh tomato and green pepper puree, sliced bread, and saucers of goose liver. She and Madame Deluc positioned themselves nearest the kitchen in order to serve, and Barbara sat next to Sophie, Didier with the men at the other end of the table. Barbara tried her best to follow the thread of what the men were saying. At first, the conversation circled around what for her were less imposing topics: Didier's family in Paris, the weather in the province, the farm. They were having an extended drought, Monsieur Deluc explained. But he hoped it wouldn't rain any time soon, at least not until all the hay was up and out of the fields. The Deluc's son, Robert, had a bandage around one of his hands which was stained with dirt and some freshly dried blood. Barbara listened as he told Didier about the injury, about how he had almost lost a finger in the baler earlier that day. When Robert held up his good hand and made a violent tugging motion on one of its fingers, Barbara felt her stomach tighten and start to roll.

Next, the men began talking about the recent elections and the socialists' fall from favor in Paris, referring to controversies and politicians about whom Barbara had never heard. Monsieur Deluc seemed interested in what Didier thought about the new government; so they talked about Mitterrand, Chirac, and *cohabitation.*

"It's hard for me to understand," Barbara told Sophie. "This accent in the south is so different. The way it bounces. Sometimes it sounds like Italian."

Sophie explained that Monsieur Deluc used a lot of dialect whenever he talked. She smiled an understanding smile and said that sometimes she couldn't understand him either.

Gradually she returned to their former topic of conversation, started telling Barbara more about her wonderful life in the United States. How little she had known when she first arrived in New York, and how much she had learned to love the place! At first, Sophie said, she would spend her spare time just wandering, walking aimlessly through the streets, reading billboards and marquees, memorizing signs that might help her to talk to people, or to find a better job. New York City was safer and more exciting back then, much more *vif.* Vivacious and full of life. Sophie said everything and everyone seemed to belong there, the mixture of people, the trolleys, the automobiles. It all seemed so alive and so ancient, too, as if it had all just sprung up one day, everything including the taxicabs and the sidewalks. She had loved the nightclubs, the big bands, and the movies. "Oh the cinema!" Sophie Veuillot said. One of the things she loved most about New York was that you could come across famous people almost anywhere. She had once seen Fred Astaire in the department store, although he hadn't danced, and Lillian Gish in Central Park, walking a dachshund and wearing a fur coat.

Their midday meal went on and on. Madame Deluc would slip into the kitchen to stir something, then she would return with another dish. After the cold tomato soup, there were omelets with onions and sausage. Then roast pork, rosemary potatoes, and buttered green beans as thin as shoelaces. She brought out another loaf of fresh bread which everyone tore apart with their hands, then passed around the table counterclockwise. Barbara realized that the Delucs were making an extra effort. After the cheese platter came an apple tart sprinkled with cinnamon, and the fifth or sixth bottle of wine—she had lost count. It was a deep gold-colored dessert wine called Pacherenc du Vic Bilu. She read the label and later wrote down the name on a piece of scrap paper, determined never to forget it. She told Sophie that the wine sounded Italian, too. But Sophie assured her that it wasn't. "You'll really like this," she promised Barbara. "It tastes like walnuts and caramel."

Suddenly, there was the sound of a door opening and a man stomping his feet in the doorway. "*Luc, mon vieux,*" Monsieur Deluc yelled, practically screamed from the other end of the table. Barbara turned and saw one of the neighbors who had come to help with the hay, a stocky man with a blurry face and a thick gray eyebrow, which moved when he talked and reminded her of a squirrel's tail.

"Take a glass," Monsieur Deluc told his friend. "Sit down and have something to eat."

Luc cast a glad eye around the dining room. He looked upset for not having been invited to such a gathering. For a few moments, he seemed to be pouting and declined the offer. No, there was work to be done. He'd better not, Luc told everyone, before reaching toward the bottle and saying that he could perhaps find room for wine after all.

The man had the air of a circus performer, Barbara thought, as he straddled his chair after the first ostentatious sip.

Luc pulled his hat back comically and sighed. Then he continued tasting the wine using smacking sounds, as if some of Madame Deluc's homemade pâté were caught in the roof of his mouth.

After emptying the glass, Luc grinned mischievously.

"Wouldn't you like some dessert?" Madame Deluc asked him, obviously familiar with his antics. "Another glass of wine perhaps?"

"No thank you," Luc said, springing for the bottle once more.

"Just a little slice, if you please."

So Madame Deluc cut another piece off the apple tart.

Sophie Veuillot kept on talking and Barbara kept watching her extraordinary eyes, the way in which they stayed focused on her own. Crystal-clear and unflinching. There was one more thing she wanted to tell Barbara, one memory she cherished and returned to always. She said she had worked in the perfume department for years and that she was always given the very best customers. One afternoon, Sophie had waited on Eleanor Roosevelt, who promptly noticed her accent and wanted to practice her French. So they sat down together in a storage room at Saks Fifth Avenue, then talked about their favorite musicals and Broadway plays. Soon they discovered how much they loved one another's country and, after that first day, Mrs. Roosevelt would always come into the store whenever she happened to be passing through the city and had some extra time. The manager was obliged, of course, to let Sophie off the floor for a couple of hours, so that she could sit knee-to-knee with the president's wife and they could catch up and speak French with one another. "Almost every single time she brought me something," Sophie Veuillot explained. "Some gift because I helped her keep in practice. She was a great, great lady. Always so kind. So very generous."

There was no weariness or regret.

No nostalgic catch in her voice.

Sophie Veuillot spoke steadily and without sadness about these memories, and for some reason, right at this point and juncture, all the others around the table stopped their respective conversations. Everyone had stopped talking. They were listening in earnest as Sophie spoke. Finally, it was Luc, the Deluc's neighbor, who first broke the silence. Raising his squirrel-gray eyebrow an ironic notch or two, Luc asked what in the world they had been talking about using *cette langue de con*. That damned, stupid English language.

Monsieur Deluc positively roared from the other end of the table, and even Aunt Florence fought back a snicker. She looked at Luc with exasperation, though, like he was a precocious child who had said something unintentionally nasty but kind of cute as well.

"I just want to understand, that's all," Luc said in his own defense.

Sophie smiled and apologized for leaving him out of the *con-versation*, meeting his indelicacy with one of her own.

"*Pardonnez-moi,*" she said to him. "*Mais la vie était chouette en ce temps là. Tellement belle, vous-voyez. Maintenant je n'ai rien à fiche sauf de sucrer les fraises.*"

Everyone at the table began laughing once more, the men and the women, and as though at the expense of their neighbor. Except for the fact that Luc was laughing too. Barbara wondered if she had really understood the jokes or not. She had caught the slight imprecation, for Sophie had repeated the word "con" quite unabashedly. But what did it mean to sugar one's strawberries? Why had she said that and was that funny too?

Sophie herself was laughing. Almost to the point of tears.

They had all drunk quite a few glasses of wine.

"Listen to me," Sophie Veuillot said, after catching her breath. "It's true what they say about having to live with your choices." She held her hand over the table to let Barbara watch as it trembled. To sugar one's strawberries was another slang expression, a way of describing someone who was growing old and gradually losing control of their body. It referred to the way that elderly people shake without wanting to, as if they were continually sprinkling out a spoonful of sugar onto a bowl of fruit.

"It's a pretty expression," Barbara told her.

"*C'est à propos de la mort,*" Sophie said. It was a pretty saying really about death.

After good strong coffee, the meal was over. Madame Deluc began clearing the dishes, then everyone agreed to have their photograph taken outside. They all rose somewhat numbly, filed out the door, then rearranged themselves beside the well-house. Barbara took a couple of pictures with her Pentax camera. Then Didier took one of her, balanced on her crutches, smiling brightly and standing next to Sophie Veuillot, his relatives and their neighbor Luc. A few goslings danced around the side of the house, clapping their bright toy bills. When the concerned goose stuck her neck from around the corner, Barbara thought in quick succession of Robert Deluc's cut hand and the homemade gray-yellow pâté. She was glad that she hadn't eaten any. Next she realized with sudden clarity how much Didier had offered, given, concretely done for her during her stay in Paris, then throughout this vacation—how difficult the next couple of weeks were going to be for them both. In private, they had agreed to go on rather than stay the night in Viella, to keep traveling and to be together as much as possible. She and Didier both wanted to avoid any awkwardness which might result over the rooms they would be given by his relatives. Three weeks just weren't enough, she thought. Not enough time to decide anything of importance.

Everyone stood around saying goodbye, prolonging any final gesture of departure. Monsieur Deluc was saying that Sophie shouldn't keep herself closed up in her house so much, that she would have to come down the hill and visit more often. He wanted to know how she was getting along, and made a point of asking about her cats.

"They're fine, fat and fine," Sophie assured him.

Then she explained about the mysterious fire in her yard.

He agreed that it was one of the driest summers anyone could remember. Perhaps the sun had started the fire. Monsieur Deluc said that he doubted it. But it certainly was possible. If he could do anything at all to help her, then Sophie shouldn't hesitate to let him know.

Suddenly, Luc said that, by god, he wanted to officially meet the very pretty American. There hadn't been one in Viella for years! And who knew when he'd have a better opportunity?

He extended an earth-colored hand toward Barbara, which felt like the bark of certain trees. "It would be very difficult wouldn't it?" Luc asked her, pointing down to her cast. "To dance ballet wearing one of those?"

Apparently, he'd asked Madame Deluc about her while she and Sophie had talked during their long meal.

Old Luc raised one leg in the air and made an awkward pirouette. "To work, to work!" he said with conviction. "The party's over. Let's go bust it." Then he staggered off solidly as a stump, his back turned now, quite determined.

Monsieur Deluc and his son said *bon voyage,* then they followed their neighbor down the driveway.

While Didier went around the house for their little Fiat, Barbara started telling Sophie how interesting it had been to talk with her, thanking Madame Deluc and Aunt Florence for all their hospitality. She explained about the rest of the vacation she and Didier were taking together. Today they were going to drive south, she told them, toward the Mediterranean and the Côte d'Azure, which was a part of France she'd never seen. Afterwards Didier would start classes in law school, and she guessed she would go back to the United States for a while, at least to visit her parents. Yes, it would be months before she could dance again, but it was what she loved. That's what she wanted to do, Barbara said.

Then she began kissing them all goodbye.

"Four times," Sophie said, giving her specific kissing directions. She placed her hands on Barbara's shoulders and they kissed on either side of their mouths. Then repeated the process.

Next Sophie Veuillot said something else to her, with the same steady look in her eyes, a smile which was warm but hard to interpret. "You know," she told Barbara. "When I go to bed at night, I allow myself the luxury of certain thoughts. I have had a wonderful life," she said, "But how could I have asked more of it? How could it possibly have been more satisfying than it actually was?"

Resting her weight on her crutches, Barbara leaned forward and hugged her. She didn't know what to say, though, and felt awkward searching to find something. From the way everyone had acted over lunch, it was apparent that this woman had been and still was a remarkable person. A very beautiful, very fortunate woman, someone who'd had an extraordinary past. Whenever she looked in Sophie's eyes, Barbara imagined what she must have looked like back then, and what New York City must have been for her. She envisioned jazz singers in Harlem and lunch at the Savoy, floppy skirts and secret gin, the middle and the end of Prohibition. She had seen all of it.

"Send me a picture of you both on the beach," Sophie told her.

"I will. I promise."

Didier brought the car around and opened the door. But Barbara was still struggling to find the right words. Some way of expressing her gratitude for everything. After a certain point, the two Deluc women seemed almost embarrassed for her, then Sophie Veuillot asked her to remember and please to send the picture.

. . . .

They drove away from the house slowly, waving all the while, then continued for perhaps half an hour until Didier finally stopped the car. He pulled onto a smaller side road, then moved over into the passenger seat with Barbara. As soon as he stopped, Didier immediately began kissing her, saying how much he had detested being apart from her all afternoon. He lifted himself up by pushing against the seat with his right arm, then pressed the lever with his left hand, so that her seat slid back then reclined.

"Don't talk, don't say anything," Barbara said as they began.

It was almost dark. A line of vine-tangled fence and willow trees enshrouded the side road and brought on the night.

She thought of the first time they had ever made love in the apartment on Rue des Blanc Manteaux. Sex had always been lovely and relaxed with Didier, had felt right from the very start. It had been her first time to sleep with someone whose language was not her own and all of the shyness and hesitation, the linguistic awkwardness gave it an added dimension, another small gulf to try and bridge somehow. You felt odd expressing your pleasure in a way which the other person couldn't immediately grasp, but less spontaneous, inauthentic somehow, if you said things you had to think about too much. She had always felt relaxed and right with him, but until some time had gone by and the essential phrases felt natural—until a new way of talking had been established about certain things—then the words felt funny whenever you said them.

But right now, after such a day, all of the awkwardness was gone.

For the most part, despite inevitable errors, Barbara and Didier communicated perfectly.

"I love you. So don't ever leave me, okay?" he was saying, softly imploring. "Promise me that, would you? Just tell me you'll never leave."

"Ssshhhh, please not now," Barbara told him. "*Je t'aime aussi, tu sais?* Don't talk, don't talk about that."

They laughed constantly together and understood one another's different needs, different desires and different fears, it seemed, and if they were really in love, then everything would work out in the end. She believed what mattered most was that Didier felt this way about her, right now, that they'd had some wonderful times together and still had two weeks ahead of them.

After this trip, she would go back to Houston and get herself in shape again. These thoughts and others—certain images from the day—raced and washed through her thinking. Strawberries and houses and the blood on Robert's finger. So many choices. Yes, Paris, she thought. Los Angeles, Atlanta, New York. Someday soon she would dance there again. All her life she had dreamed and worked so hard to achieve a certain version of happiness, a personal conception of success and pleasure which it was impossible not to continue to believe in. But she also believed that she loved Didier too. So she closed her eyes and wondered, listening to the strange familiar words. *I need you please. Never leave me, okay? You promise?* Didier kept saying, kept asking, and Barbara wished that they did have more time to be together, to enjoy their brief trip and this love in the dark.

The Sins of Jesus

When the thought of adopting first came to him, Larry Holman was taking a bubble bath, resting in the tub after a long hard day. Being in the bathtub was relaxing. The acoustics fantastic. Larry liked leaning back so that both ears submerged and all ambient sound grew muffled, watching the hairy-flesh island of his stomach, and wiggling his coral-colored toes. Resting his tired muscles. His stand-up-a-lot choir director feet. Lounging that night in the hot sudsy water, a persistent thought suddenly came full bloom: *I want to raise a child. I really want this. Someone I can help, then who can help me. A friend and buddy. Perhaps a companion for my old age.* Larry was forty-three and happy. But something was missing. He had plenty of money, despite his median salary, plenty of spare time to raise a child the right way. Plenty of love. Plenty of everything, for both himself and another human being—one of God's creatures—someone he could spiritually guide and physically care for in his off-hours from being choral minister and youth recreation leader at Lone Oak Baptist Church.

So the next morning, Larry called an adoption agency. It was an epiphany of sorts, like Paul on the road to Damascus, this decision to expand upon his personal existence. *Yes, a son. Clearly the best option. A daughter might be more iffy and trying.* Raising a little girl might be more difficult, although some parents claimed the opposite, more strenuous in ways Larry couldn't fully imagine and didn't want to think about all that much.

His yearning to adopt had hit him from who-knows-where. But it seemed to settle physically around his solar plexus, in an area just below his heart. By the end of the week, Larry had obtained a lawyer in Louisville—oddly enough, they helped arrange such things. He found an attorney who brokered adoptions with women, usually very young ones, who didn't feel they could responsibly raise the child they carried and who didn't consider terminating their pregnancy a moral choice. Needless to say, Larry was thrilled. He'd be doing his part to prevent an irreversible wrong, then he would personally raise the child he saved. How many pro-lifers would go so far? But Larry Holman was willing. He was ready to start being a good parent right away.

Such things take a while, though. So Larry kept his plan a secret.

For over a month, he didn't tell a soul.

Then one afternoon he bolted into the pastor's office:

"Brother Bill, do you have a minute?"

"Sure thing." Pastor William Copus furrowed, then quickly unfurrowed his brow. He'd been hunched over his desk, writing on scrap paper.

Larry Holman stared solemnly at the carpet's tight, Berber weave. His more playful side wanted to prolong the suspense.

"I have something to say. Something that might shock you."

"Well, I doubt that," Pastor William Copus smiled. Most of his congregation liked him immensely and routinely called him Brother Bill in passing. "You couldn't possibly tell me something that I've not listened to first-hand, or heard roundabout before. Unless you've borrowed some extra money from the offertory."

"It's nothing like that."

"Ha, ha—just kidding." Brother Bill seemed like he was in a playful mood as well. "Let your genie out of the bottle. I'm all ears."

For a few more seconds, Larry Holman kept staring at the carpet, artfully avoiding his pastor's gaze.

"Well, it appears as if I'm going to be a father."

Perhaps it was the considered pause, the stagger in Larry's timing, which occasioned the look that he had hoped to see. First, the furrowed brow again. More mild confusion. Next, Brother Bill's expression slid into an opened mouth look of astonishment.

"Pardon me? What did you say?"

"I'm going to adopt," Larry Holman said, laughing. "The agency called over the weekend. There's a healthy baby up in Louisville. He's three weeks old. Ready and waiting to be picked up."

For the third time, Brother William Copus knitted his forehead. Well, what do you know? He had been surprised indeed. Maybe even the word "shock" applied to his innermost reaction. He started to offer some pastoral advice. But the thing seemed done. Brother Bill saw contentment and resolve in his colleague's face. The matter had been decided. Most likely, very carefully weighed. Larry Holman's character and his sense of responsibility were unquestionable. He did a superb job for the church. He was good with infants, kids, and teenagers alike.

Whenever Larry substitute-taught for ailing Sunday School teachers, he could answer children's straightforward questions in a way that Brother Bill could not: "Why does God have to live up in the sky? How come the snake in the Garden of Eden could talk?" Or the older kid's levelheaded stumpers like: "Why did an all-knowing God allow an evil angel to exist in the first place? Why did three-year-old Whitney Bowland die from leukemia? Why does a sparrow-and-hair-counting deity let horrible things like African famines drag out, or the Oklahoma City Bombing happen to decent folks?" Brother Larry always rose to the occasion. He told such youngsters about the ubiquity of mankind's sin, about earthly evil since Satan's fall from grace. He was ever patient. All cards on the table. "Faith is always faith," Larry Holman told the young people. "You have to trust in what you cannot touch. Believe in what you cannot see. God is constantly watching. He loves all of his earthly children. But many things—like what happened to little Whitney Bowland—such things simply cannot ever be explained."

Yes, Larry Holman could do it. No doubt there.

While a bit unconventional, Brother Bill Copus thought, Larry's being a single father should work out fine. Quite frankly, he envied the man's courage. He himself had a stereotypical preacher's son at home, a fourteen-year-old embarrassment named Kevin, who was a potty-mouth and a masturbating dynamo. Brother Bill had caught the boy in the bathroom once, coated from head to foot with Hawaiian Tropic tanning oil, an array of lurid magazines spread out at his feet.

At Wednesday's prayer meeting, a week's vacation was announced. For the time being, no more details were disclosed. Early Thursday morning, Larry made the trip up Western Kentucky Parkway and I-65. He drove toward downtown Louisville, into what the locals call "spaghetti junction." Then he took the Third Street exit. Soon he was in his lawyer's office at the Riverfront Plaza, overlooking the slow brown crawl of the Ohio River and its smattering of wild birds—the river sat roughly in the Mississippi Flyway and always attracted its share of instinct-driven, migrating Canadian geese.

Sitting before this wonderful view, Larry looked at a photograph of the birth mother. She had made a lot of "classic bad choices," his lawyer explained. She was a little rebel. She was a little drug addict. Luckily, her drug of choice was not crack or heroin. But she had drunk, smoked cigarettes, used some marijuana during the pregnancy. She was Caucasian and the little boy's father was Caucasian. The lawyer made that part up front and clear, as if Larry Holman would have cared. Prior to the birth, the woman had specifically mentioned this fact three times in her pre-adoption interview, but she disclosed no more. All of this information was manila-foldered. Very carefully arranged. The lawyer was a tall, handsome man. Hazel brown eyes. Devout Republican. A funny name, though. Jadran Simic. His family background was Serbo-Croatian. He had a soft deep voice—probably a middle tenor if he ever sang—and took only a modest fee for this *pro bono* service. The contract he'd drawn up required Larry to pay the young woman's medical bills to date. He would assume all fiscal responsibility for the child forthwith.

"Okay," Larry Holman said quietly.

He started perusing the official papers.

"Getting a child this quick is rare," Mr. Simic said, nodding. "She picked you from a lengthy list of prospective adoptive parents."

Without an ounce of vanity, Larry Holman looked again at the photograph. Hadn't he glimpsed the woman's face somewhere before? She was nineteen years old, bless her heart. A beautiful smile. Light-filled, green eyes. A flowering of acne still on her face. She sported what some people call Kentucky Big Hair raised in a puffy mound, like a protective helmet of woven light-blonde wheat. Had she been drinking on the night when she'd gotten pregnant? Where had her parents gone terribly wrong? Larry hoped that his son's mother was a Christian, or would become one shortly as a result of this profound human experience—giving birth, then giving up her baby. He hoped she had been exposed to moral ideas at some point, although her recent behavior suggested otherwise. If only he could talk with her. But that wasn't possible. No telephone number appeared in the documents. Just the one photograph so that her son could see his mother's smiling happy face some day. No name. No means for future contact. That was the deal.

"But years from now?" Larry wondered. "What if one day..."

"Call me first," Mr. Simic told him. "I'll make contact, then we'll see."

Next, Larry Holman signed the adoption contract, the hospital documents, etcetera. He put his John Henry to the daunting stack of legal papers placed before him.

"That's that." Mr. Simic looked satisfied. "Now, let's go see your boy."

Once they arrived at Kosair Children's Hospital, they went to newborn viewing and found the infant kicking in his crib. Beautiful and bubbly. Smiling his pink-gummed smile. The grown men grinned and the little tike grinned back, waving his cherub arms and legs.

"Picked out a name yet?" Mr. Simic wondered.

"I'm going to call him Mason," Larry told him. "Charles Mason Holman. After my uncle who helped raise me."

Suddenly the little boy let out an uncanny screeching. A noise of such happy vitality that it rattled the Plexiglas. Both men jumped backwards. Then they began to laugh.

"Guess he doesn't object," Mr. Simic joked.

"Apparently not," Larry agreed.

Of course, there were a few more documents to sign at the hospital, talks with attending nurses and the physician who had overseen the birth. A final handshake with Mr. Simic. Soon enough, though, Larry Holman was heading back down I-65 with a content-looking baby dozing in his new Graco car seat, the model *Consumer Digest* suggested to be the very best. How weird, Larry thought. How strange. Only a few hours earlier, he'd driven up to Louisville all alone. Now there was this quietly sleeping, vulnerable body beside him. Hard to believe that they'd let him have him. Hard to fathom what all the responsibilities would entail.

"I'm forty-three," Larry thought to himself. "That isn't really old at all. But this little baby is so brand new." When Mason turned ten, he would turn fifty-three. At that age, Larry would still be capable of running bases, jumping on trampolines, playing pick-up games of basketball and volleyball. He was going to teach Mason sports, something no one had taught him as a pudgy, quiet, unconfident youth. He would encourage healthy eating habits, like Daniel in the Old Testament. He would teach him to think and to do good things. That was the idea.

II.

Only three days after they'd been living together as a family, Larry's adopted son began losing weight at an alarming rate. Little Mason refused to eat. He slept fitfully. When he awoke, he cried nonstop. The trend of weight loss continued for two weeks. Little Mason dropped from almost nine pounds to under seven. It was as if the beautiful boy were vanishing before his adoptive father's very eyes. First, Larry went to a series of doctors at the local hospital, then he drove down to Vanderbilt in nearby Nashville. A team of pediatric specialists kept the child alive—but barely—on IV glucose and a gastrostomy tube which pumped formula directly into his stomach. The Nashville doctors tested him for everything: cerebral palsy, various enzyme disorders, epilepsy, and AIDS. By this point Larry had grown to love the child. A strong bond had formed.

All of Mason's pre-natal and postpartum charts were faxed from Louisville. The Vanderbilt doctors considered what the charts contained. But by week's end, still no change. Little Mason soon weighed five-and- a-half pounds. The specialists finally pronounced his condition as "failure to thrive."

"Is he going to die?" Larry Holman asked point-blank.

"Yes, that's possible," Dr. Herold sadly told him. He was a bearded man with an unsmoked cigar in his pocket, nestled snugly next to a Mont Blanc pen. "No one really knows why this happens. Some infants simply do not survive. But there are certain patterns. Directly after birth, this child saw his mother for less than an hour. There's an emotional element—always an emotional element."

After talking to the unhopeful doctor, Larry began to read stories to Mason. *Go Dog Go, Green Eggs and Ham, The Collected Adventures of Curious George.* He talked aloud to the child, whenever he wasn't praying, more fervently than he'd ever prayed. Larry didn't sleep or eat much himself. Then after a few days of this storytelling and fasting—miracle or whatever else you wish to call it—his adopted son began to suck on Larry's pinky finger. Next, a proffered bottle. He gained a couple grams of weight. The Vanderbilt nurses weighed him every few hours, weighed his dry and soiled diapers to gauge input and output.

Long story short, Larry Holman and his boy were soon on the road back home. Charles Mason Holman, Jr. had survived indeed. After returning from Vanderbilt, the youngster ate quite heartily. Mason consumed everything in sight. Baby formula, strained apricots, Gerber biscuits galore.

More time passed slowly.

More time passed quickly, as earthly time is apt to do.

Weeks turned into months. Months turned into years. Just like any other terrible two and three-year-old, Mason saw to his fair share of toddler mischief: flooding the bathroom with his own bathtub water, clogging the toilet with a whole roll of paper, once cutting his right index finger to the bone with a serrated knife, something he'd filched from a drawer despite Infant-Guard fasteners installed throughout the kitchen. Luckily, the knife-wielding toddler missed all his ligaments and tendons. Some local ER doctor at Paducah's Western Baptist sewed up the index finger just as good as new.

The real trouble didn't start for a while yet.

Not until Mason turned nine-years-old.

One day Larry Holman came home frazzled and fatigued, disaffected from yet another bickering-filled choir practice. Currently there was a quiet brawl going on over solos between violet-haired Mrs. Lyles and Laurie Boaz, a talented young woman who could actually sing. Upon pulling in the driveway, Larry found his boy in the backyard, screaming bloody murder at his babysitter. Beet-faced. Inconsolable. Mason was yelling at the girl because she'd been petting his new cat named Bob. As in bobcat. Quite frankly, it was an inappropriate name for such a docile, sweet kitten. But with its vertical wisps of ear hair and brindle coloring, the animal did resemble a miniature version of the woodland felines.

"Don't touch him again," Mason screeched. "He's MINE!"

"Okay, okay," his babysitter agreed.

Yvonne Bowland tried her best to calm the boy down. Her teenage face looked more frightened than fed up.

Larry glimpsed the whole tableau from the driveway. But he waited, not wanting to intervene. He wanted to see how the babysitter could manage the child in her charge. Finally, he headed toward the lawn which he maintained himself on weekends. Of course, he encouraged his son to help with the promise of McDonald's Happy Meals, cotton candy, or giant Pixie-Stix. But his son still stubbornly refused. So Larry did the work himself, never without a shirt—but often barefoot—carefully avoiding the dark-colored honeybees and butterflies cruising across the lime-green lawn. A dangerous habit, mowing without shoes. But the yard was level, and Larry loved the feel of grass on his naked feet.

"Hey, hey, hey! What's going on here?"

"Daddy, she touched my cat. I HATE her! I NEVER want her to touch him! And I NEVER want her to babysit for me again."

The expression on Yvonne's face said this wouldn't be a problem in the least.

Suddenly, Mason grabbed the kitten from her and flung it violently halfway across the yard. The sight of this angered his father. But Larry tried his best to check such a powerful emotion.

"Don't you *ever* do that, young man."

Larry spoke firmly. But not too loudly.

He'd been around a lot of kids over the years. He'd learned the consequences of yelling at this particular boy before. However, try as he might to diffuse the tension gracefully, Larry couldn't find words to appease his son, or erase the displeasure from Yvonne Bowland's face. Her daddy was a deacon at Lone Oak Baptist. Larry knew that this event would be reported and rebroadcast in no time flat. Yet another story added to his son's fabled repertoire.

Already, Mason's temper had become quite legendary, the shenanigans of Brother Bill's son long forgotten and eclipsed. Once Mason had lost it at a church ice cream supper. He started kicking people—for no reason anyone could determine—then the reprimanded boy began to pummel his father about the face. Even then, Larry had stayed very patient, as the two men who pried the boy off him shook their heads in quiet contempt. But they didn't know the half of it. After Mason Holman became riled at home, sometimes *nothing* worked to settle him down, not once his adrenaline—or whatever it was—began to flow.

Once when little Mason was younger, Larry had slapped his hand for playing with electrical outlets, occasionally "paddled his bottom good" to teach him limits. He had tried everything to no avail. Larry had spanked and he'd not spanked. He had taken away privileges and tried "time out" one minute for each year of Mason's age. He hoped Mason's disposition would improve when he got older. Perhaps he would change his ways, for example, whenever he reached the age of accountability.

But, alas, such was not the case. Always out of control temper-wise, Mason eventually killed the brindle-colored cat named Bob. This happened the year he turned sixteen. A neighbor, Sue-Ann Spiceland, saw him do it. He strangled the full grown animal one day for tracking mud on his freshly washed and waxed car, then—not a pretty detail but a fact all the same—Mason kept squeezing downward in some fit of ineffable, mysterious rage until the poor animal's intestines protruded from its rear end. Sue-Ann had witnessed this from her kitchen window. Afterwards, Sue-Ann ran into the bathroom and vomited. Then rather than calling the boy's father, she called the local police department.

Of course, the police knew him already.

They'd had run-ins with Mason ever since he'd gotten his driver's license, and a slightly used, all white Grand Prix—his very first car.

Still, Larry persevered. He did his parental duty, his community and his church obligations. He secretly began to hope that something dire but not catastrophic would happen, so that his son's soul might be shaken-up and salvaged. Something like what had happened to him, when Larry was around his age. A year younger, actually. Fifteen years old. That's when Larry Holman had gotten saved, following a trip to the dentist to have his two impacted wisdom teeth removed. During his convalescence, Larry was given Tylenol number threes and amidst his pain-addled, slightly feverish state, God, or a God-like voice, had spoken directly to him: "Do not choose hell. Choose heaven and happiness—follow me." A visitation. A personal marvel and message: "Follow me." That part had been unmistakable and distinct. A kind, mellifluous voice in Larry's brain had told him this so clearly, and some vivid pictures went along with what he heard. That day, he'd seen an image of God's son, Jesus Christ, smiling benevolently, hovering against the cream-colored ceiling above his small twin bed. Right there beneath his bedroom ceiling. On his aunt and uncle's farm where they'd raised him ever since his own parents were killed, swept away by the floodwaters of 1963.

Later in life, Larry saw the same thing once more, glimpsed it again more or less, in some old sick person's living room. By then he was a music minister. He'd been looking at coffee table book photographs of Rio de Janeiro with its lily-white and gorgeous Corcovado Christ, roughly the same image which he'd seen at fifteen. Of course, Rio's calm marble statue of Jesus had its arms spread over some rickety slums and beachfront skyscrapers off in the distance. Copacabana. Ipanema. Leblon. Some of the book's other pictures concerned a thing called "carnival." These photos didn't shock Larry Holman, but they made him nervous, especially while sitting in a church member's home. Still, Rio de Janeiro looked beautiful.

Once upon a time, Larry had considered missionary work on the island of Tonga. He'd always dreamed of living someplace tropical. Maybe somewhere beside a turquoise ocean. But he never actively pursued those dreams apart from an occasional bathtub musing. Eventually, though, he hoped to maybe take a cruise. Perhaps when he retired from the church, because nowadays Larry's dreams and wishes centered elsewhere, around his troubled and trouble-making son. He hoped that someday Mason—who the community of Lone Oak sometimes called Charles Manson Holman behind his back—would have the blessing of a divine visitation. His own late-night "hey you down there—wake up." From time to time, Larry guiltily hoped for a slight illness, something out of Mason's control that would possibly turn him around. Something mildly painful actually might help. Something like his wisdom tooth episode, anything to scare the boy, something to make him grasp the utter truth of human frailty. The little or lot of suffering-on-the-back-burner which surely awaits us all. It sounded so *wrong*, of course.

Another sickness. For his son.

What a horrible thing to think.

III.

Larry Holman was beloved. He is still beloved. The summer he left Lone Oak Baptist—how he lost the hearing in one ear, and how he very nearly died—will never be erased from recollection, the memories of hundreds of people, dozens upon dozens of congregation members and their extended families to whom he gave so much.

Singing was his forte, if the truth be told, not choir leading, or parenting, or anything else except the sheer generosity with which he gave his time—and who on earth has much of that? But Larry Holman always found time. He always seemed to have some extra. He would take busloads of kids snow skiing, fishing, golfing, to the St. Louis zoo to see the exotic animals. When it came to the kids, Larry was *there* for them and there was nothing iffy about what he wanted or expected in return. He didn't expect a thing. You name it—if some church kids wanted to do it—Larry would find the funds to make it happen, then drive the bus himself. But it is his singing at Lone Oak Baptist that lingers most in memory. Whenever Larry Holman sang, everyone, including his adopted son, Mason, stayed absolutely still and perfectly quiet. Totally reverent. His voice could arrest almost anyone's wandering attention, lift up any lukewarm believer's bad mood, then assure the truly devout that the Holy Spirit was on the move.

He had the resonant tenor of someone professionally trained. But as a youth growing up on his uncle and aunt's hard-scrabble farm in Mayfield, Kentucky, Larry was self-taught in every endeavor he attempted. He'd not exactly had a blissful childhood. The only thing Larry was good at, which made him forget his social awkwardness, was when he stood before a crowd to sing. "The Old Rugged Cross," "Marching to Zion," "Blessed Jesus," or his signature Easter Sunday number, "Up From the Grave He Arose," featuring a few notes so low—so moving and almost spooky—that the sanctuary's temperature actually seemed to drop whenever Larry Holman sang that particular song.

When Charles Mason Holman Jr. turned seventeen, he got another car. He would drive it very fast wherever he decided to go. His new car was a black Trans-Am with T-tops—a birthday gift from his father. No doubt, a very big mistake. But Mason had fervently promised to help pay the insurance, promised to get a part-time job and that had swayed Larry's decision. How Mason got spending money wasn't all too clear. One thing was certain. He did whatever the heck he wanted to do. Mason discovered alcohol shortly on the heels of speed. Then sex. He had a cute, well-mannered girlfriend named Lynn Armstrong. She settled him down for a while, but in the end Mason's behavior didn't improve one jot. He vandalized. He lied. He shoplifted every chance he got.

Something had to happen. Didn't it?

Finally, that thing did.

One day Larry got a phone call from Kentucky State Trooper Bobby Helm. "I'm sorry to have to tell you this. Your boy is at the McCracken county jail. I'm afraid the charge is rape."

Of course, a girl was involved. Larry should have known there would be. Actually two girls and another one of Mason's roughneck friends, a local football star named Brooke Weller. After buying a case of beer, they'd all driven behind the soybean fields beside Paducah's Barkley Airport to make-out and watch the noisy jets take off. One of the young girls had been with Mason and the other girl was with his friend. That's where the stories diverged. Apparently, the girls willingly drank the beer; then it seems that Brooke's girl went all the way—but Mason's would not. So Brooke and his girl said they'd go for a walk around the airport's perimeter. They got out and left Mason and Tammie in the car. That's when—according to the girl's first statement—Mason had pulled out a small gun from the glove compartment. Tammie Murt was fifteen-and-a-half. So a statutory rape charge had been brought against Larry's adopted son.

In an effort to show his profound regret, Larry Holman visited the girl's parents' house. Once there, he learned more than even the police knew about what really occurred. Oddly enough, Mr. and Mrs. Murt seemed just as irate at their daughter as they were with Mason. Her parents had learned some things from Tammie's diary, things that made them doubt whether she'd been entirely honest with them. Both on this particular occasion and in the past. Once cornered, Tammie bragged that she smoked pot regularly and that she had a three-foot bong hidden in her room. Next, she told her parents that she'd had it ever since eighth grade. Since the event at the airport, however, Tammie had changed her story. She said that no rape had taken place. Apparently, Mason had done something else to make the girl upset. But Larry never found out what that might have been. The gun had only been a starter pistol, something Brooke Weller had obtained since he ran track for the high school. For whatever reason—perhaps a parental wish to avoid publicity—all charges were eventually dropped.

But charges or no charges, Larry Holman didn't want the lesson to evaporate so quickly. He had to devise some way to punish Mason. So without saying anything, he placed an ad in the newspaper to sell his son's beloved Trans-Am. Once he had a potential buyer, Larry arranged a meeting at the church office and accepted a certified check. Then all hell broke loose.

"Your car is gone," Larry patiently explained, just as soon as Mason returned home from school. "I sold it today."

"You did what?" the outraged teenager screamed.

But Larry Holman remained quite calm.

"You have breached my trust one time too many. Despite our agreement, you failed to get a part-time job. I bought the car as a gift against my better judgment. I paid for everything. Even your insurance."

By now, Mason was sneering in a nasty way. His face had drained off its deep-red color. But what it looked like now was even scarier. Devoid of any color, or expression, or any blood at all.

"No thanks, no respect, no gratitude," Larry Holman continued. "None whatsoever. That's the way it's always been. You fail to understand who is on your side."

The boy laughed out loud.

"Get lost," Mason coolly told him.

Larry Holman wasn't surprised one bit. "Once again," he said sadly, but in a voice tinged with intrepidity. "Once again, you have spit in my face."

His adopted son Mason laughed at him.

"Screw you, you pansy-ass nobody. I don't want anything you want, or anything you want to give me. Why don't you leave me alone? As a matter of fact, why don't you fuck off?"

So much for not losing one's temper.

Larry finally slapped him.

"What did you just say?"

"I said screw you. Screw everything you stand for. I want to be free. I want to be happy. Just as free as a deer in the woods. Goodbye and good riddance. Adios, I'm a ghost."

And he was gone.

The next Friday afternoon, Larry walked across the church parking lot to Lone Oak Baptist's newly constructed recreational center. He had to supervise a pizza-and-bowling birthday party in the facility's basement. Over thirty kids had showed up for Lisa Hancock's special day. They all ate Domino's, bowled a few games, then devoured an ice-cream cake from Baskin-Robbins. Some of the kids wanted to play ping-pong. Since Larry had no other plans and needed the distraction—he'd been worried where Mason was sleeping, how he was eating—he agreed to stay longer than originally planned. Besides, these sweet-faced children were the perfect balm. They enjoyed his company immensely. That much was plain to see. So Larry sketched out a round robin table-tennis tournament in which he participated wholeheartedly before feigning a last-minute loss.

After locking the recreation center, Larry Holman drove home in his eleven-year-old Buick Regal with many thousands of miles on the odometer. Once he'd parked and was walking around the side of his house, he saw a dull flash of yellow under the garage security light. Then he felt something hollow and hard against the side of his head.

The pain was spectacular. Totally disorienting. The wiffle-ball bat was plastic but very hard. The whistling sound alone quite horrible. Larry Holman genuflected involuntarily. He silently dropped to his knees, then raised his head to see his son Mason hovering above him. The boy's face was expressionless and pale, as he reared back one-handed, as if stretching for something on a distant shelf.

Once again, Mason swung the wiffle-ball bat violently. The second blow landed in such a way that Larry's eardrum burst. Mason swung a third time. Then a fourth. Full-force and in the face. Larry Holman's adopted son was large. He had lifted weights some, but failed to make the football or track team like his roustabout buddy Brooke. Soon Mason's shouting was constant. But its loudness varied, depending on whether Larry was being kicked. Or hit again with the bat. Eventually, several ribs were fractured. Once or twice, Larry Holman tried to stand. But he was knocked back down. Another kick made a sickening thud at the base of his nose, and Larry's upper lip exploded wetly with blood. He was about to faint. Instead of losing consciousness, though, he heard his son's battery-acid laced voice. "I HATE YOU! YOU GOD-DAMNED QUEER! DIDN'T I FUCKING TELL YOU TO GIVE ME BACK MY CAR." Nothing modulated. Nothing hidden. All of his off-kilter wrath exposed.

Eventually, Sue-Ann Spiceland and her husband, Joe, heard Mason's yelling as they lay together that night in bed. They were half-watching *The Tonight Show with Jay Leno,* and as soon as Joe Spiceland heard the yelling he understood immediately what was going on. "That psycho kid! Goddamn it! That little bastard is hurting him."

Immediately, Joe jumped out of bed, tugged on a pair of jeans, then tore out the door. His nickname was "Burly Joe," a serious gray-eyed man who drove tandem dump trucks for a living, drank beer and rarely went to church, but supported his wife's decision to make their kids attend. By the time Joe Spiceland negotiated the chain link fence, Mason had seen him. He quickly deciphered the look on Joe Spiceland's face. He saw the man's big adult eyes focusing hotly into his own.

"If I'd gotten my hands on him," Joe Spiceland later told the deputy sheriff, "you'd be hauling me in for assault. Or maybe worse."

"Yes, sir." The deputy sheriff nodded.

The deputy kept scribbling.

"The ungrateful little shit is lucky," Joe Spiceland said and he meant it. "I would have handed him his ass on a plate."

Of course, Mr. Spiceland had other reasons to be furious. He'd heard about the strangled, half-eviscerated cat. Plus a few other stories. But what Mason Holman had done to his own pet animal, well, that had left an indelible impression. His wife had been terrified of the boy ever since that day.

Actually, Larry Holman's two neighbors hadn't been watching *The Tonight Show with Jay Leno*. Not watching carefully, you might say. They hadn't been paying much attention to his lantern-jaw mugging, his I'm-such-a-nice-guy performance. ("Boy, he's sure changed," Joe Spiceland vaguely remarked at one point. "Something's happened. I used to love Leno's stand-up act"). No, they had only been staring at the TV. Actually, Joe and Sue-Ann had just finished a full-blooded round of connubial naughtiness. Afterwards, they'd been lying awake in a giddy, relaxed daze. They'd merely flipped on the set before dozing off to sleep, when suddenly the shouting began in the backyard adjacent to their own, whereupon Joe Spiceland jumped to his feet, cursed a blasphemous blue streak, pulled on his pants and ran out the door.

Sure, Mason got away. But who knows?

What if Joe Spiceland hadn't intervened? Quite possibly, Mason would have kicked his adoptive father to death—entirely possible.

Indeed, who knows?

After he recovered Larry Holman left Lone Oak Baptist. Then he accepted another job at a smaller, startup church in Myrtle Beach. Last anyone heard, he was doing okay. He married a woman six years younger. He is fifty-nine now and she is fifty-three. But what if burly Joe Spiceland and Sue-Ann hadn't been wide-awake and listening carefully? What if they had remained distant and uninvolved? Strangely enough—given the choir director's appearance when the paramedics arrived—Joe and Sue-Ann never *once* heard anyone scream in pain. Or yell out for help. They heard only a single shrieking voice, Mason's blood-chilling shouts and his deranged hate-filled accusations. Otherwise, not a single protestation, or quiet beseeching. Not a please-stop, please-don't-do-this. Not a single solitary peep.

The Angels

"Voices, voices—even the girl herself—now."

—Joseph Conrad, *Heart of Darkness*

Sometimes I think of the face Frank wore that day and imagine him jumping from the airplane. How difficult it must have been—how sad—that he couldn't indulge in the thrill of the fall. I think of what he was thinking and the degree to which his thoughts were different from those of previous jumps, different from any I'll ever know. I suppose that falling out of the sky must be an overcharged version of that tender tug you feel whenever the car you're in goes over a hill too quickly, or when your body is caught by a wave. The most vulnerable part of you is lifted up, and then there's a slow, sexy sinking.

I wonder what the scenery is like from five thousand feet with the wind in your face while you're falling. What color are Panamanian hills? Or the water in the middle of the canal miles from either ocean? Turquoise or muddy? Brown or blue? Where do all of those barges come from, and why in the world did they leave?

Whenever my mother writes me from Mexico City, my father always scribbles a few lines at the bottom of her letter. He calls me *gringa* and says how much he would like me to visit them as soon as I find the time and money. It's not cold-hearted, not really, and he means to be funny. But you have to know his code. This is my father's way of reminding me how far away from home I am and letting me know that he misses me. I know this, for my memories are solid. There were good times too with my father.

Right now it is winter in Los Angeles, and the man I loved has been killed. Frank is dead. So I try to remember my childhood, my parents, all the things that I thought about when I was a little girl and the innocent games we played growing up in the outskirts. I would skip rope on Calle Duraznos or kick a ball with my brothers and sisters, the standard games kids play, or we would invent something else to do: fasten bed sheets or towels around our necks, then jump off stairwells and pretend we could fly.

I remember becoming very ambitious, quite logical, about the sensation this flying game produced. I wondered if with a bigger cape, or perhaps some more practice, I would be able to stay afloat for a few seconds longer. Then one day my brother Ernesto snitched my grandmother's umbrella, jumped off the roof, and broke his arm. Afterwards I forgot about the idea of rigging up something that would let me glide around the neighborhood and smile at all the others. It was a blissful state to be in though—believing. Believing that for a short space of time it might actually work, that the privileges and invulnerability of youth, that these good times would last forever. It is something that I'll always remember about my childhood and that I used to tell Frank about sometimes. We didn't have television, we didn't have cartoons, but on Saturday mornings my mother's mother would bake thin sheets of piecrust with honey. We would fight over who got the biggest pieces—we were kids—then race around the neighborhood, our faces smeared with cinnamon, wearing our sheets and soaring off stairs.

We used to play so hard and get filthy from head to toe. The dust from our *calle* would get caked on our fingers, and we would chase one another around, trying to wipe our messy hands on each other, my grandmother's pastry inside us and on us, giggling and falling, the wind in our hair.

Everything's so different now. Every thing is different. The way I feel about being here, people's faces, this ocean, although the ocean is no colder than it was before because the ocean was always cold, but darker now and lifeless, somewhat bluer and entirely blind. Usually there are boats here, sailboats and trawlers, headed for the faster water or the more valuable fishing grounds. It's hard to believe, but this ocean is teeming with life: salmon and swordfish, sea urchins and crabs. There are bluefin tuna, I've read, fish which weigh hundreds of pounds and are worth five thousand dollars apiece because the Japanese consider them a delicacy. There is fierce competition for these bigger fish, but for the smaller fish too. The zones are closely surveyed, and the methods are vicious, I am quite sure. They say that love makes the world go around, but how much does what we love cost us? *¿Cuánto cuesta amarnos?*

Out on the beach the same morning they told me, I couldn't believe there was anything moving beneath the waves. Apart from the motion of the water itself, there was no activity. No boats with their fishing nets, no surfers in wet suits—nothing—and I couldn't imagine any life beneath the waves either, although I'm sure I was mistaken.

I am fluent. Capacious. I'm interested. I want to find ways of keeping the solid moments we shared together, the pleasure that Frank and I knew. One way of doing this is to remember his arms and his legs, his mouth, and his awkward monosyllables.

Frank never liked to talk much beyond the point where he'd said all he wanted. Perhaps he believed that too many words were a distraction, a slipping-away which sometimes, in their user's desperation, could constitute a loss. But I don't think Frank had enough faith in his ability to let me know what he was feeling. I would talk to him like this, the way I talk to you now, and he would listen to me, leaning forward occasionally to tell me some things I wanted to know too. Frank told me what it was like being away from me so long and what his thoughts had tended toward at night, what he had wished for and what he had learned. With a child's enthusiasm, Frank told me what was involved in learning to become a paratrooper—what it felt like to fall out of the sky.

. . . .

We used to come to the beach together and that is where we first met. On a Friday, I remember, during the summertime when I didn't have to teach. After sunset we went out with his friends and my friends to eat shrimp and drink margaritas. Frank was originally from Charlotte, North Carolina. So this place was new to him as well. He was nervous at first, quite boyish and awkward, whenever he talked to me or whenever he tried to use Spanish. Frank knew a little. Everybody here knows a little, or says they do anyway. But Frank genuinely wanted to learn some more.

So I thought of the whole Pacific coast that day on the beach, the day they called and explained that Frank was one of the first to fall. The newscasters broke the general news about the invasion, but the telephone call itself came over a week later. After the New Year had begun. After I had slid all his presents under the bed. I thought about us— about Frank and me—but also about this vast apartment.

The Pacific Coast.

This land, you know. My new home.

It's hard to believe that it happened more or less in the same part of the world. Of course, I'm talking about a huge chunk of the globe but the same continent with the same name, which is what I have to remind myself I'm actually standing on. Japan's an island. Cuba's an island. Even Australia. Only by geographical accident do I find myself on what is called a "continent," for the name doesn't fit somehow, and it does not feel like one to me.

Right now at least, I'm on the biggest island on the globe. And if you close your eyes and listen, then perhaps you'll see what I mean. Or trace your finger down the continent's coast, southward, towards where

I come from—that's where it happened, all right. We're connected, you'll realize, up to a point. There are canals between every body. Oh yes, I know what I'm writing. I'm a schoolteacher and my English is wonderful. I'm saying there are gulfs between all of us. But I'm not sure how good your memory is. I know little of your fascination with maps. So consider how the land swings down, low in a crescent, past the Baja, past the borders. The land lies on its side like a sliver of moon, something wounded or weary, propped up against an ocean the color of midnight and another name that's a lie. Or think of the land as a person's body, someone smiling and leaning on an elbow, her muscles relaxed now that it's all over, one leg stretched out into the Gulf, the other sprawled in the Caribbean sea.

If I threw myself in the ocean here I could float all the way down, depending on the current. Sometimes the idea occurs to me. I could make it if the water happened to move that way. My waist-length hair would spread out, like black seaweed or tentacles, swirl over my body and grow longer after I had drowned. I would take off my clothes to speed the journey, and who knows how long it would take, if a fishing boat or an oil tanker would spot me. The albacore fishermen might fight over me—you know that joke some men tell one another—or I could float off-course towards Japan.

Could I silently impress the sharks?

Avoid the hooks, the acquisitiveness, all the nets?

. . . .

Frank was a year younger. Twenty-three. Ironically, this is currently their official figure for what happened in Panama. He was quite young in some ways and could still be giddy on occasion, although he didn't talk much or show his excitement the way I do. Still, I'll never forget what Frank told me about jumping out of an airplane, about the rush of being airborne, what it felt like the very first time.

Worst of all were the interviews around Christmastime. Sitting in my apartment and trying to understand via satellite. Trying to see through their well-read words. Waiting and watching with telecommunicative curiosity. The commander's assurance. His general gusto. "Good evening Ted," the big voice boomed. "It's good to be talking to you." The Southern commander and Ted Koppel gave the impression of being old friends, but I got the feeling they had never laid eyes on one another, or cared to all that much.

. . . .

Sometimes it's hard for me to get up and face these happy children. Their shimmering faces. Their wonder-filled innocence. So I force myself. I'm confused and angry, but I'm not sure who to blame, who I should hold responsible for what has happened. Sometimes when I'm talking to my students, a grown man's face appears, and I hear that booming voice from the television broadcast, see the bright lights from the helicopter. The waving palm fronds. The big man's smile. I tell myself that his face is no more substantial, no more solid or more real than my own face, or the faces of these children. It is powerful but sculpted by many hands. Straightforward, rigid, and confident to be sure—but constructed. This face I see is ubiquitous and its owner's energy is everywhere. It has been built-up, put in place. And while it might sound like little or nothing right now, I assure you that what I do makes a difference. What I do here makes an indelible impression. I too have a voice that cannot be stopped, and so that face can be transformed, rearranged. I tell myself this every morning now. I can shift a few bricks.

I'll bring in the map and show them the sliding coast, put the word *pan* in their mouths, slip in *luna, cuerpo, mujer*. This is part of the earth, I will tell them, and then point to the place that hurts me. *Corazon.* Heart is not the same thing, you see, and you don't really have a word for what I feel.

Tierra, I will teach them, but that's a hard one because of the r's.

Watch closely then and listen, I'll say.

Pay attention to my tongue.

. . . .

I come from the largest city in the world. So perhaps I know a few things you don't know. But I'm not sure. Whenever people are packed together so tightly, it seems like the gaps are wider. The distances between people, between people and things. Now that I have more of it I've learned to focus more sharply on "freedom," which is just an idea like any other, you realize, the sound of which isn't worth a handful of beans. But when I use the word "freedom" don't think that I'm smiling on one side of my face. Don't think that I'm being satirical. Even after what's happened, I feel glad to be here, you see. But have you noticed the way our eyes can slide over things?

Someone's face? An ocean? Or a book?

How you never become intimate by accident?

The fact of the matter is that we're all islands. All of us. Entirely different. Distinct. There is no denying it. We are cut off from one another in the most essential ways, which is precisely why I'm telling you all of this. It is no mistake that I happen to have a pen in my hand or that you're sitting down reading what I have to tell. It is something intended, that we wanted to do, or if we are lucky, desired. Yes, that's the word, or do I speak for myself? What I'm desiring right now is no accident.

. . . .

I'm no general, no judge, no philosopher queen. But when I was a little girl I used to come home from *colegio* and sing songs and write poems. I used to dream of bursting out from that closed, stacked-up world—of living my life just right.

All the people around me, my family and friends, they basically wanted the same things. But I suspected they would likely never have them and understood that some of them never could. I wanted to be the woman who did something, who left her roots and kept them too. Who worked hard, and who made a difference. Some people say we Latinos are lazy, just passionate lovers, duffers, and dreamers. They say we pay too much attention to wishes, those gauzelike images that come to us. But I managed to move toward just what I wanted. To work my way up, you might say.

It's not perfect, by any means, in this valley either, and indeed a lot of things are quite the same: the crowds, the cold money, the *caca de camiones*. All the rushing and distance and speed. But I've got a good job in the City of Angels, which just goes to show you that there's a practical dimension to wishing, that it's one way of making things happen. So tell me this, my fellow compadres, has this other kind of desire dried up in you? Have you put up a border around dreaming?

. . . .

Personally, I'm afraid of all passionless people, their robust voices and ironic smiles. Not laughter, mind you, but smiling. Laughter occurs within a different domain.

I think a lot of times we laugh to forget, or to remember. But deep-down we laugh because we are frightened.

Personally, I'm afraid of the fearless.

. . . .

My mother never knew we were married and I can't tell her now. My future would be the color of a crow's wing, because my parents would see things from a different perspective, from otherworldly Catholic eyes. My life as a woman would be over. My father might call me worse names than he did on the day I first left his house. So I can't tell them now. Am I wrong to be silent on this matter, to prefer my form of pleasure to theirs?

No one had ever taken care of me, pleased me, the way that Frank could whenever he took the time. In spite of his big hands and his awkward way of saying what he wanted.

"Okay, *espera*. Not now," I might tell him.

But sometimes it was the other way around.

Sometimes Frank would say, "Hold on. Let's wait a minute." Occasionally I would sympathize with his strategy, and neither of us would utter a word. One morning before classes, I was wearing a yellow dress—a yellow dress with black dots—drinking coffee and reading papers from students. Frank was getting ready for work in the other room, and he came out of the shower, soaking wet and dressed in a towel. He wanted to be with me, he said. "Me too," I decided to tell him. We had to hurry, of course, and afterwards I pulled down my yellow dress with the black dots. Frank drove me to school and I taught. But then all day long I felt him kissing me and had this intimate sensation which is hard to describe, like he was still actually there. I'm not talking about something vague, some evaporated sweetness like dried honey, but some solid logic. Something tangible. Quite real.

I'll never forget that feeling Frank gave me. I want—I wish I had the opportunity right now, you know, of hearing him blurt out that he wanted me, then of telling him there wasn't enough time.

I wish I had the luxury of telling him no.

. . . .

I don't have to draw you a picture. I've not mentioned places much, or named many names, have you noticed? But this does not mean that I've forgotten the particulars of his story.

I have done what I can to be precise.

What else is there to say about my Christmas? What more can I tell you about how I feel? *¿Qué sé yo?* You'll just have to imagine for yourself what my life was like in the outskirts of the largest city in the world, the things I had to do to leave and how my life changed when I came here.

Once I finished school and when I met Frank. I've only told you part of my story, but every bit of it is true. While we can't absolutely control our dreams or our stories, there is one difference between them, I think. Our dreams, they come to us. They're not dependable or straightforward or necessarily true, so we can say what we want about dreaming. But we can't lie to ourselves, can we, about what we've done? What would be the point in something so farfetched?

If there's one thing I hate, it is fantasy.

But perhaps I will fill you in. Tell you a little bit more. I just want you to understand about my life. About the hope I had and the love I lost. About the importance of not being born important, which is the reason why I first came to Los Angeles and the reason why Frank joined up.

. . . .

I remember how one morning, when Frank was on leave for the weekend, we watched cartoons together lying on the sofa. "Oooooooh, I hate that rabbit," thundered a hot-headed prospector. Yosemite Sam was his name. Sometimes this Sam character doubled as a castaway, a pirate, or a cowboy, and he never learned a thing from his former experiences. In this particular cartoon, he had been tricked again. But he defied physics for a moment, racing off the edge of a diving board then feeling with his foot before falling.

While we were lying there, Frank explained about parachutes. He talked about his training drills while we watched Bugs Bunny and that dark Daffy Duck racing around. Outwitting each other, or being outwitted. Then came that emaciated bird who runs across highways, past rickety cliffs and huge sandstone spires. She seems so alone in the desert except for an occasional bus and that ACME coyote. He is more notorious than any of these characters for not catching the drift of things, for celebrating his indestructibility.

. . . .

I think of Frank and his parachute. The size of a man and a woman. They are playing some game together, and she's riding on his shoulders. Wide-eyed and taking it all in. Overwhelmed and still not really believing that he has jumped. But the image is wrong, I realize, since Frank was completely alone. While I have no idea what it was really like to jump out of that airplane, I see him buoyed up like a floating piece of cloth, flapping majestically against the purple Sierras, not enjoying himself precisely, or worried anymore that his chute might not open—beyond that now. Yet not impervious to the violet hills sloping down towards the sea. The blue and white buildings. The sand-colored sand.

Talk, Talk, Talk

Late Friday afternoon when Angie Thompson came home from work, she found her Air Force husband holding their sixteen-year-old daughter on her tiptoes by her peroxided waist-length hair. The day was July hot. Southern Georgia humid. Apparently tempers had flared. At first, Angie only caught a silhouette of them in the living room, while parking her Honda with 191,000 odometer miles in the driveway. She knew her husband and daughter were arguing again—the screen door's cross-hatching showed her that much. *How can I fix this?* she thought. *How can I be a more useful mother? How can I take out the guess work and make the bad stuff stop?* Angie couldn't hear precisely what was being said inside her house. But she could easily guess the gist of it. Currently, Renee refused to date white boys—a fact that drove her father crazy. Their daughter only dated African-Americans, although she positively ridiculed the term and claimed that her black boyfriends did too.

When Angie first crossed the threshold, Wayne was holding a fistful of Renee's hair in his right hand. Her thin white neck looked like it might break.

"Say it," Wayne told their daughter. "Tell me, 'Daddy you're in charge.'"

Nothing from Renee, though. Not a single word seemed to be forthcoming.

"Put her down," Angie said softly. "Please. Let's talk."

"We've talked, talked, talked!" her husband insisted. "Conversation is a waste of time. We could talk with this one until kingdom come and it wouldn't change a blessed thing."

Oh, the useless clichés, Angie thought. *The not-so-helpful shortcuts one sometimes resorted to when trying to be an effective parent. No one gave you a script or a blueprint for the job. No crystal ball could tell what the horizon held in store.*

"I said, say it," Wayne demanded. "Tell me who's in charge." The very air in the room seemed to quiver, become more solid.

"Apparently I am," Renee told him.

Her father's eyes flashed like chips of bright ice. "Have it your way. You had a choice." Wayne smiled a cool thin smile, then raised her white-blonde hair up yet another notch.

On her way toward the ceiling, their daughter grimaced. Renee opened her mouth wider and wider, until her new silver tongue stud flashed for all the world to see. She'd gotten her tongue pierced after seeing the movie *Pulp Fiction,* featuring that silly line by Rosanna Arquette. "Why do you have that hunk of metal in your mouth?" John Travolta asks at one point to which Rosanna replies, "For fellatio. You know, oral sex." Luckily her father had not seen the film. Considering Renee's wild-oat behavior in general and her recent male companionship in particular, Wayne would have really hit the roof if he'd known the most recent piercing's inspiration.

Within a few seconds, Angie had closed the heavy front door. Thank goodness, a wooden door and a screen door now separated the living room from the sidewalk and its pedestrians: kids on their bikes, after-school skateboarders, a whole subdivision of potentially strolling neighbors. Once again, Renee had pushed her father too far. Obviously she'd pushed him just like she'd pushed him in the past. Wayne's face looked cucumber-calm. But Angie knew that he was enraged.

Her daughter's expression was more inscrutable. Right now, Renee was wincing somewhat but with a faint co-mixture of delight. A wry recognition of the chaos she'd caused still played across her face.

"Honey, don't do this," Angie finally started begging. "Please let her down."

"I said, who's in charge?" Wayne repeated. It seemed like something he wanted to know and desperately needed to hear his daughter say.

"No rush, young lady. We've got all evening."

Still Renee stayed silent.

Her eyes were a more intense color than Angie's or her father's. Light-blue as well, but with an inner fire, especially when she was mad. Feral-looking. Sled dog eyes. Renee's once beautiful, once strawberry-blonde hair was now a mushroom cloud. Her mouth a mask of mirth and pain. Her daughter had real gumption to stand up to a man like her father. Part of Angie admired it. When still a baby—tiny, pink, and helpless—Renee had been her father's "precious pumpkin." She had been his "bestest buddy" once she'd learned to walk and speak. As for herself, in the beginning Angie could just take a whiff of her first born infant. Then cry for a half-hour in joy.

"Whenever you're ready," Wayne Thompson explained. "Or I'll rip every hair out of your thick skull. Repeat after me: 'You're the boss. You and Mom are the ones in charge. As long as I live under your roof then I'll gladly do whatever you say.'"

Angie half-expected Renee to tell him, "So I have to live in the attic?"

But luckily she did not.

The girl had spunk. That much was for sure. Both at home and at school, her daughter's irreverent wit had gotten her in trouble many times before. More than once she'd called her father things like "square" and "silly," accused him of being hypocritical and literal-minded.

Of course, Wayne was wrong, Angie knew. What he was doing now would only make matters worse. But she loved her husband, too. She loved him like a woman loves a man to start with if he really loves her— if the love is real, and the loving is real—if both are consistent, palpable, and allowed to grow. Sometimes Wayne could give her "the look," stare at her in a certain way, with an azure gleam in his F-16 pilot eyes. Then

Angie would feel herself wetten in three seconds flat. Immediately *crave* him. Right then and there. She still respected him as well, despite the scene before her eyes. She couldn't believe her eyes right now. Wayne Thompson was a good man. He really was. Sometimes he could be thoughtful and tender, both as a man and as a father, and deep-down he only wanted the very best for Renee. Angie just wanted to fix this. Once and for all. If she could only get them talking. Start a productive conversation. That's what she was shooting for. Except part of her also feared that talking would only make it worse—something her daughter knew as well.

Over the last few months, Renee had really tried their patience. She had consistently lied to them, repeatedly let them down. Disappointed was not the word for it. She'd worried and terrified them time and time again. Once she'd disappeared for almost two months, staying with various friends, sleeping god-knows where and living practically in the streets. She'd gotten busted with pot. She'd done some shoplifting. They tried juvenile court—even threatened military camp—but they couldn't break her legs and chain her in her bedroom, could they?

Of course, there were the boys. The marijuana. Some other drugs now, too. That was the part that frightened Angie the most. Most American kids went through the Boone's Farm and Old Milwaukee, the cheap beer and sweet wine stage. All of Angie's friends and co-workers at the hair salon, Shear Experience, half-jokingly assured her of that. Since the age of thirteen or fourteen, Renee had occasionally gotten mildly drunk. In tenth grade, she'd slipped out of her bedroom window and done what kids her age were sometimes tempted to do. She'd gone overboard. But she'd learned a lesson. Angie had found her sleeping the next morning, slumped over in the Honda Accord. Clothes ripped. Make-up smeared. A huge pipe wrench inexplicably in the passenger's seat. Angie had found a pink puddle of Sloe gin and 7-UP puke on the car's console and carpet. She'd sent Renee to the shower and cleaned up the vomit before her father ever saw a thing—their little secret number one.

. . . .

Growing up in Germany, Angie had drunk her own adolescent share of beer and wine. She'd thrown up once or twice herself, like that dance at the base in Düsseldorf where she'd first met a younger Wayne, wearing his dress blues, and she'd been wearing an orange silk blouse. They had danced and drunk all night, then kissed, then eventually done you-know-what. Sure, it had been very quick. No doubt. But she had never heard a Southern accent before. Angie had found Wayne's small-town diffidence unique. Quite charming. It added something softer to the pilot's wings and uniform. His chiseled, blue-eyed, very handsome face. No, Angie was honest about her own life. So it wasn't the teenage drinking, or the sexual eagerness that worried her. Something else was wrong, Angie vaguely sensed. But on this point, she and her husband often hotly disagreed. For her it was everything, all of Renee's puzzling behavior put together. Mostly, the drugs worried her, all the different boyfriends, too. Perhaps the confused unhappiness underlying such behavior—not the rebelliousness itself because that was most likely just a stage.

She wasn't so uptight about the race thing either. Such touchiness about skin color—whether you got a little more melanin willy-nilly—that was something that Angie simply didn't understand. She came from a broader, more open-minded place in the world. Once when she was seventeen, she had gone to Amsterdam, and she'd gotten an eye-full. Her senior year in gymnasium, German high school, she'd read an anthropology book about Samoa written by Margaret Mead. Those South Sea islanders didn't stress monogamy, and even jealousy was a cultural oddity. If you lost at love—no big whoop—because one love replaced another. Apparently in Margaret Mead's Samoa, sex was plentiful and no big deal.

Needless to say, she'd talked with Renee about precautions. She had driven that information home to her again and again. No glove, no love.

Angie encouraged her daughter to be honest and to tell her everything and anything. Still, kids needed to live. They needed to find out some things for themselves and perhaps make a few mistakes.

Renee had slept mostly with basketball and football players to begin with. But now that she was doing drugs—marijuana of course, and something else called MDA—her predilection for the high school's best athletes had gone by the wayside. She'd had a few white athlete boyfriends. But none as of late. Of course, Renee had gotten pregnant once. Supposedly from a broken condom. She'd had an abortion already. Their big secret number two. Three months earlier, Angie had overseen the process and she'd managed to keep it under wraps. She'd taken Renee across the state line to Jacksonville, Florida, a bigger city where faces could stay anonymous. The little Georgia community they lived in would have been outraged, wouldn't have tolerated an abortion. Yet most of her Bible-belt neighbors would have been doubly shocked if this particular kid had ever seen the light of day.

. . . .

For three or four eternal minutes, Wayne had kept his right arm and Renee's hair lifted toward the ceiling. She wasn't off the floor entirely, but up on her toes. His muscles looked both taut and relaxed. He was still in extraordinary shape, merely to hold his arm up that long; this had been an exertion and a test of wills for them both.

"Please let her down," Angie told her husband "Pretty please? For me?"

"Now she steals!" Wayne started yelling. "Steals from us! Can you believe it?"

"Do it for me," Angie said. Then she paused for a moment. "Steals from us? What do you mean?"

"I got the credit card statement. She's a goddamn thief."

Almost half-heartedly now, Wayne tried the litany once more. "Who's the boss? Who makes the decisions?"

Still nothing from Renee—no adjustment in her physiognomy.

Next, Wayne took a deep breath, slightly adjusted his stance, and for a split second, Angie feared the worst. Very quickly, she sought out her husband's gaze.

Angie looked for that softer part of this tough man she loved. And Wayne had one too. They had been married two decades, going on twenty-one years. Angie was thirty-nine and Wayne was forty-three. This daughter was their first. But they had another daughter named Jessie, who was now thirteen. More wild oats around the corner. Possibly not, though, because Jessie was a different girl entirely. Probably not—but who knew? Especially with an older sister like Renee. Luckily, their other daughter was at a girlfriend's house right now. But the effects of her older sister's behavior was a genuine concern. Of course, another worry was whether this marriage itself could last. Could Angie and Wayne endure this? Or would they come unglued? She knew one thing for certain. She absolutely did not want that.

"Someone explain," Angie said finally. "Tell me what happened, sweetheart."

But there was a brief moment of confusion. Neither Wayne nor her daughter—who swiveled her laughing, pain-shot eyes—seemed to understand. Neither seemed to know whom she had just addressed.

"Did you use our credit cards, honey?" Angie asked her daughter.

"Used!" Wayne suddenly exploded. "One thousand three hundred and fifty-seven dollars worth of shit. I didn't tell you yesterday because I was so upset. That's how she's used us. That's the fucking thanks we get."

"Why did you do it?" Angie asked.

"Yeah, let's keep it simple," Wayne said. "Why did you steal from your parents, who have given you life and everything you've got? Something has to change! I'm sick of talking and I mean it! Actions speak louder than words. Everybody knows that."

Just as Wayne had said this, though, another sardonic expression shot across their daughter's heroin-chic pale face.

Such bitterness. Such resentment—but over what? Angie didn't know, couldn't understand, how such an attitude could possibly have come to pass. It was as if all of her motherly alarm bells had been disabled at some invisible point along the way. All the same, something had to be done. Right now. So with a speed which surprised everyone, herself included, Angie Thompson took matters into her own hands, the same hands that cut, dyed, blow-dried and permed, worked nine hours a day, six days a week most weeks. She reached up and tugged down the root-showing blonde hair from her husband's grasp.

"Okay," Angie said. "Now everyone relax."

"No it's not okay!" Wayne complained. "She continues to get her way!"

"Honey, I know that you're upset," Angie said. She took two deep breaths. "But you know what the counselors said. Remember what they told us. This just isn't going to work."

Next, she listened to Wayne *harrumph* in defeat and weariness. Then he stomped off toward the kitchen. Angie heard the hermetic sound of a refrigerator door, the release of gas from a hastily opened Bud Light, then the automatic garage door opening. Suddenly, Wayne was no longer in the house. He was in the garage, doubtlessly toying with his new motorcycle. His pride and joy. A new Harley Davidson that Angie had bought him with her hair-stylist salary for their twentieth wedding anniversary. She'd spent over twenty-three thousand dollars on it, because Wayne worked hard, because he'd been through a lot of stress. Because she loved him. Because he deserved it. Plus, there was something else—just one other thing. Didn't the mid-life crisis sometimes happen even to happily married men? Angie had saved up nearly two years, planned it carefully down to the spruce-green paint. Recently she and Wayne had gone to a motorcycle rally in Daytona Beach. Jessie and Renee had stayed with Wayne's mother for the whole week that they'd been away.

Lately they'd had a ball riding the Harley Davidson together. They would go cruising most weekends through the Georgia countryside. Saturdays and Sundays were their days to ride. Her husband needed to relax. Angie knew that—who didn't? Getting out on his Harley was diverting, provided some excitement, now that Wayne no longer regularly piloted F-16s. His job was mostly a desk job now that he was getting older. Sometimes he could be so uptight when it came to their oldest daughter, and especially when it came to Renee's recent boyfriends. Suffice to say, whenever the subject came up, her father wasn't inclined to use the term African-American. He used a different word, something else made in the USA.

. . . .

"Now it's only us." Angie said, leading her daughter over to the couch. "Tell me what happened, sweetie. It's just you and me."

Renee's face had brightened somewhat. There were still no words.

Only the uninvolved, blank cold-fish gaze.

Also, a smell now that Angie was closer. A sweet-dirt, evergreen, ashy smell. Just great. More marijuana. Her daughter had come home high again. That was what made her expression seem so distant. So happy and hurt at the same time.

"So you did it? You made those credit card charges?"

"You really want the truth, Mom?"

Now Angie was starting to lose her patience. Her eldest daughter wasn't even trying. Sometimes in such moments she wished this ever-renewing adolescent problem, this millstone-like emotional burden would disappear and go away. At least for a while. It had been so fun to escape for bike week in Daytona, to get away from their military friends with whom they usually barbecued and bowled. Even the name of the place—Moody Air Force base—gave Angie the heebie-jeebies whenever she thought about it for too long. They'd bought T-shirts and black leather bracelets while in Daytona. Costumes of sorts, you might say. During the seven-day bike rally, Wayne had given her "the look" more or less around the clock. They'd made love in the Florida surf, then in the room, enjoying the sunshine beaming through their balcony's glass door. It had helped them both, let them forget their worries, helped them forget that they were at a loss—at their wit's end—completely in the dark about what was bothering Renee. They had sneaked down to Florida by themselves, gone to the turquoise oceanside for a week of something almost adulterous. Hidden and all-embracing. Angie had really enjoyed herself. Felt sexy. Younger. They'd felt happy again. Very close once more.

"So you used our credit cards?"

"Uh-huh."

Only the slightest vibration of a voice. Yet the nod from Renee was clear. Later on that night, Angie would scrutinize the list of charges. A set of serrated titanium knives. Some household cleaning products featuring citrus oil. A lot of expensive jewelry Renee wouldn't likely wear herself, then a professional, chef-quality set of stainless steel pots and pans. Fortunately, this merchandise could be returned. But her daughter had sure racked up quite a bill. She'd intercepted the packages from the QHS shopping channel, then stowed them away while her parents were at work.

"Tell your mom. Why'd you do it, sweetie?"

"Just because," Renee explained.

Finally, a brimming of tears began. Human water. The fat drops stacked up on her daughter's eyelids, yet they would not fall. She was not a baby girl—not anymore. Now at sixteen and five-foot-five, Renee could sometimes be just as hard as nails. Her body language that of a tall live oak.

"I just like dating different boys—why can't Dad accept that?" Renee said. "Why can't you both love me for the way I am? My grades are good, and I like to party after my work is done. I like a lot of the same things you do, Mom. But you two just don't understand."

"Well dear, I try," Angie began. "I certainly do."

But in truth, she felt at a loss for words. Looking into her daughter's eyes, through all the stacked up tears, Angie couldn't decide what she needed to say. It was as if part of her daughter were standing twenty feet away—in another house or in another state—and part of Renee wanted to whisper softly in her ear.

"Just tell me. Why'd you use the credit cards?"

"Do you really want to know?"

"Yes, I would like to know."

"Okie dokie. Are you sure you're ready?"

"Yes I am."

"You do fun stuff with Dad—but what about me?"

Angie noticed how the tears had started down her daughter's cheeks, how brimming others had replaced them and were on their way.

"I love you, Mom. I miss you."

"Oh, I love you, too."

A few quiet, elongated seconds passed. Suddenly, Renee shook her head back and forth, as though something had been skipped over—misconstrued or poorly conveyed. She reached behind Angie's own shoulder-length, naturally blonde hair, then pulled her close by the nape of her neck.

Her daughter leaned forward some more. Closer, closer, until their foreheads pressed. Bone on bone. Only a thin layer of skin between. Renee kissed Angie lightly on the lips, then kept gently kissing her, as her tear-streaked expression slid from hurt and anger, towards something else, something harder to detect. Still crying, still very upset—but knowing precisely what she wanted to say—she opened her mouth, closed her eyes, then forced a hard, steeled tongue inside her surprised mother's mouth.

Angie pushed her away. Lightly at first, then with more vehemence. Her exasperation rose from her stomach, then moved palpably into her throat. Now she was definitely upset.

"And what was *that*, young lady? Just what are you trying to tell me now? That you're bisexual as well? On top of everything else?"

"What do you *think*?" Renee said, her tone highly sarcastic. But she kept on quaking and sobbing. "Sometimes you are so lost. Sometimes you're just like *him*. You don't pay attention. Not really. You don't listen or care about what I say."

"Oh, whatever—whatever!!!" Angie Thompson finally raised her voice. She felt overwhelmed by all of this act-out behavior. Just how much outrageousness could any parent be expected to take? "I swear to God, Renee, I'm so exhausted. So sick and tired of all this me, me, me! Notice me! Notice me!"

"You can say that again," Renee quietly observed.

Her daughter's tone had changed anew and Angie felt confused by the strangely muted, slightly frightened voice. Almost a whisper. But it contained something else, intangible and human, something besides decibels and mere sound particles alone. Because suddenly, Angie Thompson stopped herself, immediately checked an impulse to yell or talk some more, as her daughter's wild blue eyes drilled silently into her own.

Instead, she pulled Renee's head onto her shoulder, the same one she'd routinely used after feeding her over a decade and a half ago.

Then Angie held her there. On her shoulder.

"Thank you, Momma," Renee said softly. "That's it—that's exactly right."

First Love

My cousin hung on for nearly three months, so when my mother told me yesterday I just couldn't believe it. Why, just last summer we smoked grapevines in our fort beside the creek, talked about girls and played flashlight tag in granddaddy's cornfield. Then showed off the pubic hair we'd grown since Christmas. Almost every single holiday, Theo and his parents would drive down and we would catch up on everything, think up new pranks to pull on his older brother, tell wild stories laying in our bunkbeds till two or three in the morning. Or until my father came in with his belt. My cousin was the first person outside of my immediate family—my mother, father, and grandparents—who I revered and adored. We always had so much fun together. He enjoyed my company. So if Aunt Elizabeth tries to make me look in the casket, I'll tell her to leave me alone. To stop and just think for once in her life.

Besides, one memory is bad enough. His chest crushed. His eyes like someone else's. After the accident Theo looked like a full-grown man, someone who weighed three or four hundred pounds, because of the horrible swelling around his face and neck. When I leaned over the hospital bed, he grinned like we had just stolen a few beers, or had snuck off with an armful of his brother's magazines, then climbed up the mimosa tree in our backyard. That day in the hospital, Theo recognized me from the first. He smiled when my eyes watered up. Then he grinned even wider and whispered: "Hello, squirrel." Just barely a whisper. He was hurting and looked so tired.

The VW he was in had slid on some gravel going around a curve, dropped off an embankment and rolled over twice. The doctors said that it was a miracle Theo had survived after being thrown halfway through the VW's sunroof. So I felt very lucky and made several silent promises. I promised to do anything, anything at all, if Theo would live. Then vowed to devote myself to some worthy task. I remembered to ask and it shall be given and to believe with all my heart.

Sometimes when Theo visited we would all go to church together and whenever he came the strangest things would happen. One time in the middle of an Easter service, the preacher opened his mouth and this huge black wasp flew straight down his throat. Next, Brother Sailor went into some kind of shock. His throat swelled shut and he would have asphyxiated and died, I suppose, if a registered nurse hadn't put a little hole in it for him. But that's not all. A couple of summers later, the same preacher stood up before the entire congregation and announced that he was leaving the ministry. He said that he was very, very sorry. Then he started down the aisle against the left side of the sanctuary and kept on walking right out the door.

Well, everyone was surprised to say the least. My cousin and I liked Brother Sailor and we were sort of sad to see him depart. On Saturday afternoons, he often played basketball with us. Once he had even beaten Theo in a pancake-supper eating contest, which was not an easy thing to do at all. The man had our respect. He told funny jokes and preached real good. He always saved our favorite sermon for the hottest day of the year, usually around the first week in July. This was when Theo's family would drive down with a trunk full of fireworks from across the Kentucky-Illinois border. That sermon went on and on and even had a title I'll never forget: Ten Things to Do if You're Going to Hell. "Well, the first thing I'd do," Brother Sailor would say, "The very first thing is drink a taaaaall glass of ice-coooold water." He was from even farther south and those Arkansas vowels really tickled Theo. Whenever Brother Sailor got to that part about the ice-cold water it just about killed us both.

Generally during the service, we would start snickering and fidgeting. We could hardly sit still in the pews. That's why peppermint Lifesavers were always in my mother's purse. But that day when Brother Sailor apologized before the entire congregation, a whole lot of other people had the same problem. Everybody was shocked, but they soon started acting fidgety. Everyone stayed put in their seats, twisting and turning, silently watching our preacher walk out the door. Next, they turned back around and began staring at the empty pulpit, gaping and gawking—at a real loss for words—all except for Theo, who observed that the Lord moves in mysterious ways.

Well, I thought Aunt Elizabeth was going to whack him a good one, right then and there. Then the head of the deacons boomed out a great big "Amen!" He seemed to agree with Theo for some reason, and who knows what that old geezer was thinking.

Outside in the car, we rejoiced some more. This meant we could go swimming in the creek, maybe light some firecrackers, and ride the horses sooner. Suddenly out of the blue, Theo piped up again: "He's run away with the organist!" Well, that's all it took. Aunt Elizabeth started screaming and became furious, a little madder than she should have probably. Her face turned beet-red. She slapped Theo across the face and made his lip bleed. Aunt Elizabeth told him to act right. She said that he'd had it coming for a long, long time and we had no business blaspheming and making fun. After we got home, though, and had finished dinner, our aunt's Sunday School teacher called up and said that's what had happened all right. Brother Sailor and the organist had already left town.

When my cousin came outside and told me, we both couldn't believe it. I was playing around in our little peach and apple orchard, trying to knock down some still-green fruit using bottlerockets. Theo had gotten a good look at Aunt Elizabeth's face and he'd heard a little of the conversation coming through the receiver. The deacons were calling an emergency meeting and you can just imagine all the commotion.

The Most Beautiful Day of Your Life

A distinct, broken glow came through the trees and could easily be seen from the highway. The kitchen light still on. Halfway along the red-gravel road leading up to his house, Barry Pruitt shut off the eight-track and killed the engine, then coasted along with the gearshift in neutral so that Diane, his pregnant wife, wouldn't hear him coming.

It was Saturday night and he wanted to surprise her. From the right side of the truck seat, the smell of tomatoes, onion, melted cheese and baked crust emanated from a grease-flimsy cardboard container, a confluence of smells which had tempted him for miles. More than once he'd considered flipping open the lid and eating a slice of the pizza while he drove, but he wanted to leave what he had brought home intact, still untouched for them both to enjoy. Pruitt was tired, half-starved. But he wanted to wait. His battered pickup crunched slowly along, rolling quietly toward the faint patch of light. The little driveway dropped off Route 68 at an angle and descended through a stand of oak trees, hickories, and sumac which stayed filled with squirrels and blue jays from March to December. He had built the driveway himself, cut through the tight cluster of hardwoods using a friend's bulldozer, graded and shaped the road bed, then spread the gravel with the same friend's landscaping tractor. He hadn't bought his own at the time, hadn't yet started his business. That was almost three years ago, he thought, only a few months after he'd returned from Vietnam and gotten married.

They had dated since their junior year in high school. Diane was in the marching band's rifle corps, and he played flanker and cornerback on the football team. In 1971, when he was nineteen years old, he had flown from Fort Campbell to Fort Lewis, then on to Saigon, where he worked just outside the city in requisitions near the Tan Son Nhat airport. Pruitt had wanted to see some of the world, and he'd managed just that, for what it was worth. He had only witnessed the tail end of Vietnam, the ass-end of the war, as one more experienced veteran friend used to say. Troop withdrawals soon started, and the U.S.A. was cutting back its ground commitments. If ever pressed and asked what he had seen first hand, done in the way of actual fighting, Pruitt always grinned and told people that he'd rarely left the supply hut, his bunk, or the bar. But even his war wouldn't go away. Mostly, it had been a willed adventure, a free ticket out of a small community in a still small town, to a larger, exotic world which everyone was talking about at the time. When Pruitt had joined up, on what had essentially been a whim, he hadn't thought through his reasons for going, hadn't measured the ratio of risk and gratification. Now, of course, he couldn't keep from looking over his shoulder without a measure of fascination from time to time. But in the end Vietnam had not thrilled him. Still, though, it constituted a certain lure, an inevitable tug like any other strong memory. Why was he sitting in his truck alone? Thinking back on it? Tonight of all nights?

Whenever he talked to his brother's boys, his nephews Terrell and Brian, Pruitt answered their wide-eyed questions about Southeast Asia like any good storyteller at bedtime. He made it sound exciting and rare. "You can't imagine how different everything is over there," Pruitt told them. "All the flowers and the plants they have, their food, and the way the water tastes. Once I took a nap leaning against a casurina tree and when I woke up guess what I saw?" His nephews shook their gorgeous blonde heads. They didn't know, they told him.

"Well," Pruitt continued, "When I woke up there was this big cobra right beside me, flicking its red tongue and staring at me with black, glassy eyes." Terrell said he wouldn't have been scared so long as he had his gun with him. Besides, he was smarter than any old snake and would have killed that mean cobra in a jiffy. "I couldn't move though," his uncle explained to him. "I have never been so scared in my life."

Of course, the phrase carried a sane, veiled admission of what being there had really been like for him. While he had never seen enemy fire or faced any disguised threat during his brief tour— he didn't even know for sure if there were many cobras in that part of the country—Pruitt had walked around desperately sensing death, feeling vaguely threatened, out of place and surrounded by venom, coiled indigenous danger. Some of the others he knew had thrived on it, gotten a kick out of the adrenaline-filled living, the untethered R-and-R. All the foreign women and foreign color and speed which got mixed up together in their heads, kept them interested, and perhaps helped keep them alive. But he was never excited by what they were. A strong visceral fear and an unanticipated conviction that he might find himself in a senseless situation which could end instantly and conclusively—a clutched sapper bomb out of nowhere, a phantom bullet from the foliage—such thoughts kept him from enjoying his time in a place that could change the way you thought about vegetation, rain, and color for as long as you cared to remember the various things you saw.

Tonight as he sat in his truck, Pruitt could still recall the physical dread which had kept him from seeing more of the Vietnamese countryside, volunteering for pick-up patrols which would periodically sweep the fringes of the compound, looking for stray mines, or woebegone Vietcong. That late in the war, chances were slim they would find any that close, but Pruitt didn't want, or didn't need, to drum up such adventures. Not if others were content and willing to devise them, and there were plenty of people who were. From the first minute he'd set foot there, what Pruitt wanted out of Vietnam was out. If he got thrilled about anything it certainly was not another weekend in Bangkok, or a rip-roaring helicopter ride across a verdant jungle canopy. All he wanted was a long, slow, blue plane ride home.

After ten minutes or so, he climbed out of the pickup. Pruitt pressed the door closed, then quietly started toward the house. That's what they both called it, although it clearly wasn't one, not a *house house*, but only a stepping stone, a planned detour on the way to actually affording, building and having what they really wanted. Using a concrete block which served as the rear staircase for a footstool, Pruitt reached down and untied his boots. Carefully, he eased open the back door then slid the cardboard box onto the floor before going in himself.

A light sound of splashing water came from the far end of the trailer. She must be in the bathtub, he thought, which was why he hadn't seen her moving around. Pruitt was hungry and tired. He began taking off his dirty clothes, leaving his grime covered jeans and shirt, his socks caked with sweat and the fine dust from pecan-shells, lying in a heap by the entry way.

All afternoon he had been setting out vinca minor shoots and wading through crushed pecan shells, spreading these around plants in the border garden he was building for an attorney in Heather Hills. "I wonder if she'll want pizza tonight," Pruitt suddenly thought. After undressing completely, he lifted the box and walked quietly toward the sound of the moving water. Then he stood still and paused, listening before the bathroom door. Diane was moving around in the tub, swishing the water, shifting her weight.

"I gottcha," Pruitt said, jumping into the room.

His wife had been reading. After her initial start, she continued focusing on the book.

"I heard you," Diane told him, faintly smiling. "Don't you know any better than to go around scaring innocent women and children?"

"Listen to you," he said. "Just how did you end up like that?"

Pruitt was still naked and dirty, standing by the bathtub as if he might hop in, something he liked to do sometimes whenever his wife took a bath.

"I might sit on you if you don't watch it," Diane said.

Pruitt raised his eyebrows and began grinning lecherously, rubbing his hands together in the manner of a cartoon villain.

"All right," he said.

"Think twice buster," she told him. "I'm not kidding."

Diane slid down further in the large green tub, then spread her arms and her legs to fill up remaining space. Her round stomach rose out of the water like a sand-covered island. Tan and floating, faintly marked. She was seven months along. This child would be their first.

. . . .

After returning from Saigon and lollygaging around for a few weeks before their marriage, Pruitt had gone back to doing what he had always done during the summers before he joined the service. Throughout high school, he had worked construction since it kept him in shape and always paid well. The same company gave him his former job and he'd started off as an apprentice operator, driving dump trucks and learning more about excavating equipment. They taught him how to take grade, operate a backhoe and a bulldozer, how to dig basements and swimming pools. After fourteen months of abiding by someone else's schedules and expectations, he had started a little landscaping business of his own. Nowadays their future appeared bright green. Red, white, and blue. While they didn't have much to show for themselves just yet, they were young and energetic, brimming over with solid plans and down-to-earth expectations. Work was steady. The baby was on its way. One day, Diane was talking on the phone with his mother, and she mentioned the restlessness which was beginning to confound with the serene and more satisfied feelings of imminent motherhood. She was starting to feel anxious, bloated, somewhat harassed and quite frankly annoyed.

"I am ready to have this baby," she'd told her mother-in-law.

"There's only one thing to do about that," Pruitt's mother had replied. "Just try to relax. You'll just have to wait honey. It'll be the most beautiful day of your life."

That night when Pruitt returned, Diane told him she would be doubly relieved once the baby was born. She didn't know which was worse, carrying a baby around, talking about being pregnant all of the time, or listening to the silly things people sometimes told you.

When the two-month early labor pains began the second week in May, Pruitt was still working in Heather Hills, a subdivision several miles from his wife. Diane was at the university in Carbondale, trying to keep up with her course work, hoping she might finish the semester. Around eleven o'clock he heard a shrill, concerned voice coming over the CB radio he'd installed in his pickup, just in case Diane needed something during the long hours he was necessarily away. *"Barry. Barry. This is Carla Richards. Barry…How do you…? Goshdarnit…Am I doing this right? barrypleasecanyouhearme? Does this damn thing even work?"* He rushed over to the pickup after hearing the excited voice. Using the radio base he'd set up for Diane back home, his neighbor explained that she'd driven over after receiving a call from Carbondale about a half-hour earlier. She had broken a window to get inside the trailer. "They told me to use this to get ahold of you," Carla Richards said. His wife was being taken to the hospital, and Carla hoped it wasn't anything serious. She said that he shouldn't get upset or assume the worst. Diane had collapsed in the parking lot and that was all she knew for sure. Someone had found Diane and called for an ambulance, and then they called Carla over at her house. "They're taking her to Western Baptist," Carla said. "Drive safe. Try not to worry."

Heather Hills subdivision was ten or fifteen minutes from the downtown hospital, but he weaved through enough traffic and turned right at a sufficient number of red lights in order to get there faster. All the way there, Pruitt juggled with potential outcomes, possibilities and alternatives. Different phrases and scenarios jockeyed back and forth, looped through his thinking. Low blood sugar. Diabetic shock. Possible heart failure. A premature but healthy birth. Would the baby be fine after all of this? How could he know?

What could've happened to Diane? What could have gone wrong? Over the past few months he and his wife had poured through some baby books she brought home from the S.I.U. library, but these books explained about baby problems, diaper rash, hiccups, what to do if she had a fever, or if she choked on something which she'd swallowed by mistake. She, her, a baby girl. Whenever he imagined looking at or holding their baby, Pruitt always imagined a little girl. Not that a girl was what he wanted most or expected necessarily, rather, this was what his mind's eye told him to think of whenever he imagined holding their first child.

Still a few miles from the hospital, for the first time since the radio call, Pruitt wondered about the long-term effects of Diane's condition. What exactly was she experiencing? What would it be like to be a woman? To go through what they experience and men never do? Could they get what some Vietnam Vets suffered from? Go through combat fatigue or shell shock after something like this?

Something clicked in his mind and Pruitt thought of a trip he had taken only a few years ago, although, right now, it seemed like decades. Twice he made an exception to his policy of lying low and playing it safe in Vietnam. He had spent a long weekend in Thailand, then later toward the very end, he had gone on an unofficial helicopter flight with Allen Borders to a remote peasant village—something he would never forget. Only once had he flown to Bangkok with Chad Ramage, Jay Williams, Jimmy Smith, and Allen Borders for a weekend's leave. The five of them stayed in a massive three-star hotel by the expanse of a wide canal off the Chao Phraya. You walked into the hotel from the water off the taxi-boat, right into its bar, which was an immaculate, highly polished establishment full of mahogany, English ivy and marble tiles. Then past the bar tables, there was a transparent far wall, a plate-glass window behind which two or three dozen young Thai women sat watching television, playing cards and smoking Marlboro cigarettes. If you liked the way one of the girls looked, or the way she looked at you, it was necessary to tell the server the color of her dress, or the number in turquoise paint on her shoulder. Sometimes there were men who went MIB, that is, Missing in Bangkok, and watching Jimmy Smith in action he suddenly understood why. Pruitt had argued with him for a couple of hours, but never managed to get his point across. Yes, the girls were attractive. Sure, they could wear a condom. Still, the thing was not right. There were gradations of death, Pruitt tried to point out to him, but talking to some people was like talking to yourself if you were drugged, half-drunk, or otherwise willfully numb and stupid.

Just inside the emergency room entrance, Pruitt talked with a nurse who listened to half of his story then pointed to a large woman wearing bifocals sitting behind a counter and drinking coffee from a Styrofoam cup. Yes, his wife was there, this woman confirmed. She made a quick swivel movement in her chair, then placed a call. Soon another nurse came to the admissions desk and asked him to follow her upstairs. "Where is she?" he asked, as they stood together waiting for the elevator. For some reason "where" and not "how" had come out. His immediate concern was to locate, merely to find Diane.

"Your wife is on the third floor, postpartum," the new nurse explained, as if he should have known this information. "That's where we're going right now."

She smiled pleasantly, though, a big calm woman with hazel eyes and graying hair, an older nurse who gave the impression of having seen everything over the years, but who would still be moved by pain, by other people's joy, or by their loss.

Upon entering the room, Pruitt found Diane sitting bolt upright. Her dark hair was slick with sweat and brushed back roughly, still very wet, as if she had recently washed it in the sink. Her expression was blank yet tense. Neither sad, nor relieved, nor confused. She looked at him strangely, still without speaking, with a terse and strange intelligence he couldn't quite grasp. Her eyes seemed to say enough, Pruitt thought. *Why weren't you here with me? Regardless of any obstacle? Why couldn't you have gotten here sooner?* Pruitt felt his own eyes tighten and fill as he walked over to hug her. Perhaps a minute passed. Still neither of them spoke. With his arms around his wife, he sensed some tiny resistance, a cautious coolness which somehow presented itself and separated him further. He began asking her about the details of what had happened. What could he say, though, when Diane was through talking? What would he do then?

"Well, it wasn't supposed to be like this," Diane said in a crumpled voice. Her body was quaking now. Her grief becoming visible, breaking up and slowly surfacing.

"No one ever said..." But she stopped and didn't finish the sentence. She quit shaking and began to stare at the folded blanket on the foot of her bed.

A doctor wearing a navy suit and a bright, hand-painted tie with a macaw on it came into the room. He took Diane's pulse, then had a look at her chart. With a glance and a nod, he indicated that he would like to speak with Pruitt out in the hall. Before he and the doctor left the room, Diane said there was something she wanted him to do. She wanted him to promise that he wouldn't call anyone, not a single person. She didn't want people to start visiting and consoling her after what had just happened.

"I can't face their disappointment," Diane said. "I can't take that."

"All right," Pruitt promised. "Just a minute."

Out in the hallway, the doctor introduced himself and shook his hand firmly. "I'm Lewis Chumbler," he said, still holding Pruitt's hand. "Son, I'm afraid that this looks pretty bad."

On the far end of the maternity ward, there was a crib isolated from the others, surrounded by eight or nine doctors and nurses, all of whom were leaning over and looking at his child. Pruitt and the main doctor joined them briefly. He looked at the tiny red body full of IV tubes and probes, then he turned away. He found a chair and quickly sat down. He thought that he might faint.

"We're still doing everything we can think of," the doctor assured him in a kind, even voice which made him nervous. "But it looks like we might lose the baby."

Taking a thick fountain pen from his suit pocket, the doctor started making a list of all the things that had gone wrong and led to their decision to do the C-section, going over all of the possible consequences of what they knew so far. At some point, the child had defecated in the womb. When exactly they weren't quite sure. Perhaps before the fall, or perhaps because of it. Maybe this had occasioned a systemic problem which caused Diane to feel weak in the first place, Dr. Chumbler explained. The child had been taken out by Caesarian but had not breathed for the first ten minutes. He eventually began breathing for a little while. Then they had trouble keeping the baby's breathing constant. The phrases "systemic problem" and "mioxin drugs" kept coming up as the doctor talked and wrote. Dr. Chumbler said the names of some chemicals generated within the womb, then mentioned "spinal meningitis"and "possible brain damage," noting down all the possible outcomes on the yellow legal pad. It was hard to believe and difficult to make out what this person Pruitt had never seen before was saying to him, that despite the fact *this* had happened, and although *that* had not, their baby technically was still living.

"I'd like to go talk with my wife."

"Yes," the doctor said. "Of course."

He went back to the room and held Diane's hand, asked her if the doctor had spoken with her. She nodded and said he had. They discussed all the details very quietly for ten or fifteen minutes, as if the other tiny person concerned had matured and could hear them, or someone else they respected a great deal was in the room and listening. Afterwards, Pruitt went to look for Dr. Chumbler again. After speaking with him, he returned to Diane, and they sat there and stared out the window throughout the afternoon, a strained, wordless time during which Pruitt hoped it would all end. Maybe that would be best, then they could start over and try again. At one o'clock, a nurse brought in a tray full of food. They could not eat. A little later, he and Diane agreed to call their parents. At three-fifteen, the doctor in the blue suit and the outrageous tropical bird tie came back.

"I'm very sorry," Dr. Chumbler said. "We did all that we could."

Diane buried her face in her hands.

Pruitt pushed back his chair and shook the doctor's hand for the second time.

Unintentional, hard-to-control inflections of voice, little different details, made the curiously formal return home unbearable for them both. The weeks and months to come would be a time of small altercations, subtle bitterness and unspoken accusations.

On the first day they came back from the hospital, Diane swallowed the Valium the doctors gave her and then slept all day.

"Mother's little helpers," she joked weakly.

Then she cried some.

Diane's feigned hardness dismayed him and it would get worse. That very first day, Pruitt ate a bowl of cereal with milk and bananas, then went to bed early, taking care not to disturb her sleep, for some reason staying on his edge of the bed all night, like she was a stranger he barely knew, or a very fragile, elderly woman. This was the way he remembered sleeping with his grandmother after he was nine or ten and would occasionally still spend the night with her. At some point, when the sedative wore off, Diane got up. Pruitt stayed in bed and listened to her movements. He was tired too and didn't realize exactly what Diane had done, or how long she'd been gone from the room.

The next morning, he started to take out the garbage under the sink and discovered that she already had. Stacked up neatly by the trash bin on the porch, he found several cardboard boxes full of the presents Diane had received at the baby shower her friends had thrown a few weeks earlier. He reopened a few of the boxes and discovered some navy socks and a rattle, a pair of little red and white shoes. In one of the plastic garbage bags Diane had taken from under the sink, he uncovered the yellow crib blanket his aunt had crocheted, tumbled in with cantaloupe peels, paper towels soaked with bacon grease, coffee grounds and the empty Raisin Bran box he'd left on the kitchen table the night before.

Pruitt shook off the greasy papers and removed the scraps of food. He left most of the packages where she'd put them but tucked the crib blanket under his arm, then stuffed it behind the seat of his pickup truck. Before starting the engine, he leaned his head against the steering wheel for a few minutes, tried to control his breathing, his quaking chest.

Several weeks passed, but Diane's mood stayed essentially the same. Pruitt wished he knew what he could do. What could he say, invent, or imagine—a trip to Florida, or was there another book they could read together—what could he do, solidly and practically, which would turn her face from the past? Something he took pains to avoid was any over-ly pat solution, any indirect accusation of self-pity. He didn't want to pigeon-hole her grief. He tried not to resolve the problem too rapidly or assume that he could solve it for her. There had been a tragedy. They had lost their first child. It was a loss that ran deep and would leave an irrad-icable groove, a thick white scar on both of their memories. But wasn't the terrain of the past oftentimes like that? Full of freak pieces of fate, surprise raids, and heavy bombardments? Wasn't most people's mental baggage comprised of more bad memories than equally potent, equally vivacious ones? Or was it just the way his own mind worked?

"I can't stop," Diane told him one night.

They had consumed a whole meal in virtual silence. Fried chicken, mashed potatoes, sliced tomatoes, and green beans. Pruitt had sighed, only sighed, raising up from his seat to clear the dishes. Diane immedi-ately grasped his exasperation and he'd seen it in her face.

"Its okay," Pruitt told her. "Me neither."

"Then why that big lungful of air?"

"That what?"

"That world-weary sigh of yours," Diane persisted. "I mean, if it really is okay."

"I'm only tired," Pruitt weakly tried to explain. "Like I said before. It still gets to me. I think about it all the time."

He walked into the kitchen with the stacked plates and started to run the dishwater. She stayed behind at the doorway watching him, silent past the point of casual interest, the mental inertia which can come from watching someone do almost anything, or from watching water.

"You're bored, I think," Diane said finally.

He noticed her voice was quicker. More speedy and with an edge.

"Maybe you were quiet so that I would carry the conversation," Diane told him. "Tell you what. I'll entertain you. Finish the dishes and bake a cake. I'll run out and buy some balloons."

And she left, slamming the aluminum door with the cheap, hermetic trailer sound he hated to hear.

Three months earlier he wouldn't have known what to do—now Pruitt just stayed still. The car started outside and he heard Diane open its door while the motor was still running. Next the sound of the trailer door unsealing itself once more from the door frame.

"Think about what you really expect," Diane said, entering the room again. "A more resilient woman? Someone who would get up a week later, put on a smile, go out to buy some new clothes?"

He didn't think so. No, it wasn't just him. Working your way back to the good memories, making them stick, took some doing and considerable effort. Once upon a time, Pruitt had lived overseas, gotten through his twelve months there, and even that was enough to partially erase nineteen years of a mostly contented stretch of time, years and years full of football games and baseball tournaments and good food, houseboat parties, water-skiing, fond memories of the Pontiac Firebird he liked to drive and still owned back in Western Kentucky. Yes, you had to fight your way back toward such memories. It helped you go on. On hot sleepless nights, he would lie in his hammock and imagine driving out to the lake, listening to a favorite song on the car's stereo, some Creedence Clearwater Revival. It would be a strenuous, productive mental effort, a kind of fleeting transcendence which no one else had to benefit from but himself. Twelve thousand miles away from the car or his friends, an ocean or two from Diane, Pruitt would listen to a Creedence cassette with desperate joy and abandon, seeing himself or an image of his younger self with her, both of them, himself and his fianceé, willfully intertwined in its images: An emerald-green river and the sound of bullfrogs, a barefoot girl dancing under the moon, and he was there watching her dance.

A loss. Yes. A tragedy. Full of heartbreak, suffering and blood. But wasn't it better to look at the thing head on, face it for whatever it was? And then, after this stage, move on? To him it seemed like a greater loss to give up all quotidian hope and effort, to forestall getting over something which you could never get over in the first place.

People simply didn't let go of certain memories and associations; they weren't built for a black and white world. Pain could certainly swirl together, though, with the former happiness, and there were dozens of shades of gray. While she didn't accuse him openly, at some level Diane would always remember how she had gone through the worst of this all by herself. She would always remember that he hadn't been there with her. But wasn't the opposite also true? Although the intensity and the pain were by no means equivalent, how could she know what he had felt, while listening to their next door neighbor on the radio, or about the drive to the hospital scared and alone? Couldn't he convince her that any shame or lingering regret would only slow them down, perhaps jeopardize all their prior happiness, all their future plans together? Was it an empty-headed cliché, a sappy greeting-card sentiment, to tell her they really *could* start over?

The summer warmed, grew hot, then hotter. And as the days grew longer, Pruitt devoted more time to his new landscaping business. Ideally, if the work week went smoothly and the hours passed by unnoticed, yet significant tasks were still accomplished, he would have left at six o'clock most mornings, then stopped working eleven or twelve hours later. Often he got home long after sunset by the time he'd finished fueling-up the equipment and dropping off Antonio, the forty-year old Mexican who now helped him. Tony often needed a ride back and forth to the job sites, since his own car never ran reliably.

"Save up for a new one," Pruitt joked with him. "Stop drinking all your paycheck and spending your money on American women."

"Bueno, bueno," Tony said laughing. "They keep me out of other troubles."

Some evenings he arrived home around eight-thirty or nine. He would find Diane doing what she seemed to have turned to and enjoyed the most now, reading books, thick novels or her anthropology and history texts from the courses she had dropped spring semester. Pruitt would come home and find her holed up in the back room, propped up and reading on the bed, or talking on the telephone with other students. She had started socializing again with her friends at Southern Illinois University.

For weeks, they hadn't spent time with one another.

"But she's happier," Pruitt told himself. "She's getting happier and if this helps her, then fine. It's okay. She's working a way through what has happened."

But another part of him, his most hopeful and gregarious side—the part of him that would jump into her bathwater or sing a whole CCR song out of tune for her, exaggerating his singing voice since he didn't have one, anything to encourage her to laugh, to get her to be relaxed and immersed—this more hopeful and playful side said no, it wasn't entirely okay. After his long days, he wanted to come home and find his wife ready to spend some time with him, to reflexively drop what she was doing only for five or ten minutes. If he was honest, Pruitt guessed, that's what he really wanted. That's how he actually felt about it if he was emotionally precise, because he needed to forget too, needed to relax with her, to grow whole and feel sane again after working in the sun and talking to persnickety chiropractors' and dentists' wives all day long, installing sprinkler systems and pruning their trees, sowing grass and sculpting these rich people's earth mounds, making their backyards so comfortably green. He needed Diane back with him, but he needed the work too in order to keep himself moving forward, and more and more of the better jobs were coming in.

"I want to finish this degree," Diane said. "Can we afford it?"

"Of course," Pruitt told her. "I'm glad you're going back."

The summer afternoons slowed and the nights became insect laden and brimming with moisture, hotter and hotter, thick with crickets and mosquitoes and lightning bugs. Suspended, unfallen water. The tomatoes he had planted out back beside the wash line ripened. This was the only version of a garden he'd had time for this year, a small plot he sometimes scraped around in while Diane hung their clothes to dry. In keeping with their general plan to save and save—to put off buying anything they could possibly do without until they started their dream house—they had agreed not to buy a washer and dryer. They were still taking turns doing the wash at Owen's Laundromat. These little chores connected them, kept them focused to a degree. However, every weekday and some Saturdays, an hour or so after he'd left every morning at six, Diane drove the Volkswagen beetle away from the old cattle and soybean farm, then over the river to Illinois. She had her work. He had his. Sometimes she would get back even later than he did. Pruitt would be asleep already, stretched out on the floor, the blue cast from a police serial or sitcom bouncing off his sunburnt face and arms.

Then one Saturday, after a thunderstorm dropped rain on the job site all morning, Pruitt drove home around noon. The torrential rain had lasted for a couple hours straight, and it would be too wet to work later, despite the hot blue sky.

"Do you want something?" Diane called from the kitchen.

He lay down on the floor, exhausted, and doubled-over a couch cushion for a pillow. The day before he and Antonio had torn down an old fruit house on the farm, a thick squat building with walls four-feet thick to keep out the heat and the cold. They had worked past dark using the pickup's headlights, gathered bushel baskets full of Bell canning jars and chipped the mortar off three truckfuls of bricks, free material which he could use for borders, or to build patios and brick walkways.

"I'm fine, thanks. Just wet and tired."

A room away from him, Diane was moving about briskly.

From his position on the floor, Pruitt listened to the thin trailer floor rumble, shake the way the sky had shaken earlier, or the roof on the metal tool shed he had played around when he was a little boy, thundered whenever the stray cat jumped onto it from an overhanging tree limb, an old orange tomcat named Tim. This place, the farm, was filled with such stacked-up memories, and it had been the perfect place to recover the time they had lost while he was in Vietnam. Soon, he hoped, they could start a house here. "Why give away money that we'll need later," Diane had explained, when he'd first proposed getting an apartment. "Why pay somebody else's mortgage and remain homeless?" Finally, Pruitt had agreed. His wife had been absolutely right. Soon perhaps, maybe in a year or so, they could sell the trailer and find a contractor who would build what they wanted, start making house payments of their own.

"Don't you want something to eat," Diane called out. "I thought you might come home early. I bought some things for lunch."

Then the silence. Again. Once more. Pruitt kept his eyes closed. Why couldn't they sit quietly and peacefully together as they had in the past? Did these edgy, restive moments change that former peace into a joke, transform it retrospectively into some deceived contented lull?

After a while, Diane came into the room wearing a black cotton sundress and carrying a bag of tortilla chips. She plopped down on the couch, munching them while she talked.

"Tell me something," she said. "Why didn't you ever learn Vietnamese?"

Pruitt laughed. Vietnamese was not a snap of a language to learn, and he'd known few people who bothered to try. There were perhaps one or two men he remembered who could say whatever they wanted, tell jokes to the people there, speak naturally to them, off-the-cuff. "I did a little," he told her. Then he counted to twenty for her in Vietnamese, and said he would like a liter of bottled water please. Asking politely for potable water was something he had learned to say in the Saigon restaurants.

"Not bad," Diane told him. "I'm impressed. What a gorgeous place that must have been."

"Yes, it really was."

"Is, you mean," Diane said. "After all, it's still there."

"That's what they're telling us. Are you interested in seeing for yourself?"

"Sometime, perhaps, why not," she said. "You know, I learned something very interesting today. It made me think of you."

In her civilization class, Diane told him, they were studying the Korean war. She tossed the half-empty bag of tortilla chips onto his lap, then started explaining the basic principles of an ideogram, outlined the ones for "east" and "contentment" on a piece of paper she picked up off the coffee table. The word and idea for east was made from two other symbols drawn on top of one another to suggest the arrival of dawn, the symbols for trees and for sun. Contentment was also made from two superimposed symbols, the symbol of woman drawn under the one for roof. "Did you know that forty percent of their language is derived from Chinese," she said. "That the three most common words in Korean are country, gold or money, big and great? Gold means the same as money," Diane explained. "Big means the same thing as great."

"Live in country," Pruitt said. "Amass big gold. Have great contentment."

She started laughing and in that very moment, some veil or partition was lifted it seemed, miraculously and instantly removed.

"You sound like an Apache in a bad western," Diane said, hitting him on the arm, her eyes glittering and focused on his own. "Why don't you start counting to twenty again? I liked that very much."

Perhaps she had understood his other question after all, Pruitt thought. And if only she'd known how thirsty he had been, how long it had taken for that look, for that one laugh. Perhaps now they could talk again and say what came to mind without pausing and hedging, or acting like they were walking on glass whenever they talked. Now that she seemed interested, he wanted to tell Diane about some things he'd never told anyone. Had he told her, for example, the real truth about the cobra and the Vietnamese casurina tree? Surely she had known all along. But there was something else he had thought about recently, while they had gone through what they'd gone through. He didn't know how Diane would take it. Partly for that reason, he had hesitated.

Men would do the strangest things in Vietnam, desperate and incredible things Pruitt would never forget, which spanned an entire spectrum and extended to all extremes. His friend Allen Borders was one of those people who had seen it all. In the early sixties he had done LURP reconnaissance missions in Cambodia and along the border of Laos. During their weekend together in Bangkok, Al had been the only other soldier in the group who had not picked out one of the Thai girls, yet he was precisely the kind of guy who you expected not to give a damn about what they felt, someone who lived out his tours at a tough-minded, quite instinctive level. There wasn't a sentimental bone in his body. For years, he had snooped around in some of the most threatening places, spoke the language fluently, even a couple of indigenous dialects. He was the kind of guy who had some complex attitudes about the war, the kind of soldier who once sat on a high bank above a river, then watched a Vietcong patrol walk along the river edge below him. He told Pruitt how he held one of the VC in the sights of his rifle for a minute or two. Just watched him. Until he was out of view. Had no intention of shooting him. Allen Borders said all he could do was envision the guy's life unfolding as he watched through the sights of his M16. He'd discussed the Alpha, Delta and Theta states of mind with Pruitt, some of the key concepts of Buddhist thinking. Their method of concentrating on any action or daily task—whether it be holding hands with someone, shelling green peas for supper, or brushing your teeth—something Buddhist monks called "bringing the mind home."

Eventually, Allen Borders quit carrying ammunition entirely and started carrying an air mattress instead. He said getting a good night's sleep was the most important thing he could do to stay alive. Another time he argued with someone who started whining about being on point and cutting through the jungle. Sgt. Borders took the guy's place. Later on he told the guy that the next time he didn't immediately walk point he would shoot him, but that the guy wouldn't know when. So he could just worry about it and worry about it.

After the war was over, Sgt. Borders had stayed and as far as Pruitt knew he was still living there. Just two months after their excursion to Bangkok, Al had become a father to a Vietnamese child. The mother was Montagnard, from a part of the country in the mountains toward the north. Following a tradition of his wife's village, a practice which aimed to distribute the profundity and discomfort of childbirth, to deepen the experience for the father, Al had witnessed his wife's labor and son's birth from start to finish. He waited for his first breath and watched the rest of the labor process. Then he went into the next room, boiled then consumed the placenta, with his hands held over a wooden bowl.

There were obvious reasons why Pruitt hadn't told Diane about this recently. But why hadn't he ever mentioned it before? The story about Al had to do with devouring pain and all that life gave you, accepting willy-nilly discomfort and pleasure too perhaps. Just like the wind, the rain, and the stars. Certainly Al's story had to do with belonging and fitting in, Pruitt thought. Maybe about the ineluctable risk and potential loss you necessarily gave yourself over to at some point. Perhaps that had been his brief lesson in Vietnam. That and this. If he ever got to the point where he might fail to do something in civilian life, something another person expected from him, simply because he was unsure, ambivalent or frightened, then there were some things he had seen over there which still helped.

Vietnam, Kentucky, Thailand—wherever. The world was a gorgeous, interesting, danger-filled place, especially if you stuck around and kept your eyes open, worked hard enough at whatever it was you worked towards, whether you were trying to be a good ER nurse, ditch digger, school teacher, or a good parent. But you could never quit and cringe. You could never lie down. He had learned that much from Al Borders and from a few others. There would always be snakes, either real or imagined, but perhaps his little nephew Terrell was right. If you thought carefully about snakes were they really all that frightening? In spite of everything one is sometimes told?

Diane slid off the sofa, joined him on the carpet, draped her arm over his chest.

"I love you," she said.

"I miss you so much," he told her.

They lay there on the floor, kissed and held one another. He kept quiet and was relaxed again in this different sort of silence. Who knew? Who knew how long any human life might last? He believed that the ten or twenty, possibly forty or fifty years he and Diane had left together were incapable of being safeguarded. Never utterly organized. Never completely guaranteed. They spread out before him like a lush, but not limitless jungle, full of green vines and monkeys and trees, moss-covered limbs and clusters of strange vegetation he'd never seen before, which concealed much beauty, probably more pain and more real suffering. But in order to glimpse the beauty, you had to risk entering the jungle then be willing to work your way across to the other side. You had to go through the thick of it and admit that you might die there.

Pig Summer

Most of this happened the same year as Skylabs I, II, and III, the cease-fire in Vietnam and sleepless nights for Richard Nixon, something my Uncle Ed always referred to as that shit-eating lawyer's *coup de grâce.* It was 1973 and I had just turned thirteen. School was out and the hay-fields were green, all the swimming pools had opened. The weekly routine of lawn mowing, the pesky mosquitoes, and humid Kentucky heat, the loquacious long days had begun. But my summer break really started with two long distance phone calls, first from Springfield, Illinois, then chilly Chicago, distant snow-filled worlds of sin, booze, and crime.

"There's less chance of him finding trouble there," Theo's father told my mother. "I'm telling you beforehand, he knows the quickest ways of finding it."

"Well, don't you think they'll find it together?" she asked laughing. "But bring him down anyway. I know someone who'll be thrilled."

Of course I was. My wild-assed Northern cousin was a year and a half older, and now he was coming to Kentucky to stay for a whole month. Plus my father had just bought me a brand new motorcycle, a Honda SL 100 that would fly—so who knew what would happen? The telephone call from Chicago came from our favorite Uncle Ed. As chance would have it, he was coming to Grandma's too. She lived alone now on seventy acres beside the northern end of Clark's River. Toward the back of her property there was a stone-lined creek, a bluegill pond, and a patch of trees which gradually thickened until it became a full-scale woods—hickory and black gum, persimmon and ash, another wild complete world in which you could get lost and discover things. If you broke open one of the creek stones using another stone, for example, there were swirls of pink crystal which Theo's older brother called quartz. Most importantly, her big white farmhouse was nearby. My parents had built on four acres my grandfather gave my father, a welcome-home gift when he returned from the Marines.

The farm was a working farm, but only in the *laissez-faire* sense of full-time farming. I would help cut hay, rake, and bale twice a year. Occasionally, my father and his brother would spread lime and bushhog. They let a herd of cattle graze and fornicate randomly, and there was a family of vicious hogs behind one of the barns. The pigs were constantly getting loose from their rickety holding pen, destroying our grandmother's tomatoes and chasing us kids. Needless to say, we tormented them. Mostly, we'd throw dirt-clods, or dirt-clods loaded with rocks, worthless crabapples and hard little pears. Then whenever Theo came down from Springfield, we'd switch to fireworks, BB and pellet guns. The firecrackers were supposed to be illegal in Kentucky, so this added taboo and danger, heroic luster to his descent. Every Fourth of July, he would arrive bearing contraband, something illegal one way or another: skyrockets, Roman Candles, packs of M-80s and whole bricks of Black Cat firecrackers which we'd painstakingly unroll to make bombs.

But this particular year, Uncle Ed arrived in Kentucky first. He was fifty-one, an iron-worker, who'd lived in Chicago for nearly thirty years. A coffee and beer drinking life-long union man, and a voracious reader: magazines, the Holy Bible, Louis L' Amour, or what have you. Earlier that same year, Uncle Ed had surprised us on Easter by arriving with a woman he called his wife. The newlyweds seemed happy, so Grandmother humored him. While she couldn't fathom the impulse to be marrying at Uncle Ed's age, she welcomed his new spouse into her home with open arms. She understood that for Uncle Ed this might be practical. And besides, Rosalia fit right in. Throughout that Easter weekend, she wore tasteful blouses and a pair of white wool slacks. Poised and formal, an almost olive-colored woman, Rosalia impressed us all. She played the piano for Grandmother and knew the second verses to some well known hymns. Her perfect hands didn't prevent her from helping.

So all went well. Until now.

Because this time Uncle Ed came all alone.

"Where in the world is Rose?" my grandmother asked him. "You didn't leave her at home by herself, did you? Why Ed...," she said, her voice trailing off.

It wasn't a question. The word "why" before your name was her idiom for censure, which meant you better start explaining, and you probably ought to be ashamed.

Grandma stayed silent and he watched her face. Uncle Ed knew she was upset from the look in her eyes. Next, he said that there'd been an altercation, some disagreement involving rest stops and a thermos full of hot-lemon tea.

"I set the cruise on seventy-five and told her she'd have to wait," he explained. Uncle Ed said he hadn't stopped until they reached the bridge spanning the Ohio River. By this time, of course, Rosalia had peed in her pants a little. So they had started to fight again, parked right there on the Illinois-Kentucky bridge. "Rosalia got out of the car," he said, "and before I knew it she had jumped." Some passersby had watched her climb the railing, and they had surely seen the license plate.

"You might say I drove her to it," Uncle Ed confessed. "A court of my peers would send me to the pen."

This was a favorite reference which meant the penitentiary. One distant dull-hot day when I was twelve years old, we were watching *As the World Turns* and eating Fudgesicles, and Uncle Ed explained to me that he'd done some time in "the pen" for murder. "Yes, son, I've killed three men. But they did me wrong, and I had no choice."

Of course, when my grandmother overheard this, she told me not to pay attention to him. "Why Ed," she said, "don't tell the boy lies."

So this time, as soon as she heard something about "the pen," my grandmother's expression tightened.

And everyone listening suddenly understood.

What Uncle Ed had done offended my grandmother—over the Easter weekend she'd fixed up their bedroom real special. But for an entrenched Southern Baptist, she possessed a rare thing. Almost always, my grandmother refrained from casting blame, even when she knew what she knew and Uncle Ed was involved. Even when the first stones were flying.

Uncle Ed finished what he had to say, then lit a cigarette.

Then my Aunt Elizabeth, who was hair-triggered, waved her hand back and forth. Unlike my grandmother, she didn't adore her brother.

"Really *must* you?" Aunt Elizabeth said.

Uncle Ed started smiling and taking these huge brimstone drags.

"What did I *tell* you? What did I *say*?" Aunt Elizabeth told my grandmother. "Not under *my* roof in a million years. Not without holding the wedding license in my own two hands and witnessing the ceremony with my own two eyes."

. . . .

So the next day when Theo's father drove their new Chevrolet up the driveway, Uncle Ed had made himself scarce. I'd been waiting for two hours in the front porch swing. After the shiny-new car had stopped, Theo's older brother helped unload. Apart from the pigs, he'd been our object of contempt for years. He had been a good student all his life and a little chubby for most of it, rendered even more of a nerd because for the longest time he wore these thick-lensed Clark Kent glasses. His name was Greg, but sometimes his mother called him Gregory-Joe, and whenever she did we just about lost it. Throughout his adolescence, we'd called him Pig Man or Four-Eyed Pig Boy to his face. He'd had a complexion problem, too, and we called him Pimple Man as well. That is, until Theo's brother suddenly transformed. A couple years earlier, Greg shot up to six-foot-two, then he started lifting weights. His senior year in high school, he won all-city tackle and got a trophy. Now he was going to a liberal arts college in Chicago. Plus he'd learned to play the acoustic guitar.

Quite secretly we admired him because now he was a hippie. He could play Iron Butterfly's "In-A-Gadda-Da-Vida," "Stairway to Heaven," and sometimes "Kumbaya" to please our grandmother. From time to time he came down on holidays with a knockout girlfriend named Joan Lawson. She treated me and Theo just like insects but braided clover in her waist-length blonde hair. She and my older cousin shared a house together and were double-majors at De Paul. Religion and history. Intellectuals. But I'll just mention here in passing that Theo's brother's major eventually changed. During his junior year in college, Greg would switch his concentration to pure philosophy, then write an article examining some of the deficiencies of Western metaphysics. The article dealt with traditional thinkers' responses to grief and mourning, then considered various Tao and Buddhist alternatives. Although written by an undergraduate, the paper got published in *The Existential Review of Psychiatry*. It would have gotten him in any graduate school in the country, his professors told him. But they'd missed the ardent-hearted emotion behind his argument. He eventually went to law school instead because he wanted to buy a sailboat, and, rather like the young Siddartha, he could still be philosophical on the side.

While his brother and father unloaded the car that day Theo stayed in the back seat pretending to snore. Once the trunk was empty, he opened his eyes and hopped right out. "Let's get those bags," he said, vigorously rubbing his hands together. Everyone laughed except for his brother. So Theo stretched and yawned some more.

"It's good to be here, Grandma. Thanks for letting me stay."

Then he started hugging people, first her, then my mother, then me. His heat-seeking personality turned on high.

"Hello, faggot," Theo told me.

"Hello, squirrel," I replied. "You have a nice snooze?"

"Thank you for asking. It was lovely."

Next we helped take the luggage inside. Then Theo chit-chatted with various other relatives he'd not seen in a while. But as soon as we could leave, we got on my new Honda motorcycle. Within a very few minutes, we were miles away, lying on our backs in the uncut hay, the SL 100 cooling and resting on its side. We each smoked a cigarette from a pack of Winstons that he'd filched from a carton in Uncle Ed's room.

"That's some ride. What else you been doing?"

"Not much," I said. "There's nothing to do."

My cousin languorously exhaled a giant blue cloud of smoke. One of the reasons I admired him was that he never coughed.

"I doubt that," Theo told me. "There's always something."

Instantly, I knew that he was talking about girls. My hormones had just started to kick in, too. When I'd shown Theo my first pubic sprout-ings in the attic that prior Christmas—as he'd done with me only a year before—there was just a little itchy patch of them, darker and thicker than usual, rather like the mane hairs on a horse. "Hey, check this out," Theo told me. Then he closed his eyes and started thinking about kiss-ing a girl, whose name was Laura Hapanowitz, until he got what he called a "boner." I'd had them myself. But his took ten seconds. Of course, none of the rest of the family members knew about this partic-ular feat, or that Theo—who lived in a big suburb and whose father was a GM executive—had taught his rural cousin a few other tricks as well. Like how to blow smoke rings. Or how to play nine-ball for money. Or how to shotgun a can of Budweiser in two seconds, by puncturing the aluminum bottom with a sixteen-penny nail, then quickly popping the tab. Still, surely our parents suspected from their own pasts—not to mention their past with us—how new avenues of mischief would effort-lessly open up. In entirely different ways, we were both learning about human ecstasy: the wonderful scary feeling that girls and gravity caused if you just risked doing things.

Recently, I'd learned to go fast on the motorcycle, preferably shirt-less in the rain. My cousin didn't have a dirt bike because he lived where you couldn't ride one. But he'd told me all about his life in Springfield, Illinois. How he rode his ten-speed bike to parties held in his girlfriend's parents' basements, big comfortable ranch styles surrounded by mercury vapor lamps and well matured boxwood shrubs: an ideal place for first love, shag-carpeted havens for Spin-the-Bottle and Truth-or-Dare. His best friend, Blake, came with him, too. They made out with Laura Hapanowitz and her best friend Aleisha. They made real drinks. They played strip poker. Then later in the evening when Mr. and Mrs. Hapanowitz got back from having dinner, they removed their bikes from the boxwoods and raced back home.

"Any good looking ones live nearby?" Theo asked me.

"Beth McConnell and Kathy Reed," I said. "But they're older."

"Beth, Beth, Beth," he said. "Names are important."

"I know a few others," I lied.

Theo put a green sprig of fescue in his mouth.

"Beth McConnell," my cousin said. "I bet she's something."

A couple of crows circled over, jet-black against the high sapphire sky. The nicotine made my stomach queasy. But I liked the colors. For awhile we stared at the sky and didn't move. Then I showed him how to flip the choke and start the motorcycle. "This is really cool," Theo told me. I'd always loved the way he said the word. It sounded better with his non-Southern accent, pronounced with the "O's" drawn-out and rounded, like he actually had some ice resting on his tongue. The sun angled down fiercely, burning a sheet of tangerine on the bluegill pond as we raced by. Three-inch winged grasshoppers were everywhere and we sent them soaring in our wake.

When we finally arrived at the tree house, we used tomato stakes to prop up the windows and let out the trapped heat. The view overlooked a creek bed with some huge trees and tangled undergrowth, poison oak, spider-plants, and maidenhair ferns. My cousin promptly lit another cigarette. Then I explained about the trouble Uncle Ed had caused. Theo laughed and said that Uncle Ed was cool but that Aunt Elizabeth was still a ditz. Mostly we just talked about what had been happening since we'd last seen each other. The light slowly left the sky, turning the two-by-four windows slightly orange, increasingly crimson, then a bruised and much darker reddish brown. The hot summer of 1973 stretched out before us. Later during his visit, camping out one night under the ink-dark sky, we would talk of some things that we'd never discussed before: the end of the universe, the size of stars, what someone we knew a thousand miles away might be doing at that very minute. But that first day we just chatted in general.

"Let's hang out awhile longer," Theo said. "Alright with you?"

So I said okay.

"I really like coming here. It's completely different."

Riding back on the trail beside the creek, the motorcycle headlight's beam flicked past the drifting blackness, the trunks of hickory and biblical sycamore, persimmon trees, maples and hard pin oaks. Intensely lit, just off the trail, these strange-familiar trees appeared like massive barriers. Then they dissolved behind us into invisible trees and our flung-up dust.

There was no moon whatsoever that night and I remember when we got back home it was so dark. Entering my grandmother's house from the screened-in porch, we saw a woman standing in the kitchen. Rosalia, our uncle's wife! She wiggled her fingers at us from beside the sink where she was scraping some carrots to make a carrot-raisin salad. Everyone else was in the living room, out of earshot, but as we approached their conversation, it sure seemed like they were having fun. Theo's father was scarlet red. He had out his handkerchief to wipe his eyes. My parents were sitting on the couch together, holding hands and laughing too.

"I've had it with you, Ed." Aunt Elizabeth was saying. "I'm sick and tired of all your nonsense."

But Uncle Ed said, "Now wait just a minute. You ought to think a little about what has happened. Suppose I told you that my wife's mother's mother had married a black man. A man so black that he was blue. Or say some Mexican?"

Aunt Elizabeth's eyes widened, then narrowed.

"There you go again," Uncle Ed said. "It's none of your cockamamie business. Why, you're just like the man who shoots himself in the foot, then still puts the thing in his mouth."

"Well, I never..."

"I know you never," Uncle Ed told her. Then he quickly changed the subject. "Hey, it's good to see you boys," he told us both. "Getting about time to eat isn't it?"

He walked over and gave Theo a swat on the shoulder.

"Rosa and Mary!" he yelled toward the kitchen, like he'd lit a fuse and wanted to warn them both.

"What now?" my grandmother screamed back. "It's almost ready, Edward! I've told you twice!" Then she said "dammit" under her breath.

But Uncle Ed formed his mouth into a pleased little shocked expression, like he'd caught a jolt of electricity or burned his finger. "Yes sir, I should have seen this coming." Then he turned around and eyed Aunt Elizabeth.

"If you ask me, Sis," Uncle Ed said calmly, "Sometimes you're just too hard on people."

. . . .

My cousin's parents and his older brother left after a couple of days. Uncle Ed and Rosalia stayed a few days longer. His wife had family to visit in St. Louis, which was the reason for the second car. But my uncle said he had to get back to work in "wind-bag city." He said that while Richard Nixon wasn't from there, a place like Chicago could sure produce him. On the night before they left, Theo fixed a bowl of raisin bran for a snack. But when he went to the fridge to get the milk, Uncle Ed tossed two tablespoons of Folgers' coffee into the bowl. Grandma accused my cousin of throwing out her food, so Theo made a face and said that she should try some. "Why, there's not a thing in the world wrong with this cereal!" Grandma improbably told us, because she tasted it and there were coffee grounds floating, and the milk had turned brown already. Next Uncle Ed held up his hand, like he was going to make a speech. "It's okay, Mary. I'll eat it myself. If there's anything I deplore, it's a needless waste." Then he ate the whole bowlful and never blinked an eye.

After Uncle Ed and Rosalia had gone, we had the farm all to ourselves. Two summers prior to this, we'd stolen some strawberries and peaches from Mr. Langston's farm. He'd not caught us, so we stole some cantaloupe too green to eat. All child's play, we now thought. This year was different. We used the motorcycle to barrel race and do wheelies, then occasionally Evil Kenevil-jump into the bluegill pond. It was blistering hot and all my cousin's idea. First, we built a ramp then practiced at half-speed. After a few rounds of that, though, we went around to spread the word. Robert Harned came to watch us, Tina McKinney and her brother Bobby, who brought along his Sting Ray to try whenever we were finished breaking our necks. On the most spectacular jump of all, since Theo didn't effectively gauge his speed, my cousin soared twenty feet or so then landed violently. He pitched wildly over the handlebars at the last minute, headfirst and cockeyed into the muddy water. But he bobbed right up and tugged the Honda out. The SL 100 was lightweight, easy to push from the shallow pond. But the motor wouldn't start again, so we all took turns on Bobby's Sting Ray bike.

Occasionally, our escapades took us beyond the boundaries of the farm. One day we went floating down the Cumberland River with a group of teenagers. They'd made a raft from inner tubes, plywood and oil drums. So we swam out and hopped on. They had day-glow dunce-hats and noisemakers, laughed like hyenas, and we all had a lot of fun. They were really nice to ask us along insofar as we were just kids. After we got back, though, Theo told me that they were probably doing some LSD. Another time we hitchhiked home from Cardinal Lanes, where we'd gone to bowl and play some pool. It took forever to get picked up, then Larry Snow gave us a ride. Larry was six-two, a natural leaper, the only basketball player on the team who could dunk. He was a big deal on the all-white county team because during the early seventies dunking was still fairly rare. Since it was Friday, we stopped at the car wash, and on its flimsy aluminum siding we saw some graffiti in black spray paint: LESLIE POWELL'S A WHORE. No one understood why she left it there, or why her father didn't shoot somebody. We gave Larry Snow a hand vacuuming his used Grand Prix, so he gave us two Budweisers. Then while we were drinking the beers, Beth McConnell drove by and waved. She had the t-tops on her Trans-Am down and shot us all a big summer smile: water-ski blonde hair, a killer tan, her teeth real white. But Larry Snow just raised his Budweiser, half an inch, maybe an inch tops. Then he tilted the aluminum can toward her and nodded his head in a lukewarm nod.

Needless to say, we had our annual assault on those foul-smelling pigs. One day as we gave them their table scraps, one of the biggest hogs whirled on my cousin. Nipped at his leg. "Did you see that?" Theo said. "He tried to bite the hand that feeds him. That just won't do." The boar had really scared us both. My cousin was breathing quickly. But there was a playful spark in his brown eyes.

"Come with me," Theo said. "I've got an idea."

We ran to the garage at my house and he explained. "Go look in the fridge. Find something to feed him. That pig will pay."

But I thought of the warning Uncle Ed had given us a few years earlier. "I'm telling you boys for the umpteenth time," he'd told us. "Don't fool around with those hogs. If a mad sow pins you down, she's liable to kill you. That's how my brother C. D. lost his ear, and if you don't believe me, just ask your grandmother." So we had asked her, and it was absolutely true.

We couldn't believe it! Those stinking pigs!

Once inside the house, I concocted a gallon ice-cream bucket full of old mashed potatoes, some vile green peas, and a whole package of Oscar Meyer hot dogs. Out in the garage, my cousin Theo had found a five-gallon can full of gas. Then we ran back to the barnyard. The idea was to set the food out in the middle of the sty, in a hoof-worn, virtually grassless area, well away from the barn itself. First, we dragged out a garden hose from one of the horse troughs, just in case the fire got out of hand. Next we found a tile spade and dug a circular trench, maybe twelve or thirteen feet in diameter. After the trench was ready, we poured the bucket of slop inside the circle. All the other pigs were casually lolling in the mud, trying their pig-best to escape the heat. But not this boar. He'd smelled the slop. And once we called him, he trotted right over. My cousin told the boar, "I'll scare you just like you scared me. You're an ungrateful good-for-nothing. Sooey, sooey, you big fucker. I've got your number." When the boar started for the food, Theo walked around with the can of gasoline, thoroughly dousing the trench. As soon as the circle was complete he joined me on the fence. The pig ate on obliviously—just like a hog—like an animal.

"Bon appetite, you vicious bastard!"

Theo lit a strip of rag, then tossed it on.

It worked like a charm. Within seconds the big boar was encircled. The fire in the trench ignited with a wind-like *whoossshhh*—like a whole crowd gasping at a cold winter football game—then the pig stopped chewing and started to squeal. "Poor little porker," my cousin mocked and whined. But after a few more seconds, the pig could tell that he was in real trouble. So Theo jumped off the fence and manned the hose. We wanted to be ready if the sucker bolted.

"If he starts running, his goose is cooked," Theo told me. "You know, I read somewhere that pigs were smart. The third most intelligent animal in the world."

Soon the wall of fire subsided, though, and I jumped down from off my perch. It had been some show. But now that it was over, the boar still wouldn't budge, and to our great dismay he didn't seem to realize that we were the agents of his terror.

Theo kept spraying down the barnyard, and the pig leaned back down to finish up the food. "It's not true revenge," he concluded. "But I guess it will have to do."

. . . .

On the penultimate day of his stay—and somehow I'd sensed this day would come—we went to the tree house with Tina McKinney. She was Bobby McKinney's sister. Until the day of my cousin's pond-stunt, that's how I knew her. Tina was exactly my cousin's age. She would soon be fifteen, she told us. She came to the farm with a friend this time, a girl named Carla from Minneapolis. The McKinneys originally came from Minnesota. They owned a swank, all-wood, very modern-style house on the biggest lot of Green Acres subdivision. They liked to drink and socialize at the country club, and they often played golf there on Sunday afternoons. Their dad sold real estate and was part-owner of Polynesian Pools. I forget exactly how Theo set the ball rolling—something about how cool it was, how they'd never see another tree house like it—but we ended up with these two neat girls back in the woods.

My father had built the tree house for me. He was always wary, perhaps a little jealous of my cousin's visits. He'd built it on weekends, for my tenth birthday, using a skill saw hooked to a generator. It had two main floors and a roof terrace, three levels in all, with trapdoors, even a Plexiglas skylight. There was an elevator of sorts, a pulley and platform to haul things up. Since there were two of us to hoist the rope, the girls decided to use the elevator. Tina went first and Carla followed. They both agreed. It was pretty cool.

Well, before you know it, my cousin and Tina McKinney were mashing big time. And there was Carla. There was me. I remember watching a while before nervously kissing her, desperately looking for pointers. Carla didn't need them though. She kept her tongue moving in quick wet circles. Her mouth was soft. After twenty minutes or so, she put my hand up her untucked shirt. She'd done the untucking. So I touched her warm back and the strap of her bra. Tina and my cousin had managed to get supine at some point. I recall looking in their direction more or less constantly. Then Carla from Minneapolis started making some strange sounds too, like she was imitating Tina McKinney. Theo gave me a thumbs-up sign and smiled, then he leaned down toward Tina's mouth again and closed his eyes.

Before we left the tree house, he'd taken off her shirt, and their hands were everywhere. Just to see what happened, I'd touched Carla's belt buckle once, and she'd not stopped me. That's when I froze. What if she grabs me, I thought, and discovers my itchy patch of horse hairs? She would laugh and point, I felt quite sure. So I just kept kissing her and patted her soft warm back a little more.

Once we'd climbed down, Tina says, just as pretty as you please, "You guys want to come over? My parents are out of town."

Theo shoots me another look, like Spanky's double-take in *Little Rascals.*

The girls both laughed.

"Sounds groovy," he said. "You guys lead the way."

So the four of us walked over to the McKinney's house. First, the girls made us all ham-and-butter sandwiches, some Minnesotan concoction which even my cousin had never heard about. We ditched the sandwiches while the girls put on their bathing suits, and Theo presented olfactory proof of his tree house conquest. "Check this out," he kept saying. "It's nectar of the gods." But I kept slapping his hand away and he kept laughing. Then we all went swimming together in the Polynesian pool. That's when I had the opportunity to kiss Carla again. The bright underwater lights made our summer-brown legs shine, our glowing bodies seem even younger, embryonic, and feather-light. I remember thinking, "What could be nicer than to hold *this* girl? Why another?" We all climbed out of the turquoise water, drank shots of Mr. McKinney's scotch, then jumped back in, like giddy dolphins.

Our tongue muscles were tired.

But so what? We kissed some more.

On the very last night before he went back to Springfield, my cousin and I camped out in the hayfield. Since the tree house was so far away, my mother didn't want us to stay there by ourselves. We made a fuss at first but finally agreed. After all, those woods got so dark. Besides, the hayfield was much better. Laying under the stars on our Coleman sleeping bags, we talked about everything we had done so far, and what we wanted to do in the future. Theo talked about visiting foreign countries. He thought it would be really cool to learn some Spanish. We talked about our parents and our favorite music. Girls and God and outer space. What would it be like to live for a while in Skylab? Or to be able to say that you'd actually walked on the moon?

"There's no way the universe can end," Theo said. "What would be there?"

"A wall?" I suggested.

"But a wall is something, too. You see what I mean?"

I wasn't sure.

"Well, there must be something behind the wall, Theo said. "Even if it's just more wall. Infinity necessarily exists."

My cousin said that he'd gotten this insight from his older brother, who was currently majoring in the humanities.

"What's humanities?" I asked him, because I honestly didn't have a clue.

"It's all the stuff about being human," Theo told me. "That's what I'm going to major in, too. Where do you think you're going to college? Have you decided?"

"I don't know. But I'm going to go."

Although in truth, the thought hadn't taken shape, or ever been made palpable and appealing. Other options seemed equally solid, growing up where I grew up. There were plenty of good-paying professions which didn't require college. Jobs at B. F. Goodrich, or Union Carbide, or perhaps the small construction company my father had started. Most of my high school friends slipped happily into them. After graduation, a lot of them worked at the B. F. Goodrich chemical plants because of the wonderful benefits. They bought their first houses, started their families and began their lives.

"You should go," my cousin told me. "I wouldn't miss it if I were you. Don't you think that going to college sounds like a lot of fun?"

. . . .

During the summers, we had that farm and so much time. Hours and hours to wonder over the straightforward puzzle of adolescence. The quick veers of energy it gave you—a harmless urge to roam or run away. We would be sitting after supper at our grandmother's house, then very faintly my cousin Theo would smile. "Ready-set-go," he would say. Then we'd race out the screen door and hightail it. Zany. Unflagging. Our hearts pumping wild.

Well, more time went by for both of us.

Seventeen summers for him. Fifteen for me.

Then his car crashed just north of Springfield on Route 14.

Things changed because I loved what he'd loved. In the beginning, sheer silliness and companionship at all costs. Any adventure. Virtually anything new.

But then toward the very end, Theo loved ideas. In January of 1976— the same year he died— he wrote his older brother at De Paul: "Send me some books to get me ready, sucker. I promise to read them word by word." So his brother sent four doozies. *The Rise and Fall of the Third Reich*, *The Varieties of Religious Experience*, *Romeo and Juliet*, and the collected poems of William Butler Yeats. I've often appreciated my older cousin's sense of humor. Four books by guys named William. I've often appreciated the various other things Greg gave me, because after Theo's death those books became mine.

I inherited them. His mother told me that Theo would want me to have something, so I took a leather jacket and a few albums he'd played for me. Led Zeppelin's *Stairway to Heaven*, Pink Floyd's *Wish You Were Here*, and The Rolling Stones' *Goat Head's Soup*. And I took those books. It took a few years, I should mention, before I did more than flip through them. This story concerns an aftermath. Like many true stories, change is at its core. It's about my Aunt Liz and Uncle Ed and a girl named Carla from Minnesota. It's also about Theo's brother, a friend for life, and inevitably about my father too.

A couple years after Theo's death, my father discovered a fifth of Bacardi 151 in my first car. A brown Camaro. Another gift which I later sold for tuition. It was football homecoming and I'd bought the rum and cokes for friends, I told him. My sister was in the room, so he called me out to the garage. When I turned the corner, though, he hit me hard and knocked me down. Daddy hit me in the face with his fist—very important details—but that's not all. While adrenaline-filled, the scene was oddly calm. There was this feeling of restraint hard to describe, a sort of slack-jawed violence, something which a wolf or lion might use to whisk an offspring from certain threat. A firm but sharp-toothed touch. "I'm your father, and I always will be," he told me. "I'd rather do this and have your mother know it before I let you ruin your life." His very words. So weirdly brutal.

But for the first time I saw real fear in my father's eyes.

When I tried to stand, he knocked me down again.

"I don't care if you're bigger than this house," he said.

I was seventeen and football-strong, and these two thoughts went through my mind: *Perhaps I should fight him. What he's doing is wrong, wrong, wrong.* But after a while I just stayed down and he kept raging.

Then finally, he stopped.

My cousin's accident occurred north of Springfield on Route 14. It happened on May sixth, just three weeks before their high school graduation. His best friend Blake was driving. They'd just bought a case of Coors. In those days, anywhere east of the Mississippi, such beer was hard to find, and since it was rare, of course, it tasted the best of all. So they were drinking Coors and listening to music on their way to Summit Lake with friends. Then Blake's blue Volkswagen Rabbit skidded going around a curve. Loose gravel. Too much speed. Their friends in the other car were well ahead and they drove on. They didn't notice as the blue VW left the highway, rolled twice, made another quarter turn, then propped itself sideways against a tree. After a little while, a passing pickup stopped because of the new skid marks and ripped up vegetation. A couple of Illinois corn farmers on their way to lunch, some local people who knew the road.

Both boys were alive. But my cousin's body had been thrown halfway through the sunroof as the car began to roll. The VW's propelled weight had crushed his chest. Then he flew free. When the Illinois state troopers arrived, they found some unopened beers and cubes of ice, still unmelted, strewn over the ground and throughout the car. They took out the ashtray and, sure enough, discovered a joint.

"It's a real miracle he even made it to the hospital," the doctors told my aunt and uncle.

On the way to Springfield, my mother prepared me for the truth. No one expected him to survive. A week had passed by, though, and Theo still hung on. A registered nurse herself, my mother wanted me to understand things. Not much had changed. All his ribs were broken, like so many soda crackers, one of the doctors had explained to her. One lung still functioned, and he could breathe, but not without a ventilator. Ideally, he could have been hooked up to a PEEPs, positive end expiratory pressure machine, but this was a device still fairly rare at the time. Unless he got stronger, they wouldn't be able to fly him by helicopter to see some specialists at a better and bigger hospital. All the way there, my mother's tone was calm. Quite professional. But once we were at the hospital and she'd visited the intensive care unit, she came out crying. I noticed a fleck of blood on her lower lip. A little wound on my mother's mouth from where she'd bitten it.

"But will he live?" I asked her.

My mother paused. But she didn't hesitate. "Don't go in, son. Not unless you really want to. You might remember him this way."

"No I won't," I told my mother.

But she was right.

The whiteness of the sheets. And those purple-and-yellow bruises. It's like one remembers a few Renaissance paintings of favorite martyrs, or any kitsch thing really, something you loathe but hangs so persistently in selective memory. My cousin's head and neck were very, very swollen, and his eyes looked like somebody else's. The face a sexless face of a stranger weighing three hundred pounds. A man's or a woman's.

And I remember his long hair. Those too white sheets. The lime-green plastic translucent tubing. It was only a matter of time, we'd all been told. The talk of helicopters was now hollow hope.

On the twenty-sixth day of Theo's miraculous survival, our Uncle Ed came down again from Chicago. He'd been to Springfield before me and my mother arrived.

Then the thing dragged on.

When Uncle Ed came into the lounge, the others had gone back home to rest for a few hours. So I was alone. He said hello, then tried to find a nurse. He left me sitting on those thick-vinyl chairs the color of French's mustard. There was a coffee table with a few magazines, mostly *Reader's Digests* and an old dictionary. I'd looked up "miracle," a word rich with meaning, from the Latin *mirari,* "to wonder," and the Sanskrit *smayate,* meaning "he smiles." Needless to say, I'd done a lot of praying. I remembered to ask and it shall be given you, and to believe with all your heart. To this day I recall those mustard-yellow chairs. Some chrome cylindrical ashtrays filled with fine white sand.

After visiting my cousin for the last time, Uncle Ed came back into the lounge. He said, "I don't know all the details. Did they really find some drugs?"

"Some marijuana," I told him. "Aunt Helen says it wasn't his."

Uncle Ed nodded and sighed wearily.

"Let's go get some coffee."

There was a cafeteria one floor down. So we went there. As we were moving through the line, he asked if I'd eaten anything, then put a few things on my tray: an orange, some kind of sandwich, a piece of pecan pie with gray-colored whipped cream. I ate the sandwich while Uncle Ed drank his coffee and smoked.

"Listen here," my great-uncle told me. "No one on this earth deserves that."

The steam from his coffee mingled with the cigarette's fumes.

"I can only imagine what this must be like for them," Uncle Ed continued. He was talking about my Aunt Helen and her husband. "But there's no need to point fingers. Not at the other boy. Not at anyone at all. There's no reason to blame anybody or anything for what has happened. It's no one's fault, son. I want you to remember that."

"Well I don't know," I told my uncle.

Suddenly he started coughing. Then to my amazement the cough transformed.

My Uncle Ed began to laugh.

I looked up at him quite surprised. His eyes shone from all the coughing and from whatever had just occurred to him.

"Do you remember that time when you both peed in my shoes?" Uncle Ed asked me. "Oh, I was *hot* when I put my foot in there. You two boys were really something."

This must have happened the summer of 1970, the year of Apollo 13 and Kent State. We'd been horsing around after dark, as usual, shooting off bottle rockets and trying to stick lit sparklers down Theo's brother's shirt. We'd make Pimple Man mad as a hornet, but when it came to catching us he didn't have a prayer. Anyway, at some point between the bottle rockets and starting a game of flashlight tag, Theo spotted Uncle Ed's lawn-mowing boots sitting on the porch. No one was around. Just the crickets, lightning bugs and us.

"Let's surprise him," Theo said.

So we unzipped and laughed the whole time.

This was the same year of the Roman Candle Wars, that summer we declared a full-fledged assault on those mud-caked hogs we loved to loathe. I can still see those bright orange and sulfur-yellow, those brilliant carmine bursts of light. I can still hear my cousin laughing as we fired away. *Thwump, thwump, thwump.* Boy, did those pigs squeal! The scalding balls of light were evenly timed, but easily dodged if they came right at you. We had put on some extra clothing to jack things up a notch, because we'd learned from before not to wear shorts whenever we had Roman Candles.

We didn't think we were indestructible.

Like most clichés, that's imprecise.

Indeed, I can still hear my cousin screaming as that strange-looking man grabbed him in the dark. A girlish scream of utter fright. Uncle Ed had been hiding in the horse barn all the time, watching the fireworks, dressed up in hobo clothes. He had a cigar and a floppy hat. Also a burlap sack. When Theo got close enough Uncle Ed jumped out and shoved the sack over his head. Then the hobo's deep voice apocalyptically filled the night.

"What are you boys doing to those poor swine?"

I backed away. My eyes like saucers.

"I've seen it all," the mysterious deep voice boomed. "Don't you think that hurts?"

After a little while, my cousin's body slackened.

However, soon the bum was tickling him.

"They're pigs! They're just pigs!" Theo screamed. "Turn me loose!"

I ran forward and jumped on Uncle Ed's back, but he peeled me off effortlessly and grabbed me too.

"Aren't you going to say you're sorry?"

"Yes-yes-yes, we're sorry."

"We won't do it again. We promise."

Around and around we went—we thought it would never end. Uncle Ed locked both our skinny wrists in one of his huge steel-worker hands, and he kept tickling us with the other. We could see his smile from the cigar's orange stub, and deep down we knew that we hadn't hurt the pigs. They had thick hides and were caked with mud. Besides, we'd been hit many times with those Roman Candles ourselves. Yet a vague guilt filled us, and we rejoiced over having gotten caught. "You're cuter than buttons but meaner than snakes," Uncle Ed told us. Theo wriggled out of the sack, and we tried to kick our great-uncle in the shins. Our stomach muscles aching, the pain delicious. Uncle Ed just kept tickling us. He showed no mercy. We couldn't stop laughing and he wouldn't let go.

The Life and Death of Stars

A map is small, flat, and limited to a page in front of you; the sky is huge, domelike, and all around you. It will take time to absorb and remember constellation shapes, their relationships with other star groups, the names of stars and other objects. But the reward for doing so is great.

I.

Resting quietly in the hospital, unable to sleep, Jimmy Duvall could see over his chrome-plated bed rail, then through the plate-glass window off to his right. He had broken over two dozen bones from his fingertips to his shoulders. It was one A.M. and the halls had emptied. No cleaning staff just yet. No well-paid doctors and nurses. No life-beat-up folks taking constitutional strolls, or wheelchair rides to quell their boredom. No one at all. Just Jimmy Duvall, the room and the moon.

"Where will I work next?" Jimmy wondered. "What will I do now? What will I be?"

Just overhead, sat the gibbous lunar surface. Looking so close that you could drive a car there. High above Western Baptist Hospital's parking lot the midnight sky was dark. Over in the western part of the sky, Jimmy could see a rare conjunction of planets he'd heard about on *The Today Show*. Jupiter, Saturn, and Venus—shining and not flickering. Fainter Mars and Mercury, then all of those cold-hot stars, blinking off in the distance. Kiloparsecs. That's what the book said. Millions and millions of miles away.

Once more, Jimmy had been injured, so badly hurt that any desire to walk, or take a diversionary wheelchair ride, was entirely impractical. Not something he craved to do for the moment. He was hurt real bad. He'd had a mishap at the Super Wal-Mart where he worked forty hours a week, stocking shelves and doing maintenance. An accident at work luckily. Such a strange thing to say. But true enough. He had been lucky in a sense. This time there would be no problem paying sky-high medical bills or fretting about coverage of an insurance policy he did not have. Jimmy had been standing on a thirty-five-foot ladder. He'd been changing fluorescent bulbs, perched high above the shelves full of merchandise, when he reached for a pack of Wrigley's spearmint stashed on his tool belt. He lost his grip then fell over twenty-five feet. He'd hit hard. Very hard. But Jimmy Duvall was from the school of hard knocks. First, he'd broken his fall on a top shelf of assembled children's bicycles, next on the floor itself by sticking out his flailing arms and hands.

Yes, he'd hit the Wal-Mart floor after falling over twenty feet. But he'd been at this hospital before. Boy oh boy, he knew the place quite well. In fact, Jimmy Duvall was born here. And his mother had died in the cancer ward. He'd breathed his first breath here, and she had breathed her last.

He recognized certain doctors' faces at Western Baptist Hospital. He knew certain nurses and they knew him. When he wasn't noticing the yellow-faced moon—or this rare massing of planets—Jimmy was thinking how he'd like to see one of the nurses in particular.

Lee Ann Riddle, that was her name. Someone he knew from high school. When he'd been checked-in on Thursday she'd not been working. She had been on vacation, but once the weekend was over Lee Ann Riddle returned. How good it was to see her. She couldn't believe he was hurt again. Lee Ann even said so. He'd had the accident on a Thursday, and she'd returned to work the following Monday after a snorkeling trip in the Caribbean—her first time away with some new, sweet man. Her first vacation in a couple years. Nowadays, Lee Ann was charge nurse for an entire floor in a different wing of the hospital. A classy, intelligent woman. No longer a girl. Someone who had been more popular than Jimmy had ever been, someone who only recently had gotten engaged.

Back in high school, Lee Ann had been the Prom Queen and Valedictorian. She'd been voted most popular because of her personality, and her no-matter-who-you-are beautiful smile. My god, she'd been so pretty. And she still was. After his first bad accident—during the four months Jimmy had been in the coma—Lee Ann Riddle had visited regularly. Talked to him while he lay unconscious. Dead to the world. Then miracle of miracles, when Jimmy finally woke up, Lee Ann's had been one of the very first faces he had seen. She wasn't a friend. Not exactly. But she wasn't a stranger either. He'd kidded with her in high school, and Jimmy always loved to make her laugh. He'd copied her geometry tests before she'd gone on to trigonometry and calculus. He'd winked at her and flirted in his own way. Once before they graduated, because someone on the football team put him up to it, Jimmy had signed his handwritten note in her yearbook "cunnilingusly yours." What a jackass he'd been. Even to do such a thing on a dare. But Lee Anne was smart. Too intelligent to make a fuss. She'd read the yearbook entry, blushed one second tops, then laughed good-naturedly right in his face.

Lee Ann Riddle was so nice. Quality all the way. Every Sunday, she went to Lone Oak Baptist church with her family. She was a good person. Jimmy had known it in his bones even way back in high school, behind his closed adolescent eyelids at night, and the I'll-never-even-hold-her-hand pit of his yearning teenage stomach.

Isn't life so strange? Unpredictable and unpatternable. Because years later, they would meet up again. Right here. Twice already. At this same hospital. Who would have thought it possible? One of the first things Lee Ann Riddle said to him when he'd recovered from his four month well-of-nothingness had been: "Thank God, Jim. I've prayed and prayed. Thank goodness, you're going to be all right."

II.

Yes, Jimmy Duvall had recovered from the first accident. He'd bounced back from the coma and regained consciousness. Gotten back his very existence. Of course, he wasn't ever the same. Afterwards, Jimmy didn't feel or think or talk the way he had before that first accident. And it was certainly depressing to go from what he once had been: his father's son, so utterly confident—a natural athlete who'd set a record at the Air Force obstacle course, someone who had led the elite corps chants whenever he and his buddies hit the Panamanian cantinas:

> *Two old ladies lying in bed*
> *One rolled over to the other and said,*
> *"I wanna be an Airborne Ranger*
> *Live a life of death and danger*
> *Blood and guts, sex and danger*
> *That's the life of an Airborne Ranger!*

His first accident had made him a slow-motion person. Not a split-second decision-maker. Not a graceful arc of movement, like when he'd soared out of C-130s. Back before his coma, though, all of Jimmy's decisions had been lickety-split. He'd felt more alive than most people ever dare to feel. Everything had seemed so effortless and piece-of-cake: *para aquí, para allá,* right-hand, left-hand, physically smooth as silk for him. But nowadays, Jimmy Duvall drooled a little when he talked. Actually drooled his spit. Sometimes when he got tired, or very nervous, and sometimes when he talked to strangers. Also, the flesh on his face occasionally jumped around on its own, like the summer skin on a horsefly and heat pestered horse.

Tourette's Syndrome. The doctors had a name for it—for what the muscles on his face did—for almost everything else that had gone wrong. How weird and amazing! How bad things could happen to any-body, then one day they suddenly happened to him. Sometimes, Jimmy would stare into the mirror with fascination. Deep interest and disbelief. He couldn't be sure what the next expression would look like. And if he fought too hard to control the jumping-around, then it seemed like the jumping-around would just get worse. Once at the Super Wal-Mart, some of the teenagers at the loading dock had mocked him. Some grown-up men, too. Jimmy had secretly seen them giggling during their lunch break, until another, even older man had made them stop. He'd seen his co-workers contorting their faces, talking slow, mocking the way he talked. Slurring like Jimmy slurred while spitting up their Pepsi-Colas and laughing their tomato-red laughs.

Of course, during the coma, Jimmy hadn't had to see such things. Didn't have to think or hurt or watch anything at all.

But that was that. And this was this.

Right now, Jimmy was arranged in a sitting position. But once before, he'd spent four months at Western Baptist flat on his back. He'd been in the Air Force Rangers when it had happened. He'd been twenty-four years old, living life and loving it, raising general hell in Panama City. Central America. Jimmy had lived a kind of dream of sorts. He'd gone away from Western Kentucky and seen some of the world. Then one sun-drenched day on Lago Gatun, the speedboat he'd been operating drunk-to-the-gills had flipped. Those three or four seconds were a rapid-fire blur. Also, something in cinema-like slow motion. Even now, Jimmy remembered every whirling one of those seconds, and he recalled the couple minutes following with big-screen-like precision: how he'd been thrown clean, how rock-hard the lukewarm blue water had been, how when his body landed he'd scooted, bounced, crashed along the man-made lake to a totally dazed and limp-bodied halt.

Then he began to drown.

He could not swim.

He could not move. Jimmy's well-conditioned, hard-muscled young body began to sink. His neck had not been broken, but he'd received a major concussion. His spinal cord had been damaged. Therefore, he drifted downward, see-sawing back and forth with the current, eyeing the translucent green-blue surface of the Central American lake. Unable to breathe. Unable to believe this thing had happened. Knowing in a split-second, flying above the water, that it absolutely could not be reversed.

That day Jimmy Duvall wanted to get to the surface and feel the sunshine once more, gulp fresh air and not sixteen ice-cold beers. But Jimmy could not. His arms and legs would not allow him to live. So Jimmy just watched the tropical light filtering down through the water, allowing a kind of calmness to replace the horror. He had a son. He had a Panamanian wife, a beautiful, brown-skinned woman named Petita. A wife who he had sometimes hit. Never closed-fisted, like you would hit someone who invaded your house or who hit you first—say some man in some fistfight a bar—but Jimmy had slapped her hard enough to make her nose bleed twice, more or less the color of roses. And Petita always cried. Cried each time.

Sinking to the bottom of Lago Gatun, Jimmy could tell her he loved her and really mean it. Except that now he wouldn't ever get the chance. Now he would never get to watch their beautiful boy, his black-haired, almond-eyed son grow up. He just watched the sunlit surface of the lake. Growing darker. Slowly less translucent. The lake's surface grew farther and farther away as his body zigzagged downward on its way toward the watery floor.

Some other boats had been nearby, or he would have died that day for sure. Finally, someone from the base zoomed over in another speed-boat, dived in, then dragged him back up. Then what-do-you-know, Jimmy Duvall was shipped back home to the little town in Kentucky where he'd been born. Raised or reared, or whatever you want to call it. At any rate, while he was growing up, Jimmy's family situation had been chaotic to say the least. Just another fact. A solid, certain fact. Hardly an excuse for his own mistakes.

His father, Junior Duvall, was a tall, muscular man. Six-foot-four with eyes the color of wet cement. The son of a cattle farmer. Someone who owned the local livestock auction barn. His father was very handsome. Very a lot of things. Especially whenever Junior Duvall got mad. His father was a chip off the you-know-what. Jimmy's grandfather's name was Eugene "The Bull" Duvall, and Junior was just like his daddy and his daddy's daddy before him. Jimmy's French great-grandfather first came over with the family name. A legendary man himself. He once stabbed another man to death over a five-dollar debt in a cornfield. Later in life, he died from a shotgun blast coming out of a window. Climbing out the bedroom window of his neighbor's wife.

His grandson, Junior Duvall, had the grace of a cowboy and used it to good effect with horses, all his lady-friends, and his three ex-wives. Hell-raiser and womanizer, yes. But loved just as well by his boisterous male friends. Eventually, Jimmy's grandfather had lost the livestock auction barn betting on racehorses. He'd squandered virtually all of his money, his vast farm acreage, his wife's affection clean away. Then Junior Duvall had done the same thing.

Peggy Murphy was Jimmy's mother's maiden name. Irish and red-headed. Friendly, smart, fun-loving. She'd died of ovarian cancer the year her son turned fifteen. But she'd divorced his father when Jimmy was only four-years-old. At any rate, Junior Duvall had married a good woman—for a while there. He'd married a woman who'd loved him in the beginning. But he'd made poor choices. Junior Duvall pussyfooted around when it came to keeping that love intact. Taking her for grant-ed. Staying out weekends till two A.M. Never complimenting any of her substantial efforts at homemaking, or her taking the time to cook won-derful meals. Sometimes hiking his leg to fart at the dinner table. Creating a mood of disaster. Creating chaos. Doing whatever he could to lose what he'd once had with Jimmy's mother, making more real with each passing day the not-to-be-toyed-with connection between very bad luck and very bad taste.

But Jimmy Duvall's luck was of a different order. A cursed cosmic dice-roll. Something written in the stars—or so it seemed. When Jimmy had been in the coma, his father Junior had come up from Little Rock, Arkansas, just to stare at him in the bed one weekend. One Saturday morning. That was all. And Jimmy had lain there for four whole months. Slowly getting better. IV drop by IV drop. His substantial need for his father's presence just wouldn't go away; it wouldn't disappear despite everything Junior had done and had failed to do, despite his father's more-or-less disappearance act in the not-so-distant past. Sometimes Jimmy *still* missed his father terribly and he still loved him. Jimmy couldn't help it. He just did.

During the coma, Jimmy's two aunts on his mother's side, a couple of old friends and Lee Ann Riddle would come to visit. But Jimmy did not know that. Wasn't conscious of it until afterwards. Then after recovering, Jimmy just wasn't the same person. Not the same Jimmy Duvall he once had been. He would have a stagger, not a swagger, when he walked. You had to laugh, though. See the lighter side if possible. You had to spit into your palm and go back to the drawing board, bounce back from a situation which would allow you to bounce. Ha. Ha.

Be able to grin and bear it.

Not simply hang your head. Or stare idly off into space.

. . . .

At least Jimmy was still alive—this time as well. Time to get it in gear. Just like they'd learned in Air Force basic. Time to hump it, because time was short, and only time would tell. Jimmy Duvall certainly knew that. If he'd just slowed down some of his movements while standing on that Super Wal-Mart ladder. Etc., etc., etc. Because sometimes even post-coma Jimmy still did things too quickly. Like he'd always done. Instinctively. Just like his explosive behavior with his pretty, cinnamon-skinned wife, Petita. However, what beautiful black-brown eyes she had given to their boy. Yes, he'd moved too fast up there on the ladder. Sometimes Jimmy Duvall did things without thinking beforehand. That was simply the way he'd been built. Wired or taught. Or whatever the right word is.

III.

Tonight, he'd been looking for these planets on purpose, and they'd suddenly come into view, not too far from the moon. Wasn't that something? Extraordinary. Venus, Saturn, and Jupiter were the biggest. The others mere hints of light since he didn't have binoculars. All five planets were within a handspan of each other, but Jimmy couldn't hold up either hand right now. He'd mentioned hearing about the planets on TV. He told Lee Ann Riddle about it when she returned from scuba-diving in the Cayman Islands. That was three days ago. On Monday afternoon. Lee Ann hadn't said much at the time. But early Wednesday morning, she'd brought him a book, *The National Audubon Society Field Guide to the Night Sky*. She'd taken her own copy on the Caribbean vacation with her new fiancé, the eye-doctor, although there was a fancier name for what he did at the hospital.

Lately, Jimmy had been reading the book. Not just looking at its pictures. Lee Ann had given the book to him as a present, thought he might be interested, after hearing about what he heard on *The Today Show*. All the photographs were very beautiful. No telling how much those telescopes cost that took those pictures. The photographs of individual stars, well, they were absolutely gorgeous, resembling something like flowers. Red roses blooming. Mid-explosion.

Some of the writing confused him. Jimmy knew most of the words, what they meant separately, but sometimes not what they meant together. For example, "fuzzy set theory" and "fuzzy logic." He'd never once given Petita flowers. Once her nose had exploded with blood. Maybe that's why during the coma she'd not exactly been keen on staying in Kentucky. Maybe that's why she'd decided not to have any more to do with him. Then she'd gone back to Panama. All of Petita's family lived down there. She had found another man—not another American. Oh, how Jimmy would like to look at his son's face as soon as possible: see him grow up, learn how to write his name, score a touchdown, or hit a grand-slam. See him right now. Lay eyes on him period.

Oh, the regret and helplessness in Jimmy's heart, the sadness in his head, which these doctors and all their instruments could not gauge. But time always allowed for more surprises. More transformations. And who really knew what time held in store? Almost anything could happen. Couldn't it? Things no mere human being could know—or possibly foretell. Maybe someday Petita would soften-up a bit. Perhaps some day she would forgive him, then change her mind about Jimmy ever visiting their boy. Yes, he had definitely made some mistakes. But who knew, right? Maybe something unexpected would be discovered by the scientists and the doctors. Perhaps something to help him with the twitching. Perhaps he should start asking God for help.

Meanwhile, certain things still gave him hope. Daily upliftings from the depths. There was the fact that his Aunt Yvonne and his Aunt June still visited him regularly. Also, the concern on Lee Ann Riddle's kind, smiling face. And the things that her mouth said that her mouth didn't have to say. Now Jimmy Duvall was only twenty-seven years old. Once, Lee Ann Riddle had said that she'd prayed for him. He had been twenty-four and twenty-five-years-old, passed one of his birthdays at Western Baptist during the coma. Only a few years earlier—say, at twenty or twenty-one years old—that praying stuff would have struck him as corny.

He'd been here less than a week this time. But the word "corny" didn't fit the way he felt about prayer and health and luck. Not now.

Words were important—but they were never enough. Like when he'd told Petita that he was "sorry." Or like when Jimmy's father used to say he "loved" him.

Right after the coma, his father sounded funny on the telephone. When his aunts asked Junior Duvall if his recovering son could live in Little Rock for a little while, Jimmy's father had gotten embarrassed. Then he'd hem-hawed around.

Yes, words were important indeed. Once he'd spoken Spanish pretty good. Jimmy had learned some Spanish from his wife. Petita had made him listen to a song once, right after they'd had a horrible, horrible argument, a song in Spanish which said that actions were fire, words were ashes, and feelings, well, feelings could be rather like smoke. Jimmy hadn't liked the song very much at the time. Hadn't cared for it—or cared to think about whatever the hell it meant. It sounded like poetry. That is probably why Petita liked it. She'd told him that once in *el colegio* she'd won a poetry prize. She won an award for something she'd thought up and written down. Something she'd written long before she'd ever met him.

Yes, Jimmy was hurt again. He'd been hurt quite bad. He was in another hospital bed here at Western Baptist. He wasn't a whiner, though. Jimmy was a winner. Maybe he'd get some other books at that new bookstore Lee Ann had told him about downtown. Because Jimmy Duvall was *interested* in the book she'd bought him. He wasn't a quitter. So what if people laughed at the way he talked, or mocked the way his neck and face muscles jerked around. That was a decision those people made, like those bad decisions his father had made sitting at the dinner table, while everyone else in the family ate their meals.

One way or another, Jimmy would get through this new setback. One way or another. And time would tell. He would do his therapy, by golly, regain full movement in his arms and shoulders. Both hands and all of his fingers. So what if his father had never called back from Little Rock this time? Maybe he thought that his son was going to ask to stay with him again. But Jimmy didn't want to be a burden. He hadn't been one in the past, and he didn't want to be one now. Besides, Junior Duvall owned a pawn shop and he had a business to run. He had his own health worries, his liver problem, the rest of his own life to live.

. . . .

Jimmy Duvall exists. He briefly considers forcing open the hospital window. Perhaps breaking out the plateglass with a chair when he gets well enough. Then stepping out onto the ledge. He briefly considers doing this. But this just won't do. What would Lee Ann Riddle and his two aunts, what would the three people who care for Jimmy think if he did that? He has broken seventeen bones, the doctors have explained. That is, if you're counting what the doctors call metacarpals. Seventeen bones total. But he would bounce back.

Land upright, by golly. Yes he would bounce back. All by himself. Because who else on planet earth could Jimmy Duvall rely on now?

He'd survive as usual and be okay.

The dice and the odds be damned.

The Enduring Nights of Sidney Wingcloud

Once upon a time but not so long ago really, a baby boy was born in the sun-drenched desert, on the steep slope of a canyon grooved by a river the color of rust. The day was blamelessly blue and clear as a bell, but the child's entry into the world was prolonged and occluded. Opaque. You could say that. This boy's birth was opaque—uncertain, ambiguous, unclear. All he had to do was get his head out of the womb and all of his worries would be over. Yet the child's mother had lain on her back in vain, screaming in Athabascan for seventeen hours, cursing her husband and clutching a quilt, loathing all fathers before him.

"If you ask me, those are hooves," she declared through clenched teeth. "I tell you he's the size of a colt."

All the preparations for the birth had to be remade throughout the long wait. Around four in the afternoon, during the twenty-third hour, one of the women helping the young mother-to-be had gone to the river for another kettle of water. She had just refilled the container and started back up the switchbacks which led to the house when she heard a high-pitched wail coming from inside it. By the time she scrambled up the zigzaggedy slope the poor woman on the bed was unconscious, but still breathing. Her first child, an elongated baby boy with spindly legs and a jet-black mane of hair, had crawled over her stomach and begun to nurse of his own accord. The two midwives, who were inexperienced and rather worthless actually, but who had come to learn what they could, stood pressed against the wall in a stupor. They told somewhat conflicting stories about the birth.

"It happened in a heartbeat," one of them said, claiming that the boy had shot out at the last moment, like a greased kernel of seed-corn pressed between one's forefinger and thumb.

"A blink of the eye is the right way of putting it," the other girl maintained. "He stuck out his head and yawned, then winked at me like a dirty old man."

The proud father was called in, and he ceremoniously cut the umbilical cord with his antler-inlayed hunting knife, then sponged his wife's forehead until she regained consciousness and opened her eyes. After she came back to life, he promised that they would decide on a name together, a process, as it turned out, which took longer than the gestation period itself. The boy's mother fought hard for a traditional, ancestral appellation, some warrior's name like Red Feather, or something romantic and more resonant, along the lines of White-Sky or Running-Brook.

"White-Sky Wingcloud," the father said, mocking her. "That's redundant, that's silly. What about John or William, or how about Paul?"

"If you're dead set on a traditional name then there are hosts of others to choose from," he added. "Like Christopher or Robert, or oh-I-don't know. My point is this. Who's gonna do business with some guy named Red Feather?"

"Whatever. I've had it," the boy's mother said wearily. "But this child needs a name and he needs one now. Let's stick to your father's idea. We'll call the kid Sid," she told him.

So Sidney Woodwater Wingcloud it was.

The old chief was elated to be given a grandson and a namesake, and the year-old boy responded positively himself to having finally been given a title, after so much wishy-washiness and patriarchal wheel-spinning. He began to eat more and to put on some weight, devouring everything within reach or that was given to him, which was precisely everything a child could want.

His family were by far the wealthiest Apaches in all of New Mexico, and they spared no expense when it came to molding strong bones and teeth, vigorous boys, and able-bodied heirs. From the time he was weaned and started to crawl, Sidney quaffed bottles of Angus milk or peach nectar mixed carefully with the milk of his wet-nurses. He downed bananas and mangos, fresh pineapples and tangerines, snacks which were tastier and much better for him than the bulk licorice sold at the concrete-block market owned by one of his uncles, exotic tropical fruit which cost a pretty penny to be sure, but wouldn't endanger his smile. These delicacies, of course, were rare in the Southwestern desert and the envy of other children's eyes. But this was only one of the many luxuries which the Wingcloud clan could provide for their sons and which distinguished them from all of the other Indians. Every one of their children was wealthy and wise, they believed. However, there was something exceptional and even more impressive about Sidney Wingcloud. All the tribal leaders and all their wives, everyone had their eye on him from the start. He ate the choicest cuts of Iowa meat, the finest Latin American fruits, and eventually Sidney grew up to be a beautiful boy.

"He'll heist our daughters' hearts," prophesied some of the women, who themselves felt weak and envious looking at Sidney's olive-colored skin, his blue eyes and high cheek bones, which made him look like a little Italian movie star.

"He'll inherit our earth," said his father's father.

. . . .

Early in the century Sidney's grandfather had occasioned a break with the rest of the tribe when he took all the money he had made selling sad blankets and bogus cougar teeth to desperate mountain men and cringing pioneers, then commissioned a huge wooden house to be built on the encampment's far fringe. Chief Sidney Woodwater Wingcloud I, who had nothing but scorn for his customers and often proclaimed that they were "such nincompoops," was the patriarch of Wingcloud millions. The house he built endured.

This house, of course, was very beautiful and very, very white, towering three stories above the cliff rising over the desert floor. On each side of the structure were two long verandas and a series of ivory columns which lent a classical aspect to the mansion's facade. Comfortable wicker swings hung from the ceilings of these lengthy porches, and the boards beneath them were painted blue. By the time Sidney was ten, his grandfather had installed a slate pool table on the top floor of his house and tall French windows overlooking the backyard, where he played horseshoes while his wives hung the laundry. He was getting older and wistful by this point and would occasionally take his grandson up into the attic to play pool, then tell him stories about the old days when the land had seemed much larger.

"Cochise was too stubborn and thought with his heart," he told Sidney. "It took a while, but by the time they shipped him off to Florida, even Geronimo had finally caught on. The trick is to know when you're outnumbered, then to act like you're beat when you're not."

"Merge, merge, then diversify," Chief Woodwater I advised. "Lay low in the system and scrape bits of it over to your side."

Sidney nodded and took the next shot. He devoured these financial insights in the same way he gobbled down food. These talks with his grandfather helped turn him into a budding entrepreneur at an early age, a lifelong socioeconomic pool-shark who knew the advantages of carrying a big stick, but walking softly and acting like it wasn't.

Once when he was twelve, Sidney was teaching some of the other braves how to smoke cigars and play cutthroat when his first shot sailed off the table, into the air, and out through a closed French window. When the pool ball dropped that day, the old chief was sitting in the backyard, scanning the financial section and watching his Japanese gardener work in the flower bed. While most people would use a lawn chair, the old man preferred an upholstered office model with inclined back, comfortable arm rests, and cabriole legs. Upon hearing the glass shatter and seeing the ball fall, Chief Woodwater I shifted his weight to the opposite side of the Cogswell chair. Then he crossed his arms in thought. But before he could decide what to think or do about this odd occurrence, young Sidney burst around the side of the house and explained to his grandfather what had happened. He and his friends were playing hooky from school and the cue ball had flown off on the break. Sidney said he was sorry for smashing the window, and in recompense for the damage he offered to exercise and brush down every stallion in his grandfather's stables.

The old Indian chief laughed, then patted his grandson on the head.

"No sweat," he told Sidney. "Go back and enjoy your game."

Later that evening, the old man chuckled some more about the mishap and readmired his grandson's honesty. Old Woodwater decided that he loved the youth considerably more than his other two grandsons who had been born in the meantime—the granddaughters being, lovely and lovable as they were, an altogether different matter. On that very night, he extracted his will from the bowels of a wall safe and arranged it so his grandson would never want for anything that money could buy, whether it was prestige, more money, or more love.

It would not be superfluous to note, at this point, that old Woodwater Wingcloud enjoyed these last two luxuries in particular. He often boasted that he would die, in fact, while fiddling around with one or the other. "Either at the bank," he would bellow, then pause. "Or in the saddle," he would say with a snort.

Indeed his boisterous prophecy panned out. For on the very night Old Woodwater amended his will, he died poised on his elbows, and more red-faced than usual, while panting above one of his squaws. Old Woodwater had possessed an uncanny knack for moneymaking, though, and he knew when to retrench or spread out. From 1880 to the day of his brain hemorrhage, he had amassed land and power and loot, always shuffling around his capital, like a desert Frank Cowperwood, whenever confronted by some frigidity in the marketplace—then switching his methods and finding some hot spot, whenever opportunity beamed back at him and lavishly opened her arms. When trading post commerce slowed to a trickle with the decline in Westward expansion, he branched out into jewelry and beads, which his wives manufactured and, later on, he shipped to Los Angeles in freight trains. His workers would unload the box cars while the locomotive was serviced, before heading back east via Denver, bulging with profits and Central American bananas right off the boat. The old man had sat out the thirties like most everyone else. But after the war he was one of the first to consider selling automobiles secondhand. On a grand scale. By the mid 1940s, Chief Woodwater Wingcloud headed a chain of used car lots which spanned the Sunbelt and were run by his legitimate sons.

Soon, the Wingclouds were ghastly wealthy. So when Sidney turned twenty-one and gained access to his share of the estate, it had grown considerably since the time his grandfather had inserted the percentage-based clause. The first thing he did with his wealth was to part with a considerable chunk of it. He bought extravagant presents for his extravagant friends and arranged to send one of them to Europe in order to study sculpture or aeronautics. His best friend, Thomas Bigsky—the most insatiable and profligate Native American of them all—could not really decide what he wanted, what he would do there, or what he would learn. All of his life, he had suspected that something fateful awaited him on the other side of the ocean.

"Call it destiny, call it fate," Thomas Bigsky told his fortunate friend. "I've got an insatiable urge to see the land of our forefathers. It'll be a sort of backwards discovery."

"But our ancestors came from the other way," Sidney reminded him. "You'll need to cross the Pacific Ocean instead."

"Depends how you look at it," Thomas Bigsky said with a smile. "It's no thanks to a bunch of savages that your grandfather left you sitting in the catbird seat. I mean you gotta rain dance with who brung ya."

Thomas Bigsky was overwhelmed with directionless desire and an itch for the intercontinental, he explained. So Sidney Wingcloud gave him ten thousand dollars for the trip. After all, they had grown up together, and both of them had always been rambunctious at heart, healthy and handsome and capable of, well, you name it. As boys they liked to cut class and play pinball, or go up into his grandfather's attic. They loved riding the old man's thoroughbred and Appaloosa stallions bareback in front of the young girls, so their long hair trailed behind them like smoke or the wings of certain birds. On more than one occasion, these two cooked up a diving contest with the other boys, a dangerous sport which began at dawn on the highest cliff, and then terminated in a turquoise canyon pool, just deep enough at its center to receive the arrow of their falling bodies without inflicting harm—but you had to hit that mark.

This was a foolhardy enterprise to begin with and a tragic one in the long run, for Bigsky fractured a collarbone, and Sidney lacerated his forearm. Ultimately there was even a death. After attempting a double pike to win the cliff-diving tournament one weekend, Billy Freefire snapped his neck, and the elders drained the water from the canyon pool. Once they were older and considered themselves men, Sidney and Thomas Bigsky forgot about swimming holes, and they rarely went to the stables together. They began devoting themselves, instead, to the lighthearted acquisition of women, a more playful and absorbing enterprise, they both decided. In the beginning, Sidney complained about not riding the horses anymore. But Thomas Bigsky would coyote-laugh and remind his friend of the superior glee which women afforded them, as the sun affords warmth to the earth.

"But those Appaloosas," Sidney explained. "I'll miss the sensation, the speed."

Placing a hand on his friend's shoulder, Thomas Bigsky bared his teeth like some parched desert animal that has discovered an oasis full of persimmon trees. "Sid," he would say with a ravenous grin. "Isn't it time for someone else to play horsy?"

Great care had to be taken, of course, so that the girls' families were kept ignorant of these nocturnal rampages. But this detracted in no way from the boys' pleasure. In fact, Bigsky believed that eluding their fathers—most of whom had ceremonial hatchets lying around somewhere or another—added an extra dimension to their sport. They would sneak in through tent flaps on their bellies, wriggle through windows and doors, then charm what they could from their girlfriends. Some would refuse to do this or try that, yet their reluctance seemed to decrease should the social and economic niche of their father be higher and seemed to augment with their level of poverty. Other factors intervened, of course, such as the proximity of their parents' bedroom or sleeping mat. The time of the year, or the moon. A big part of these quests, therefore, involved seeing just what could be achieved considering the various permutations of such constraints. Undeterred by such barriers, Thomas Bigsky seemed to enjoy them, and he even devised an intricate system by which they competed and kept score.

After Bigsky left for Europe, though, Sidney felt the dull pangs of boredom. He become curiously less confident on his solitary warpath for love. To console and comply with the colossal yearning, which he had also inherited from his grandfather, he hired an architect to construct a huge nightclub on the outskirts of the area where all the Wingcloud families dwelled. Of course by this time, the United States Government had established a reservation for the regular members of the tribe. But the region occupied by the elite Wingcloud families had long before distinguished itself. So much so, in fact, that the rest of the tribe devised a name for it, *palo-fe-thad*, which is a running-together of a demonstrative adjective and two other Athabascan words meaning "soft place."

. . . .

During the time it took to construct the nightclub, Sidney kept spending money and throwing lavish dinner parties where butlers served cocktails until everyone had his or her fill. Flamingo pâté and swan soup were then featured on handwritten menus designed by one of the most exuberant chefs from the coast who was, as they say, gay, screaming, on fire, flaming and great fun to have around. The famous chef's appetizers were followed by tiger steaks and watercress salads. In order to arrive at his dinner parties with flair, Sidney purchased a convertible, needless to say, a 1951 Ford with ivory-colored upholstery. And he began the rare wine collection which would later be stored in the nightclub's cellar. Apart from the cost of commissioning the new building, his chief expenditure, Sidney bought himself some Scandinavian furniture, a cappuccino machine, and a gigantic futon filled with pheasant feathers. He added a Finnish sauna to his house's vast spa and for a while his vague loneliness and translucent sense of loss was abated somewhat.

Once again, Sidney was a happy man. Really, he was. While many claim that people who become instantly and particularly wealthy lose their ability to go out of themselves, their capacity to love indiscriminately, and to have fun with anyone at all, this was not the case with Sidney Wingcloud and his friends. They laughed and loved a lot, in fact, and were contented, because they did have the good things with no illusions about having them always. Markets crumple, vessels burst, necks will snap. Thoroughbred horses and people will die, Sidney knew, from growing up where he grew up and from having long talks with his grandfather. He and his friends would not be hoodwinked into some phantasmagoric belief in eternal perfection, a promised world to come, full of milk chocolate dancing girls and unblemished fruit. They just wanted things perfect while they lasted, while they could still be bought and solidly obtained.

Sidney Wingcloud could see it now. Once completed, the nightclub would be a main attraction, renowned throughout the country, so he had the construction crew work double time. In a half year, the exterior was completed. Soon enough, there were just some finishing touches to be put on the seventeen bars and various dance floors on every level. It was an intricate modern structure whose green marble facades were reminiscent of those buildings built by the Fray Bentos corn-beef kings in Montevideo, held together with a burnt orange mortar, the color of the surrounding desert. Entirely unmoved by the ecological and strategic advantages of the wiped-out Indian dwellings at Palo Verde, the architect had conspicuously set his creation on top of a cliff—in a place where everybody could find it—rather than into one where nobody could.

A few weeks before the grand opening, Sidney's best friend returned from his stint overseas to begin his new job as the bar's general manager. A self-propelled, ingenious fellow, Thomas Bigsky had given up his initial ambition to design and test airplanes while in Paris and had chosen instead to study art. He performed his course work shabbily, though, and much preferred life in the streets. When he left the fine arts school, he couldn't paint a profile or sculpt a woman's shoulder—much less explain Bernoulli's principle or fly a lazy-eight. But he had picked up argot readily. He mastered the morals of the Marais, reveling until dawn, as he used to brag with a snicker, in the more sumptuous *boîtes* of the Right Bank.

Once established in his new position, Thomas Bigsky became a sort of twentieth century pleasure merchant and a regional celebrity to boot. He helped hand-squeeze limes and lemons to mix his mean margaritas, taught his staff various other recipes from his trip toward the East, using magnums of champagne and crates of rare, concupiscent flowers. In no time at all, people came from miles around to drink deep and see for themselves the Apache disco where sparkling wine and tequila were also standard. Every night, from the perspective of his office's two-way mirror, Sidney and his assistants would glean the gorgeous from the crowd that formed in front of the neon sign which bore his name. These customers alone were admitted by bouncers wearing tight buckskin trousers, who took their coats and their cover charge, then gave them a ticket for a complimentary drink.

At Wingcloud's nightclub all the cocktails were served copiously in inverted glass teepees which Thomas Bigsky had managed to design himself in a burst of practical inspiration. In those long-ago days, when everyone laughed ceaselessly and danced lithely till dawn—so unlike his later life, those postponed and more dissipated times to come when he would drive out into the desert, strap himself to a road sign riddled with hunter's bullets, then wait—Sidney Wingcloud and Thomas Bigsky would circulate among the club's clientele, pouring refills into the glasses of women and winking ambiguously at their dates. When they were particularly interested in what they saw, one of the bouncers would whisper the code to the elevator into the girl's ear, then ask her escort to skedaddle. Sidney's henchmen were prepared, of course, to offer these startled young men recompense for their inconvenience, but some refused to leave and had to be persuaded. There was some gunplay, a few broken bones. But finally, the women who left their dates to go up into the glamorous offices always made this choice themselves, a fact which their dates tended to ignore.

Like his father and his grandfather before him, and so on, Sidney Wingcloud enjoyed feminine companionship. He shared this passion with all of his other friends who helped him at the nightclub. They would sit around for hours discussing the intricacies of feminine aesthetics. During his time abroad, Thomas Bigsky had become an expert. He had held long conversations with some knowing and savvy Arabs concerning just what constituted true art, true beauty in a woman.

"A woman should look good naturally," he insisted. "Naturally, a woman should look good."

Thomas Bigsky admitted, however, that in certain psychological states most men—a category into which he fell squarely—could be attracted to paint. Occasionally, even Bigsky himself liked the type of women who used conversation, clothing, or some other feeble covering to give a fleeting impression of beauty. There was something about the intelligence of artifice which fascinated mankind as a whole. Generally speaking, though, Thomas Bigsky believed that discriminating males required a woman to be gorgeous "as is."

Sidney Wingcloud disagreed. Hadn't Bigsky himself preferred paint, and not merely from time to time? Hadn't he championed the night-wealth of Rue Saint Denis or the Bois de Boulogne in the summertime?

After listening to such arguments, Thomas Bigsky draped his ponytail over the back of his chair like a long mink stole. He acknowledged these aesthetic lapses, but pointed out that in those days he had been somewhat younger. More curious than anything else. He had indeed gone through thousands of dollars wandering along that supine street of sense. He attributed these visits not to sheer lust, or an inclination to experience art, although some of his acquaintances there were skilled artificers and artists of a sort, but rather to his genuine interest in quelling the myth that these prostitutes possessed a mystical grace with their clients, to an earnest urge to refine and clarify the scientific study of woman to which he felt personally committed. "Just think where we are in the course of things," Thomas Bigsky said. "You never can tell when those Japs might retaliate—or you might get picked-off by a truck. Why should you die lonesome in this dangerous world we live in? It just doesn't make any sense."

"Besides," he added. "It was cheap."

"Oh really?" Sidney asked. "How much did it cost?"

"Well, I forget," Thomas Bigsky admitted.

These chuckleheaded conversations commonly occurred at night, and eventually Sidney was inclined to agree with the gist of his friend's theory about natural beauty. Thomas Bigsky kept pressing his point. He reminded Sidney that his prodigious grandfather, Chief Woodwater Wingcloud I, had held similar views and forced the women of his household to look the way that he wanted. The squaws discontinued wearing customary beads, or highlighting their facial features with blue clay and the paste of certain berries. While Thomas Bigsky conceded that several dozen European strumpets had made the flea buzz about his youthful ear, they put their makeup on like professional plasterers, proof that they themselves sensed how true beauty was immanent. As he finally observed with uncharacteristic pith: "A woman should be able to dive headlong into a body of water, then step out dripping and looking her best."

. . . .

During those first few years, there were some wonderful times after-hours. Once they'd closed the club at dawn, Sidney and his friends would invite a few women home for breakfast on the twin blue verandas. As the sun crept cautiously over the full-sized landscape, then spread itself shyly over the smaller houses and mobile homes below where they sat, these select few would sit on the porch of the huge white house, drinking and laughing some more. Bowls full of cantaloupe, then king crab omelets were served here, but everyone ate half heartedly and seemed distracted. They all seemed more interested in what would happen next. Hating to see an evening end, but not wanting to force matters, Sidney Wingcloud occasionally suggested that they all watch a movie together in the private projection room, or play croquet in their underwear on his carpet-like lawn.

Oftentimes, things became more risqué. The person who instigated these more salacious activities was, of course, Thomas Bigsky whose hell-bent-for-leather tactics surprisingly seemed to work. The rich meals of melon overlooking the tumescent panorama were sufficiently mood-setting, and he knew this. After everyone had left the table and gone inside, Thomas Bigsky would set the ball rolling. "I think I'll unwind in the hot tub," he would say casually. Then undress with a yawn.

Once the others had joined him, Thomas Bigsky would smile with a peculiar sweetness, then control the atmosphere in the spa by selecting music on its built-in, waterproof stereo console. He seemed to generate the best results with classical pieces but kept the volume light at first, playing quiet sonatas and flowing string quartets. After the others had splashed-around, toweled-off, and paired-up, Thomas Bigsky enjoyed staying in the water with his date. This certainly was no sweat lodge or calefactory. Bigsky prided himself on being musically prepared for any situation, any weakness, any whim his guests might have. Personally, he liked to conclude the *soirée* with a bit of Bartok or Wagner. He would wait until all the others had gone to their respective rooms, then, should his girl for the evening be willing, he would fill a syringe with a concoction of poppy juice and cardamom, the recipe for which he had obtained from an Iraqi prince while in Paris. Then absorbed in his own music, as he loved these women, Thomas Bigsky would inject this mixture into the blue veins which invariably trickled down their thighs.

Eventually Sidney Wingcloud found him out. He often rebuffed his friend for this habit and for the extremes he would go to in general, saying that they were dangerous and pointing out that they were contrary to ideas about forthright beauty and pleasure. But Bigsky couldn't help himself. He was hooked in more ways than one. He tried quitting cold turkey, but he started gaining weight and losing his self-confidence.

One afternoon, following a week of bad living, Thomas Bigsky convinced a seamstress and her twin brother to indulge along with him. Bigsky had secretly been on a binge, roaming the reservation like he had in the old days, throwing his salary around and swilling mescal with the locals. He hadn't seen Sidney Wingcloud or any of his other friends for seven nights and seven days and had entered his rich friend's house using his own key.

The next morning, Sidney's maid woke up her employer in tears. After serving him coffee rather shakily, she took him to witness the disastrous tableau for himself. There the three of them were, asphyxiated by one way or another. The young seamstress and her brother were still holding hands, floating facedown in the water. Thomas Bigsky was equally motionless, leaning back on the whirlpool's stairs, covered with vomit, surrounded by various vials and floating lemon wedges, still smiling uncouthly and clutching a bottle of liquid gold.

After the funeral, Sidney shut down the nightclub. He traveled north into the LaSalle mountains to mull over the mishap and consider revising his life. Food was plentiful in the late summer forest, and Sidney felt one with the land. He ate wild green salads and drank root-enriched teas along with the peanut butter, bacon, and jelly sandwiches which he made from the stock of groceries he'd tossed in the car trunk. He returned to the reservation one month later, having gained twenty pounds and sworn off the all-nighters for good. He banned each and every user of the poppy seed and cardamom mixture from the nightclub,

a cleanup operation which took no time. These addicts were easily iden-
tified by the tincture of their pupils and palms which turned
rose-colored shortly following an injection. Afterwards, Sidney began
business as usual, living pretty much as he had before, but more carefully, with a resolve to enjoy himself immensely and to avoid going too
far.

Some claimed he did though.

Some people said that Sidney never really came to grips with his
friend's death and that he remained trapped forever in his own lit-up
world, a comfortable and well-mannered realm for the most part—but
a violent one.

"That's just what they say," Sidney would assert in his own defense.
"They're jealous, but they don't know it."

Louise Flyingbird, who dated him briefly, claimed that he liked to
stand in the bathtub and have her throw leftovers at him, salisbury steak
and mashed potatoes, handfuls of lima beans and lemon meringue pie.

Also, just ask the reservation's sheriff, Earl Littlefeather, who caught
Sidney Wingcloud out on Route 537 at three o'clock in the morning,
huddled in the backseat of the convertible, crying fiercely and watching
a fire over five miles long. According to Sheriff Littlefeather, Sidney had
started the blaze himself and burned away all the tall grass by the road,
which the rest of the tribe usually cut for hay.

However, both of these accounts could possibly be misleading and
slanderous: the former being the fabrication of a gold digger, belatedly
grasping at straws, and the second a plausible misinterpretation of what
had really happened on the night of the fire. The individuals who began
and perpetuated these stories were the same kind of people who started
them everywhere, bored and emotionally-starved individuals who
cooked up whatever it took to make themselves feel morally superior,
blessed while they really were miserable. Sidney had Linda Flyingbird
lured out to Hollywood by a rinky-dink movie producer who he'd met
in Santa Fe and who owed him a big, big favor. Once she was out of his
hair, Sidney paid no attention to what anyone else said and considered

his critics to be envious of his wonderful life. He continued to carouse and ostentatiously consume just like he always had.

Once, he fell in love.

On the night that Sidney met Sarah, Thomas Bigsky had lain in the earth for five years, a stretch of time during which the club had become even more famous. Since its owner was now an indigenous success story—flesh and blood proof of certain right-wing theories about what could be done with one's boot straps—Sidney Wingcloud made the cover of *Life*. Needless to say, there was a blurb in *Town and Country*, and an entire article about his nightclub in *Santa Fe Today*, a comprehensive story which got reprinted in the travel section of the *New York Times*.

Oh yes, Sidney Wingcloud had made it.

Then what happened next went like this.

Sidney glimpsed a woman from his office's two-way mirror and immediately suspected that she was an exception to Bigsky's theory.

A fair-skinned girl from Vermont, Sarah had freckles and corrected vision, and she was entirely different from the girls to whom Sidney usually found himself attracted. He descended and talked with her briefly. He soon realized that he'd been right. They felt entirely at ease with one another and talked ceaselessly. They talked about the desert and baseball, John F. Kennedy and his ham-fisted dealings with the Soviet premier.

"Those Kennedys are always on the make. That's why they frighten me," Sarah told him. "They always watch for the camera, then look out for number one."

Here was a woman who wouldn't be toyed with, Sidney realized. Someone who was in control of her opinions, someone who had made firm decisions about the way she wanted to live. Sarah had a soft, orangy voice and cream-colored skin, which was thickly rouged and smelled of sandalwood. Beneath a thick foundation of base, a few girlish freckles were still visible. Her eyebrows were plucked then drawn back on gaudily with a marker, her eyelashes curled, her eyelids caked with layer upon layer of sparkly robin-egg blue eye shadow.

For three weeks, Sarah would come in and just talk with Sidney. This fascinated him and brought out the best in him. Two months later, after he'd won her confidence, after her cosmetic fortifications had been flanked, steamed away with her permission by the heat of his hot tub, Sidney saw that he had been right. She was not naturally gorgeous. But her voice and her hands were extraordinary.

To say that Sidney Wingcloud fell in love with Sarah's voice or hands alone would be reductive and preposterous. But he thought of their talks together constantly, and her hands were lovely and strong— unlike any woman's he had ever held before. Perhaps androgynous, certainly skilled, Sarah's fingers were graceful whenever their owner interlaced them with his own, or moved them to make a point in con-versation. The way she used them to express herself, to start a cigarette, or to flip off a light switch, such commonplace movements fascinated Sidney to no end. Sarah wasn't the most financially driven girl he had ever known or the most lovely. While there were many other much less resistible clients, who would do anything to have a shot at his fortune, Sarah seemed superior to and oblivious of all other competition. She would occasionally refuse to see Sidney when he wanted her, saying quite frankly that she had made other plans. Sarah wore makeup year-round, like some people wore slickers or overcoats, thick gobs of goo and overbearing chemicals, which covered the scars she once sustained in a horrific auto accident and made her feel better about her appear-ance.

On the first night they slept together, Sidney noticed the wire of a dental plate curving around each of Sarah's bicuspids. She removed this and made a snaggle-toothed face which frightened him terribly at first, and then reminded him of a jack-o-lantern. He listened to stories chock-full of calamity and brimming with uncommon resilience, ghastly tales of broken bones, lawnmower mishaps, grease fires, bicycle wrecks, and an unfortunate spate of muggings. Her fate hadn't been stellar. No,

Sarah's luck had not been good. Once when she was thirteen, she had gone on vacation with her family to Glacier National Park where she had been mildly gored by a bison. As for her front teeth, they had been gone for most of her life. Sarah told Sidney in detail, but without bitterness or remorse, about the day she had volunteered to tend goal for her brother, who had recently taken up lacrosse but hadn't acquired all the necessary equipment.

"Having bad luck, getting a bad draw. These things happen to everybody, and they will happen to you," Sarah said. "You wasteful and wanton boy."

"Yes, I suppose," Sidney sighed.

Then he winked at her.

Just like he'd winked on the day he'd been born.

"Always remember the Kennedys," Sarah told him. "Calamity is something you can't completely avoid. It just proves how tight-knit we all are. Instead of what keeps us apart."

These two made love so well and laughed so hard together, especially after the jack-o-lantern incident, that Sidney Wingcloud discovered what he really liked about Sarah. The way time transformed whenever she was around. The way it sometimes seemed to disappear entirely. The way Sarah could make almost anything funny and believed that most things, including losing one's front teeth, including love, were perhaps best endured from a tragicomic perspective.

Something clicked in Sidney Wingcloud's soul. Sarah was the only woman who could make him laugh, and whenever she made him laugh in bed, Sidney could feel his bones float. Eventually, he learned to love other parts besides her hands: her wrists, her shoulders, her words, her rust-colored hair, which turned out to be beautiful on closer inspection, glistening like the sun hanging on the Western horizon, glowing like an orange-brown-reddish ball. They would take trips together or spend entire weekends at home, face-to-face, and away from the nightclub. Pleased with one another's company, they felt no obligation to appear in public or to assure anyone else of their happiness.

But alas, only a couple of months after the onset of their courtship, one of Sarah's best friends from Burlington, Vermont, came out for a visit. Just when he'd realized the value of what he and Sarah had together, just when he'd grown accustomed to certain people's quips about her false teeth, Sidney Wingcloud lost her forever merely because of a whim. It happened on a Wednesday evening while Sidney was going over some invoices and supervising the set-up crew who were preparing to open at eight o'clock. Sarah had gone to the grocery store and left him and her friend Cozette at the club. He and Cozette, a vain dipsomaniac when you got right down to it, got drunk together, and that's all she wrote.

Now it should be noted that Cozette McKenzie was the antithesis of Sarah, evenly tanned, with a perfect mouth, and no scars whatsoever. Furthermore, she had never handled a lawnmower or ridden a bicycle in her life. In a word, she was gorgeous "as is," and when Sidney slept with her he screwed up his life. After Sarah had left on her errand, the two of them began drinking Singapore Slings and telling jokes, which became progressively more insufferable, playing games which were sillier and sillier: pinball, bumper pool, and darts, then drinking games like Thumper, Prince of Wales, or Spin the Bottle and Empty It. The employees went silently about their work—folding napkins, sorting silverware, and slicing fruit, separating eggwhites for the Singapore Slings—while these inane activities escalated and their participants forgot themselves beyond all measures of public decorum.

The night before, Sidney had taken Sarah and Cozette down to Santa Fe for a big Mexican meal at the Pale-Faced Adobe. He had eaten the *chile verde* combination plate and a side order of *frijoles* and had been suffering all afternoon from sharp pains in his side. While he was laughing at one of Cozette's stupid jokes, a little gas had squeaked out, and she jumped. Nothing hideous but audible. He apologized in passing and promised to light the next one for her.

"You'll do what?" Cozette asked him in stitches.

"You heard me," Sidney promised.

He seemed quite serious and committed.

Her incredulity was evident, so a few minutes later, when an opportunity presented itself, Sidney sent forth a torch using his cigarette lighter which singed his polyester golf pants and scorched a small swath of the nightclub's carpet. Of course, why such behavior would be considered irresistible by anyone only confirms the degree to which Cozette's judgement was clouded whenever she drank Singapore Slings.

Shortly thereafter, they were in each other's arms.

Much to the initial amusement of a waitress who found them there, Cozette and Sidney snuck off and coupled in the nightclub's walk-in refrigeration unit.

"I'm sorry, sir. I didn't see a thing," the waitress said, quickly excusing herself and trying to keep her job.

"Please shut the door," Sidney told her wearily.

Already ashamed, the two picked themselves up from the crates of pineapples and maraschino cherries onto which they had dived in the confusion of their lust. Then when Sarah returned only a half-hour later, Cozette broke down and promptly confessed what they had done.

Twelve months and three days later, Cozette gave birth to Sidney's son. He never knew about the birth. He never heard anything more from the woman with the sandalwood skin and the high, citrus voice who could make him feel orthopedically light. He hired private detectives and offered rewards for any information which might lead to her whereabouts. But Sarah had completely withdrawn from society. And for good reasons too. Cozette McKenzie had gone with her and dried out. Disillusioned with men and their inclination for abbreviated forms of love—a force they believed could be practical, like gravity, or the earth's twin magnetic poles—Sarah and Cozette remained friends. They weathered the tragedy together. The two women raised the boy by themselves in a lean-to by a river. Outcasts, they grew their own crops, and the child grew sturdy on meals of oatmeal and okra.

After a while, Sidney Wingcloud got over the loss. He thought secretly of Sarah on a regular basis, however, and often missed her a great deal. From time to time throughout his life, particularly at dusk and the cusp of night, Sidney would occasionally remember her hands, her laughter, or her sunset-colored hair. Not only did Sidney never again laugh in bed, but unless he passed out from excessively cheering the inner man, which sometimes became necessary after two or three days of insomnia, he found it difficult to sleep in one either. Sometimes Sidney wanted to close his eyes and keep them closed, but he didn't have the courage or the strength. He would occasionally, it is true, lapse into a sort of semi-consciousness at the appropriate time and place, that is, at home in his bedroom, but this became equally frightening for him because of a nightmare. His one and only dream. There was this little movie which constantly flickered before his eyelids. On several occasions when he wanted to sleep deeply but couldn't, Sidney Wingcloud saw himself situated in a strange landscape that he'd never seen before, a kind of hellish limbo full of characters from his past. A prison without walls, you might say. Many people he had known or had heard about were there with him, his own father and Thomas Bigsky, the Iraqi Prince, and some of the other practitioners of Bigsky's private religion. Old Woodwater was there too, of course, the granddaddy of them all, with a handful of his more gullible squaws.

There were no guards, no ostensible barriers which kept people in this place, yet they stayed on silently, and no one attempted to leave. The building was built of the oldest materials, dried adobe, and grooved partitions of wood.

"It's like a vast barn," Sid would tell you. "But not exactly."

For example, this building was filled with people instead of live-stock. It had streets and alleys crisscrossed by even larger thoroughfares and was divided up just like a city. Alongside these roads lay the carcasses of various beasts. Suspended from rafters or propped against beams, the bodies of halved animals and plucked fowl were carefully displayed. There were round hens on hooks, fat shiny geese, and glistening sides of beef. The people Sidney Wingcloud recognized and knew from before, outside of this mental landscape, looked thinner here and acted like per-fect strangers to him. He sometimes wondered why they never ate anything, never built a fire and roasted some of the meat, or dried bits of it in the sun which shone brightly through a few openings in the building's sides. But no one attempted to use this as a source of food, and the animals lay wastefully dead.

All the people in the dream would sit around in groups, staring at large televisions and playing inscrutable board games. A lot of the men walked around shirtless and smoked. Occasionally, someone would begin a languid contest of tag or blind-man's bluff. The dream lent itself to these silent sports, for its streets were labyrinthine, and the building was maddeningly large.

One could, however, glimpse another world through a few openings in the building's sides where the dried mud had cracked and fallen off. There were various shops, booths, and market stalls, and sometimes Sidney could make out a few faces in the crowd. He discerned the sounds and smells of a festival, a carnival or a fair. Once, as Sidney stared at them, the people who ran and frequented the booths began looking back through the openings, staring at him and the others on the inside. What these people were really watching, though, was a man who had suddenly appeared. Some skinny man with a beard who Sidney had never seen before was flying around the building using a hang-glider he had fashioned from a series of sticks. With no breeze to support him, the mysterious man fanned out these twigs with his hands, then soared about the thick wooden rafters, weaving in and out of the area under the building's thin, tin roof. After the man had landed, there was the polite sound of clapping from the crowd outside, then Sidney glanced over and saw Sarah looking on with all the others.

Seeing how impressed she was by the demonstration, Sidney ran over and asked the man for a lesson. The stranger smiled and said sure, "Nothing to it."

He agreed to give the bundle of sticks to Sidney with no strings attached.

It wouldn't cost him a cent, the man promised.

Following a few tips about balance, concentration, and so forth, the man showed Sidney how to hold the rickety apparatus, spreading the twigs out effortlessly like a magician fans a pack of cards. He fluttered about the rafters one last time, turning a few loop-de-loops which drew more sighs, then another burst of applause. Then the man descended. He wished Sidney Wingcloud the best, then he was gone for good, never to appear again in the recurring dream.

Suddenly, the crowd shifted and seemed anxious. They had the air of a nervous circus audience watching a highwire act or a trapeze artist, and Sidney had the distinct impression that he was now expected to perform. But the bundle of sticks felt useless in his hands as soon as the stranger had disappeared. He held the wooden device up incredulously. Then placed it behind his back. Nothing happened. For the first time, all of the people inside of the building made some sounds in the back of their throats. They laughed at Sidney and began chanting his name in harsh monosyllables—Sid! Sid! Sid!—as he stood there squatting and straining, trying to remember everything the mysterious stranger had told him. He held the wings loosely but firmly, trying desperately to ignore the people who seemed to be tormenting him. Then Sidney believed he distinguished Sarah's low, orangy laugh. But when he spun around, he heard a unified moan of disappointment. Some laughter. Some jeering. Then the shuffling of feet. As the crowd turned away, Sidney noticed her voice once again. But the laughter and the jeering had become thunderous by this point, and whatever she might have said to him was swept away by the caterwauling. Sidney couldn't ever be sure whether she had laughed at him or sighed. Perhaps she had walked away in disgust. However, Sidney couldn't be sure because of the noise from the others inside and outside the barn-like building, and this was yet another point of pain.

The dream had different durations and many variants. But the place, the people, and certain other aspects were always the same and felt so real to him. To his utter dismay, for example, the dead animals were a dependable feature in Sidney's dream. Also, every time he got the chance, Sidney would try out the sticks he'd been given and would witness his flying failure anew.

Invariably, the dream would end in one of two ways. Most often, after the crowd on the outside moved away, first in disappointment, then in mirth, Sidney Wingcloud would watch himself pacing idly, walking up and down the network of alleys and streets, amid all the conversationless game-players and the clean, quiet carcasses. But occasionally the dream ended another way. In this version, Sidney saw an impish double of himself crouching with the wooden wings in a corral-like area that lay behind the building that seemed like a barn, or a prison, but was not. In this open area, beneath spacious skies, Sidney fiddled determinedly with the bundle of wood which the soaring stranger had given him many dreams ago. Poor, poor, Sidney Wingcloud. These were feverish nights, as he practiced and practiced. Although a few times—just before he bolted upright and startled his dozing wife—Sidney Wingcloud imagined himself to be suspended briefly, possessor of the knowledge which would make the wings work. He could feel his body shedding something. Losing its density. He imagined himself not flying exactly, not actually leaving the ground, but becoming lighter and moving upward, rising gradually onto the tips of his toes.

His dozing wife? Why, of course! Just a few years after the tryst in his nightclub's refrigeration unit, Sidney Wingcloud did meet someone who pleased him. She had sour, inchoate eyes as they both grew older, but in her youth she was the kind of woman Thomas Bigsky would have killed for and who could dive naked into a body of water, then step out dripping and looking her best. Sidney had watched her do so many times, just to be sure, and although this woman couldn't do for him what Sarah had done with her conversation or her extraordinary hands, she did not cake on makeup, wear dental plates or corrective lenses. She was well received by Sidney Wingcloud's friends and business associates. So naturally he married her.

They never once giggled together, but they had a large family and were quite comfortable in the very, very white house on the hill. In order to avoid his dream, though, and anesthetize his enduring nights, Sidney started staying at the nightclub, more or less around the clock. Often he neglected going home for weeks at a time. This is around the same period the rumor began about Sheriff Littlefeather's having found him beside the highway on the first morning of deer season, perched on a stool with his back strapped to a speed-limit sign. Since the hunters had taken potshots at it in the past on their way up into the mountains, or coming back out of manly hunter frustration, the speed limit sign filled with bullet holes left little doubt what Sidney had been up to. That is, if you believed anything Earl Littlefeather told you, a rather gin-soaked individual himself who was deeply disturbed partly because of his name, the biggest boozehound and most screwed up native North American of them all.

The nightclub's popularity dwindled. While they had opened in tuxedos and buckskin trousers, then eventually shifted to three piece suits, Sidney Wingcloud's managers finally stopped wearing ties altogether. They resorted to plaid Bermuda shorts, T-shirts, flip flops, and an open door policy. Finally, it got to the point where Sidney oversaw the place himself with only a skeleton staff. Business was steady, but slow. A curious passerby would occasionally stop his or her car, then stare into the thick desert darkness where Sidney's building glowed fetchingly off the highway, a weird neon bloom.

Sometimes a cross-country truck driver or a client from the old days would pull off for a drink and take a few snapshots of the once-famous discotheque. They would often find the owner himself still sitting at the bar, wearing rumpled golf attire, and drinking salty dogs from the glasses Thomas Bigsky had one popularized. Because of his swollen, rather pleasant appearance, they often bought drinks for Sidney, thinking that he was one of the walk-ins from the reservation, or perhaps some other compatriot down on his luck. Sometimes Sidney would come over to their tables and talk, or chat with them over a game of pool. He still had the sharpshooter's touch.

He would talk about growing up in the desert, about the breath-taking open spaces and the quality of light, all the reds and the whites and the rust. About skipping school with Thomas Bigsky and riding Appaloosas till dusk. Although his facial features were puffy now and his muscles turgid from drinking, there were still vestiges of his former beauty, his high cheekbones, his white teeth, and his inexplicable Mediterranean coloring. These vestiges were apparent whenever Sidney Wingcloud smiled, which he still did frequently and always would, or when he motioned toward you from the other side of a room. If they wanted to sit around and throw back a few cocktails, Sidney would tell his customers anything they wanted to know.

"I'm happy by golly," Sidney Wingcloud would tell them. "But I keep having this dream and it bothers me."

Upon hearing this, many of the customers, who had been patient to a point with the man's memories, became fidgety and expected him to get teary-eyed. They often stood up and started to go. But Sidney tried to persuade them that he wouldn't get sentimental, to stay with him and to talk awhile.

"Everything's fine," he would tell them. "Except for sometimes at night."

Of course, you'll be glad to know, and it must not be doubted, that Sidney died a happy man, a successful man, a winner. A man who loved his country and was truly thankful for all of the breaks he'd been given, just by being born there. Apart from the usual contractions in the stock market, which from time to time hurt his investments, aside from an occasional spasm in the GNP, apart from the grief he experienced over Thomas Bigsky's death and the sadness caused by Cozette McKenzie, contentedness was Sidney Wingcloud's state.

Not New Mexico.

Towards the end he stayed drunker and drunker. Sidney started sounding more like his grandfather and other ghosts, mixing their words together and forgetting the contexts in which they had originally been spoken.

"Merge, Merge," he would roar: "You gotta lay low with who brung ya."

Up until the very end, Sidney Wingcloud continued to buy his clients' first drinks, and he mentioned parts of his life with nostalgia, others with resilient regret. Because of the way he intermingled the happy and the less happy parts of his life, these people invariably listened and they always remembered his story. They were moved and had no reason to doubt what they had heard.

Flood

Some days whenever I get a moment after work over at UPS, I drive my pickup down Highway 133, the little road which skirts Oldham creek, winding toward Joy, Birdsville, Salem and Tilene, Kentucky. They're itsy-bitsy country towns. Out in the middle of nowhere. There's nothing much to see except this thing called the Nada Tunnel, a little roadway blasted through a limestone mountain. Oftentimes I'll stop my pickup. Roll down the window. Just sit inside that tunnel and think. The Nada Tunnel's long enough for headlights, then you pop out on the other side, leaving kitten-sounding bats, green-gold moss, night-black darkness in your wake, and then, right then, the poor people's houses start to unreel: white trash rednecks and colored folks mostly, living cheek and jowl. Their impoverished homes sit hunkered down in the hollow, and the poor souls inside them live fairly dead-end lives. White folks, black folks, and everything in between, people who despite their mutual problems still can't get along together and stay at one another's throats over nothing.

Wellsir, what I'm about to tell you about didn't cause no shining light from the Heavens. No burning bush, or spotlight from God. Not nothing like that. Still, all the same. The main thing I'm going to tell, maybe you heard about it on the news already, up in Connecticut or Massachusetts, or wherever else you live and think yourself safe and sound. High, dry and cozy. Maybe you read it in the newspaper, *Time* or *Newsweek*. Hell, I don't know. Yeah, I'm going to talk about the high-water we had a while back. Then I'll get to the kind of funny part, which ends with me and this niggra boy stuck up in a tree.

Thought I was going to die that night for sure, and that black kid, too. Me and this young Afro-American teenager, name of Aaron Smith, who lives with his family three or four miles above us on Oldham Creek. Yes sir, I figured it might be my grand finale, especially since I wasn't feeling so chipper as when I was fourteen year old like him. Why just the prior September, I'd had some open-heart surgery in Nashville, which didn't help matters one damned bit. Pardon me. You'll have to excuse my language. Because some old ways, they sure die hard. First, my gosh-darned bass boat crumpled up, like a tinfoil piece of foolishness, right when I was trying to save him. Aaron Smith's teenage eyes spooked wide. Looked white as far as I could tell. But not once you got close up he didn't. A little papery-colored and frightened to death. Nappy-headed as can be. Yes sir, what they used to call a "yaller nigger." Up in a tree with me! Soon as my boat folded in two like a clasp knife then got swept downstream.

Hot-Almighty! Just the thought of it!

Over six thousand dollars down the drain. And the two of us shivering with cold—darn near holding hands at times. Waiting till daylight and trying to stay afloat.

All this flooding began with a string a thunderboomers, one on the coattails of another, until Oldham creek below the hill me and Dorris live on, jumped its banks and started coming our way. Who in the world would have thought it possible? Who in the world? Not me. That an act of God could wreak so much havoc in little ole Blanton, Kentucky? Lots of people lost everything. More than sixty-eight died in all. Of course, we'd had some prior notice, watching the news and on the radio. Soon the Ohio River hit an all-time high in Louisville, seven feet over flood stage, that pansy-assed TV weather man kept saying. Then the teak-colored water on Oldham creek kept creeping toward us, Bible-proportioned rain streaking down from a slate-colored sky.

By early Wednesday, Dorris wanted to hightail it, abandon our hill-top home. Can you imagine? She wanted to leave the house and stay at her mother's and sister Janice's. Now don't get me wrong. My wife's fantastic. She's a pistol. But that mother of Dorris's, well, I ain't even going to bark in that direction because it wouldn't do me no good. The old gal's here for the duration, I reckon. Besides, Dorris has made it worthwhile in more ways than one.

"Just stay with me, honeybunch," I told her. "Afraid that I might grab you? That water won't even *think* about reaching way up here."

"Don't go jabbering about something you won't finish," Dorris said. "If you got a mind to grab, then grab. But tomorrow morning I want you to take me to Momma's."

"Will do," I told her grinning.

But Dorris didn't grin back.

"Let's see what the rain does tonight?" I quickly added. "Maybe we can go skinny-dipping in our own front yard. Waddya say?"

My wife wasn't fooling around, though. "It's got to where I can't sleep. And you know that I hate swimming, even in a chlorine pool."

That Dorris! Don't know what I'd do without her. When I got out of the Marine Corps in 1955, I went over to see this old gal whose husband had up and died on her. He'd been killed when his truck flipped hauling pulpwood in Waycross, Georgia, leaving her twenty-three years old and in a family way. Me and Gail Hawkins—that was her name after she got married—we'd gone steady for a while in high school. We'd been tight all senior year and went together to basketball and football homecoming. Anyways, when I come home from the service, I heard about Bobby Hawkin's accident—he played ball with me and we'd horsed-around some—so I went over to ask Gail if there was anything I could do. Lands, I'll never forget that day! When I walked into Gail Hawkin's kitchen, she was frying Smithfield ham. She had one of Bobby's button-down shirts stretched over her taut stomach, standing at the stove and talking to me, while the biscuits were sweetening up the room. Talking to me and her friend named Dorris who'd just moved to town from somewheres up north. Come to find out, it was Minneapolis, and this new gal was something else I could tell right off. Not a giggly-shy-silly bone in her body, and it sure was a good one too. Once, Dorris leaned over the stove to check Gail's biscuits for her, and I had to start wiping off my palms. Caught me checking out her behind. Dorris didn't bat a lash though. Looked me smack dab in the eye. "She's a keeper," I could tell right away. That's what I said to myself. "That gal's a keeper."

So I said what I'd come to say to Gail Hawkins with her watermelon-big belly. How I was real sorry to hear about her loss and how I'd come on Saturday morning to mow the lawn. Be glad to help out any way. And that yeast biscuit smell! And that Smithfield ham's sweet-salty aroma! All the time thinking that I knew what I really wanted, and the girl named Dorris had seen it in my love-struck stare. I wanted to set up house with her right on the spot and do what dead Bobby Hawkins couldn't do no more. That is, his neck being snapped when the pulpwood truck flipped, leaving poor Gail, his pregnant brave young wife.

Long story short, it took some time for me and Dorris to get together. I had a wild hair back in them days and was full of Parris Island nonsense after the Marines. Plus, I had me a cherry-red Ford convertible and enough money to jackass around. Out until dawn. Candle at both ends. All that that entails. Here's two things for your hip pocket, just like my Daddy once told me: "Never can tell when somebody will up and die on you. Or when two folks might take a notion to hanky-panky." I don't know. Maybe my Daddy wasn't right about a lot of things. All the same, the dying part's true.

Wellsir, the weeks turned into months. Little by little, I managed to get the time of day out of Dorris from Minneapolis. She had me crawling the tower walls for it! Courtly love, my big old patootie! Young Dorris had smooth brown skin from water-skiing on Kentucky and Barkley Lakes, cute little butt on her, and a couple perky little you-know-whats. Had her this stunning summer smile which she'd lip gloss, showing off her pretty, very white teeth. We went to the drive-in using my Ford convertible, backseat-petted and smooched some, but Dorris wouldn't let me across the moat. She had been reared by that Lutheran mother of hers. She had principles about certain things. Just like us folks raised-up Southern Baptist. When I first asked Dorris to get engaged—kindly hoping she'd let down the drawbridge—her answer was another flat-out "No." First things first, Dorris explained, arching her back and smiling. She showed me that Calamine-lotion pink tongue and those perfect pearls of hers, so that my palms and feet and everything else perspired all at once. That night my future wife told me: One, I had a lot of growing up to do. Two, there could be no other girls. Three, I had to know I loved her, and Dorris had to believe it, which is always the tricky part. Then maybe, just maybe, she'd decide to accept an engagement ring.

Like I told you before, Dorris hung the moon. It's going on forty years that we're a couple. Thirty-eight years exactly. Nearly four decades since I forswore all others, except for looking, which a red-blooded grown man can't help. Iffy prostate or not. Yeah, my wife has been trying for eons to steer me from my contrariness and all of my ass-backward ways.

So when Oldham Creek disappeared, and Dorris told me in a certain tone that she wanted to leave the house, I readily agreed. Teased her about being scared some. But not too much. Now this was on a Tuesday around suppertime. Down below the hill on which our yellow brick house rests, our sentinel concrete lions had already gone underwater. Sure enough, the flood was easing its way up the asphalt slope. You see, our house sits perched on a knob-hill with maybe a forty-degree gradient. Naturally given our high location, I figured there wasn't nothing to fret about. Still with Highway 133 sunk and all, my wife wanted to be gone. Dorris said she would feel more secure with her gossiping mother and sister. They could listen to the local news, then CNN, once the flood went national.

So early next morning, we put on two of my yellow fishing ponchos. I hooked up my bass boat trailer and backed the pickup down our driveway. Soon enough, we'd set sail for Blanton, Kentucky. During the boat ride, though, we commenced to have a friendly spat:

"Why don't you stay with us tonight?" Dorris told me. "You know you're welcome. What if the flood reaches up to our house?"

"Like I told you before. It won't."

"Anything's possible, Norman." Dorris huffed and puffed. "Don't you realize that yet? Have you ever seen it rain as much as it did yesterday?"

"Well, it ain't raining now."

Dorris rolled her eyes heavenward. "That isn't how it works."

I looked up too, as if she'd spotted a white dove, or something like it. Perhaps a bald eagle bearing a laurel branch or some other rare bird of prey.

"Are you deaf?" Dorris asked. "Didn't you hear the weatherman? Or are you just dense? Thirteen inches in two hours. That's a half-century record."

"Well, I'll be."

Dorris didn't grin this time either.

As we approached Blanton's main street, we saw what the flood had done so far. Luckily, you could still see the cabs on the water-trapped pickup trucks, which was the only way to keep from hitting them. Couldn't hardly believe my eyes. On the town's east end, Hank's Hardware and the Dollar General had already succumbed. I'd figured most businesses were high enough to be okay, but it just wasn't so. For now the rain had slacked off. But maybe Dorris was right. This half-century flood stuff was for real. Already, we could cruise downtown in my bass boat, just as pretty-as-you-please. We'd had a worse flood here in 1937. Just the year after I was born. But this one sure looked big-time. On the TV they'd reported a total of sixteen inches in Carrolton, and the town of Falmouth, Kentucky, was a silt and brown-water memory. Now the Ohio River was surging its way toward Lock-and-Dam #52 and #53.

Yes, more rain. More water was coming.

Dorris and me, well, we'd both staked out our ground.

That's how married life gets sometimes. Besides, I recalled what happened when those tornadoes hit Bullitt county last summer. The floodwaters might not reach us—but the looters sure could.

Shoot-fire, I wasn't fixing to stay with in-laws. Not when I could stay at home and protect my property. Guess I'm still like my Daddy in some ways, who used to say about traveling: "If I can't go there, come back and sleep in my own bed, then I ain't going to go." No kidding. God's honest truth. Once my old man didn't leave Livingston County for a period that lasted over nineteen years.

"People do screwy things, pumpkin," I told my wife. "But me staying at the house ain't one. You'll see. Everything is gonna be just fine."

"All right then, hardhead."

Dorris stepped daintily from the boat. "I'll call you tomorrow," she told me. "Don't drink too much and fall asleep, in case the water starts lapping at your bed sometime during the night."

"Give me a peck...Pretty please?" I added.

"Okay then," Dorris said, smooching my check. And let me tell you something. I sure would remember that kiss during the long, cold, wet night to come.

. . . .

It was nearly 8 A.M. next morning when I heard Cleveland Ramage shouting at the top of his lungs, yelling my name from the bottom of my hill. Darn good fellow and a lifelong friend. Old Cleveland's salt of the earth. He leaves out the "v" when he says his own name. Strong as a stud bull in May, but he wouldn't hurt a fly. Good thing. Once right after I'd come back from the service, we was shooting pool over at The Twinkling Star. I saw Cleveland Ramage pick a man up off the ground with his left arm, using the guy's Adam's apple for purchase. All because this bonehead had pushed some woman, a waitress who'd thrown a drink in his face. Wellsir, Cleveland lifted that piss-ant bully clean off the ground, and what he said next probably shut off that boy's pee for a week. But we was in our late twenties then—not late fifties and early six-ties. Okay, I'm sixty-one if you want to know for sure. The vim and vinegar has mellowed with age. Nowadays, old Cleveland's a real pussy-cat. Just like me. He told me once that his prostate flares up too.

"Wake up quick, Norm!" Cleveland yelled at me. "The Ohio's on the way!"

"All right, all right," I started muttering from my bedroom. That Dorris had been right on the money. The night before, I'd overdone the Jim Beam and Coke.

"Hey, sleeping beauty!" Cleveland kept shouting.

"I hear you bellering," I told him, sticking my head out the front door.

Lands, what a sight. Down below the house, Oldham creek looked frightening, like one of them white-water rivers somewhere out west. Maybe the Colorado River during snow melt with a rubber raft full of people in it. A bunch of lawyers and anesthesiologists wearing plastic helmets, paying for danger and spicing up their lives. Holy cow, I just don't understand it. Of course, I'd never do that kind of stuff myself, especially considering my jump-started, rewired and replumbed new heart.

Anyhow, Cleveland was right. The Ohio River had jumped its banks. So I put on my Northerners and a long-sleeve flannel shirt—if I'd a knowed what was coming I'd have taken wool sweater like they rec-ommend in *Field and Stream*. I grabbed my rubber poncho and started toward the boat. The night before, figuring the flood might rise a half-foot, I'd left the trailer tied to a forearm-sized dogwood, which wasn't all so bright. Right away, I saw that all the slack I'd left had gone taut. In a matter of hours, the water had surged fantastically.

"Gonna lose that shiny toy," Cleveland started ribbing me. "Or fill it full of mud. Thought I'd stop to say howdy. Wake your hind end up."

"Appreciate your help."

"Have a toddy or two last night? Watch you a little HBO?"

"No sir, not me. Doctor won't let me drink."

Leaning slightly from his jonboat, Cleveland started to snicker. Then he cupped his hands, trying to light one of his Marlboro filters.

"How y'all been?"

"Took Dorris to town yesterday. She's gone to her mother's and sister's."

"Not a bad idea," Cleveland surmised. "Just look at those clouds."

"You never know," I said.

"That's right."

Cleveland tucked his cigarette in the corner of his salt-and-pepper beard, which had miraculously escaped the Zippo's blaze. "Maybe it's stopped. But maybe not. Anyhow, there are a whole bunch a people stranded. A lot of folks need some help."

"Let me lock the door," I told him. "We'll take my boat, too."

So that's how this whole mess started, just as simple as shooting eight ball, or catching a spawning crappie. Me and Cleveland and some other boys, Tim Langdale, James-Lee Hancock, and Hunter "Crazy-Cajun" Bacot—who supports the North Carolina Tar Heels, for godsake—we all went scouting the low-lying homes on our side of Oldham creek. That took half the morning. Next, we sputtered out to Forest Oaks and Rosedale Hills subdivisions, those new developments southeast of Blanton. Lord have mercy, the wild-looking, foolish things we saw! The Davidson and the Staten families from our church had gotten themselves stranded on top of their big new ranch-style homes. We used all three boats and got them to safety. What a sight to see, though, how all these more-educated-than-me people had gotten themselves into such a fix. A lot of these folks worked downtown in Paducah, or out at the new shopping mall, and they didn't have a single boat amongst them. Not a lick of common sense either, if you ask me. On top of another subdivision rooftop, there was a thirty-five-year-old schoolteacher. Her name was Julia Peck. She was shaking from cold and sorrow, two show-dog Irish Setters by her side. Her crying came because the third one named "Missy" had taken a log-raft ride down Oldham Creek. Redheaded sweet thang, that Julia. Pardon my manners, but it's the truth. A real good-looking lady. Attractive woman, that's what I mean.

Before quitting-off at Rosedale Hills, me and Cleveland came across this old man. He was actually dangling in the floodwater. Hanging on a drain spout beside his house. Didn't even have enough strength to pull himself up. He was a few minutes away from joining "Missy" the Irish Setter, I reckon. That's when we came by in the boats. Luckily we came by, the old codger told us, because he was losing his will to grip. Well, I couldn't believe those words. But the day was young. I had a lot to learn.

Some of the other men from around Blanton helped out. We all took our boats in different directions, then rounded up whoever we found stranded. Afterwards, we all met back in town. By now it was around four o'clock. Soon it was cats-and-dogs again. More ice-cold rain coming down in sheets. Must have dropped ten degrees.

Luckily by now, the Red Cross was setting up at the local high school. They had the gymnasium for unlimited cot space and were using the cafeteria facilities to give folks something hot to eat. We rescue-types got out of the rain and had some Campbell's chicken noodle to get the chill off our bones. Everybody was standing around shaking their heads, drinking soft drinks and smoking cigarettes. Saying they hadn't ever seen it flood this way, not even old man Rudolph Cope who has lived in Blanton for nearly ninety years. Yeah, I must admit that I was feeling pretty "heroic," or whatever you want to call it. Rescuing all those people made you feel right proud.

Before leaving the gym, I saw Julia Peck, that pretty woman I'd pulled off the rooftop with her Irish Setters. She gave me a smile that did a whole lot more good than the chicken noodle soup. A little while later, Hank Staten told me that he sure appreciated my Good Samaritan assistance. Of course, he said it grinning, kindly ironic, since I'm not a regular in church lately. But I figured he meant it too.

"Okay then," I told everybody, "Time to go to the house."

So around five-thirty, I pressed the boat's ignition. It must have rained another couple inches while we were pussyfooting around, but the most recent deluge had stopped. Now everything looked okay—still plenty of daylight.

Gradually, I worked my way up what used to be Highway 133, when suddenly I made out something in the skeleton-armed, mostly leafless March trees. What in tarnation could that be? At first, it seemed like one of the limbs was waving at me. So I pulled back on the throttle to take a closer peek. Out in the middle of Old Man Langston's submerged soybean field, I made out two boots and a pair of tattered blue jeans.

Hellfire, it was a human being!

Soon I could see him clear as day, some young fellow with barely half a shirt on, all tuckered out from fighting the flood. That scared kid was hugging the oak tree like it was his momma. Perched on a limb barely above the water. Slowly but not-too-surely, I veered through the muddy force. When I got into Old Man Langston's soybean field, the copper surge looked like it was trying to gobble that oak tree right up. During the summer that little island of vegetation would be bone-dry. Full of greenness. Wild foxgrape and trumpet creeper, poison ivy and kudzu. A splotch of color or two from the white and mustard honeysuckle blossoms. But that day mid-March, things sure looked bleak. Mother Nature's something. Life's so tricky. Most times they never give out reliable directions for what you should do or what you ought to think.

What made trying to get him out possible was that I had plenty of room to steer. Underneath the water, it was flat as a pancake. Out in that soybean field snagging-up wasn't a threat. But how to plan my approach? And what should I do after I got close? Should I try to toss him a line? Maybe throw out a lifejacket?

Finally, I decided on a plan. A couple of pine saplings stood on either side of the oak tree, so I figured I could jockey between them. Then I'd reverse the motor long enough to float one of the lifejackets over on some rope. So that's what I tried.

The teenage kid was silent. He watched me closely. I could see both his hands ironed tight around the tree.

First, I circled around once more, then came in at an angle. I yelled and gestured. But because of the outboard's noise and the rushing water, me and the boy never heard each other. Still, everything went just fine. That is to say, the first twenty or thirty seconds. By reversing the motor I started directly toward him and the tree. Things looked like another successful rescue, sure enough. Then lo and behold, my outboard died deader than a roadkilt skunk. So I figured I'd head on sideways, drift against the base of the tree. That was another big mistake. When my bass boat popped against the base of the oak tree, it hit about midway and I was ready with another line. Except the front edge of the boat lodged on one of those pine saplings. Wellsir, I grabbed the oak tree's trunk—yelling for the kid to scooch around and climb off that limb—then the bassboat's left side dipped downwards and the right side flipped straight up. Took approximately three seconds for the boat to get swamped, for me to yell "hot-damn," or something like it.

As I slid into the muddy water, the flood's force astounded me. Woke me up right quick. It felt like a monstrous icy-brown wave. A gargantuan unseen tide, because there wasn't no ocean. Then hellfire, if that aluminum alloy piece of shit boat of mine didn't fold clean right in two! I yelped-cursed-scampered-hopped onto the oak trunk, taking the blow of the jump full in the family nuggets and my chest. Then both of my lungs went *kaaaa-whoooosssh*. So in a jiffy, I was hurt. Gasping for air and freezing already. Just as wet as a drowned Siamese cat. But it wasn't over yet. Once I'd gotten clamped on good, what else did I witness? Well, my crumpled bassboat bobbed up, then thrusted between those pine saplings, shot out from the coffee-with-milk water, then slammed me a pretty good one in the hip. All I needed was a broken leg. Luckily it missed joint and bone, hit rump-meat and thigh. But it didn't feel so hot and I didn't particularly enjoy it.

After the white-lighting flash of pain passed, I looked up. Sitting on the limb above me was my would-be rescuée. His expression didn't look too sunny.

"You all right, mister?"

"I'm okay."

"Sorry I got you into this."

"That's all right," I moaned. "It's my owned damned fault."

"Thanks for trying."

After a while the boy added: " Hey, I'm sorry about your boat."

"Me too," I told him.

Then I uttered another son-of-a-bitch. Leaned my head against the tree. That was all either one of us said for a good spell. Both of us looked to the downflow side of the soybean and sorghum field, watched as my fancy Bill Dance bassboat twirled in the six-foot floodplain, like a colorful kiddy toy in the moiling brown murk. Had me a fish finder and a depth gauge too. Even some bright red Astroturf on the deck. Oh, it could have been a whole lot worse. Luckily, I hadn't gotten sucked underwater right when the boat got trapped and started to bend in two. Sounded Godawful, like the crunching of a auto-compactor I seen once at a junk yard. Wellsir, twenty or thirty minutes passed. I got back my breath. That kid sitting on the limb above me looked younger by the minute. He told me he was fourteen, going on fifteen years old.

"You doing okay, son?"

"All right, I guess."

"What's your name?"

"Aaron Smith."

"I'm Norman Childress."

Another half-hour or so swooshed by. It was hard to see and quickly getting darker. No one in sight—just as I thought.

Both of us rested some more, listening to the flood's white noise. A sound-erasing sound that gave a body the willies, and too much time to think. Of course, I didn't know yet that I was up a tree with a yellow nigra. But naturally, I realized that we both were in big trouble. I'd gotten soaked to my armpits, scrambling from the floundering boat. We would grow chillier, then miserable, then dangerously cold. And the dark night loomed large. Off toward the west, above the barely budding tree line, some bruised-looking clouds caught the last color from the sun. Knowing the dusk-light would soon disappear—maybe forever for me—I started to get mad. Sorry and sad and angry all at once. Very regretful for all my stupid mistakes. Like I said before, I'd recently had open heart surgery down there at Vanderbilt in Nashville. My chest had gotten hit hard whenever the boat ricocheted off the pine sapling then filled with water, and that scar over my clavicle felt like it might come unzipped.

"Well, I'm damned sorry," I told the boy. "Son, I've really messed things up."

"It's not your fault, mister."

I didn't say a single word to that.

"At least you tried your best," Aaron told me.

"Well, I don't know," I said. "Anyway, now you've got some company. We'll just have us a slumber party up in this tree."

And right then, that's when I noticed it, despite the dusky light. The kid appeared to have caught my sense of humor whenever I looked over. Still, his eyes said that he had expected more of me. That is, as an adult and an older, more mature person. I seen that much from his expression. But that wasn't all. Something else had begun to dawn on me, and you can guess what that thing was, hugging the tree, damning my own misjudgment, and wishing time backwards. The something that come to me was that the boy above me was and wasn't what I took him to be from afar. Yes, a young lanky kid. Yes, a light-skinned teenager. Someone trapped and scared. His flesh tone had no doubt been influenced by his own ordeal and the crumpling bass boat spectacle that he'd just witnessed. But once I got my breath back, upon closer inspection, this white-looking boy sure weren't white.

His skin was off-yellow, kind of taupe, like one of Dorris's favorite purses. Yet his kinky-haired head showed his true origins. So what I had to contend with now and face all-night—me sixty-one and with a Vanderbilt retuned ticker—was a papery-colored niggra teenager. Luckily it was an oak tree, though, kind of like it had been planted for this one purpose. Because if it was a dogwood, or some mangy weedy mimosa, we would have been swept off for sure.

Second by second, the sunset petered out. Soon enough, but torture-like—so that you could study on it. The bruised violet clouds turned deep purple, then eggplant, then jet-black. Maybe this really was the end, I'd started thinking. All the power in the Livingston County had failed. No man-made light would be visible all night long.

"I'm getting really cold, mister," Aaron Smith told me.

"Yeah, I don't doubt it."

"Do you think someone will find us?"

"Not tonight. We'll just have to wait."

I looked down at my wristwatch, and that didn't cheer me up none. Funny thing, time. Ain't it all messed up? How it twists around and surprises you? How you got too much time on your hands for long stretches, then all of a sudden not nearly enough? Back in my rip-roaring twenties it was like all time was *today, today, today.* Never yesterday. Over the years, though, the yesterdays slowly started to matter more. Everyone has to speak for himself time-wise, but it wasn't until Dorris and me had our kids together that time started feeling like *today* and *tomorrow* and *yesterday* all at once.

"We'll have to stay here?" Aaron asked in disbelief. "Until morning?"

"Probably so. Nothing else we can do."

"But I'm getting cold."

"I know it. Me too."

Since it was night now, I kept studying more on time. Yes, I might have done what you might call some praying, thinking on Matthew 17:20, imagining how that oak tree might just skedaddle across the soybean field if all I had to do was really, really believe. Sure, I still read the Bible. Just don't like going to church with Dorris and her mother. Back before our twins came, you know, everything was planning for myself. Maybe I'll do this. Maybe I'll do that. Then after little Deborah and Kevin, all the planning for tomorrow changed and included them. Three months later, I started driving deliveries over at UPS, then wadda-you-know, thirty years zoomed by.

"How long you been here?"

"Don't know," Aaron said. "Maybe a couple of hours. I'm getting cold."

"Cold and hungry won't kill you," I kind of snapped at him. "Don't worry, though. They'll find us come dawn."

"You think so, mister?"

"Sure thing. Don't doubt it for a minute."

Of course, soon as I promised Aaron we'd be okay, I sneaked me another look at my Timex Indiglo. That thirty-five dollar son-of-a-gun still runs like a charm. Only a quarter after seven, and us on daylight savings. That meant any potential rescue boat was still eleven hours away. Luckily, that oak tree stood sturdy. Had to be seventy or eighty feet tall with an oval-shaped truck, just like on an empress tree, then the thing continued up and divided into a Y-shaped fork. The water kept rising. Soon it shot through the Y-shaped crotch, like an opened water hydrant. We could hear a horrible gurgling-swooshing below us in the moonless dark.

Sure wish you could have seen it. Me in my yellow poncho, and him barely wearing a shirt. I was on the first hefty limb after the tree forked, and the black kid was on the next big limb up. The field itself measured fifty or sixty acres, rich bluegrass soil that would be doubly enriched following this big flood. Me, I've lived in Kentucky all my life. But what would a person from Tokyo, or a New Yorker, think if he or she could have seen us stranded like that? Old Man Langston's soybean and sorghum molasses fields bordered Oldham creek, but years ago he'd left this island of vegetation in his field for white-tail deer. Good thing that oak tree was there. Already, the biggest pine sapling had leaned over. Neither one would last the night.

"Okay then," I asked. "How'd you get out here?"

"It's was real dumb," Aaron said. "Real stupid. It's all my fault. And it's my fault that your boat got ruined."

"Heck with the boat, son. You forget that all right?"

"You ain't cold, mister?" Aaron asked.

Wellsir, I sure was. But what was I supposed to do for him? Tell the truth. Just what would you have done if you were me? No sir, this young black kid was younger and tougher so he'd have to buck-up and face the rest of the night.

"Your shirt is almost dry," I said. "Roll down your sleeves and button them. Let your sleeves dry some. That'll keep the wind off."

"Okay," Aaron said.

"Like I said before. We'll both be just fine."

Hellfire, it wasn't even ten o'clock. I'll be derned if I wanted to let him have my rubber poncho. Me sixty-years-old and fresh out of open-heart. Less than eleven months ago. I'll never forget that day. What they do first there at Vanderbilt hospital is they send in a nurse to get you ready. My nurse's name was Tammy Wilson and she'll shave you clean as the day you were born. Yeah that's right. Down there some too. Down way past your belly button. Really embarrassing. Kind of tickles, though. Then scratches like sand fleas once it grows back in. Next, they'll give you one of those feel-good IVs just before the lights go out. Then they buzz-saw your sternum in two. Boy, those doctors and nurses, they can sure save lives. Thank goodness, some folks got the stomach for it and have a better education than me.

"Aaron, you all right up there?"

"Sure, I'm okay."

"Still haven't told me nothing. Why were you out here?"

This was just something I had to know, how come he got caught in this high water in the first place? I figured maybe he was goofing off in a canoe or something, then suddenly playing turned into something not-so-pleasurable. You know, how life will do you? Something really fast will happen, then suddenly fun ain't fun no more.

"My sister got in trouble. I swam after her," Aaron explained. "That's how it started. I got her out all right. She was trying to get to Rusty."

"That your brother?"

"He's our dog."

"You swam out in *this*? After your dog?"

Well, I couldn't believe it. Another trouble-causing mutt. Naturally, I thought of the pretty schoolteacher and her Irish Setters.

"His pen sits on a ridge behind our house. Other side of a gully."

"So you were going after Rusty?"

"Going after my sister, who was going after him."

Little by little, the floodwater was inching up the oak tree. By now the fire-hydrant sound effect at the Y had stopped.

"What if the tree gets swept away, mister?" the boy asked me next. One question after another. "What will we do then?"

"Swim, I reckon."

"Don't know if I can. I'm too tired."

"No you're not. Besides, this tree ain't going nowhere. We'll just have to be miserable for a while, that's all."

"I'm scared, mister," Aaron told me. "Ain't you?"

Then hot-damned if he didn't start to cry a little. The sobbing was quiet. But the kid knew I heard him, and he tried his best to stop. His persistent teeth-chattering kept on.

"My daddy's going to whip me," Aaron told me. "If we make it out."

"No he won't. He'll be tickled you're okay."

Wellsir, the time had come. I peeled the yellow poncho off. Might as well let him have it. I told Aaron Smith that I had a big fat gut to keep me warm. The kid took the poncho without a word, but he thanked me once he'd gotten it over his tattered shirt. God's truth, I wasn't scared one bit. Isn't that strange? In fact, I'd started thinking that maybe I'd try to swim for shore. That is to say, the edge of the soybean field. Maybe I'd just slip down the tree trunk and ease into the flood's flow. Let her take me wherever she wanted. Pretty soon, my mind was like that Y-shape trunk, one part going this way and another going another. The thing about trying to swim for it was that it was mid-March. That water had felt cold. But it sure wasn't toasty either, sitting exposed up in that tree. Sure, Dorris wouldn't want me to swim for it. Deborah and Kevin would miss me if something went wrong. So maybe I should just stay put. Still, there weren't no guarantee stamped on that oak. More I thought about it, just dropping down and letting the mud-colored water take me, that sounded kind of relaxing. Suddenly, I was cold. But I was warm, too. And that relaxed, warm feeling was a warning. Somewhere, I forget where, I'd read what you feel if you're dying in a blizzard; the magazine said that if it gets real bad you just want to lie down and go to sleep in the soft-warm snow. Well, it wasn't exactly like I felt wrapped in a down-quilt from Mother Nature or anything. No sir, I didn't want to give up the ghost. There was a lot of things I'd miss, like my Ford pick-up truck and my now nonexistent bassboat, a few of my favorite rifles and pistols, and my satellite TV so I can watch the Kentucky Wildcats win basketball games just about wherever they might be playing. Yeah, a heap of stuff would surely be missed. But that was if I *didn't* make it and I'd about made up my mind to go with the flow.

Better not just jump, though. That might scare the boy.

So I decided to explain what I aimed to do.

My plan was that I could take off my Levi's then tie off each pant-leg, like they showed us at Camp Currie, when I was around this here kid's age. They taught us how to make a lifejacket by swooping each pant leg full of air. Kissed my first girl that summer. Learned how to shoot a bow-and-arrow. Anna Chumbler was her name. Wonder where'd she go off to? Who'd she settle down with and did she ever have kids after kissing on the likes of me? Well, I thought about Camp Currie, and Anna Chumbler. Soon, it was eleven o'clock. Eleven-thirty. That Timex Dorris gave me for my birthday said that we still had a long ways to go. Just didn't know if I could last it and now I didn't even have my poncho.

Time, time, time. No time-outs in life. Or second chances, if you ask me.

Longer I thought on it, taking that watery ride really seemed like a good idea. Come what may, at least I wouldn't croak from hypothermia, sitting like a goonybird up in that tree. Bottom line of it, I wasn't going to let Cleveland Ramage or Crazy Hunter Bacot find me squatting up there come morning. Especially with a shivering-crying black kid beside me. Don't get me wrong. I'm just saying that I'd never live it down. Plus, like I explained before, my chest felt like it might come undone. Not to mention the fact that my old acorns had been darn-near pulverized and they still kind of throbbed. Maybe that cold water would feel good.

Seven or eight more hours—that's what I started thinking.

Gradually, making up my mind.

Suddenly the kid starts whimpering again. Still afraid.

Perhaps you're wondering what the big deal was? How come being up in a tree overnight with an black-skinned person meant all that much? Made it any different? Well, how can I say it clearly, so you'll listen, then maybe understand? To start with, I reckon it has to do with my upbringing. Things that happened in the past and that didn't happen between myself and other races. "Nigger" was a word we sometimes heard. Maybe it was my "mentality" or "outlook" and the times in which I was raised.

Shoot, I don't know. Let me tell you this much, though. A couple things happened to me in the service, back on Parris Island, that I'd just as soon forget. After they tear your ass down in boot camp, you start to work and claw yourself back up. Pretty soon, it's kind of strange how much you start to like, really enjoy, feeling like a US Marine. That training swells you up some. You do feel proud, believe it or not. Once a US Marine and so forth. But those bad things that happened with that jet-black drill sergeant behind the barracks. That man looked just like Idi Amin. He told me "forget my rank you hillbilly-shitbird-faggot." Just trying to make me madder. He told me his rank didn't matter diddly squat because he didn't like my "insolence," or my smart mouth. This in

1954 and him black as the ace of spades. Told me to go ahead and hit him, which I decided to do before he hit me. Then that sergeant slammed me once in the face, like a ten-pound sledgehammer, and the second time right square in the throat. Stopped things right there.

Around midnight, Aaron Smith started talking funny again. Saying that he was hungry and freezing. That his daddy was "going to kill him" for getting half-drowned. My treed companion sure wasn't making any sense. But I figured if his daddy was anything like mine, then he might get a spanking sure enough. My old man he'd hit on anything whenever he was drunk. Take his belt to a corpse. And boy, did he hate what he called "uppity blacks." You ought to have heard Daddy talking about men like Martin Luther King and Malcolm X,Y, Z. That's what Daddy called him. He liked to call them uppity. Growing up, I had to hear how my Daddy hated niggers. That's what he invariably called black folks, like he was looking at blue sky and calling it blue sky. The idea of a strong, big black man. Wellsir, that put an extry-nervous edge in his voice. He thought they were all threats to every white woman and potential backstabbers to any white man who did them favors. He used to say they were taking over the country. "They're taking over," Daddy used to tell me. "You'll live to see the day." That's all I used to hear, especially when he got drunk.

Little by little, maybe the old ways change. But you know how you'll say things. Just talking and joshing around. Shoot, I've been known to tell a racial joke here and there. It's like when you get to talking about anything really, U. of K. basketball, deer hunting, chasing redheads, or trying to catch yourself a lunker largemouth bass. You exaggerate then you understate. Play the magpie and opt for hot air. What I'm saying is how sometimes we all say things we don't really mean, or change words around just to get a laugh.

My old man, though, he was different. I'll never forget the time before Daddy passed away from emphysema. Right before they officially put O. J. on trial. Lord, the things Daddy called O. J Simpson and him lying in bed and dying. He said that somebody ought to just shoot him in jail. Save the state of California some money. You couldn't tell the old man a thing. By December my Daddy was gone so he didn't see O. J. walk. He didn't see the Kentucky basketball team win the NCAA with their pin-stripped I-talian coach, Rick Pitino, who's from New Jersey. Just a few white faces on the starting squad. That stuff about an extra tendon? Don't you believe it. Me, I figure it's like they've been held down so long that they have to jump a whole lot higher just to get aloose. Take this here new black kid Ron Mercer, out of Tennessee somewhere, who carried them to the 1996 championship. Barely nineteen-years-old. But that kid can sure play his ball.

Long about one A.M., I'd had enough of waiting in that oak tree. The time had come to go. Another ten minutes was all I could take. Just like that give-out old man hanging off the drain spout, I'd done made up my mind to swim or sink.

"You asleep up there?" I asked Aaron Smith.

"Uh-uh," Aaron said. "I'm just quiet."

"See that light over yonder?"

"What light you mean?"

"Right over there, don't you see it? Somebody must be running a generator. But it's not that far. Maybe a couple of miles."

"Are they coming to look for us?"

"Yeah maybe." At first, I lied to him. But that didn't seem right. "No son, I don't think so. They're just probably putting out sandbags."

"They don't know we're here?"

"Probably not."

Then after a pause I told him that I was going for help. "You know what? I think I'll just head downstream. Old man or not, I'm a heck of a swimmer."

"Huh?" Aaron said.

"You just stay put, all right?"

"Are you going to leave me here?"

Suddenly that young boy's peepers looked solid white. Even in the past-midnight light I could see his eyes shining. Sclera it's called. One day when I didn't have nothing else to do I checked the World Book under "eye." Wellsir, no matter what I told him, Aaron Smith kept begging me: *Please, please, please mister, don't leave me by myself, all right?* He tried to give me the yellow poncho back. But I said no and that I was feeling fine.

"Okay, I won't leave. But you start talking."

"Talk about what?"

"Shoot, I don't know. How many brothers and sisters you got? Tell me about your family. Let's just try not to stop. That way neither one of us will freeze."

"All right. What do you want to hear first? "

"What does your momma like to cook for supper? You got a girlfriend yet? You like to play basketball? You're from Kentucky. So you'd sure better like it."

"Yeah, I like it."

"There you go. Just talk."

So we conversed. It's hard to remember everything we talked about. That floodwater's sound kind of lullabyed you. We just talked to keep from going to sleep then maybe *kerplunking* into the drink. All night long, I wanted to ask Aaron Smith whether it was on his mother's or his daddy's side. You know, that white blood link of his. Although somebody once told me that both ends could be black and still produce a light-skinned kid. Don't know if it's true. Anyways, Aaron Smith told me he'd turn sixteen soon. He wanted to save up and buy himself a car. Wanted an Oldsmobile. Told me that his daddy was a mechanic, and if I ever had any car or truck problem, then his daddy would fix it real good—maybe for free. See what I mean? The boy was young. He was still feeling bad about me getting myself stuck on his account. Aaron kept on repeating that part about the free car work until I finally told him to stop.

After all, it was me who screwed up royal.

So I had to stay put and help all I could.

Besides I'd lived a lot longer, horsed around some, drank my share of Jim Beam and kissed a few spare women until Dorris came along. Shoot, I'd already had myself more good times than this young kid had even wet-dreamed. Even had me a couple of redheads. Then I married a good woman to make me forget 'em all. So the way I see it, I've had a lot of breaks. Yes, my life has been all right. Don't know what my beautiful wife ever saw in me and goodness knows why Dorris puts up with me now. Prostate the size of a grapefruit. Sometimes can't pee enough to fill a thimble. But when things are flowing fine and dandy, sometimes I can still get rangy, especially after we've both had us a couple margaritas. That's living, if you ask me. Put shame on a shelf unless it's real shame.

. . . .

Wellsir, we both made it out okay. Long about daylight, I started hearing some boat motors, tinny buzzing sounds off in the distance. Rescue workers, I started thinking, or maybe looters starting out early. I hoped someone would hurry up and find us because I'd started worrying about my home. All the stuff left in it. Ain't that something? Me still clinging to that oak tree and thinking about my *things*: a collection of model VWs I'd been working on, football trophies from high school and my diploma, all my Bob Seger and Willie Nelson albums, over twenty-six in all, counting the bootlegs. My fly rods from when I'd almost gone to Alaska for king salmon once but didn't, because twin babies sure are expensive. My Winchester 30/30 and my silver plated Reuger nine-millimeter that I still ain't ever fired since it's so nice. They don't make that thirteen-cartridge clip kind no more. So it's a collector. Why in the world was I thinking of all that crap and not my wife? If Dorris would have known it, she wouldn't speak to me for a solid week.

Anyhow, I heard the purring outboards. So I figured me and Aaron Smith would be all right. During the wee hours, prior to daybreak, the floodwater had eased down maybe a couple of feet. Now that long-legged kid above me looked even younger, half-asleep and wrapped in the yellow poncho, my leather belt under his armpits then fastened around the limb so he wouldn't fall.

Pretty soon, Aaron was moving around and waking up. But he still looked drowsy. He glanced at the chocolate-milk water swirling below us. Then he grinned once he heard the boat motors. He was no longer afraid. Suddenly the kid looked completely different, like he'd had a good night's sleep and a really good story to tell.

"We got to get ready son. Look lively."

"Did you see any boats?"

"Not yet."

"All right. I'm awake."

"Me too."

The morning sun felt scrumptious, warmer and warmer. Miracle-of-miracles, the raining had stopped ever since I'd left the high school gymnasium the night before. Of course, I was hoping against hope about who might find us, praying that of all people it would be Cleveland Ramage, whose ribbing I could take. Slowly, I was feeling better. The bone-chill and vague sick feeling had started to fade. Then suddenly I remembered something. Just then it came to my recollection how there were two packets of Lance's cheese-and-crackers in my poncho's pocket. But I hesitated and didn't say anything right away.

Leastwise, we had our breakfast, waiting for some boat to spot us. Them Lance's cheese-and-crackers sitting right there in the outside pocket of my poncho. Wrapped tight in cellophane so they'd still be okay. Silly cracker that I was for not thinking of it earlier. Shoot, it don't take a *Field and Stream* or *Outdoor Life* writer to know that when the cold sets in you should have yourself something to eat. Wellsir, I felt plumb ignorant. It deep-down embarrassed me all over.

Anyhow, we made it out, and I learned a thing or two. No spotlight from the heavens or anything. Just like I said before. Sure glad I didn't give up and swim for it! Dorris wouldn't have ever been the same if my old carcass never floated to the top. She'd worrywart herself half-sick and drive the State Troopers crazy.

Later in town I touched Aaron Smith lightly on the head. Now don't you laugh, because I figure there are a lot of folks just like me. Personally, I'd never touched an "afro" in all my days. Not until that flood. It wasn't like steel-wool at all. But fuzzy and real soft. Different than my hair or Dorris's. So what? Once it was over and we were both safe and sound, I just wanted to touch his head. So that's what I done.

"You take care, all right?"

"Thanks again," Aaron Smith told me.

"For what?"

"For trying your best. For trying to save me."

That sure was nice of this kid to say that. All the coldness and soreness aside, I was feeling pretty good, looking forward to more life with my brand new heart.

Of course, it was James Lee Hancock and Hunter Bacot who found us. But it didn't bother me a fig. Luckily, that crazy North Carolina Tar Heel lover was smarter than me. He got us out of that oak tree and into his boat with no trouble. So these days, I try to be thankful. Give praise in my own way. Can't say I'm a religious man, unless March comes around and UK makes it to the Final Four. Ha. Ha. Just kidding. Seriously, I'm grateful. My boy Kevin's wife is pregnant. So I'm excited about being a granddaddy. Little by little, maybe the old ways change. For example, I've always been a Ford pickup man. Always drove a Ford. Recently, though, I took me a test-drive to see about them Japanese trucks, then I bought me a Toyota.

Shoot, where I live is like most places. There's good and bad people, better and worse-off places a body can be. They say the youth of today are the world of tomorrow, but us older folks can steer and help them out. My Daddy, he didn't always help me. That's for sure.

Anyhow, I'll go riding in my truck some days. Just cruising and relaxing. Doing me some thinking. One time I saw Aaron Smith, his brothers and some white neighbors of theirs, I guess, shooting a rubber kickball through a barrel stave on a electric pole. Playing h-o-r-s-e together in their hard-dirt backyard. So I pulled in to say howdy. Aaron seemed pleased to see me. He introduced his older brother and his two friends. The other boys were older and had a height advantage. So I watched them play for a while, and Aaron Smith did okay. Seemed like the kid had a good jumper.

Once this here flood was long over and everything had dried out, I took my sister Helen, who's a lawyer up in Louisville, driving along Highway 133. That day we saw the most depressing sight soon as we passed through Nada tunnel. There was these three young kids, standing next to each other beside the road. A head's difference between all three of them. Ages maybe ten or eleven, then twelve, then fourteen or thereabouts. The girl was the oldest. She was pregnant. Fifteen years old, tops. God's truth. And the ten-year-old boy had a snake, a four or five foot king snake hanging around his neck. Just sauntering along. That king snake was draped right across his throat. Me, I've never been overly fond of serpents. But a snake can change his skin. Ain't that the damnedest thing?

The Windmill of Happiness

Just over nine weeks had passed since she'd left Kentucky. His wife Genevieve had accepted a new job—thus virtually sealing their divorce—and now, sitting in the 737's bulkhead seat with their four-year-old, Mark Wilson thought how strange it was to be feeling so confused. Still unsure. Still ambivalent about ending a marriage that had never functioned smoothly. Never worked after a certain point. Never soothed that much. Never really *zinged*. Or was he just soothing himself to think that? Ah, but he'd loved her. Deeply loved her. So Mark's over-all attitude toward seeing his wife again wasn't anything too neat and tidy. Various truths kept him from being sentimental about the demise of his marriage. Yet the beginnings of what went wrong, its etiology, wasn't all too clear. Still, facts were facts. They had both sinned, so to speak. Many people's lives had been involved. His wife Genevieve had slept with someone the last year of Mark's oncology residency at Louisville's Humana Hospital; she'd felt ignored as he grew obsessed with work, all alone, isolated from her family in France. Afterwards there had been a period of emotional chaos. In short, his life with Genevieve was over, and now Mark was delivering Sam to Corvallis, Oregon, where he would live for the majority of the year.

Their flight from Cincinnati to Portland was direct. But for some inscrutable reason they had been delayed, stuck for over two hours on the runway like a gigantic, air-conditioned bird in a coma. But at least the breathing worked. Needless to say, little Sam became rambunctious. While Mark might hum and sing Bob Marley or The Pretenders in the operating room, to relax and get others to relax—he still listened to *Exodus* regularly, but loved Chrissie Hynde's raspy vocals, her bittersweet "Stop Your Sobbing" best of all—he was struggling now to keep his cool.

First they colored in Sam's *101 Dalmatians* coloring book, then sang "Down By the Bay," then they played with his *101 Dalmatians* sticker book. It was always a pleasant chore keeping him occupied. However, doing so away from home in strange, cramped quarters amounted to a Sisyphean ordeal which truly vexed the spirit. As soon as Sam became interested in something, he'd want to get up and mill around the aisles, jabbering at a few granite-faced, curmudgeon passengers. If Sam stayed put for five minutes straight, he wanted to change seats with his father for a hoot. Then quickly switch back.

Finally, the runway horror was over. Some gravel-voiced pilot, who sounded a lot like that low-throated, African-American singer Barry White, came over the intercom with some sultry, I've-kissed-a-lot-of-stewardesses assurances. There'd been a snag or two, the pilot intoned. They'd soon be underway. True enough, they were soon in the air. But just as the plane took off—surprise, surprise, surprise.

"No! No! No!" Sam began to howl. His lower lip peeled back into a petrified rictus. All of his beautiful white teeth exposed.

"Settle down, buddy. Tell Daddy what's wrong."

"It too high! Too high!" Sam continued keening.

Outside the plexiglas window, the engines screamed too. Every muscle in Sam's body, especially his face muscles, looked tense. His hands had become fragile claws, shaking and held tightly above his shoulders. Thirty-seven pounds of pandemonium at his father's right side.

"Let's get off now, Daddy! I don't like it! Let's go back home!"

"It's just the engines, buddy. I thought you liked to ride in airplanes. We're going to watch a movie and eat some chicken."

Of course, around this point, the plane hit a wind sheer, something or other that made it career earthwards. Then jolt back up violently. "Everything's just fine," Mark said unconvincingly, more than a little unsure himself. "Look over there, you see those clouds? Did you know that they're made of cotton candy? You remember eating *barbe à papa* at your grandmother's?" Little Sam nodded, conjuring up the memory. During one of their annual visits to Genevieve's parents in France, the Christmas that Sam turned three, they'd eaten some cotton candy and ridden a mange-stricken pony in Luxembourg Park.

"You want some cotton candy in Oregon? How does that sound?"

"Is Momma going to be there when we get there?"

"Yes, that's right," Mark explained and would keep explaining. "We'll see your mother two days from now. First, we're going to get a car, then drive to the ocean."

"Where Keiko lives—right Daddy?"

"That's right. And if Keiko's at home, maybe we'll pay him a visit."

"We're going to see him for sure?"

"Yes we will. We're going to see Keiko tomorrow."

"Okay, Daddy."

His son smiled brightly, looking appeased for the moment. Apparently, the prospect of ingesting pure sugar and seeing a Killer Whale had a sedating effect.

Gradually, the take-off thrust subsided. Little Sam calmed down. Usually Mark's son liked airplanes, hadn't been bothered by flying in the past. He'd already been across the Atlantic three times to visit his grandparents. All the same, Sam had gotten petrified when this particular plane took off. The subtle beginnings of neurosis? Ah, the family romance! Did he and Genevieve have a nascent little Woody Allen on their hands because of all the things they had already unconsciously put him through? Not if Mark could help it they wouldn't. He was going to be a good father. He was going to spend time with Sam every summer and every other December. It wasn't ideal, but what they'd agreed on. Unlike his own taciturn ex-Marine Corps father, he would talk to Sam about anything under the sun or moon. He was going to let him follow his desires and dreams. He'd be faithful to what was best for Sam. *Semper Fidelis* to that!

Of course, Mark would teach him sports, for the sake of work ethic and team effort. Baseball and basketball. Soccer instead of football. Maybe track. Hell, classical ballet if the cards fell that way, which they probably would if Genevieve ever carted him off to France. Yes, sometimes anger still crept into his moods. His constantly shifting emotions. Genevieve would probably see to it that Sam took ballet classes, just like she bought him a complete Betty Crocker kitchen-set, not to mention every goddamned Barbie model manufactured in Asia by undernourished ten-year-old waifs.

"Are they going to give us lunch, Daddy?"

"Not yet, buddy."

"When are they then?"

"Pretty soon. Do you want some potato chips and apple juice?"

"I don't want to see my mother in two days," Sam suddenly decided. "I want to see her right now. Why can't she be here on the plane?"

"We'll see your mother soon," Mark promised, feeling the attendant sadness he'd doubtlessly experience in the months and years to come.

Kids had such amazing insights. They perceived so much right from the very start. Already, little Sam knew how to play his parents against each other. Whenever he was staying with Genevieve and she denied him something, Sam would weep woefully and say that he wanted to be with his Daddy. At first, Mark had fallen for it. Over the last two months, though, Sam sometimes whined for his mother, especially whenever he didn't get his way.

During the time it took Genevieve to get settled in Oregon, working as a software translator, Mark had kept their son in Louisville for nine weeks. He'd overseen his little human needs, cravings, and moods. While he did his rounds at Humana hospital, Sam stayed at the hospital's day-care. But they spent every night together having loads of fun: lots of coloring and drawing, playing endless bouts of Go Fish, or watching videos like *Free Willy* from Mark's spring-bar North Face tent which he'd erected in the condo's living room. He'd enjoyed his time with Sam immensely. But pretty soon, his son would no longer be a daily presence in his life. Mark Wilson didn't like that one damned bit. But what other solutions existed? Especially in a year or two, when Sam started going to school full time?

Perhaps they could have tried harder. Perhaps they married too late. Ah, the perhaps-this's, the perhaps-that's were endless! You just couldn't go into some kind of nostalgic tailspin or you'd most certainly crash and burn. What was the divorce cliché? Too much had happened for it to work? Well, it was true, Mark thought. However, such clichés were useless. Only unlived words. Thinking and feeling about Genevieve still hurt. Seeing her face would just make it worse. Because henceforth, whenever Mark looked at her face, the love-light had left her eyes and vice versa: their past wasn't the present, their faces would never look the same to each other, their love had been transformed.

Once upon a time, things had been quite different. Years ago in Paris, when they'd first met, Mark and Genevieve had been quite young. They first laid eyes on each other when he was fresh out of college, only twenty-two years old, and Genevieve a very mature nineteen. More adult. More educated. She'd grown up with classic novels, poetry collections, and good newspapers. Well-educated, funny, older brothers. Indeed, one of them was currently the head of Renaissance studies at the University of Rouen. The man could read classical Greek, Latin, and Arabic, then speak five other modern languages like he was crossing the street. His little sister, Genevieve, had impressed Mark from the very start: eyes, smile, humor, smarts. They fell quickly in love without expecting it. Then Mark returned to the United States. He'd gone back to work in his father's urology office, doing basic patient prep work, running urine and blood samples to the lab, seeing if a career in medicine really interested him.

Their relationship had survived long-distance. But by the next spring, Mark could stand the distance no longer. Before starting medical school, he had lived in Paris for half a year. One last fling before the grind. However, Mark's father had called it "a frivolous waste of time." He'd not funded the trip one *centime*. So money had been tight. Ah, but what memories. Mark and Genevieve had never been happier than that summer of their still wide-open, still so young lives. He had worked full-time waiting tables to pay for living expenses. He'd made a good friend at the restaurant, Daniel Clairmont, someone from a small farming community in a *département* called Le Creuse—sort of like the Kentucky of France. And that wedding at Daniel's father's house that distant, gauzy summer was something Mark would never forget.

In recompense for the runway debacle, the Delta Airlines attendants passed out free headsets. That way, everyone could watch some movie called *The Truth About Cats and Dogs*. At first, Mark had welcomed the opportunity. His son had gotten very excited. After all, Sam loved movies with adorable animals. Unfortunately, the previews soon made it pretty clear that this movie wouldn't be featuring the likes of Flipper or Keiko, Thumper and Bambi. Instead, it was about modern human behavior. Men and women. Boys and girls.

None of the other passengers seemed to make Mark's mistake about the film. Particularly two loudmouthed fraternity types only a few seats back. Apparently, they were ski-bums despite their fraternity regalia. A couple of yahoos headed for some resort out West. Perhaps Sun Valley for a little glacier skiing, although the summer ski season was getting late. They wore sunglasses attached around their necks with chum cords, one lime-green, the other fuchsia. Both of them had blonde hair, although one of them had over-bleached his slightly orange.

Before the movie started, lunch was served. Next, some tepid coffee which seemed to have been flavored with smoked fish. Then approximately thirty minutes after the rubbery chicken and bounce back at you carrots, the in-flight film finally began. Uma Thurman came onto the screen.

"What an utter beaver!" one of the ski bums said.

His sidekick agreed.

"My god! She's death!"

"Did you see *Jennifer 8* with Andy Garcia? That film where she plays that really hot blind chick? There's a bathtub scene in that one that you won't soon forget."

"Viewed it, dude! They were mongoid! Not shabby at all!"

Both of the ski-bums had beers going.

They'd obviously been drinking for quite some time.

"I heard they used a stand-in. Just for that one scene."

"No way, man. It's Uma's face."

"So what? They can get away with anything out there in Hollywood. I'm telling you. Just because it's Uma's face doesn't mean that it's really *her*."

Since the airplane was half-empty, Mark and little Sam had moved from their bulkhead seats to a couple of better vantage points—anticipating at least a pet or two, maybe a parrot or gerbil, perhaps as minor characters. Peace reigned briefly. That is, approximately six minutes. Once Sam had established that the movie didn't interest him one jot, he started trampolining in the vacant, cushioned seats. Next, he began scattering potato chip crumbs like confetti.

By now, the two ski-bum types had ordered more Budweisers, and they were really getting on Mark's nerves. One of them had on mukluks for some reason. And it was nearly June, for godsakes! In addition to his Day-Glo chum-cord, the other wore a white headband covered with violet-colored snowflakes.

A half-hour into the film, Sam began to wind down for good. Grow tired. Woozy with sleep. Soon, he'd crashed completely, Tasmanian devil to angel on the turn of a dime. He laid his blonde head on Mark's right leg and immediately began to snore. Drops of sweet-pungent baby sweat formed on his temples. How his father would miss that smell! Only a few days from now, Mark would find one of Sam's T-shirts in the laundry, bury his nose in it, then place it in the chest-of-drawers unwashed. On the midget four-foot screen, blonde Uma Thurman began sauntering around again, wearing a tight-fitting, shiny "retro" blouse. She was walking down some sidewalk beside that machine-gun-talker Janeane Garafalo.

"Boink me silly!" violet snowflake said.

"She's *killer!*" the other Rhodes scholar observed.

They were really starting to make Mark upset. No, to really piss him off. If he'd only brought his medical bag. Maybe he'd fill a syringe with Demerol or liquid valium. On his way back from the lavatory, he'd stumble into the snowflake kid's shoulder, then whack him full of knock-out dope. Just palm the syringe and trip flamboyantly, like that pickpocket he'd encountered in Venice during the *lune de miel* with his soon to be ex-wife.

On their honeymoon, they'd taken the TGV from Paris, rented a car in Lausanne, then driven through the Aosta valley for memory's sake, where they'd eaten a delicious raclette and chocolate dessert fondue. Hardly a cake walk, even then. Not quite enough honey in the moon. Right from the beginning, they'd always argued a lot, although now Mark couldn't remember what they'd argued about precisely. Still, Venice's reeking canals and zigzagged narrow alleys, the cafés in Saint Marcos square, all those bellinis and excellent meals and the sex had been quite nice. He and Genevieve had locked muzzles all day and made wine-fueled love at night. Indeed, a template for their marriage as a whole. Yes, facts were facts. Even towards the very end, if Mark was really honest, sometimes the *zing* was still intact. Same gleam in their eyes. Same shimmer in each touch. But whenever the sun was shining, they bickered like children and stayed at one another's throats. Whenever they had quotidian, fairly straightforward problems to solve, they staked out their territory and simply couldn't get along. But ah, the nights.

Quite wearily, Mark glanced up at the in-flight movie. Once again, Uma Thurman was steaming up the tiny screen. Hadn't he read somewhere that Uma was the offspring of the father of American Buddhism? Some secret daughter he'd had back in the 1970s? A love child with the then-love of his life?

Soon enough, violet snowflake felt the urge to speak. "I thought this was going to have animals in it. You know, a Disney movie. Something like that."

"You're not complaining are you?" his friend replied.

"What do you mean?" violet snowflake asked.

"Just looky there," his friend said in a vile half-whisper. "Don't you see those two puppies fighting under that blanket?"

Next, Mark heard the distinct sounds of some rowdy high-fives. Both of them began to cackle like idiots. Oh, if he'd had that syringe!

It was a flagrant Hollywood butt shot to be sure. The two puppies in question were tightly encased in Uma's jeans.

Raising up carefully, Mark slipped his hand under Sam's sweat-wet head, the hot crook of his knees. He carefully carried him to their reserved seats. Thirty-seven pounds exactly. Recently, they had been to the doctor's for a checkup. A pediatrician friend had weighed Sam, measured him, pronounced him fit as a fiddle. When the stewardess came their way, Mark started to order a bourbon and water. But he changed his mind. Let her pass on by.

Instead, Mark fantasized what he might have said or done, for example, if one of the ski-bums had drunkenly stumbled into his son. They'd gotten up to use the bathroom twice. What if one of them had knocked Sam's head against the metal seat's edge while he wobbled joyfully down the aisle? Would Mark have come unglued? Like that father who exploded during a Humana Hospital softball match? It hadn't been a pretty sight to see. His team's first baseman, a dermatologist named Larry Steensma, had been practice swinging rather absentmindedly, when a boy about his own son's age had wandered up from behind. There'd been a sickening, dropped-cantaloupe thud. Next, high-pitched sounds of horrible pain. The boy just kept on screaming and screaming until suddenly his father came charging at Larry Steensma like a bull out of a chute. Eyes the color of beets. Others tried unsuccessfully to intervene. "Watch what you're doing, shit-for-brains!" the little boy's father had threatened. "Don't you say one word! Not one fucking word! I ought to take that bat away and split open your own stupid fucking head!"

Children changed your life—that was a true cliché for you. And there was little doubt that parental wiring ran deep. Like when Mark and Genevieve had argued over his son's growing collection of Barbie dolls, whereupon she'd purchased the kitchen set perhaps just to goad him. At least, so Mark thought. That Barbie business had really upset him. But did he buy his son GI Joes or Power Rangers or plastic guns? No, Mark did not. Of course, parents couldn't help doing what they thought was best—but sometimes you ultimately didn't know what was. One book said one thing. Another book said another. Yes sirree, having children changed a person. Some primordial alliances took hold.

Shortly after his son's birth, Mark's father had wordlessly sent him a videotape. It contained a four-minute excerpt from a TV program featuring home movies, memorable images shot by amateurs. The footage his father sent had been shot by a tourist at a zoological park on the Isle of Man. It showed an agitated, somewhat silly-looking father in Bermuda shorts, watching after his six-year-old had fallen off a boulder-and-mortar barrier into a natural habitat for upland gorillas. Very riveting! Amazing stuff! Three females, one male, and two baby gorillas had also watched the boy fall into the compound. The female gorillas were only curious at first. However, the male became immediately agitated. The boy had fallen maybe fifteen feet, then hurt his head. Fresh, crimson blood flowed from an open wound. The videotape showed the boy quietly moaning, letting out periodic half-conscious shrill cries which made the bull gorilla race nervously back and forth. Soon a large crowd had formed; the father in Bermuda shorts was frantic; someone on the Isle of Man zoo staff ran for a tranquilizer gun and a pistol, depending on which would be required.

Suddenly, the female gorilla bounded over toward the wounded child. Not aggressively, but instantly, with fluid unchecked animal speed. At this point, a park official restrained the father from going over the wall. But the female primate merely sat down beside the boy. She kept glancing over her shoulder, as if to keep her adrenalized mate in check. Next, the female gorilla reached down—her black leathery hand twice the size of any human's. She lifted the boy into her lap and cradled his injured, bleeding head. In the end, they'd tranquilized the bull gorilla then entered the compound. The kid emerged all right. Mark would never forget those images and others no less intense, like witnessing Sam's birth. Yes, being a parent was an emotionally powerful thing.

A few days after the videotape arrived, his father called. He asked Mark if he'd seen the footage. Yes he had seen it, Mark told his father. That's good, his father responded. Next, they talked briefly about what it had been like for Mark to be in the delivery room with Genevieve, something his father the doctor had never done given three opportunities. Their conversation ended with Mark's father saying nothing specific about why he'd sent the videotape in the first place. It was as if his motives were clear, the matter obvious and already understood. He liked to be an enigma whenever possible. Very cryptic. Very ex-Marine.

For over twenty years now, his father had been the only parent in Mark's life. His mother, Elizabeth, had died of ovarian cancer the summer he had turned thirteen. Watching the tenderness of the muscular female gorilla—that image of her cradling the little boy's head—it had actually made Mark cry. Too bad his own mother never saw her beautiful grandchildren. Sometimes, he still missed her so much.

During the rest of the flight, Mark slept deeply, sweating lightly himself.

Ah, such slipping away into non-thinking heaven!

It was hard to do of late. His marriage was ending. His wonderful Genevieve had had an affair—a thought that continued to churn and burn in memory. Then he'd been unfaithful too.

His last year of specialist residency had put a strain on his rocky marriage. Ridiculous demands. Inhuman hours and stress, stress, stress. Preparing to be an oncologist was time consuming. Perhaps his wife had felt taken for granted. Perhaps she'd felt ignored, but there was something else as well. There was Genevieve's substantial melancholy over the fact that she couldn't get pregnant, might not ever bear a child. She came from Catholic roots, a French-Italian tradition with strong family inclinations. For the longest time, they'd tried and tried. She had been tested. Mark was tested too. He had done The Dance of the Dixie Cups twice to establish whether or not, from a sheer numerical standpoint, his spermatozoa could do the job. First try, he'd been a little low, a couple million sperm shy of the norm. Second time, above the average. Maybe an enzyme wash would be in order, Genevieve's doctor explained. Sometimes a couple's reproductive cells needed a bath before they would join and fuse.

So they tried that too. No dice. Eventually, Genevieve grew depressed. She didn't expect to ever get pregnant, at least, not without potent fertility treatments like some of the Mormons out in Utah were using. They'd both read a few scary articles about those fertility methods. Finally, her doctor had recommended a fairly mild drug called Clomid to regularize her somewhat irregular menstrual cycle—perhaps that was the problem. In the end, however, the drug Clomid hadn't been required. Two months after Genevieve had terminated her affair, she came back to her repenting, now no longer angry, finally outright begging husband. At one point, Mark had wept in public, even sung some Jacques Brel to her in a local restaurant: *Il faut t'oublier, tout peut s'oublier. Laisse-moi devenir, l'ombre de ton ombre. L'ombre de ta main, l'ombre de ton chien. Ne me quitte pas. Ne me quitte pas. Ne me quitte pas.* Finally, the begging succeeded. He had worked hard at winning his wife back. Yet her affair still bothered him. It had humiliated him and been an emotional tutorial. Oh, how he hated that dipshit Hungarian! Her fencing coach had been much handsomer. But compared to the fencing coach, Mark thought, he had more love for Genevieve, more determination, more wit, more overall good will, in the piece of foreskin his mother's obstetrician had cut off then thrown away.

Yes, Genevieve had come back. And ba-da-bing, ba-da-boom! Miracle of miracles, his spermatozoa could. Perhaps at the most unpropitious time—still during their mending period—Genevieve suddenly became pregnant with their son. Shortly afterwards, Mark pulled his own harebrained stunt. He had gone to a class reunion at Vanderbilt, where he slept one night, one round, with Sharon Lawrence, his old girlfriend from college. Ah, if he'd only known then what being Sam's father was going to be like. What being a father to him would mean. Afterwards, he'd felt horrible and eschewed round two. But Mark's old girlfriend had called a month later and said guess what? That's right. She was pregnant too. Instant popsicle of the spine! Regret to the second power. Shame squared.

Although Mark took sad comfort in the fact that Genevieve had her affair first, with her svelte and dark-haired fencing coach from the local YMCA—who was a Hungarian for godsakes, from a town named Pecs, as in pectorals—there was no denying that his one-night affair had turned out to be infinitely more complex. From the point of Sharon's phone call onward, just like the Bob Marley song on *Exodus*: "Guiltiness pressed on his conscience. Oh yeah! Oh yeeeaaah!" But there was nowhere to flee.

So Mark shouldered the guilt and knowledge of what was coming, trudged that boulder up a very slippery slope. He'd wanted a grace period, a chance to have a family. He'd wanted to try and make their marriage work. He didn't want Genevieve to worry during her pregnancy or to be unhappy during their son's first year. He made Sharon promise to stay quiet and keep the secret awhile, then approximately one year after Sam was born Mark told his wife the truth. As for the affair itself, Genevieve took that in stride. No problem. Tit for tat. But why hadn't he been more prudent? She and the Hungarian had used condoms for their month-long fling. However, during their one-night skip down memory lane, Mark and his old girlfriend from college had not. Of course, his wife was French. Half-Sicilian on her father's side. Apparently Mediterranean-types have different ideas when it comes to questions of lovemaking. Questions of right and wrong. Genevieve reminded him of AIDS. He was supposed to be a physician, for goodness sake. The word "sin" didn't come into play for her, but phrases like, completely irresponsible, *bête comme la lune,* and *absolument con* seemed to apply.

Despite his occasional MD ego, Mark Wilson felt quite humbled by it all. Of course, the Humana nurses and nurses everywhere were right; doctors could certainly be a swaggering, cocky lot. But sometimes cancer patients needed to see certainty in your eyes, absolute confidence in your demeanor. God-knows, human beings produced a lot worse things than professional assurance. Or lustiness either, if you really thought about it. The so-called Christian penchant for humility, he had never fathomed or particularly trusted. The meek will inherit the earth? What the hell was that supposed to mean? He'd grown up Southern Baptist and met a lot of born-again "believers." Quite frankly, he preferred the Jewish ethos and a lot of the doctors which that culture produced. Over the years, he'd crossed paths with a lot of Bible Belt types who'd do their humble-meek bit in public; however, some of them needed the phrase "judge not lest ye be judged" sutured in gold thread across both eyes. Maybe, just maybe, that would help the goody-two-shoes lens through which they saw the world. He'd met a lot of people who would say nothing to your face—flash a saccharine smile, use a flat, uninvolved gaze—then bury a knife to the hilt between your shoulders. Many craved money and pleasure out the ying-yang. Then they voted for politicians against welfare or raising the minimum wage. Of course, he'd met some Christ-emulating Christians as well—his mother was one of them, forgiving and loving. So were many of the pastors, the wonderful church-going folks, he'd seen while treating his cancer patients. The way those good people soothed the dying was essential. Generous, selfless, and indefatigable. They were some of the bravest, most gifted, most important people in the Humana halls.

Yes, Mark felt humbled. Fate had certainly intervened. The plot of his life had veered off course. Yet considering all he'd seen over the years in the medical profession, he knew he'd better thank his lucky stars. While he hadn't chosen his destiny, Mark tried to accept it. His old girl-friend Sharon Lawrence insisted that she still loved him; therefore, she could *not* not have his child. At first, Mark had pleaded with her, mouthed some idle protests. But you were either responsible for your actions or otherwise. Ultimately, you were either "pro-choice" or not, a good-hearted friend or an ice-hearted stranger. In short, some knight-errant sperm, some lucky seed, had struck gold twice. His children weren't twins exactly, but darn-near when you looked at them. Sharon had named their daughter Elizabeth after his mother. Little Sam and Little Lizzie. His children were only four and a half months apart.

Two perfectly healthy, beautiful children. Neither quite expected. What a real mess he had unintentionally wrought. A bumper crop.

II.

Soon they were in Portland, taxiing on solid ground. It was nearly six p.m. Pacific Time. Little Sam stayed zonked-out until the unloading chute had been hooked-up and all the interior lights flicked on. Then Mark showed him the Valsalva maneuver to equalize the pressure in his ears. Due to the runway delay, they wouldn't make Oregon's coast until tomorrow morning. Mark didn't want to make the scenic drive at night.

Since they had only brought carry-on luggage, they grabbed it and headed to the rental counter, where he obtained a four-door Subaru Outback. He'd heard good things about Outbacks from Brent Stoltz, the medical physicist in radiology. They played squash together sometimes at the Pendennis Racquet Club, drank beer occasionally, schmoozed in the Humana hallways with the nurses. What a hound-dog! What a card! Although Mark really hated the nickname Brent had given him of "Doctor Death," the guy could be quite funny from time to time. When he heard about Mark's upcoming divorce, Brent Stoltz had quipped that he wouldn't ever get married, not ever, not even if they threatened to burn him at the stake. Then again, maybe being burned at the stake wasn't all so bad. At least that way, the fire would stay hot. One's demise would be quick and comparatively painless.

"Okay buddy, " Mark told Sam. "Hop in and buckle up."

"Are we going to get a hotel?"

"Yes we are."

"Yippee! And can we have pizza? Just like you said?"

"That was the deal. Tonight you can sleep with me, okay?"

"Yeah," Sam said, showing his pretty white smile. "And I won't pee in the bed, Daddy. I'll pee first. Because I'm a big boy, right?"

"That's right."

So for dinner that night, they had Domino's in their hotel room.

Little Sam ate three whole pieces, crust included, plus any stray pepperoni he could filch from his father's plate.

The next morning, they got up early. Sam always saw to that. The landscape between Portland and the ocean was lovely, a few Quarter Horse farms, lots of agriculture, yellow-tinged fields of sunflower, corn, and mustard plants. In Newport, Oregon, they visited the aquarium devoted to Keiko, the killer whale in the film *Free Willy*—another promise that absolutely must be kept. When Mark found that the line at the entrance was two football fields long, he became a hundred dollar sponsor of the Oregon Coast aquarium. Easy as pie. They waltzed right on through, saw the movie-star whale and laughed at the penguins. He took some darling pictures of his son, posed next to a couple of sea otters dozing in a plexiglas habitat window. Little Sam had a blast. He ate a hot dog and Haagen-Dazs ice cream bar. Then he pitched a hissy fit in the souvenir store because Mark refused to buy him two stuffed killer whales at fifty-seven bucks a pop. After the hissy fit, though, not a chance.

Later that afternoon, they found a hotel further down the coast in Florence, Oregon. By six o'clock, the sea's edge was windy and sand-strewn, like it had been covered over in beige-colored gauze. This hotel was resort-like, much nicer than their first hotel. A celebration of sorts was in order. So an hour before sunset, Mark ordered room service. Fresh halibut for himself with a bottle of white wine, and for Sam a small prime rib and baked potato. They had a "picnic" on the bed, then took the leftover bread onto the balcony to feed the seagulls—another treat Mark had been planning all along. He keenly remembered doing the same thing in Fort Lauderdale with his mother and father, the very first time he'd seen the Atlantic Ocean as a boy and thought to himself: "Too big! Too big!"

Out on their hotel room balcony, the view looked stunning. Traces of tangerine light now spread over the Pacific. The birds were virtual acrobats. Quite amazing to watch. It seemed that Oregon seagulls were much better in the wind than East coast seagulls. They had the ability to move in all directions, pinwheel on a dime, virtually hover in place, zoom up or zoom down, if it meant catching one of the bread chunks.

"Let me," Sam yelled. "Let me throw some!"

So Mark scooted out a chair and held Sam up on it while he pitched bread. A gull would soar in and grab it mid-air, only a few feet away. His son would squeal with delight, laugh his beautiful raspy laugh.

"Those crazy birds! They're crazy, Daddy!"

"Yes, they are, buddy."

The gusty wind hadn't died down. Plenty of orange-violet, slanted light remained. Out on the sand colored beach, people were shuffling around, wearing windbreakers and heavy sweatshirts. Hard to believe it was June because it was getting really chilly.

"Let's go back in. Okay Sam?"

"Okay," Sam said. His son dutifully climbed down from the chair. "Can I jump on the bed now if I want to? Please, Daddy, please?"

"If you be careful not to fall. Watch out for the corner of the dresser. You see how sharp this is?" Next, Mark showed him the place, touched the dresser corner with Sam's own hand. "If you fall and hit your head here, you might get hurt."

"Daddy, uh, Daddy," Little Sam said. Something familiar was on his mind. "When I come back to live with you next summer, I can have a dog, right?"

"That's right. When I get a house."

"Do you remember Melinda's cat? That cat where we used to live before with Momma? That white kitty-cat that used to live next to us?"

"Tater Tot? Was that her name?"

"Uh-huh, that's right. And whenever I get a cat, I'm going to name her Fishstick. Then I'm going to get another cat and I'll call her Tater Tot, okay?"

"That's a good idea," Mark said, then laughed.

He thought his son was smart. He loved his loopy, playful connections. Such wild leaps in thought. Quite involuntarily, he kept laughing about the Fishstick and Tater Tot line, the idea of having domestic pets named after Sam's favorite foods. Two seconds later, he thought he was going to cry. Instead, he grabbed Sam, then threw him on the bed. Dr. Mark Wilson tried his best to stay young in life, thus the North Face tent still set up in the living room. He always tried to retain a sense of playfulness. A high degree of rigor, professionalism mixed with informality. For example, most everyone at the hospital avoided what he considered a *blah* last name. They agreed simply to call him Mark or Dr. Mark instead.

"Don't Daddy, don't tickle me! Please, please—PLEASE!"

He would tickle him some. Then stop while his son caught his breath.

"Do it again," Sam would say, then laugh his laugh. His shiny little teeth were like the nubs on candy corns.

Seeing such mirth in his child's face was infectious. Quite ineffable. It made you so happy and was impossible to describe. When would the innocence that fueled such a smile begin to fade? Ah, it would fade. Nothing could bring it back either. The hurting would happen, but what form would it take? Perhaps a goldfish would die. Perhaps a playground bully would dispense some pain, and what would a sagacious, good parent do then? When would the permanent smile, Sam's adult face, take shape?

"Tater Tot and Fishstick," Mark said, laughing some more.

"That's right!" Sam squealed.

"What kinds of names are those, you silly goose? How would you like it if I started calling you 'Pizza?' Or 'Barbecue Chicken'?"

"Yeah, okay," Sam giggled. "Sure, why not?"

A short while later, Mark ordered a movie called *Indian in the Cupboard*. Very well done, he thought. Both of them enjoyed it. They watched it together until Sam went to sleep. Afterwards, Mark drank the rest of the white wine. His mind wandered. He considered the "freedom," the extra time, all the possible experiences now opened up before him. He and Genevieve had been separated for a year and a half. Now she would be living on the other side of the country with his son. Part of him felt vaguely angry about it. Still very guilty too. Being apart from his children saddened him. Since Sharon had a physics background, she and his daughter, Lizzie, lived in Oak Ridge, Tennessee. It was like having three hearts inside your chest, a miraculous bloom of emotions which you could pull the petals off, then scrutinize with thick fingers. But you could never understand the flower as a whole.

Over the past four years, Mark had seen his daughter regularly. To Genevieve's credit, she'd welcomed Lizzie into their home. After all, why punish or place aside a perfectly innocent, loving child? Little Lizzie had even spent a couple of holidays with her half-brother. They were two peas in a pod. Partners in crime. Once, they'd completely flooded the upstairs bathroom and laughed like hyenas. Of course, it had been a strain too, having her in their house; and, sure enough, at the local Winn-Dixie, everybody had asked Genevieve if her two cute children were twins. Only a strong marriage could have withstood the blow.

So during the past year, Mark and Genevieve had lived apart on different sides of Louisville. He had tried dating occasionally. He might as well get used to it. After all, his wife was dating. Boy oh boy, she hadn't lost any time. Therefore, Mark started searching around himself, looking for some way to anesthetize his sense of what he'd lost. Rejecting the possibility of meeting someone at Humana hospital—someone he'd like, like a lot perhaps, but have to work with daily—he decided to take Brent Stoltz's advice and place a personal. He called the *Courier-Journal's*

Singles Connection line and recorded a "voice greeting" just to see what surfaced.

The first person who called was Meg. They met for sashimi and sake. She loved science fiction and horror novels. She held a heartfelt conviction that Stephen King didn't get the artistic respect which he deserved. She was okay, pretty and well-spoken, despite her belief that Steven King deserved a Pulitzer Prize. They didn't really hit it off, though. Not really. When he walked her out to the car, Meg didn't seem to enjoy being kissed goodnight. At least, not by him.

The second woman's name was Debra. She returned his message, then met him in a downtown fern café on a sunny Saturday morning. They'd gotten along from the start for some reason, got drunk on Bloody Marys, and talked for a couple of hours. She spoke Spanish and had lived for half a year in Montevideo. Things moved fairly quickly once she heard he was a physician, something he had failed to mention when he'd met Meg. Ah, the human heart! Later at her place, they watched a University of Kentucky basketball game at his request; they switched to champagne, and Mark watched her puff on a spliff-sized joint. But Debra's true sports interests lay elsewhere. Not with UK basketball. By the second quarter, she'd taken her shirt off and encouraged Mark to reciprocate. She was a minor league hockey fan who had nipples which hardened into two-inch projectiles that she insisted he gnaw on with vigor and relish. He had feared hurting the woman, actually drawing blood. But Debra shouted out clear instructions on the matter, telling him please not to mollycoddle her body, just to do what she said and to clamp down hard. She wasn't fragile. She was a big girl. She said that she wasn't going to break. After their first date, Mark and Debra saw each other a couple more times with the same efficacious results. A kind of primal affection developed, which was perhaps something you could never really trust. So finally Mark decided that the personal ads weren't the way to go.

Soon enough, a third prospect loomed. A twenty-seven-year-old redhead moved into his apartment community. Her name was Kimberly

Goshen, as in land of Goshen, striking green eyes, skin the color of milk. Prior to architecting a garbage dumpster *rendez-vous,* Mark noticed her comings and goings, the blue rhythms of her TV, her living room lights across the way. Then one day they chatted briefly while dumping their trash. Mark found out that she'd just recently moved from Cincinnati. She was a shy, slightly unconfident woman with an absolutely beautiful green-eyed gaze. Not a stunner figure-wise, but weight and height proportionate, as the personal ads would say. So they had lunch. Next, dinner and a movie. After he'd bought Kimberly Goshen dinner the third time, she invited him over to her apartment. They kissed passionately for a couple of hours. He touched her bare breast and the bony ridge of her coccyx. Mark knew his way around human anatomy. He felt the mound of soft flesh—so lovingly named in Latin—behind her jean's zipper whereupon Kimberly stopped the proceedings by holding his hand in place.

Since she'd not acquiesced, Mark decided it best not to push matters. Better not lead her on. Start something that could not be finished. Yes, Kimberly Goshen was a wonderfully adroit kisser. She had a beautiful face. But if the truth be told, a rather sloppy behind. She absolutely never exercised. After she had held his hand in check, Mark recalled all of her allusions to food over dinner. Plus, he'd peeked in her refrigerator when he went for ice. Kimberly told him at some point that she positively hated to exercise, and her emphasis astounded him. Hated? Why not outright loathed? For godsakes, couldn't she get on a stationary bike? Go for a walk, or jog like everybody else, move her carcass before she became one sooner. Ask any cardiologist—case closed. Why couldn't she have an occasional carrot or eat a carton of yogurt? He did. Others did. Why the heck couldn't she? He wasn't being a sexual snob so much as honest and forthright about what wouldn't work over time. Sure, heredity was a factor. Some people simply couldn't help it. But a willfully fat butt just wouldn't cut the mustard. Did Kimberly think his idea of ecstasy was doing sit-ups or that he loved jogging the way he loved chocolate eclairs? Get real. Be consistent. Be fair. Also, why the double standard when it came to being *called* an ass? Didn't women prefer their men in decent shape? Did they flock in droves to see full-figured Chippendale Dancers?

Desire is. Was. Will be. Genes and glands were one thing. But lying to yourself and growing bitter about the opposite sex was another. Sure, being "a good person" and having a "good heart" mattered. Mark knew that intelligence and humor were important. He'd married Genevieve hadn't he? He just couldn't involve himself with a sweet-faced couch-potato, despite the wonderful tenderness Kimberly exuded when they kissed. Therefore, until he got lonely for such kisses—ah, the human heart—he never returned her calls.

A couple of weeks passed.

Finally, Mark dialed the number, but when Kimberly answered he cringed and hung up. A cold sweat formed on his forehead. He prayed she didn't have caller ID.

. . . .

Soon the hotel room's digital clock read two A.M.

All the white wine was long gone.

In the end, he'd only had protected sex with Debra the hockey fan. But she'd been a little too raucous for Mark's taste. Yes, some of it had been tender and it had soothed. Some of the Eros was for real. But Debra had a kind of darkness which was a shadow of her sweetness. Some of the things she'd said and done had shocked him. Frightened was perhaps a better word for what he'd felt with her. But what could it be that he was vaguely scared of *right now*? Why had he waited so long to marry Genevieve anyway? Was he in love with love? Or the conditions of irresolution? Also, whenever you got down to the bedrock truth of it, what did Sharon Lawrence—who claimed she loved him—think, hope, and ultimately expect from him? Would she have had the baby if he were a plumber? Or a semi truck driver? Or if he were unemployed? Perish such thoughts, Mark told himself. One should never look a love gift-horse in the mouth. If indeed, there was such a thing. How many times had he learned that you could think too much, be too smart for your own good?

Soon the digital clock passed three A.M.

Mark Wilson listened to the waves from out on the balcony, where he'd fed the seagulls earlier with his ecstatically happy son.

Out past the windswept beach, the Pacific Ocean heaved and crashed with rhythmic insistence. Implacable. Very powerful. Quite dark.

III.

The next morning, little Sam woke him up at seven-thirty. Very early as usual. Fully rested and chipper. Ready to wrestle and eat. What naturally contented beings four-year-olds were, Mark thought. So healthy and happy, and it was a good parent's duty to try and insure these qualities. Try one's best to lay a solid emotional foundation, prepare them for being reasonable, responsible, happy adults. Because happiness in the long run, well, that was a very subtle, very delicate thing. When would the real complications kick in for Sam? What if he turned out to be gay? That wouldn't be so bad. What if he committed a horrible, horrible crime? Again, perish the thought. But seriously, it had to happen to some people and what would a good, devoted parent do then? Continue to love, of course, because what else could you possibly do, what other emotionally valid options existed? There was no turning back in this earthly ride.

Outside the sheer drapes, the sun was very bright. Already hot looking. Prior to being roused by his four-year-old, Mark had pulled the sheet over his eyes. "Get up Daddy, I want a Pop Tart," Sam kept saying. He kept burrowing for attention, head-butting his father under the sheet. During his short life, he'd already crunched two pairs of glasses and bloodied Mark's nose once with such roughhousing.

"How about some scrambled eggs, buddy?"

"Scrambled eggs are yucky."

"I don't know if we can get a Pop Tart here. How about some cereal?"

"Do they have that Batman kind?"

"You win again," Mark said. He swung his legs over the bed's edge. "Hand me the phone. I'll tell them to bring some breakfast."

"Okay, Daddy's getting up." Sam's voice sounded triumphant. "And we're going to have another picnic? Like last night?"

"That's right. Do you want some cereal with bananas?"

"Yeah, okay. The Batman kind."

Actually, this was his code for Raisin Bran. Lately it had been easy to get Sam to eat less sugar for breakfast, and if he had his way it would be Pop Tarts for sure. Prior to an upcoming summer blockbuster, some Kellogg's folks in Battle Creek had paid some folks in Hollywood to put the Caped Crusaders on their Raisin Bran boxes. Another Batman sequel was on the way. Apparently, Uma Thurman and one of those bogus, hunky doctors from the television show ER would star.

"And orange juice? You want some orange juice?"

"Sure, okay."

"And toast and jelly?"

"Yeah, that's alright."

Outside, the Oregon coast looked gorgeous. The wind had died down in the wee hours. Now the skies were a deep azure. By the end of the day, several heat records would be established all across the state.

. . . .

Once they'd eaten breakfast, packed, driven inland, then crossed a series of knob-like hills that shielded cooler air from the sea, it was eleven o'clock and 102 degrees Fahrenheit. Such hot weather in Oregon was an anomaly. *Would he grow up thinking in Celsius? Meters instead of yards?* In an hour or two, Mark would see Genevieve's face, then hand over their son. *Very soon, Sam won't be with me. Not on a permanent, daily, continual basis. Off and on, I'll see him for a while—then he'll go away once more.* Mark Wilson glanced in the back. Once again, little Sam had fallen asleep in his Graco car seat, lullabyed by the winding mountain roads. Zonked out anew.

Their family had ceased to exist. Its duration had been too short. Recently, he'd seen a TV magazine special on baby-boomer parents, the generation prior to his own, whose myths of individual secular pleasure and freedom from consequences had been passed on. Perhaps too deeply imbibed. The TV show focused on "empty nest depression," something baby-boomers experienced after their kids had all gone off to college or been cast like dandelion spores to wherever the modern job market winds coldly blew. One fifty-year-old stockbroker, a Rogaine-using former member of SDS, confessed that after his son left for Dartmouth, he'd kept a pair of his dirty track shoes in the front vestibule. At the end of his Wall Street day, he simply couldn't stand the sight of a vacant-looking house. Apparently, a six-figure-salary didn't help with that. Another dry martini wouldn't fill the void. Or a cigarette boat. Or a condominium in Cape Sans Blas, Florida.

Over time, Mark's three-heart feeling, all the distance, would just get worse. Of course, both Sam and Lizzie would be a constant feature in his life. He would provide very well for them. Take them fascinating places. Show them exciting things. Spend a lot of quality time with them both. No mysteries there. After all, their future relationship was up to Mark now wasn't it?

As for what would happen with the mother of Lizzie, well, this was a decision that simply could not be rushed. Sharon claimed she loved him. But he still felt manipulated. Part of Mark loved her too—whatever that meant—because part of him distrusted love: marriage statistics, human nature, his and his first wife's past. Besides, scientists had chemical names nowadays for what caused people to be in love. Hell, they could map out the neurological patterns in your brain. All over the world—the Amazon River basin, the Serengeti Plain, Sri Lanka, Iran, Iraq, you name it—cultural anthropologists were studying mating patterns; nowadays they were theorizing that the seven-year itch should really be more like five. He and Genevieve had made it almost eight—not too shabby. However, perhaps they hadn't hung in there quite long enough. Because after a few decades of marriage, so the love scientists claimed, some golden-year endorphins came barreling down the pike.

Soon, their divorce would be official. After Genevieve lived for an entire year in Oregon, the lawyers would be engaged and they would be well paid. Luckily, it wouldn't be painful financially. Mark's wife just wasn't that way. She spoke four languages fluently, a rare thing in the USA. Genevieve was smart and talented. Very proud and plucky. Of course, he would always support both his son and his daughter. To do otherwise would endanger his spirit. Besides, pigs get fat and hogs get butchered, as any good lawyer knows. Mark worked very hard for his money. His branch of medicine wasn't for everyone. He'd made $186,000 dollars last year. The partnership he'd recently joined had income tax and malpractice insurance advantages.

Needless to say, it was never easy watching a lot of patients die from cancer, and a certain number of them died regardless of chemotherapy, despite the powers of "the healing beam." Sometimes Mark wondered if he'd made the best choice, following his mother's death. But he also knew that he'd been quite fortunate in his chosen career. He could take nice vacations, buy any car, most any house he wanted. He could afford an accountant who more than earned her keep. Her name was Sally Cleavenger from Birmingham, Alabama. Sally was pretty and intelligent. Lithe-limbed and ringless. Soft and sultry, all sexual readiness—Mark just knew it—under the silken robe of her Deep South, be-kind-to-strangers, mint julep voice. Sally was about his age. Thirty-four or thirty-five. In September, Mark would be thirty-seven. (That meant he was half-way dead. Given the current male life expectancy figures, if his luck held out, he had approximately thirty-five more years to go). Ah, the human heart—*tick tock, tick tock, throb throb*. Sally Cleavenger's southern accent could melt down iron filings. Her breasts did not look real, though, come to think of it. And Mark saw no point whatsoever in that particular surgical procedure. He enjoyed their conversations, though. She was pretty and quite witty. Perhaps he should give her a call.

Suddenly, from the backseat, Little Sam made some mewing sounds. He shifted in his car seat, then dropped back off to sleep.

Yes, Mark was going to miss Genevieve, miss seeing her face on a regular basis, talking with her, knowing what she thought about things. Ah, what a mess they'd made of it all. She'd known him at the beginning of medical school, then she'd had her affair with the YMCA Hungarian toward the end. But what all Mark had learned from her that wonderful summer in Paris, before he'd decided concretely to become a doctor. Genevieve had shown and taught him so much. He'd gotten a job waiting tables in order to improve his horrible college French. He'd worked at night to make ends meet. There was the city's treasure trove of art museums, architecture, history during the day. And they'd made love around the clock.

At the end of August, when Parisians left the city in droves, he and Genevieve had watched Daniel Clairmont and his fiancée Luce-Marie get married in the country. It had been something, that wedding in Le Creuse. Quite unforgettable. He had never seen anything like it back in the United States. One of the distinct things Mark remembered about Daniel's wedding was how Genevieve had acted among the people in Le Creuse. How they had treated Genevieve and vice-versa. She was from Paris. Attractive, educated, very outgoing. They were just farm folk, like some of Mark's rural relatives, his great uncles and aunts back in Kentucky. For example, Daniel's brother was the size of an NFL lineman. He actually looked as if he walked behind an ox all day, or perhaps pulled the plow himself. But Genevieve had laughed, drank, and danced with him and others like him all night long. Mark had loved her for it. What a wedding! What a joyous occasion it had been!

First, there was a church service, then a civil service. Half the little town from Le Creuse attended and the other half watched from their windows or from along the village's cobbled sidewalks. Next, the celebration festivities began at Daniel's father's very humble house, where various snacks had been placed out on tables: doors from the house had been removed from their hinges, then propped on empty oil barrels and saw-horses. Later, there was a game they played called *les gages*, a little bit like Truth or Dare. After drawing her slip of paper, Genevieve had to drink three glasses of red wine out of Daniel's huge, sweaty brother's shoe. The conviviality alone was something to witness—even if you chose not to participate. Lots of wine, whiskey, and Ricard. Everybody drank some. Farmers, housewives, even the local priest. Afterwards they all clambered in their cars, lights on, horns blowing, and merrily drove off to a local *relais* to eat. That meal had lasted nearly till midnight. Appetizers. Four full meat courses. Eight vegetables. Cheese and salad and fruit—anything you could possibly want. More red and more white wine. Oodles and oodles of champagne that Daniel's farmer father couldn't practically afford. Still, he'd gone in debt to do things nicely. For his oldest boy and for Luce-Marie. Following the cheese and fruit, came another sweet wine and dessert. But instead of a wedding cake, there was a *moulin du bonheur*, a meticulously built meter-high "windmill of happiness" made from vanilla creme-filled pastries that had a very sweet, caramelized coating, like a candy tortoise shell around the exterior to protect what was inside.

Watching the heat-seared Oregon landscape pass by, Mark Wilson suddenly wondered something. Had Daniel Clairmont and his wife ever had children together? Where were they living now? And how were things going for them? Very good, he hoped. He felt sure they were together and hoped they were both okay. Because that faraway summer when he and Genevieve had fallen head over heels for each other, Mark and Daniel had gotten to be quite close. He waited tables and Daniel chopped vegetables in the kitchen of a restaurant on Rue de Temple. They drank beer together after work. They talked. They told jokes. They discussed their respective futures.

His friend Daniel had not been able to finish high school since he had to help his father with crops. He'd not been very fortunate. He'd not been given many chances. At twenty-five, his teeth were rotten. Really horrible. Daniel had no money and he probably never would. He'd crossed paths with Luce-Marie, who'd come to Paris quite poor herself, hoping for a brighter future. That was something silly tourists didn't understand or think about nearly enough, how big fancy modern cities like Paris, Los Angeles, or Tokyo could be some of the hardest places to live on earth. One night while drinking beers, Daniel told him something. A personal secret that Mark would never forget. Before chopping vegetables at the restaurant, Daniel explained, he had drawn tarot cards near Beaubourg for tourist pocket change, and his wife, Luce-Marie, had worked as a prostitute on nearby Rue Saint Denis. Daniel said that he'd told her fortune once. They'd had coffee together afterwards. That was how they met.

Just another true life story. But it had moved Mark deeply. What made his upcoming divorce so wrong was that he and Genevieve had been so damned lucky. They'd been given oodles of chances. But all those silly arguments. Such intransigence over nothing. Ah, the petty stubbornness! Ah, the squandering! That was the part that bruised his heart and made his soul so sick.

. . . .

Driving the rest of the way to Corvallis—not wanting to arrive where he was heading—Dr. Mark Wilson, the successful oncologist, thought back on it all. He keenly recalled his and Genevieve's wide-open youth. He had lots of photos somewhere. Of course, there were more pictures in Mark's head. Later, there would be questions, various things Sam would need to know. Sometime in the future his father would try to explain everything. "Things just got too messy, buddy," he might say to start with. Only a few months from now, for example, Mark would tell Sam over the phone that he missed him. Little Sam would say, "Well, Daddy, that's why you and Mommy should love each other." Ah, but they had and in a way they still did.

Suddenly, Mark recalled the very first day he saw her face. A friend had given him Genevieve's phone number, because she'd been dating that friend's brother at one point. Mark had been planning to do Eurail the summer just after college, but he knew no one at all in the various foreign countries he wanted to see. So he'd casually dialed the number once he got to Paris. Then Genevieve showed him around the city. He recalled her bright smile and bright eyes that day. He remembered how they'd effortlessly fallen in love, or whatever you want to call it, how they'd argued about politics for hours on end. Really arguing, mind you. Her brothers were card-carrying Communists, pavé-throwers of 1968, and Mark's father the urologist voted like a devout Republican. He'd grown up pampered. He thought everyone had boot-straps or the means to earn them. In short, he had a lot to learn. They disagreed about a lot at first. But they talked, talked, talked. One thing led to another. And they finally kissed. Four days later, Mark jettisoned the Eurail idea, and he and Genevieve traveled by car instead. They drove her family's little Renault all around Italy, Switzerland, and southern France.

Back then, Genevieve had turquoise blue eyes. Jet-black hair and olive skin. At almost twenty, she had wisps of a distinct mustache which she needed to wax. She smoked a pack and a half of Marlboro Rouge, read two books, drank ten or twelve cups of espresso a day. She was funny and smart, more than a little pudgy. Quite overweight in fact. But the extra weight didn't matter. Not at all. Not a single bit.

In the valley of Aosta, at a place called the Hotel Roma, they made love for the very first time, and the most memorable thing about it for Mark had been afterwards—what it felt like simply to hold her hand the next morning. He was twenty-three. Genevieve barely twenty. Sure, they were both young, but old enough to know what that feeling meant. Maybe just not mature enough to preserve it. Of course, in the years that followed, perhaps their needless arguing was just love with the volume turned up. Yet the more Mark thought about it, this was merely a nice idea. It could not be lived. Certain limits had to be observed. His son Sam needed to know that part too, because love was fragile. Possibly quite rare. But love was real. Love could water that dry part of you that needed watering—or it could slip through your hands like sugar-fine sand.

Yes, Sam needed to understand that work was important in life. But not the most important. He needed to hear the whole story of how over the years his mother's and father's love had been botched. How little by little they'd let each other down by bickering. By being selfish with time. Human time.

Ah, time was precious, Mark Wilson knew. He was currently feeling it in his bones as his son lay asleep in the rental car's backseat. The only certainty in life was death, and its arrival was a dice roll. How many times had he seen it while practicing medicine? A beloved family member irrevocably whisked away? Like that nice guy, Mario Rodriguez, a peach picker from Mexico. He worked in the Eison orchards for how many years and for *frijoles*? Then testicular cancer—usually a quite treatable metastasis—knocked on his family's door and took Mario from them forever. Like Kathleen Tomlinson, who had a mastectomy four years ago. In March, though, he'd done another mammography and found out that her cancer was back. Flourishing wasn't the word for it. She wasn't a DES-daughter. She didn't have a breast cancer history, but her aunt had had squamous cell carcinoma. Kathy's children were nine and eleven years old. So he'd "hit her hard" as they say in the trade. Most likely, the chemo would be worthless. But you still had to try. Now the stuff was in Kathy's remaining chest tissue, her armpits and glands. Her bones, lungs and liver. They'd even found a cyst growing on her left retina, causing her vision to fail. Luckily not both eyes, though. Consequently, Kathleen Tomlinson could still see her children, right up until the final curtain.

Yes, living got messy. Sad changes happened. But there were always survivors, other people who needed affection. So you couldn't give in to sadness either. After a certain point—a necessary mourning period for loss—the perhaps-this's, the perhaps-that's were worthless. Ultimately, Chrissie Hynde was right. Finally, the sobbing had to stop.

Glancing back in the car seat, Mark admired his beautiful boy some more. He pulled the rental car over simply to watch Sam sleep. Head drooping. More crystal-clear sweat on his brow. Unfurrowed and care-free. So perfect and precious. Little Sam was still a baby in many ways—but growing up so fast. And now his father wouldn't get to see the process in its entirety. Not day by day. Living had gotten messy indeed. Planet earth was blue, just like in that other song from his college days. Some amazing stuff, though! Some amazing stuff was out there! Improbable weddings in the countryside and resilient couples like Daniel and Luce-Marie. Killer whales, seagulls, and gorillas. Looking into your children's bright, shining eyes. Or just holding Genevieve's hand that day in the valley of Aosta, as they walked together chastely through the streets.

At some point, Mark Wilson would have to tell his son that part for sure. How he'd never forget that feeling and many others. Never in a million years, that is to say, not for the rest of this one life on earth. Yes, someday, perhaps in the distant future, the near-adult Sam needed to hear the whole story. Mark would try to explain it. All of its minute details. He would always tell the truth, and hopefully the story's details would make Sam a better person, a more generous individual. Perhaps a better father himself someday. A kinder friend. A sweeter man.

Malololailai
or *Discovering the World*

"To create is greater than created to destroy."

—Paradise Lost VII, 606-607

. . . .

"The refusal of men to take their wives into their confidence at such times accords with their apparently total disregard of women's opinions about warfare. When Joan Meggitt talked to Mae women about these matters, all of her acquaintances—without exception—said they detested the frequent clashes, no matter how just the cause. As one woman phrased it: 'Men are killed but the land remains. The land is there in its own right, and it does not command people to fight for it.'"

—*Blood Is Their Argument: Warfare Among the Mae Enga Tribesmen of the New Guinea Highlands*

. . . .

"The beauty of the living world I was trying to save has always been uppermost in my mind—that, and anger at the senseless, brutish things that were being done."

—Rachel Carson, *Silent Spring*

"We figured if we had been over in Vietnam fighting for our country, which at that point wasn't serving us properly, it was only proper that we had to go out and fight for our own cause. We had already fought for the white man in Vietnam. It was clearly his war. If it wasn't, you wouldn't have seen as many Confederate flags as you saw. And the Confederate flags were an insult to any person that's of color on this planet."

—Reginald "Malik" Edwards
Phoenix, Louisiana
9th Regiment, Marine Corps
Danang, June 1965–March 1966

. . . .

"I have adhered closely to fact in every particular, and endeavored to give each thing its true character. In so doing, I have been obliged occasionally to use strong and coarse expressions, and in some instances to give scenes which may be painful to nice feelings; but I have very carefully avoided doing so whenever I have not felt them essential to giving the true character of a scene. My design is…to present—the light and the dark together."

—Richard Henry Dana
Two Years Before the Mast

Malololailai
or *Discovering the World*

I.

This is a story about one of the most amazing human beings I have ever met. He was someone I had the pleasure of knowing in my slightly wayward youth, a loyal friend and travel companion, someone you could count on whenever the chips were down. We first met in Ventura, California, the rainy spring of 1984, working construction during the day, then later on, as Fitzgerald grew to trust me—after my own loyalty had been eked out and earned—we would talk for hours at the local marina.

Robert C. Fitzgerald was an expert sailor and open-water navigator, a carpenter by trade. A plumber and electrician who spoke fluent Spanish, plus some fair Italian. A shade-tree mechanic and Jack-of-all-trades *par excellence*. He was well traveled, both Continental and Pacific Rim. Supremely curious. Prodigiously busy. He was a 173rd Airborne ex-soldier turned neo-Remarque pacifist, a veteran of what he often adamantly referred to as "The American War" against the diverse geographical and cultural region known as Vietnam. He was DLI trained at Monterey among other places. So he spoke some Vietnamese as well. He stood five foot seven and weighed around one-sixty. Fitzgerald had this calm but ever-attentive, always-arresting gaze. Brightly colored, inwardly-lit gold eyes. Very light brown with fleckings of amber. Once I found him sitting in his pint-sized Datsun pickup reading a textbook on Calculus. Riveted by, zeroing in on it. Scratching around the margins with a chewed up pencil. "Why in the world are you reading *that*?" I asked him. "Because I never learned before," Fitzgerald told me. This was his quick, no frills response. He lived and worked out of that Datsun pickup for years, then slept at night in an eight-by-six wooden toolbox he'd built near the local marina. This toolbox had been his home for goodness knows how long. Just a waterproof wooden box. A poncho liner and a pillow.

He kept a ragged North Face sleeping bag nearby, just in case the temperature should drop. Everything else, all of Fitzgerald's books, a few family and combat photographs, select letters, and so forth, he carefully organized, then placed in storage. Every spare minute, every spare cent, went into his current sailboat in progress. The Chó-Fú-Sá. This was one of the sailboats which would change things in ways too complex for me to quickly communicate. It was a thirty-two foot, exquisitely hand-built beauty, which he skimped and saved for and slowly brought to life.

For about two years, we remained good friends. Then Robert Fitzgerald turned up dead. So that was that. One day he was irrevocably gone. Thus ending our friendship except for these good memories. Thus ending Robert Fitzgerald's quasi-charmed, geared-to-his-own-time life after he'd made it through: a typhoon off the northeast coast of Australia, another man-killer storm in the Caribbean, and the surreally horrific battle of Dak To. That's right. November 1967. Of course, if you're a sentient witness of those troubled times and its alchemy of issues, if you're not allergic to history, then perhaps you have an idea about just what this means. That battle fought for Hill 875 had one of the most tragic instances of friendly fire during our entire involvement. The firefight at Dak To was a pivotal moment for many forever brave and forever dead young men, many so-called theorists of "limited war," and dozens of still-surviving American soldiers. However, as anyone who actually lived the war knows all too well, any pivotal moment in Vietnam didn't change that much—or change it nearly soon enough. The French had their tragedies at Haiphong, Cao Bang, and Dien Bien Phu. And we learned well from their catastrophes which cut both ways.

Next, we had a long list of our own. The battle at Dak To was a turning point in a war replete with so many turning points they form a monotonous dizzying gyre: Bien Hoa, Ap Bac, Pleiku, Song Be, the various battles at Hue, the bad-trip standoff at Khe Sanh, and the lie-filled massacre of innocents at My Lai.

Let me be the first to say that I didn't have a blessed clue about what Vietnam or any other war was like. And I still don't. I was born in 1960. So I spent the early part of the decade eating Captain Crunch and Pop Tarts and occasionally peeing in my bed at night. Other things on TV commanded my toddler, then my adolescent attention. I ignored the combat footage and stayed glued to *Gilligan's Island.* I watched *Star Trek* and *Lost in Space* from behind my mother's knees while she ironed the family's clothes, getting a cheap rush of outer space danger and "scary stuff" from between my fingers. Go ahead and laugh. That wavy-armed robot really gave me the willies. By the time I'd turned ten, other things like riding my SL70 dirt bike, then later on Pac-Man, commanded my time. No sir. No ma'am. I didn't have an inkling. Not until I hit twenty-three and ended up in Ventura, California, where Robert Fitzgerald generally befriended me and taught me some things, partly by putting me in my place. He taught me how to sail and invited me to the South Pacific to help repair a hurricane damaged boat. He talked to me forthrightly about his combat experience. Really talked, mind you. No holds barred. No swinging-dick tall tales.

But this guy was *dauntless*, I'm telling you. Not nuts or berserk or supermacho. He was always thoroughly engaged—no matter what he was doing—and in love with life down to its last drop, fascinated by all of its kaleidoscopic particulars. Once we were at sea in the Fiji Island group when this vicious thunderstorm came out of nowhere, and there we were, off Malololailai, maybe half a mile from a waterspout—this freaking tornado full of saltwater. Well, let me assure you that I was scared and trembling. Yet Robert Fitzgerald was genuinely unafraid in a wide-awake, stoic, uncocky way which this particular war had taught him, and this was the general attitude he'd managed to bring back home.

But how did the USA end up over there anyway? Talk about an oil-drum size can full of slick and wriggling worms. Perhaps any point of origin is something hard to determine. Any eschatology is also flawed, ultimately doomed to failure. Consequently, how to begin and end this story, which comprises American politics and culture as a whole, stems from our habits, practices, beliefs, and ultimately also the teller of the tale? How to separate being from becoming? When did you start to be the person you are or aren't right now?

When does a good marriage begin to fade?

When does a star begin to become a black hole?

. . . .

Robert Carlton Fitzgerald was originally from Fairfield, Connecticut. He was born in 1947 and was an only child. His mother worked as a registered nurse. His father was a dabbler. According to Fitzgerald, his old man was a real piece of work. Somewhat of a ne'er-do-well. Possibly a genius in his own way. Officially an inventor by trade. Ever known one personally? Someone who makes his living on patents? Well, that's what his father did. Apparently, Robert's childhood was typical enough, fairly comfortable economically, although there were some tight times, too. He was publicly educated. His mother and father were both big readers who instilled a lexical appreciation at an early age. Also, they both loved the sea. While he was growing up, Fitzgerald's parents had a Morgan thirty-eight, which they kept docked in a rented slip at Stonington, a coastal town in eastern Connecticut with a deep harbor and an open view of the Atlantic. They would go out there most Saturdays, even if it was just to sand or paint something on the sailboat or generally clean up around the dock.

His parents loved each other. They both liked their jobs. His mother worked in the local Catholic hospital, and his father kept his own odd hours. On the weekends, though—ocean winds and swells permitting—the three of them would sail.

His mother would pack a picnic lunch with garlic-and-rosemary roasted chicken, maybe a bottle of chilled Chardonnay. His father would have maybe a few beers tops. He was never a big drinker, according to Fitzgerald, and his son turned out the same. But that didn't always matter, insofar as his father could be quite wacky. Moody and unpredictable. I could tell you some of the things he invented: those ceramic fittings for halogen bulbs, a type of backing for adhesive tape, an innovative fiber used in most air conditioning and heating filters. Also, I could tell you about the job he had working for a company that implanted specks of gamma sensitive matter inside of skeletons. Sounds wild, right? Maybe so. But no less true. This company in Stamford, Connecticut prepared the skeletons into human facsimiles, then sold them to medical schools to train oncologists and radiologists.

The skeletons were real, mind you. They came in burlap bags from Bombay, India. Another hearty gift, if not a gratuity, from the so-called "third world" to the sunny future of the so-called first and foremost. This particular job was only temporary, something Fitzgerald's father did to get the family through a rocky time and allow them to keep their Morgan thirty-eight. Since he was between inspirations and patents, he made these training dummies. The bones came into the factory from India. But they had to be reassembled into skeletons because they arrived all loose. Next, they were placed in a person-shaped Jello mold—as if the person were lying horizontal—then the bones were positioned with dabs of clay to hold them away from the lower surface of the mold. This Connecticut company made ninety percentile, seventy percentile, fifty percentile molds, depending on the size of the "the body" desired. Male or female. Adult or infant. Once the bones had been laid out in the lower mold, a special plastic goo was poured into it then allowed to harden. The assembly was then flipped, clam-shelled onto the upper mold, then more of the muscle-like, plastic goo was injected. After it all cured, "the body" was popped out and unceremoniously sawed crosswise, parallel to the ribs, with a meat cutter's band saw. The slices were then returned to the mold, stacked back together, then reconnected with plastic registration pins, so that they could be held together intact, or disassembled one slice at a time. Once they were shipped to the various medical schools, the teachers could hide germanium pellets anywhere in "the body," and their students would then have the task of finding the offending location using the x-ray equipment.

Robert Fitzgerald's mother was very devout. Roman Catholic. She worked in the local Catholic hospital's pediatric cardiac ward, having opted to specialize in intensive care, work with children who were struggling to live with their imperfect, variously malformed hearts. Personally, I can't imagine having parents like these. Much less growing up with a family sailboat or spending sun-drenched weekends upon the Atlantic Ocean. Robert's father died in a commuter plane crash his senior year in high school, and the year after that Fitzgerald lost his scholarship to Dartmouth, joined the Army, then volunteered for paratrooper training.

As for myself, I'm from the South. My hometown is a place located near no place at all. But it means a whole lot more than that to me. I was born at a hospital in Paducah, Kentucky, named after the eponymous Indian Chief Paduk who, legend has it, once consorted with Merriwether Lewis and William Clark. George Rogers Clark had been given a land grant for surveying along the Ohio River, then before he died he willed all of his plotted lands to his brother, William Clark, who eventually changed the town's name from Pekin, Kentucky, to what it is today. We had a farm and a small house. My father worked incessantly. There were no boats on the coast, no hobbies, no pastimes really. No regular family outings on the weekends with garlic-roasted chicken and chilled Chardonnay. But while growing up, that farm and some the older ways surrounding it was a boyhood paradise. I loved the possibility of the woods and would go there often with my cousins and my friends.

Right now, it seems idyllic. Our home place was an adventure just waiting for the right gang of boys and girls to make it happen, full of ongoing green-spaces, tree houses, forts and creeks, a pasture for my pony named Candy—who would routinely shit then buck me off in it. There was a nearby gravel pit where I could ride my SL70 motorcycle. No helmet, no shirt, no shoes. Just a pair of Levi cut-offs and that was it. Oh, I was fortunate. Looking back, I wouldn't want my kids to do the same. But all of that wide-open, verdant space does something to you, and they haven't got that, or anything close to it, over in Paris, London, or Barcelona. All of that freedom, or whatever you want to call it. That wind from a galloping horse against your skin and in your hair. Well, it's just something you never forget.

My parents were not rich. Not even solidly middle class to start with. All we had was all we had, but everything we had seemed like enough. Absolutely fine to me. There were those seventy acres of fescue, a few horses and that dirt bike, also this nearby U-PICK-EM strawberry farm which my friends and I would sneak into at night then gorge for free. Since I mowed and maintained the owner's lawn all summer, he didn't really mind about all those purloined strawberries. That childhood. That farm. I wouldn't trade it for anything, any other upbringing in this world.

My mother didn't work. She stayed at home, cooked and cleaned. Typically Southern perhaps. Typically 1950s. Ozzie and Harriet. But society was transforming quickly since World War II, changing fairly rapidly for many women in particular. My mother was very pretty. Dark black hair, olive skin, hazel eyes. She was attentive and loving, fiercely loyal to her children whenever Daddy's temper got bad. She was a true Christian. The real thing. My mother hated gossips with a passion, and if she didn't have anything kind to say she would just stay quiet. She was particularly good-hearted if someone had made a mistake in life, always compassionate, always hospitable, which is still one of the best things about the best people from the South or anywhere else. She loved the so-called unlovables. There was this woman in our vicinity who once set a fire to make some insurance money. She made a very bad mistake, though, and one of her kids was badly burned. Afterwards everybody shunned the very sight of her, but my mother always spoke kindly:

"That poor, poor woman. Just imagine how she must feel." My mother walked the walk. Nothing for show. Real W.W.J.D. hard stuff. Perhaps you've seen the slogan and the knickknacks with these letters, which stand for that healthy gadfly reminder, "What Would Jesus Do?" designed for any interpersonal situation. Now, I'm not saying anything about people who are proud of their faith, or who announce it on their T-shirts or key chains. What I'm saying has to do with my mother. Her depth versus surface approach. You could ask anyone who has met her for five minutes, or has known her for fifteen years, and they will tell you precisely the same thing.

My mother was a native of Savannah, Georgia. She came from a more well-heeled, urban, Old Southern family. But my father, he was full-fledged country. He'd grown up on the same farm where my brother and sister and I were raised. There were three of us siblings total. For the time being, we still have the place. Yet another traditional family farm swirling down the drain. It's located about two miles off I-24, two and one-half hours from Nashville, three hours from Saint Louis. There are a bunch of corporate-owned soybean farms and peach orchard operations all around us. Either them or "the home developers" are always calling Daddy and cash-thirstily waiting in the wings. But so far the bulldozing and subdividing have been forestalled. Who knows what will happen when my father passes away? Siblings bicker. They have families and financial needs: braces, college funds, vacations—maybe a third car. Being the oldest, perhaps I'm the most sentimental, the one who can still picture my mama standing against the backdrop of our horse and cattle pasture hanging the laundry out to dry. Those crisp, white sheets swirling around her pretty suntanned legs.

More than anyone I've ever met, my mother took the needs and feelings of others into account. She was a "lady" who expected me to be a "fine young gentleman." She didn't dislike these terms per se, but thought they could definitely be misnomers. Evidently, there were a lot of so-called ladies and gentlemen in the world, people who were really what my Aunt June called "snooty toots," fashionable folks who cared more for their cars and clothes, their country clubs and social ranking, rather than being well-spoken, graceful, and gracious to other people. We had a few relatives, for example, a couple of cousins who lived in Baltimore, Maryland. They were actually native Louisvillians, though, with heyday Brown and Williamson tobacco stock. Some thoroughbred horse money in their bluegrass pasts. Not exactly embodiments of *noblesse oblige.* They sometimes made fun of their country cousins' accents and seemed full of metropolitan prejudice in various ways. Do people in the Bronx think they sound mellifluous? Oh, there's many flavors of provincialism, don't you think? One of these cousins even has an Ivy League education. But on the subjects of poverty and crime in inner-city America, I have sure heard some callous things come out of his paleolithic mouth. To this day I still can't help but feel that there's something off-kilter and ungrateful, something unimaginative about how he sees things.

My father joined the Marine Corps in 1952 when he was seventeen. These days he's a friendly, more relaxed, quite perceptive man. But when I was younger, he was very tough. He was head of the household. He called the shots. My father has worked hard most every day of his life and gave me a keen appreciation of a job well done. Physically, he was very strong. He had bad eyes, though, and his myopia kept him from combat service in Korea. I've heard many co-workers compliment his strength with amazement, tell me about various feats, like how my father kept jumping into a caved-in sewer line to save another man who had been buried alive, how it took several people to hold him back, how my Daddy kept risking his own life after he'd been partially buried himself. Another time I saw him single-handedly lift a half-filled hundred gallon diesel tank onto a flat-bed dump truck. This was quite impressive, a little frightening. Those veins standing out on his neck, such absolute determination, those rock-hard arms that sometimes held a belt after I'd fetched it from the closet; that diesel tank was going on that dump truck, by-God, and that's all there was to it. Perhaps my father's being demanding was good in some ways, and occasionally I deserved his sternness. He was always generous with his scant spare time, always willing to throw for batting practice, or shag some grounders. He was the undisputed, official leader of the family, like Paul says in his epistles to the Corinthians—or so my mother let him believe.

They got along okay. Despite some rocky times, they've held on to their marriage. Nowadays, my mother and father take good care of each other, which is fairly rare, and that's the way a husband and wife team should be. Of course, both of them have changed over the years. But while I was growing up, my parents were conservative. Quite reactionary, you might say. My father was further to the right. Gender-wise, race-wise, across the board. And speaking of race, here's a quick anecdote, an embarrassing occurrence from my youth.

When I was seven years old, I was over at my granddaddy and grandma's. They had a two-story wooden house with a verandah brush-painted blue. My grandmother was one-fourth Cherokee which I suppose makes me one-sixteenth. She always kept a big garden, lots of canned vegetables in her fruit house. Like a lot of Southern women, she was a devoted, marvelous cook. Many of my recollections circle back to her great food. Anyway, one day I'm reading the local paper's comic section in their house's breezeway because it's summer. Very hot and humid. I'm eating one of my grandma's corn muffins when suddenly there's a knock on their screen door. Well, I get up to answer and there's this black girl. Maybe ten or eleven years old. She wants to know if she can have the newspapers. At first I didn't know what she meant. This was a request which confused me. Perhaps I thought she wanted the comic section I was looking at. And what was she doing anyway? Peeking at me eating my muffin through the windows? Maybe I didn't like getting interrupted. Maybe I didn't want to be bothered period during my cherished visit to grandma's house.

"We don't have any newspapers," I told her.

"Sure, you do. I always get them."

That's what the little girl said. But I didn't believe her.

"We don't have any newspapers," I repeated huffily. "Leave me alone."

Well, just about that time my grandmother asked who was at the door. Oh, it's nobody, I told her, it's just some—then I said the n-word. Of course, I knew enough to sort of whisper it. But the little girl certainly heard what I said. Mind you, I was seven-years-old. Still, that's no excuse. Next, I prissed back to my comic page and my plateful of corn muffins, thus dismissing this sunny-faced girl just a year or two older than me. Her name was Shydonna, and the way she looked at me afterwards sure was a lesson. Another tutorial was on the way, though, because my grandmother's face was a whole lot worse.

My grandmother came around the corner, all flustered and apologizing. Next, she gave that little girl an armload of old newspapers which they routinely saved for her family to read. Apparently, they didn't have money for a subscription, even though a paper back then cost around ten cents. After Shydonna left, my grandmother really let me have it, even threatened to make me "go cut a switch." They liked their black neighbors just fine and this little girl named Shydonna in particular. My granddaddy even let a few of the black families make summer garden plots on his farm, because he had a little extra land and didn't really miss what they used for their gardens. However, this is also the man who stood up in his little country sanctuary and said he would strongly oppose any black person taking membership in his church. Oh, the hot and cold morality of it! The whites and the blacks both who still pour salt, pick and claw at this country's most horrendous scab! The sheer ignorance, partisanship, and bad faith!

So there it is, an embarrassing story from my childhood. But I'd heard that word before and whose fault is that? The most complicated thing is that I'd heard my grandfather say it as well, someone who I loved and who overall was a good man. But here's something else important. I have never once heard my mother use that word, not ever, or call someone a "faggot" or a "queer" either. Not once in my whole life. Not even in relaying what someone else had said. Also, one time I saw my mother get disgusted, then turn the channel, all because of this very popular black comedian's language coming from the TV.

Who knows, maybe you're a Southerner, too. Maybe you didn't experience stuff like this. Personally, I'm just shooting from the hip about the region where and when I was brought up. Because if you love and do not loathe a place, then isn't it best if some hard-truths get told? In short, I was raised in a rural area of the Bible Belt, located in the south-central part of the United States, a place that needed to transform a thing or two, like improving its education standards and philosophy. For example, stop saying that evolution is bunk, that maybe dinosaurs didn't really exist, and that the fossil record in Africa is invalid. Stop intimating that Charles Darwin, Marx, and Freud are simpletons, easily-reducible, or utterly evil fools. This was a region that needed to heal some racial scars, and it still needs to modify some of its state flags, insofar as the semiotics are hurtful. Perhaps it was a place that needed to loosen up that belt a notch or two. Then lay down on the sofa and read some bright books of life. Some novels by Nathaniel Hawthorne, D. H. Lawrence, Herman Melville and Djuna Barnes. It was a place that needed to be less absolute about what it took to be the "truth." A place that needed to have what it "knew" fruitfully challenged and confused.

Partly what I'm suggesting here is that I didn't learn very much in high school. Before its recent successful reforms, my home state ranked forty-eighth in education in the nation. Sure, yours truly is partly to blame—but all the same. Not one teacher taught a foreign language with a native tongue, and our single Spanish course was not encouraged or required. No one ever told me it was good to read the entire newspaper or care about who was in Congress, know who made the important decisions that affected millions and millions of people. All my high school buddies and I ever focused on was getting a Trans-Am or a Camaro, passing classes, and sports, sports, sports. Football, basketball, and baseball were about all we lived for, that and our puritanical obsession with getting laid.

So after I graduated from high school with my virginity intact, despite my best and clumsy efforts, frustrated by various things and worn-out by my father's stern vigilance, all I could think of was getting far away from Kentucky. And once I left, I pretty much stayed gone. For a few years I traveled around out West, living on a shoestring, working odd jobs. But no complaints. You meet some interesting folks that way, and a Sheraton Deluxe hotel suite is more or less the same in any capital of the world. But you know, it's strange. How different people from different backgrounds all over this country—for my mother's parents were more comfortable, more urban, more party-line Republican—how very different people often share similar views of how the world is or should continue to be. Double standards and duplicity still reign. The overall ideology can be quite fluid, yet granite-hard at the same time. Rules, rules, rules, and barriers. If a girl loses her virginity it's one thing. For a guy, well, it's not so bad. Makes him a "man." White people over here, Hispanics and African Americans over there, Chinatown unto itself, gated communities all the rage. Everybody in her or his own place. Of course, some of it's socioeconomic. Some of it's by choice. But not nearly enough.

My father had his own views. That's for sure. He sometimes voted Democratic, but he generally distrusted welfare and looked askance at raising the minimum wage. But that's not all. My father also got suspended from high school once for refusing to pray. Apparently, Daddy didn't object to the principle in general, he just didn't feel like bowing his head when they told him to do so publicly. Praying was personal, between him and God. That's how he'd been raised. Back in his own wild-oat youth, though, he once peroxided his hair, even got a USMC tattoo in 1953. Later on, he had it removed. But given various aspects of Daddy's sometimes maverick personality, it might or might not surprise you to know that he was a teetotaler. He hated the use of alcohol in any shape, flavor, or form, much less other versions of personal indulgence, like smoking marijuana, that the Vietnam era and the 1960s held in store.

So my Uncle Walter, my mother's younger brother from Savannah, was a source of consternation and a modicum of family shame. Uncle Walter really threw my father for a loop. He was cut from a different cloth entirely. Following the tradition of doing one's duty, Uncle Walter enlisted in the Navy. My grandfather from Savannah had done the same, fighting in the Pacific theater during WWII, where he'd served briefly in French Indochina. An entirely different war, though. A very different time, context, and generation. Uncle Walter began his own time in the service in 1962, shortly after the first CIDG camps were established, a couple of years before the first incident in the Gulf of Tonkin. He was on the fringe of the Vietnam war and that's where he stayed. Out of harm's way. Due to a Southern Georgia senatorial connection—I'll not name a specific name, but I could certainly give you one—let's just say that due to a solid political tie on my mother's Savannah side of the family, he managed to get a billet on the turquoise wave-washed shores of our paradisiacal fiftieth state. Dear Uncle Walt. What a humdinger. He had dark brown eyes, jet-black hair, and the efficient body of a swimmer. He didn't have the nearsightedness which kept my father out of Korea, so theoretically they could have sent him anywhere they wanted over in Vietnam. But that's exactly where my Savannah grandfather, who knew a thing or two, did not ever want him to go. Instead, Uncle Walter served out his Navy stint in a kind of Eden, and he happened across the woman of his dreams. She had been selected Miss Teen Hawaii a few years before they met. Her father managed a hotel. Her mother was a schoolteacher and a rather stunning ex-nun. Of course, it was many years later, not until I was nearly thirty years old, when I found out how the Navy had kicked my uncle out of the service for allegedly selling grass to tourists on Waikiki Beach. Anyway, there's a little bit about my Uncle Walt.

Perhaps that's a side note.

But it figures in, too, as you'll soon see.

II.

Before I arrived in California, I'd been wandering around out West a while, fleeing my upbringing, looking for adventure. My first source of income had been with TWA Services, the corporation overseeing all aspects of upkeep in Yellowstone National Park. I'd worked as a dishwasher, hiked on my off-days, and met a lot of friends from all around the country who'd come to Wyoming for the summer. There was this guy named Jim Paruk who had a degree in forestry and biology from a small college in Sault Ste. Marie. He was of Polish descent and his father was a judge in Hamtramck, Michigan. Jim liked to call grizzly bears *ursus horribilis* just to show off and make me laugh. He refused to wear bear bells and knew the Latin names for most plants and birds as well, like our very favorite bird to watch, the water ouzel. We lived in the employee dorms and played eight ball in the TWA employee pub, swam in crisp, cold rivers and went "hot potting" in the geyser pools. We camped under the stars whenever possible, set off on our hikes just as soon as our menial work was done. Oh, that sky out there! My goodness! You could even see the planets, Jupiter and Mars, shining steadily off in the distance. Slightly orange and powder pink. The color of baby aspirin.

Pretty soon, I'd fallen in love with this Mormon girl from Salt Lake City. Cheryl was pretty, very sweet, and I was a goner. That's where the idea of college started for me. But it was mostly just an idea. Still I gave it a whirl after moving down to Utah and finding a cheap apartment. Cheryl lived with her parents. She had worked at Old Faithful Lodge as well that summer, and I just started taking some of the classes on her schedule. My girlfriend was a marketing major, who eventually wanted to get an MBA, which seemed to be a very popular degree. I signed up, attended lectures, and did my part. That is, until my first encounter with a business class called "quantitative methods." Unlike Cheryl, and later my friend Robert Fitzgerald, I did not have a thing for math, not even this particular class, which was supposedly an easier one specially designed for the core curriculum.

To tell the truth though, I wasn't serious about studying. Other interests prevailed. Since my Mormon girlfriend had grown up snow-skiing, come mid-November of my aborted freshman year, Cheryl had me snow skiing some as well. Eventually I became a ski bum of sorts, skipped more classes, then met a very non-Mormon skiing partner by the name of Cinnamon. I kid you not. Cinnamon Taylor. His parents had been hippies. His father lived in Key Largo, and he had gone to prison once for counterfeiting. His son also told me stories about growing up and seeing an Igloo cooler in the living room filled to the brim with top-notch weed. Can you imagine? Being raised up by yahoos like that?

Anyway, we skied a lot together, occasionally smoked pot and had too much fun. Our shenanigans high in the Rocky Mountains, so to speak, all of our leisure activities put considerable pressure on my relationship with Cheryl, then sealed the deal on my forthcoming failing grades. After one semester, I'd had my fill of college. Soon, I'd gotten frustrated again with my overall life's trajectory. But there was something else. How should I put this? I'd gotten disenchanted with my brown-haired girl. Her sweet-then-sour, hot-then-cold, occasionally fiery then suddenly frosty attitude toward our two young bodies.

Frankly, I didn't know what to make of this. Just what might it portend? Cheryl was a kind-hearted individual. Her sense of morality and goodness—how she always treated other people—that was something I greatly admired. That part of Cheryl reminded me of my mother. The point I'm making has to do with shame, how the whole self—the fuller picture—is what should really count. Often in America, it still does not. Sure, the young need guidelines. They must be instructed. They must be safe. They must be taught the difference between right and wrong. But have you ever considered how some of our youthful promiscuity, some of America's gross indulgence, is directly linked to our enduring taboos? Forbid it absolutely—then it's absolutely thrilling. The juiciest carrot of all. Perhaps visit other places, check things out. See how they educate their children, then put the Ten Commandants in schools all you want. See how Japan and England have legislated their handguns, how their kids don't have fraternity hazing or get alcohol poisoning just as soon as they leave the nest. Go walkabout like the stepped-upon aborigines. See what you find out there, but don't get me wrong. Please don't put words in my mouth. What I'm saying begins with this story's first sentence, then continues in seven parts. What I'm saying about the war and everything else cannot be easily distilled or quickly summed-up. Robert Fitzgerald refused to dummy-down. He understood that with certain subjects less-is-less, like that bumpersticker slogan—"Fighting for God and Country"—and the problematic, outside of history, transcendent sentiments that sometimes go with it. Because surely everyone who has considered the matter knows that the Ten Commandments, or the six hundred and thirteen of Judaic tradition, the overall ethics of the Holy Bible, the Talmud, and the Apocrypha all put together, didn't have a single solitary thing to do with what went on over in Vietnam.

Once again, Cheryl was a fine young woman. She and I were raised with more or less the same values. My mother was Southern Baptist, clearly the more religious of my parents. We went to church on Sunday twice, for what it's worth, and usually on Wednesday evenings as well. Oh, I'd heard my share of guilt-and-terror, fire and brimstone from the pulpit. While working in Yellowstone though, Cheryl and I had sex sporadically. In one form or another. Then we would have one of our long, long talks. Her method seemed to be everything but "the deed" itself, and the more I think about it that's an intriguing guideline. After all, Cheryl was twenty-one, starting her senior year in college. She was attractive, fit, and healthy. One of the very best kissers I've ever encountered unto this day. Boy, she could get you riled and would be all worked up herself. Then in the next bated breath, she wanted to talk about "eternal marriage." Apparently what had been okay up in Wyoming caused her second thoughts once she'd returned to the land of milk and honey.

On the one hand, she could be enthusiastic. Then this crippling, torturous guilt came back to roost.

Seriously, what's the solution? How to ease the sexual millstone from around our necks? And if it doesn't feel like one yet, just wait until you have children. What's the answer then? Getting married very early, like Marie Osmond, so you could have legitimate intimacy—then get a fairly quick divorce? There is no easy answer. No single appropriate age. But consider this as well. My great Aunt Bessie got married at fourteen. Years ago, that was considered a-okay. Absolutely moral! My great Uncle Paul never let her get a job, learn to drive a car, have indoor plumbing, or cut her long hair. Following his funeral, though, Aunt Bessie learned to drive in their tobacco field, cropped her waist length hair, installed a bathroom and bought a piano for her living room. Then she found a job at a barbecue restaurant. After a two-year wait, Aunt Bessie briefly dated a man who sold her some furniture, dated him until her brother, the good deacon, razzed her so much about being "hot-to-trot" that she lived alone for the rest of her long life.

· · · · · · · · · · · · · · ·

After botching college, it was back to work. Odd jobs once more. I'd always done various kinds of manual labor. My father was someone who instilled a respect for people who got dirty, folks not afraid of a little elbow-grease, not disdainful of rolling up their sleeves. He bought a backhoe and started a gravel business to supplement our iffy farm income. Daddy dug footers, swimming pools, septic tanks, and his slogan on the dump truck proclaimed: "I dig ditches for a living." Sometimes I thought this was kind of corny. However, the more I thought about it and saw how my father looked around eight or nine p.m. most nights, well, it made me very proud. Since I could do a little carpentry, I got a job framing and roofing for a company in Park City, Utah, where they'll be having the Winter Olympics in a couple of years.

That construction job lasted a good while, then after some white-water rafting near Moab, it was off to California. Los Angeles. My first big city. I worked at *Acapulco y Los Arcos* in Westwood until I was fired for giving away flan desserts to boost my tips. Oh, the various and sundry things I contrived to give away! Marxist dining at its finest! A lot of students from UCLA came in, and it would be anthropologically correct to say that some of the young women in California were something else entirely. Salt Lake City this place was not. Not the Bible Belt either. Compared to their tertiary education equivalents in the land of that sly old devil Brigham Young, some of these California co-eds didn't have qualms about removing their raincoats, their wristwatches, their bathing suits, or their undergarments either. Therefore say whatever you want to say, it was a gigantic breath of fresh air.

My best friend at the restaurant was a Chicano named Frank Corona who had the sweetest, most lady-like girlfriend you can imagine. Her name was Julia. I had this huge crush on her. But Julia was in love with my friend Frank. Then there was this black guy named Barry, who I always played ping-pong with after work. He was from Peoria, Illinois, and his father had been best friends with Richard Pryor before he became even a glimmer of a rising star. Speaking of which, that was something else about L. A. Growing up in the rural South, I'd never been around famous people, never seen anyone up close I'd seen on TV. Much less dealt with them face to face. So that was interesting as well. While working in Westwood, I served the following people and they were all very nice as I brought their food and drinks: Dick Van Dyke, Jim Nabors, Mary Lou Henner and Cliff Robertson. I even saw my after-school buddy, Bob Denver from *Gilligan's Island,* the basketball coach Pat Riley, and the comic Steve Martin.

One rainy afternoon, the writer Norman Mailer came into the restaurant, and somebody pointed him out to me. He was sitting with a young woman who looked, but didn't act, like his granddaughter. They drank a couple margaritas while Norman Mailer gave her the eye and scarfed down a few baskets of free chips and salsa. Then for some odd reason, he challenged Frank Corona to arm wrestle. But Frank Corona declined.

Anyway, after my brief turn as a dessert stealing garçon, it was back to wearing a tool belt. Doing what I liked the best. Working outdoors. Being in the sunshine. My new group of construction friends and I used to hang out at Gladstone's on the tail end of the Pacific Coast Highway, and we had a real clique going there for a while. The seafood was good, the beer domestic and imported, and they had real sawdust on the floors. The Pacific Ocean was only two good Frisbee hurls away. You could see the surfer-types going out to sea before the sun went down, dressed in black neoprene suits during the colder months and looking dangerously like seals. Green Acres, thank you very much. The Golden State seemed like the place for me. At least, that was my thinking at the time. I liked my new life in California because of its sheer difference, just as I'd liked backpacking in Yellowstone's Thoroughfare region, snow skiing in Park City, hiking in the gorgeous Uinta mountains or the red-rock regions of southern Utah. People can say whatever they want about the Mormons—tell that joke about Joseph Smith's statue with his back to Temple Square and his front facing the ZCMI bank—but they're good people, they love their families, and they live in one diverse and absolutely gorgeous state.

Anyway, the sheer newness of it all, living out West was so exciting. I'd grown to love the mountains, the thrill of meeting different people, not knowing what the next page might contain. Through a friend, I eventually heard about a better job further up the coast. The pay was $13.50 an hour, really great back then. I'd been sharing an apartment with three other guys, and I had a girlfriend named Stephanie, who choreographed and taught ballet. She knew stuff I didn't know, and we'd recently become very interested in film, especially foreign movies, really good ones, which would come to The Vogue or be shown at various screenings at UCLA.

Stephanie and I dated for a few months, and we watched *400 Blows* by Truffaut, *Gallipoli* by Peter Weir, Weija's *Man of Marble* and *Man of*

Iron, then this fantastic wedding movie by another Polish director named Zanusi. Also, a lot of stuff by that huge-hearted Frederico Fellini. Some of Kurosawa's films like *Yojimbo* and *Rashomon*. The trilogy by Satyajit Ray and his masterful *Days and Nights in the Forest*. No doubt about it. Stephanie taught me a lot. I made her watch *Coal Miner's Daughter*, since it was about my home state, the eastern part of it anyway, which I didn't know too well. She agreed that it was a fine film. Stephanie was really wonderful and I thought we were wonderful together. Then something happened. She briefly broke my heart. Briefly, I say, because mostly it just enraged me. One night Stephanie and my roommate Rick did this man-made drug called "ecstasy," then they slept together while under its influence. Stephanie cried. And I cried. Another first—having my heart confused that way. Then something else happened with my roommate Rick. I didn't plan it. One night I got drunk and fought the guy. We both got hurt. Another waste of energy.

Time to hit the road again.

Start that job further up the coast.

When I first arrived in Ventura, I had no idea what lay in store or just how much my life would be changed. The new construction company I worked for built about everything, just so long as there was a profit to be made: apartment buildings, fast food franchises, strip malls, office space and condominiums. But I worked exclusively in a subdivision north of Ventura, in the direction of San Buenaventura Mission. This new company was building a new development, dozens and dozens of private homes. Once again, the pay was righteous. Besides, I really did prefer blue collar jobs over waiting tables. One of the problems with waiting tables is that you constantly have to "step-and-fetch-it," occasionally take a smart-aleck customer in stride. Do it all with a big plastic smile. I finally figured out the game, then did whatever was necessary to get good tips. It took a while, though, because I tended to wear my emotions on my sleeve. In short, I was still quite young. So wet behind the ears. Sometimes I took so much for granted, as we North Americans are often prone to do, and here are a couple very important things I misunderstood: my good health, which I thought would last forever, and my occasionally pugnacious, feisty temper, something which had been cultivated to a degree and which I thought could be pretty cool.

A lot of young men all over the world are taught that this can be a desirable trait. But this feistiness, such ready aggressiveness, had caused some problems. Something about my jejune sense of self—perhaps something about my father—had led to two or three fairly serious fights. And isn't this related to our principal theme? Personally I didn't feel out of place in California. Not oddballish like I sometimes felt in high school, not bizarre, not lamentably alien, which is the way we often saw the Japanese in World War II, the Russians, the North Koreans—then the Vietnamese.

Yes, the story of Robert Fitzgerald and the Vietnam war is coming in which, rounded off, we lost 60,000 young American lives. Average age nineteen. Average tour of duty one year. The Vietnamese lost four million. Some of their teenagers fought for an entire decade. A good majority of Vietnam's young people, both men and women, ended up in coffins. Some of their older soldiers—those who had fought the French before us—fought virtually their whole lives. Perhaps over 300,000 of their solders are still MIA. Napalm and white phosphorous, all of those huge blasts, you know. Quite often, there was nothing to be retrieved. Let's leave aside the on-going Operation Hades and Operation Beef-Up details—just who are the jokesters who made up this stuff—the Operation Ranchhand horrors, or the fact that not a single hometown in America was ever mined, shot at, or bombed. Perhaps you know all of this. Please excuse me if you know all this, and that some of our leading generals wanted to use nuclear weapons during our South-Asian "police action," the longest, never officially declared war in all of US history. Some say twelve years. Some say twenty-five. All depends on how you count.

But these figures are boring, right? Well, don't worry. Like I said, Robert Fitzgerald's story is just around the corner. I only thought we should get the historical ball rolling. In case you didn't recall some key details. I'm not saying what needed to be done or what didn't. Just pointing out the numbers.

. . . .

Since I'd been working out West, various wonderful things had come my way, and I tried not to take them lightly: some good friends and some so-so, new experiences like snow-skiing, backpacking, hiking and whitewater rafting. Also, waiting tables in a big city of perfect strangers, who certainly weren't angels-on-earth, which made them more or less like me. Folks in California were friendly. I don't know why. Open sesame. The doors kept opening. Most people were interested in where I came from, occasionally tickled by my accent perhaps, but really on the whole quite nice. Until the Stephanie and Rick encounter, which threw a monkey wrench in things, I'd been doing all right emotionally. Then one day on the Ventura construction site, I finally lost my composure. Let my feistiness surface once more. There was this yellow fiberglass hammer I'd recently bought. Suddenly, I couldn't find it anywhere. Of course, sometimes things go missing around construction sites. Little thefts are made, not-so-funny jokes are played, and I felt wholly convinced that I had been ripped off.

"That's mine," I told this guy. His name was Robert Fitzgerald.

We'd not spoken a lot yet.

"That yellow hammer. Did you find it somewhere?"

"Yes."

"Well, it's mine."

"I don't think so."

"You just said you found it."

"This morning in my toolbox."

Well, the crowd of onlookers—they really liked that one. Robert Fitzgerald suddenly looked amused himself. His gold eyes flashed. His lips made a thin, straight smile. All I knew for the moment was that he was using the same yellow hammer I'd recently bought, and he had the gall to let me see it in his hands. That day, Fitzgerald was wearing a red bandanna, sort of pirate-style, you might say. Oftentimes, he wore a bandanna to keep the sweat out of his eyes. He always wore T-shirts and jeans, good leather boots, occasionally shorts if the weather permitted. Once I asked him about the silk-screen on one of his T-shirts which seemed to be a favorite. There were these big fish eating little fish, then bigger fish eating the eaters, then in the right lower corner this guy wearing eyeglasses eating sardines on two slices of bread, and the T-shirt's caption read: NULLUM GRATUITUM PRANDIUM, which in Latin basically means that there's no free anything and this world owes you jack-shit.

Robert Fitzgerald had a receding hairline by the time I knew him. Thirty-six going on thirty-seven. He was shyly forthcoming, quietly candid, but you noticed what he said whenever he decided to talk. He wasn't handsome or unhandsome. But he was not bland. Fitzgerald was someone you invariably noticed. There was no ignoring him when his unavoidable topaz gaze and his intelligence suddenly filled a room. We just happened to be outdoors on this particular day, and while I didn't know it yet, we would spend a lot of time outdoors together in the future. Sure, I knew a few things casually gleaned from the other workers. Apparently, this Fitzgerald guy had fought over in Vietnam. But that didn't mean whoop-di-doop to me. Quite frankly, his taciturnity, his habit of eating quietly by himself, got on my nerves. Who did he think he was? GI Joe? Someone who'd seen and done things heretofore not done, not seen?

Soon the other workers thought what was going on was funny. A few were long-haired types. Josh and Mike and Al. There were a few hippie holdovers who drove Harley Davidsons and had wallets affixed to their belts with chains. Some belonged to the Grim Reapers, a local motorcycle gang. There was Louis Ruiz and his brother Gabriel. Also, Tony Hayden from Alabama, who was the only other Southerner among us. Now they were all watching. Son of a bitch, I was going to have to get tough. That's what I realized right away.

"Okay, asshole. That's my hammer."

Robert Fitzgerald smiled again. "Say what?"

"Give me back my mother-fucking hammer"

"It's yours, huh?"

"That's right," I told him.

"Are you quite sure?"

Robert Fitzgerald asked me this question calmly. His tone was very odd. It was almost as if he expected a half-childish response. Something on the order of *mine, mine, mine.* The whole construction crew still stood poised. Waiting and hoping for a brawl. Fitzgerald kept smiling. But I said nothing. I was adrenalized, blindly determined not to back down now. Not to be considered a pantywaist while the rest of the house went up.

"Yeah, I'm sure."

"Well then, here you go," Robert Fitzgerald said. Then he laughed out loud. "If you say it's yours, then it must be."

Next, I held out my hand, suddenly noticing a tremor I'd not expected. Back then I weighed around one-hundred and ninety. I was six foot one, twenty-three-years-old, full of vinegar or whatever. Physically confident to the extreme. In high school, I'd played wide-receiver and cornerback, set a school record in the 440. Since then, I'd won the three or four fistfights that seemed to come my way. Never started a single one of them. Including the one with my roommate Rick. Not really. I just insulted him until he hit me first. Boy, it had hurt, too. That scuffle had sure been a close one.

At any rate, Fitzgerald handed me the hammer.

End of discussion. No harm done.

Afterwards, I started to work on a section of pre-fab ceiling joist which we had to raise, then nail snugly in place using some queen posts and diagonal struts. A breeze bearing sea salt and reeking of gutted surf fish blew across the construction site. The ground was muddy and puddle-pocked. An array of worker vehicles, mostly motorcycles and pickup trucks with slick, nearly bald tires, sat parked in the wisps of fraying sun-bleached grass.

Our houses sold quickly. New Bermuda sod, palmetto palms, ever-green shrubs, and bougainvillea were still two weeks, maybe three weeks away. Ventura County was growing at a clip. We built these homes lick-ety-split, pushing the boundaries of the crabgrass frontier. Money. Capitalism. Real good stuff. I sure liked that pay. But pay was all it was. Mostly, I was just biding my time, digging the littoral gals and the West Coast lifestyle. But you know what else? My Daddy once taught me two smart things: Never sit on a sheepherder's hat, son. And when you get married don't pick the flashy one sitting at the bar. Don't feel you have to search the biggest cities, not necessarily, because she might be right in your hometown. Well, my Daddy was from the heartland South and obviously liked the idea of a country gal. But I never did understand that thing about the sheepherder's hat. Not until I asked.

Back then, I mostly wanted to keep moving. Keep the wanderlust satiated. Sure, I'd skied and played around too much in Utah with my sidekick Cinnamon. We all make bad choices from time to time. Maybe getting good grades wasn't difficult for Cheryl, but those college cours-es she took just didn't hold my attention. She could say that I was irresponsible. But she couldn't say that I was unwilling to work. Besides, what was the payoff of finishing my bachelor's? Not much more money than I was making building houses. What would the outcome be? A humdrum coat-and-tie existence? Working for some land-developer in Charlotte, Charleston, or Destin? Personally, I'd rather be a lowly car-penter working beside the Pacific Ocean.

"Look here! Over here!"

Someone was yelling.

I was still on the roof. So I climbed down.

"What's up?"

"*Mira, mira aqui.*" Gabriel Ruiz was smirking beside a stack of con-crete blocks, this smooth graveled area where we often took our breaks. He was holding up another yellow fiberglass hammer. Precisely like the hammer in my hands. Apparently, I'd set mine down sometime the afternoon before. My mistake. My bad. Nowhere to run, nowhere to hide. So I had to make amends. During lunch break—two fried bologna sandwiches and a Hostess fruit pie—I apologized to Robert Fitzgerald. But he took his hammer back without much to say.

"Didn't I ask if you were sure?"

"You did."

"Okay then," Fitzgerald said.

And that was all.

Throughout lunch, the other workers talked of fishing and beer drinking, motorboats, cars, and T and A. You know, the kind of conversations construction workers are sometimes prone to have in public. The crew discussed whatever they'd accomplished over the weekend and felt compelled to brag about, the size of their girlfriend's titties, or the size of some other woman's titties they'd glimpsed in the Goat's Head Saloon, a local haunt off the main highway. Suddenly, Tony Hayden, the guy from Alabama, started to look upset. He was from my neck of the woods more or less. For some reason though, Tony Hayden seemed to draw a lot of fire in California. He took a lot of flack. A couple years earlier, his wife had passed away at a young age. He'd left Alabama to get some distance from the pain, perhaps being somewhere new would help anesthetize the memory. Anyway, now Tony was upset. The others kept up their crude talk. I don't know if Tony Hayden was thinking about his wife. But Robert Fitzgerald noticed his face. He instinctively knew, somehow sensed, that something was going on inside of Tony Hayden. So he spoke up. There was just this little thing Fitzgerald told us, short and quick, merely to change the subject for Tony Hayden's sake. He just said something off the wall.

"Hey, did you guys know that it wasn't until 1971 when women in Switzerland first attained the right to vote?"

That was it.

The bawdy talk screeched to a halt.

As I would later witness many times, Robert Fitzgerald would often say something quirky and unexpected, then five minutes, or fifteen minutes later, it suddenly made a whole lot more sense. He would effortlessly veer the conversation into a more genteel, soul-expansive vein, deflect the subject of our "postprandial chit-chat," as he once called it, then get us on topics more substantive. The Middle East. Various ways to build a yurt. The ancient presumed function of the human appendix. In this case, though, Fitzgerald just made things more comfortable where Tony Hayden was concerned. This guy was from Birmingham, Alabama. He sounded different from everyone. That is, everyone but me. But Tony Hayden lived differently as well, than most of the other guys on the construction crew. He didn't exactly fit the bill in terms of sounding "cool" or acting "hip" in California. For one thing he was quite religious. Very serious about his faith.

Ever since his wife had died, Tony Hayden was still putting his jigsaw life back together, but the process hadn't been straightforward. He'd hit the bottom of a paint-it-black, hate the whole wide world depression, and one evening, while still in Birmingham, he'd placed a shotgun underneath his chin. Sitting in a lawn chair with the gun below his head, he'd heard a distinct voice telling him to put the gun back down. That's when Tony Hayden had found God again, discovered that he needed something divine in his troubled life. He had told Robert Fitzgerald this near-suicide story once before, and that's what Tony told the rest of us after we'd eaten lunch that same day as the yellow fiberglass hammer fiasco. He'd said his piece without sounding oily or preachy. He told a little about his life. But what was admirable was how Tony didn't seem to worry about what others might think. Some of the ridicule wasn't kept secret and made its way across a number of the other men's faces. Tony Hayden's face seemed to say that they could laugh if they wanted. Personally, he felt convinced his life had been spared, sitting on the lawn chair with a twelve-gauge shotgun underneath his chin.

"Jesus saved me," Tony told us. "And he can save you all. He saw me sinking. So he came down and stopped me from doing it."

A light of relief and gratitude had reappeared and was suffusing his whole face. Then someone mumbled a wisecrack.

"That's real nice."

Tony Hayden didn't mind the jibe.

"He came to my house. He saved my life. He helps me to go on every single day. You don't know what it's like to hate absolutely everything. To really hate yourself and the entire universe. Maybe you have never had to face an evil demon. But let me tell you, I've seen them. There are demons out there to be faced."

Soon, there was another jokester.

"Were the demons red? Could you be more specific? Did they look like those ones on Underwood's Deviled Ham?"

This cynical comment came from one of the motorcycle riders, Charlie Tucker, who we sometimes called Chip. His voice made a sort of tinny sound. He was snickering through his upturned can of Coca-Cola.

Tony Hayden looked down at the gravel and dust.

"Why didn't you take a Polaroid?" Charlie asked him. "Did they have horns on their heads. Maybe pitchfork tails?"

Everyone sensed the tension. We all felt the discomfort these insults necessarily caused, and right at the end of our lunch hour when we needed to feel relaxed, recharged, ready to go back to work. Goodness knows how he did it. But what Robert Fitzgerald did next I'll never forget. He must have had his Zippo lighter going, fired it up somehow perhaps hidden behind his pant leg. He was sitting by himself over to the side, on a concrete block, and maybe he had a pair of pliers held out of view. To this day, I don't know exactly how he did it. But he certainly had that Zippo lighter going. What we all saw next was only Fitzgerald standing up, then Fitzgerald stretching, then Fitzgerald acting like he was heading toward our skeleton of a house-in-progress. A house built on California sand by these hot-shot developers, constructed very quickly in the land of earthquakes. Robert Fitzgerald started fiddling with his tool belt, then suddenly a handful of change spilled from his callused hand, a hole in his pants pocket, somehow from somewhere. Don't ask me how he did it. Anyhow, some coins emerged. He took a step toward Charlie Tucker, reached to refasten his tool belt, and it seemed like he'd accidentally dropped some change. This rag-tag mixture of nickels, dimes and pennies. Just a handful of cumbersome metal—especially if you're a working man—a half dozen to a dozen coins suddenly fell at Charlie Tucker's feet. So Charlie instinctively bent down. He reached out and picked the change up. First a nickel, then a quarter and a penny, then another penny, and then all of a sudden his face went strange. Charlie Tucker's eyes got big. He stayed very still, frozen in the crouch for a few more nerve-confused seconds, as if he were caught off balance and going to fall. Robert Fitzgerald had never stopped moving, never ceased moseying, never stopped walking casual as all get out toward that half-framed house. He hadn't acted like he'd seen the change. He just kept on walking when wham, bam, hot-damn, Charlie Tucker's whole being was suddenly rocket propelled. He was moving upward, as if from a springboard. He was saying a few choice goddamn-mother-fucking-son-of-a-fucking-bitches, drawing his arm back, then throwing that hot handful of change as far as he could throw.

"Goddamn it," Charlie Tucker blasphemed once more.

Then he held out his hand, where a mean red blister had already started to swell.

Somehow or other, Robert Fitzgerald had heated up a single dime, made it sizzling along with the rest of the change. I thought there was a quaking sound, a faint shaking of laughter, coming from his general direction on top of the house. How he'd done it we had not actually noticed. But that Zippo lighter was going. That much is for sure. Very soon we could hear him working, see his hand groping for nails up on the roof. That red bandanna tied around his head and the moving silhouette of his rhythmic right hand. That yellow hammer swinging. That cloudless blue sky.

III.

Slowly, Fitzgerald and I became better acquainted, if not close companions. There was a piece or two missing for a full fledged friendship. Still, we'd go out to Jack-in-the-Box for cheeseburgers and milkshakes because bringing cold lunch meat sandwiches can sure get old. Sometimes we'd drink a couple of beers after work. But Fitzgerald did not drink much, partly because he was always working, fiddling with something, toiling away on his sailboat nearly all the time. He talked about the Vietnam war a little bit. Told me some stories concerning the Vietnamese food he liked. Some dish called Cha Gio, shrimp on sugar cane, Saigonnais seafood soup, lemon grass chicken, and pan-fried catfish. He never once mentioned the hammer incident about which I felt increasingly silly. Oh, I had been absolutely sure of myself. A banty rooster. A prototypical ex-high school football player in his early twenties. Over time, Robert Fitzgerald became a sort of mentor figure, you might say. But our friendship hadn't solidified quite yet.

He was from the North. I was from the South. Of course, maybe we had more in common than it might first seem. Both of us were Easterners—as in east of the Mississippi River. We came from similar stern fathers, men who worked constantly, men who didn't talk much. Paternal backgrounds marked by waspish silence and Bible-Belt reserve. His father was a contemplative man, a non-practicing Episcopalian. But Fitzgerald's mother was a devout Catholic, as has been mentioned. He told me a little about growing up and going to mass. However, I would later discover the depth of his mother's Catholicism and its lingering effect on her son. Robert Fitzgerald would tell me about a dead Catholic priest he'd known fairly well over in Vietnam. He told me about the importance of this communion service he'd taken once and about Father Water's role at the battle of Dak To. At any rate, we'd both left home, temporarily abandoned the places where we'd been raised. Fled our sweet-souled mothers and our iron-willed, workaholic daddies. Of course, I'd left my landlocked origins for different reasons, because after

Robert Fitzgerald lost his father, then lost his scholarship to Dartmouth College, he went overseas to fight in a labyrinthine and mendacious war. Everybody must be humbled by something to fully become a human being. Humbled or awed, either one will do. But preferably both. And this points directly to the main difference between Fitzgerald and me. Because when we first met I was still snot-nosed. Still so young. A shit-bird, as they say on Parris Island, and I'd sure heard my USMC father use the phrase.

Since we lived in the same area of Ventura, Fitzgerald and I would sometimes share a ride to and from work. One sultry, windless day, a propos of nothing as far as I could tell, he looked me square in the eye. Then Fitzgerald told me something. He said that I had a hot fuse and a temper which needed fine-tuning. "It's like you're *vaguely* mad. You should be aware of it. That's all I'm saying. Getting angry occasionally, that's okay. That can even be productive, that is, if you get angry at the right things. Personally, if you ask me, the vague is the problem."

"Aren't you?" I asked him.

"Aren't I what?"

"Pissed off at all of the unfairness."

He considered the question thoughtfully.

"No, I'm not."

"You're not?"

"That's right. I'm not."

Naturally, this particular recollection—oh, how Robert Fitzgerald could put people in their place with a look, just a phrase or two, with such snap-your-fingers speed—naturally, this leads to the dove gray, slightly foggy morning when I first met Fitzgerald. *Really* met him, mind you. In an entirely different mood. We'd been working together for three or four weeks. We'd had the fiberglass hammer run-in and patched that up, then I'd witnessed the hell-hot dime legerdemain he'd engineered for Charlie "Chip" Tucker. Suffice to say, I'd made his general acquaintance. By now I knew some details. But perhaps one's real self comes partly from the penumbra, not our apparent self and visible deeds alone, but also the overall shadow that we cast. Of course, I knew some facts. Robert Fitzgerald was half of a generation older than me. Thirteen years to be exact. He was skinnier, shorter, quite wiry. He'd loved the sea ever since he was a kid. He'd spent a lot of time at Rocky Neck and sailing off Hammonasset Beach. I knew that nowadays Fitzgerald lived alone. Somewhat like a hermit. In that wooden box. He just required a place to sleep because most all of his money and all his spare waking hours went into the Chó-Fú-Sá.

Through some of the other workers, though, I heard about this lady who had been in Fitzgerald's life. He'd been dating this black woman, a registered nurse from Santa Paula. Word was that she'd cared a lot about him and used to come around the job site occasionally. They had finally broken it off only a couple of months before I came up the coast from Los Angeles. Apparently, they had dated for a couple of years. She wanted to get married. Paula wanted to be his wife, but only if Fitzgerald would be willing to settle down, have kids and a regular house, stop sailing off to kingdom come every so often. An African-American girlfriend. Imagine that. A registered nurse just like his mother. Later on, I asked him about her. Fitzgerald told me that if he had any single fetish, then maybe it was for registered nurses, that it wasn't so much a psychoanalytical thing as maybe a gratitude thing, perhaps a lingering attachment to a couple of amazing women whom he met over in Vietnam. He said that Paula refused to get on a boat. She disliked, distrusted the ocean. Some people, they just don't like it. It's sort of like flying. Anyway, Fitzgerald told me that his reluctance to get married and have children had ended their relationship. Paula wanted to have a family. Fitzgerald wasn't so sure. He didn't know if he ever wanted to have children, or be a parent period, given the loss of his father and everything else he'd experienced. His mother, Yvonne, was still alive. They talked together on the phone two or three times a week.

Of course, I thought this Paula woman was interesting. Not the kind of situation you saw often in the South of my youth. Hey, if two people happen to find love and affection—true commitment in their lives—then they should be together and that is that. Why, back in Vietnam there were some Caucasian and Southeastern Asian relationships, many of them unequitable, poverty-forced, exploitative, and outright wrong. But some of the GIs and some Vietnamese women actually fell in love. And if you ask me, that's a whole lot more beautiful than a lot of close-minded folks might think they think.

Oh, the brutal silliness that has gone on since the dawn of recorded time. The Irish versus the English. Hutu versus Tutsi. Serbian versus Croat. The Chinese versus the Vietnamese. The Vietnamese versus the Montagnard and the ancient people of Cham. Pat Robertson and Bob Jones III versus homosexuals. Jerry Falwell who once claimed that all of his Jewish friends are fine, upstanding people. But that they are still going to hell as far as he's concerned. Oh, the rigmarole and rules that are cooked up and re-warmed over, like Paige Patterson and Paul Pressler did in their famous meeting at New Orleans' Cafe du Monde—what were those two doing so near Bourbon Street anyway? Then at their next Southern Baptist Convention, they preached wifely submission and conversion of Judeo-Hebraic peoples. Also just the other day on NPR, I heard about these incensed rabbis who didn't want Jewish women to ever pray aloud in public. Also, there was a report about Operation Moses, this important thing our military did in the 1980s, where a lot of persecuted, dark-skinned Ethiopian Jews where taken to safety in Israel. The Ethiopian woman on the radio explained that she had "always dreamed of Jerusalem," but when she got there and started saying "Shalom, Shalom" to some of its whiter inhabitants, some of them would not say "Shalom" back to her and some would even turn their backs. Oh, the biases and barriers. Oh, the factions and castes people needlessly create.

Have you ever really wondered about the country you live in, your race, or the religious denomination you happen to practice? Isn't it the case that if your parents happened to be Iranian, then most likely you'd be Muslim? Or if their names were Fleishman or Alder, then you might be Jewish Orthodox. Then again you might not. Do you think all those

Buddhist war protesters and those South Vietnamese monks who set themselves on fire in 1963 were sincere? Quite serious about their faith? If your parents were Methodist or Baptist, most likely you're Methodist or Baptist or something very close. Personally, that's the case with me. Of course, some people convert to something entirely different—but that's not the general pattern. So what does the general pattern say about "true" religion, considering that if the sperm and the egg that made you had joined somewhere else in the world, then you would probably be like the other people in that land?

All a little aleatory. Bit of a dice roll, isn't it? Not to mention how much melanin is in your skin—whether you're white or black or brown. Whether you're from Europe, Mexico, Canada or the USA. So whenever we're feeling "free" and maybe think we deserve all we have, perhaps we shouldn't mouth the word "blessed," and merely say that we're thankful.

Oh yes—we should be thankful indeed.

But we should also recall those dice.

Once again, I knew some things about Robert Fitzgerald. But I still did not know him. Early in April of 1984, we did not have girlfriends, much less lovers or wives. After Stephanie, I'd entered another dry spell. A Gobi Desert you might say. Consequently, we had more spare time on our hands than some of our co-workers. One of the reasons he and I started hanging out—then eventually sailing together—is that we were bachelors. A lot of mornings we'd eat breakfast at a local Denny's. There was this cute waitress there named Laura. She and Robert Fitzgerald would flirt occasionally. Goodness knows why, but I got it into my head that I would start flirting with her too. Nothing obnoxious or overt. Just friendly attention. She seemed to like us both okay and had this absolutely gorgeous smile. Anyway, I went in Denny's one morning. Sat down at a booth. Ordered coffee. Robert Fitzgerald had finished his bacon and scrambled eggs, and he was reading the *Los Angeles Times*.

"What's in the news?" I asked him.

"You're early."

"Couldn't sleep."

"I wonder why."

"Yeah, yeah, yeah. So what are you reading?"

"Like you said. The news," Fitzgerald told me. "I'm reading about what's not happening to me. What didn't happen the day before today."

Well, the surly S.O.B. Sometimes he really got my goat. This breakfast thing at Denny's had started to be a kind of gas-saving ritual. After we'd finish eating, we'd take turns driving each other back and forth to work. On this particular day, hungover though I was, I ordered a Denver omelet and hash browns. Back in my early twenties, I tended to drink a good deal more Budweiser than was perhaps in my best interest, then every so often Fitzgerald would rib me a little for making myself feel bad. Maybe it's some stupid Hemingway thing, believing that it's manly to get real drunk. Certain myths of manhood abound. Also, someone had once told me that Paul Newman would drink about a case of beer a day, and I liked Paul Newman very much, ever since I'd seen that prison movie *Cool Hand Luke.* That scene where he comes out to talk to his emphysematic mother, and she smiles and coughs but does not cry. That scene nearly tore me up.

Anyway, the Denver omelet and hash browns came and I began to eat. If I could have had cheese grits and country ham then I would have gotten those, but those things are rare in California. Maybe polenta for grits, that's about it. Now it was maybe six-fifteen. Six-twenty. Goodness knows why I'd gotten up and faced this particular page of my fate.

"Let me tell you something," I told Fitzgerald, because of his *wonder why* comment earlier. "You don't have to give me so much shit."

"Who knows?" he said. "Maybe I do."

I quietly finished my Denver omelet.

A short while later, the waitress named Laura came by and refilled my coffee cup. "You fellas doing good? Need anything else?"

"No thanks. I'm fine."

Robert Fitzgerald kept reading his newspaper.

Laura stood there waiting.

"Anything for you?" she asked again.

Still, Fitzgerald did not respond. He didn't seem to hear her talking. He was so engrossed. Let me tell you, he read everything in that paper: news, sports, classified ads, sometimes the comics, then the stock page. Maybe he was genuinely interested beyond my level of comprehension in some far-flung global event. At any rate, what happened next was this. First, I made that whirligig gesture at my temple.

"Don't mind him. He's just a crazy Vietnam Vet."

Well, Laura looked a little shocked.

Fitzgerald didn't say one word.

Little did I know, though. Scarcely did I foresee what I had just done. We paid the restaurant tab, walked out to his Datsun pickup truck, and when we got inside Robert Fitzgerald silently turned the key. Four or five miles out of the Denny's parking lot, he finally spoke. "Usually, I don't do this. But I'm going to make an exception. When I shut off the truck, when I get out and you get out, that's when it starts." Fitzgerald assured me that he was going to kick my ass just as soon as the truck was stopped.

"Oh really?"

"Just be ready. Don't say I didn't warn you."

"What are we fighting for?"

"For what you said."

"Hey, I was only kidding."

But that didn't seem to matter. What was done was done.

We rode on in silence for another mile or so. I didn't know what to say. Or not to say. Or think. But the look on Robert Fitzgerald's face communicated the fact that he was serious.

Still, I couldn't keep myself from grinning. Part of me thought it was funny, something Fitzgerald noticed, as well. But he did not grin back. Part of me was amused and part of me had had it with all of his bullshit. One thing was for sure, I was bigger than him and fairly assured of my fighting ability. Like I said before, I'd played wide-receiver and corner-back in high school, and one of the proudest moments when I turned eighteen was when my ex-Marine tough guy father came out to the bench press we had set up in our garage. I knew I was strong. And I was not scared. This old-ass, nearly forty-year-old, book-loving sailboat freak didn't have a chance.

So we arrived at the job site. We both got out of his truck. It was about fifteen till seven. Still a little foggy. Only a few of the other workers had arrived.

"You ready?" Robert Fitzgerald asked.

"This is stupid," I told him. "Really stupid."

My first punch was only supposed to be a joke. Partly to show him my stance, you know. Merely one punch into the side of his arm, hard enough, but not as hard as I might really hit. Well, Fitzgerald took the shot on his shoulder, then he stepped back unsurprised, both hands loosely at his side. Then he quickly slapped me, *crrracccckkkk*. Right across the face. It made an awful sound. One of the Ruiz brothers said "ouch," gritted his teeth and winced. I looked over and saw him and the others smirking. Then I really got riled-up. How embarrassing. It was like the whole world was watching.

Now this fight was real. The stinging sensation was horrible, really painful. I don't know about you, but I'd rather be hit almost anywhere than be slapped across the face. So I rushed him. But as I approached, Robert Fitzgerald hit me in the stomach, then did something behind my knees so that I tripped and fell down. I rolled away and got back on my feet, feeling totally incredulous that the morning had gone from a three-egg omelet at Denny's, to a truck ride, and suddenly now to this. Oh, how I was wishing that I'd not had so many beers the night before. After the first rush tactic did not work out, I was more cautious. This time I reflected before my next charge. I pulled up short. Got in a couple of jabs. It seemed to be the constant little efforts, determined consistency, that worked best. Once Fitzgerald hit me in the nose as I was cutting loose with the really heavy firepower, this big-assed haymaker which didn't land. Still, the haymaker seemed to annoy him. Next thing I knew, he'd grabbed me by the balls and simultaneously by the Adam's apple of my throat.

After all, a fight's a fight. Well, I wriggled loose. But on it went. Maybe six or seven minutes. An eternity, I assure you. Finally, there was some wrestling. That was my only hope.

Those Hollywood movie fights are one-punch deals, you see, and they have nothing to do with the real world. Robert Fitzgerald was so fast. I realized that I'd have to sheerly overpower him to win. But once again, my strategy did not pan out. That hangover. All that lactic acid. Whatever. Of course, these are only excuses. Still, I don't know if I've ever been so bone-tired, my muscles so utterly full of fatigue. Perhaps I got in a couple more shots here and there. But a lot of it is quite blurry—except for that mud puddle. There was this big mud puddle Robert Fitzgerald wrestled my face into, let me take a sip from, then more or less drowned me in toward the end. I'd hit him hard a couple of times, even had him in a headlock once. He just would not quit. Suffice to say, Fitzgerald was a whole lot smaller. Quite a bit more diminutive. But utterly intent.

He had warned me fair and square, though. Later on, Fitzgerald would tell me how he'd done this "just to psyche me out," how he didn't really know what would happen because one never knows anything 100% for certain. But he definitely told me beforehand. He explained that he was going to get me. Robert Fitzgerald told me he was going to kick my ass, and that's precisely what he did.

IV.

During the next week, we didn't talk much. Needless to say, we didn't meet for breakfast at Denny's. No pancakes, no bacon, no eggs. No French toast or honey cured ham. To tell the truth, I still shun the very sight of Denver omelets unto this day. For several days I was sore and recuperating. So was Robert Fitzgerald, as he would later confess. That's the thing about any fight. Any fight that's real. Everybody ultimately gets hurt in one way or another. At any rate, we took a break from each other's company. We avoided even saying hello, refrained from speaking around the construction site. But the next Friday afternoon, just before quitting time at five o'clock—we had nine hour shifts—Robert Fitzgerald came over to where I was using a caulk gun on a window seal. He wanted to ask me to help him do something. Boy, what gall. He must have been dreaming.

"I need a favor."

"You need a favor?"

"What are you doing after work?" Fitzgerald asked. "Got any plans?"

"I don't know. That depends."

Fifteen minutes later, he was standing beside his truck.

"Hop in. This won't take long."

So I figured—hell, why not?

First, we drove toward the Ventura marina. He took me to this warehouse-like area where supposedly he was building this supposedly wonderful boat. And it was true. There was the Chó-Fú-Sá. Apparently, Fitzgerald had constructed one other sailboat from scratch before, designed it, built it, put on his own fiberglass with a high glass-to-resin ratio, sailed it to the Hawaiian Islands, then roamed the Pacific Ocean for a couple of years. He had lived entirely on the profit he made from selling that first boat. Next, he tried to start an import-export business based in Thailand, but the business did not pan out. What I saw before me now didn't particularly thrill me. Robert Fitzgerald's current sailboat-in-progress was sitting on some fifty-five gallon drums with angled wood wedges stacked on top of the drums against the hull. A thick sheet of drab olive canvas covered the companionway, the stairs leading down into the cabin. Fitzgerald pointed out a thing or two. Didn't make a fuss. He told me that he'd been working on it for about eleven months. Almost a year.

Next, he showed me the wooden toolbox where he currently slept. The box looked plenty roomy for a guy his size, someone accustomed to sleeping in a V-shaped berth. But the thought crossed my mind that it was a bit too much like a coffin. I mean, would you do it? Sleep for as many nights as he'd been sleeping that way? Inside that cramped wooden box? But Fitzgerald was building and living his dream. His philosophy was as follows: sail or go bust. He was willing to suffer a little privation. Besides, he had access to a shower at the boat yard, so he wasn't dirty or living in squalor. Fitzgerald's was an ends-justifies-the-means existence. Before he'd come up with the toolbox idea, he'd slept outdoors from time to time in McGrath State Park south of the Santa Clara River. Then he'd rented out Prosser's Day Old Bread Store since the rent was fairly cheap. But not as cheap, not as free, as this boatyard toolbox. This way all his money could go into the Chó-Fú-Sá.

Quite frankly, the whole hand-built sailboat idea didn't impress me. Given the still-embarrassing, half-public comeuppance Fitzgerald had given me, I wouldn't have been impressed if he'd been working on a rocket to take us both to the moon. Besides, what I'd seen dry-docked was months and months, perhaps even years, away from being done. He'd not used a chopper-gun or a wet-out gun. Fitzgerald had hand laid the fiberglass mat himself. He'd already applied the curatives and lacquers, then had been working on the cabin area for weeks. Whenever he was free. Virtually around the clock. Honestly, I didn't see the allure. Weren't sailboats old-fashioned? Slow and boring? While growing up around Kentucky and Barkley Lakes, I'd had some friends from richer families with ski-boats and Cigarette speedboats. Any fast boat with a motor struck me as fun. With a sailboat, you were always doing things, right? Watching and feeling the wind. Hoisting the ropes and whatnot.

Suddenly, Fitzgerald said he'd be right back.

"Just one sec."

"Okay. Whatever."

He walked to the marina's office.

Fitzgerald said his hellos to a few sea-dog cronies, then he came out-side again, holding a couple of cans of Seven-Up. His mood seemed to have changed, but it wasn't always easy to tell. He handed me a soda as we walked down the dock. A couple of kids were fishing off their par-ent's yacht, a powerboat sixty feet long named "The Epicurean." Robert Fitzgerald nodded at the name, then told me that its owner was an idiot. Some half-talent, horror-movie-making, coke hound from L. A., whose time in the brig was perhaps just around the corner. Too bad for his chil-dren, or maybe not, since their father didn't have good sense. His kids looked like good kids. They were stringy-armed boys with corn-colored hair and a beautiful actress mother, Fitzgerald explained. There was a Mexican woman who lived on the boat and kept it clean. Apparently, she looked after the kids whenever their mom and dad went out party-ing, which was probably what they were doing right now, insofar as their boat wasn't blaring music. I saw that the boys had bags of McDonald hamburgers and french fries and pieces of shrimp on skimpy Zebco rods. They waved big and said, "Hello, Mr. Robert." Then Fitzgerald and I waved back. We walked past their parents' boat with the bone-headed name, then continued walking until we reached the last boat in the farthest slip—a gorgeous sailboat indeed.

By now it was nearly twilight. A lonesome looking heron was stand-ing on a pylon, eyeing the oily film of harbor water, hoping to spy a minnow or a scrap of McDonald french fry in the water. Every now and then, Fitzgerald would take a little sip from his can of Seven-Up.

"Just wanted to talk with you."

"So talk."

"Are you really still mad?"

"Maybe a little." I shrugged. "Just tell me why."

Robert Fitzgerald sighed audibly. "Because of what you said. That wasn't funny at all and you should never say that about anyone who went to Vietnam."

"Okay, all right," I told him. "But why don't you talk more about it? Who knows? I might be interested. You never say a thing about what happened."

"Just let me finish," Fitzgerald said. "Didn't I tell you once that you reminded me of myself? Sure, you said something I didn't like. But that's not the main reason we had the fight. That was something I cooked up. Spur of the moment. Figured it might help save you some time." Then he held out his hand.

"No hard feelings?"

So I nodded and shook.

"Okay by me."

"That's good," Robert Fitzgerald said. "That's the way it ought to be. I didn't know what I was getting into, you know. Besides, what is strength? Let's say I had a sprained ankle, or just happened to have the flu that day. Everything's so relative. Now about that favor. I have to do something tonight and wondered if you might like to help.

"What thing's that?" I asked.

He nodded at the sleek looking boat floating in the water. It was a forty-two foot Swan. Scandinavian-built. Really lovely. The owner was a friend. An orthopedic surgeon. Fitzgerald told me what the sailboat cost, more money than I imagined having for leisure spending in my whole life. The doctor was a good guy. A fairly avid sailor. He and Fitzgerald had this deal. Since the owner was still mid-career and constantly busy, since he couldn't oversee the boat as much as it needed, if Fitzgerald did little maintenance things, then the craft was his to use. "A sailboat needs to be sailed," he explained. "Everything must be kept in working order." He said that he'd helped the doctor once. His steering cable under the helm had snapped, coming into the harbor at full sail on a windy day. Fitzgerald had steered alongside and yelled out instructions, helped the guy install the emergency helm since the cable could not be fixed right away. Lots of other boats had been around, and the surgeon had momentarily lost his composure. Robert Fitzgerald told me this brief story about the Swan sailboat's owner, then put his hand to his mouth.

He said that I'd really popped him one good one, even loosened up a tooth. He seemed to want to make me feel better.

"Waddya say? You interested?"

"In going sailing sometime?"

"How about right now?"

At this point, I confess to a diffident pause. It had been a long day and I hadn't eaten much. Ever since our little tussle, my appetite hadn't been quite the same.

Besides, it was getting dark.

"Golden opportunity," Robert Fitzgerald said. "Only in America. There's food, wine, beer, soda. Everything's already on board."

"Well, I gues so."

"All right. Let's go."

He started toward the boat. Within ten minutes, Fitzgerald had started the inboard engine, allowed it to idle while we untied some ropes. He told me to do this and that. And I did whatever he said. Half-incredulous that we were actually going to do this, forge out into the Pacific Ocean on the cusp of total darkness. Why couldn't we go sailing during daylight? "Isn't this a little dangerous now?" I asked him. But Fitzgerald told me, "Absolutely not. That's one rule every true sailor knows. You never go looking for danger on the ocean, and if it was dangerous we wouldn't go."

He showed me around the sailboat's cabin, turned on all the interior lights, gave me a whirlwind tour. I'd never seen him this happy, or truly in his element. Now it was going on eight-thirty. Almost nine o'clock. Clearly, he wanted to get going and out to sea.

He was having a ball already. There was no moon whatsoever although later on there would be plenty of moonlight to sail by. I did not know this yet. I did not know much of anything. But Fitzgerald taught me some basics right off the bat. Green is for going, red is returning. Left was port, and right was starboard. Think of a bottle of old Spanish wine that you're pouring with your left hand. He said that "starboard" came from some Viking word and that Lief Erickson had brought dung beetles and lice, plus some of his country's language to America. Fitzgerald kept adroitly readying things. Moving calmly and talking unhurriedly. Soon we were unmoored. We backed out of the slip, running on the propeller's force. He said it would be awhile before we actually sailed.

First, we had to clear the harbor area. Then the jetty. Once we had passed the jetty, the water got considerably more agitated and I became even less calm. Pretty soon, though, I felt the first rush of adrenaline, the good kind though. Perhaps the best of all. So this was what it was like being on the Pacific Ocean. I kept losing my balance as the boat rocked. Not Fitzgerald. He was agile as a cat. After running the engine for a while longer, Fitzgerald asked me to hold the wheel, then he began to let out the main sail. Slowly the boat leaned over, tilted slightly. A lovely lilting and soft drop downward. Except all this new movement made me uncomfortable. The waves looked larger than I'd anticipated.

"Hey, could you do something?" Fitzgerald asked me. "The hatch is open. At the front of the boat. Could you go shut it?"

"What do I do?"

"Just go down and close it. Sometimes I leave it open, but the water's a bit too rough."

He pointed down the companionway. So I followed the direction of his finger. All the lights in the galley and cabin were still on. About the time I reached mid-ship, though, the motor stopped running. Fitzgerald had cut the engine. The boat was moving quietly now, sheerly on sail, and the sudden silence was surprising.

The berth area had gotten a little wet already. Shutting that gosh-dern hatch wasn't as easy as it might sound. Every time I reached up, I couldn't maintain my grip; the sailboat kept rising and falling at the far end of the V-berth. The up-and-down action was quite intense. So I hit my head three or four times on the backside of almost every swell. Eventually, I lay down on my back, tried to pull and twist the latch into place. But it kept not sliding into position, Scandinavian design or not. Finally, I started laughing since I was getting bounced around so much.

Then my stomach did a sudden flip—this little uh-oh thing—something I'd never felt before. Very soon, my laughing stopped. In more or less ten seconds, I needed desperately to throw up. There was a tiny lavatory, toilet and shower nearby. Still, I fought the urge. Apparently I stayed below longer than seemed logical, because when I came up deckside, Robert Fitzgerald told me thanks, then immediately asked if I felt all right.

"Not too hot."

"It'll pass. It'll go away," Fitzgerald told me. "Do you want to hold the wheel? Kind of like driving a car. Sometimes that helps."

"Okay. I'll try."

He said he'd check for some Dramamine, then went below. As I began steering, I did feel a little better at first. But not for long. This newly discovered sea-sickness, the thing my stomach was doing, absolutely had to be resolved. So I leaned over the cockpit lockers and grabbed the caprail. Since I'd not eaten in a while, it wasn't too gruesome. Except the dry heaves can be rather unenjoyable. They kept coming for a while, rather robustly, after I'd put the finishing touches on rounds number one and two. Talk about green-around-the-gills. Soon Fitzgerald was back topside. He took over the wheel. Averted his gaze. If he could have stayed below, I believe he would have done so just to be polite. He didn't say anything about my throwing up, not a single syllable, until I apologized and told him that I was sorry.

"Don't worry about it. It'll pass. Try to relax."

But I was not convinced.

Next, I closed my eyes. Laid down on the flat area above the storage lockers. Tried to concentrate. Tried to be still. Very, very still. When I awoke, the moon was up. It was well past midnight. A fat gibbous lunar light, maybe two days from full, beautifully illuminated the black ocean's surface.

"You feeling better?"

"I'm fine."

"Could happen to anybody."

"Have you ever been seasick?"

"Oh yes." Fitzgerald laughed. "You bettcha."

Next, he told me about this typhoon he was in off the coast of Australia. Apparently, the worst storm of his life. He'd miscalculated the time it would take to get into port, so he was having to fight the weather and getting seasick all the while. When the first huge swells started hitting the sailboat, canned vegetables had flown out of the galley cabinets, sounding just like gun shots above the gale's force. The Australian coast guard had found him after the storm died down. The boat had flipped, turtled completely, then bobbed upright. He'd taken on a lot of water but managed to stay afloat.

"That doesn't sound like fun."

"Sure, it was. After it was over."

Once again, Robert Fitzgerald laughed his distinctive hey-what-you-gonna-do, kind of happy laugh. "A little earlier," he started saying. "Back at the marina, you mentioned being interested in Vietnam."

"Absolutely. I am."

"So what do you want to know? "

"I don't know. The truth?"

He looked at me like I was in kindergarten.

"Which one?"

"I don't know. Just tell me what it was like."

So that's when Robert Fitzgerald explained how he'd almost died the first time around. But miraculously did not. He told me about Dak To. He used words and terminology I'd never heard before, names and nicknames of men, hard-to-remember foreign places, which I'd hear about again sporadically for as long as we knew each other. Fitzgerald told me how he'd joined the Army after his father died, how he'd gone on a bender, how he'd felt so hurt and enraged. He explained how he'd stopped going to classes at Dartmouth, then volunteered essentially on a whim. He'd been at Fort Bragg and at Fort Benning in Georgia. First, he'd gone through basic, then volunteered for jump training, partly because he'd always dreamed of flying, dropping weightless, soaring through the clouds. Maybe it was in his boyhood blood. All those formative years sailing with his mother and father in Connecticut. Staring up at the airfoil of the nylon sheets. Marveling at the wind. He said that he'd made a decision. So he stuck to it.

He planned on paratrooper training from the start, because once you were going off to war then you might as well go whole hog. Full speed ahead. That had been his youthful reasoning. So Fitzgerald was trained, then retrained, then retrained once more. He told me he shipped out for Vietnam, but at first they told them it was only to Okinawa.

Still, the soldiers all knew better. They knew where they were eventually going. Apparently, his regiment was one of the elite and a favorite of General William Courage Westmoreland, who considered the 173rd Airborne Division to be his troubleshooters, his problem-solving crackerjacks for whenever all hell broke loose. Then in November of 1967, there was a vicious battle for Hill 875 in the area around Dak To. This was a bad place. The Central Highlands. No one liked the sound of it and with good cause. The second battalion had already gotten shot to pieces earlier in June. Seventy-six dead and forty-three of those were shot directly in the head, which meant the NVA had executed some U. S. soldiers who'd been to Fitzgerald's same jump school if not in the same platoon. It had taken less than twenty-four hours for that June battle to be so terribly and completely lost. Therefore, when the 173rd was ordered yet again to Dak To, many of the soldiers had been demoralized and upset.

"So we go again and what do we find?" Fitzgerald said. "Well, we find squat, nothing at first. Those NVA were spooky. They could skedaddle. While they'd been there for sure, now they sure looked gone. But there were quite a few telltale signs."

Suddenly, Robert Fitzgerald laughed. He promised to show me the boat's telltale tomorrow morning. It was a small piece of cloth tied to the rigging fifteen feet or so above the deck. The Swan had an electronic wind direction indicator on top of the mast. But Fitzgerald said the tell-tale had its advantages. For one thing it rarely malfunctioned.

"Eventually we found the NVA, or they found us. Same difference. We knew they had to be around somewhere higher up, because they had this blue wire running up the mountain, and there were these hewn-out, earthen stairs leading up as well."

On November 19th, the first big firefight started. Fitzgerald said he'd taken communion before going up the hill. He had thought of his mother, done it mostly for her, but also for himself and out of sheer respect for a man named Father Waters, the priest who was there risking his life. "They would bring in the chaplains on Holy Helos. Some of us really liked having them around and called them the Saviors From the Sky. This Father Waters was a very brave, remarkable man. He went where we went. We loved him very much."

During the days leading up to Thanksgiving, the fighting went on and on. Almost half of his platoon in the second battalion were killed or wounded. "We had guys from Idaho, Tennessee, South Dakota, South Carolina, and New Jersey. Here's one thing I'll tell you about Vietnam. We thought air mobility made us damn near invulnerable. But the thing about Dak To was that it complicated things too. So many things just didn't work out in the field like they'd been planned on paper. The helicopters couldn't land because all of the trees had been blown to smithereens. Limbs and stumps were sticking up everywhere from where the F-100 Phantoms had come in with bombs and napalm. After the first couple of days, the fourth bat was called in for backup. We were losing a lot of men. Personally, I had been lucky. I had some blood on my thigh from a Chai-Kom grenade. Just entry wounds through my pants because I'd been far enough away when the thing exploded. But the injuries on the others were often very serious. There was almost nothing we could do. There was little morphine. The choppers would fill up. Then we'd have to unload the wounded. All the while, the pop-pop-popping from AK-47s continued, and the NVA kept climbing up into the trees to get a better angle. Stay above the smoke."

"We couldn't see what we were shooting. No water. Less and less ammo. So we called in the Cowboys again and one of the helicopters dropped a sling-load of goodies right into the hands of the NVA. Those North Vietnamese, we called them rinky-dinks and gooks and slopes. But they had some smart generals running their show. Like their choice of mortars, 82 millimeter, so if they got a stash of our 81 millimeters they could fire them. But our 81s couldn't fire their 82s."

Robert Fitzgerald talked.

And I stayed quiet. To tell the truth, I didn't want to risk much movement. I was still feeling nauseous and fairly weak.

"One day something happened that ripped our hearts out. Most people don't realize just how common friendly fire could be. Bullets were flying everywhere. You couldn't see on the ground, much less from the sky. Sometimes the planes were flying hundreds of miles an hour. So one of our jet pilots made a mistake. He dropped a bomb directly on an officer and triage area. We lost our chaplain in the blast. It was so chaotic. Not being able to see—that was one of the very worst parts. Not knowing for sure what you or they were doing. They just kept shooting. So in came more of our jets dropping close support. When you were stretched out on the ground and those bombs dropped nearby, it would damn near trampoline you off the ground."

"Before it was over, one hundred fifty-eight Americans had been killed. They say that approximately 1300 to 1600 NVA had died, but all that was left was mostly trails of blood. You see, what they'd do is carry away their dead so that after an intense firefight it would look like less of a victory. They fought with their hearts and their heads. Who really knows which side lost what? But you know what? The kicker is this: we gave that mountain right back to them. Two days later, we abandoned Dak To once more. For the second time, we left it there for them to use. It really made no sense. Those Harvard Business School, bean-counting, so-called whiz-kids of McNamera's, they had no idea of the determination we were up against. You want to know about Vietnam—well, there's a whole lot to learn. But I'll tell you this. My personal story all comes down to luck. I was flat out lucky. On day number three, I fell in a trench running with a guy named Zeigler. Suddenly, we found ourselves facing a couple of dazed NVA. So I froze up. Everybody was exhausted to the point of numbness. I was fumbling around to point my gun. Maybe Zeigler shot them. Maybe someone else did. Anyway, I got out of the ditch and started running and falling down the hill. Later on I found out that I'd fractured my arm falling to catch myself. The weight of my falling body was too much for my wrist. Dozens of other scratches, bumps and bruises. That's all. That fractured wrist. The droning terror, though. What the blown-up trees looked like. I can't begin to describe it. But what it must have been like if you were hit bad. Nothing to do but wait for choppers, and they kept getting fired at and a couple of them went down. We fought, then we recovered. They fought us, and we called in close support. Once the fourth battalion arrived, we charged the hill again, and finally got up top November 24th."

Robert Fitzgerald paused, looked at the compass. Adjusted the wheel.

"So you won that battle?"

"Uh-uh. No way." Fitzgerald shook his head.

"Nobody won. That's for sure. On Thanksgiving, they gave us this turkey dinner, brought in this windbag officer without a scratch. High and tight Airborne haircut. Chiseled jaw. Firm gut. He was there to gloriously and healthily preside over the so-called ceremony of the boots. They lined up these standard-issue, empty boots side-by-side in honor of all the men we lost. 'Dear God,' this guy starts saying, 'Let us remember that death is the gateway to heaven.' Well, that part didn't sit with some of the guys. That officer who gave the speech looked over at me once or twice, looked at us all, and I hope he never forgets my face."

His story seemed over. A gorgeous, quasi-silence pervaded. But I have to admit that the human dimension, the space within the silence, was slightly uncomfortable. The prow of the Swan kept slapping the ocean and vice-versa, only the sound of fiberglass on the undulating eggplant black waves. Fitzgerald hadn't made a major change to the sail or rudder for some time. Soon I would find out that he was heading for the Channel Islands, a little junket trip he'd sometimes take on his own.

"I don't know what to say."

"Nothing to be said."

"Anyway, thanks for telling me."

"Hey, you hungry?"

He posed the question quickly, but with friendly nonchalance. Quite naturally. This was his style, Fitzgerald's way, something I would often see him do in the future, deftly veer away from any overt display of gratitude or emotion.

"Sure, I'm starved."

Then for some reason, I amended what I had just said.

"Yeah, I could eat."

"Me too," he said.

Next, Fitzgerald secured the wheel with a piece of rope, disdaining the Swan's automatic steering capacity. We went down the companionway stairs into the galley. There were a table and chairs, forks and knives and plates. Very nice indeed. Fitzgerald and I had tuna fish sandwiches, potato chips, two beers a piece. By now, over sixteen hours had passed since I'd eaten anything substantial. My nausea had been replaced by a keening empty stomach, a sick-then-famished completely improbable hunger, something which years later my wife Grace would experience while expecting our first child.

After we'd finished eating the sandwiches, we went back on deck. He asked if I had plans for Saturday night, because, if not, then we could stay out another whole day. Get back early Sunday morning. Fitzgerald explained his itinerary. He thought we'd head to the northern tip of the Channel Islands, a place called Scorpion Anchorage off Santa Cruz Island.

"Sounds fine to me. I'm along for the ride"

"Why did you come to California?" Fitzgerald asked me.

"Just kind of wandered."

"So what do you think of it?"

I told him about waiting tables in Los Angeles. My friend Frank Corona and his pretty girlfriend. About getting fired for giving away desserts. Told him that I liked L.A all right, but I didn't think I could live there all my life. Afterwards, I explained about some of the good movies I'd seen with Stephanie. Then Fitzgerald told me about a film by Kurosawa he'd seen once. He couldn't remember the title but said it was set in Siberia. He said I had to see it. That I'd really like the scene where this ginseng root hunter saves the life of the Russian captain during a snowstorm by collecting dry grass and piling it up on the half-frozen Russian to make a grass igloo over him. And thus the Russian captain survives. That scene really impressed Fitzgerald. He liked it a lot.

The sailboat moved on. Toward Asia.

Glistening dark water. Ribbons of moonlight.

Silence except for the wind and waves.

Soon, we talked some more. In particular, the story of Robert Fitzgerald's ex-wife still intrigues me. After returning from Vietnam, he decided to leave the United States awhile because he couldn't stay and couldn't tolerate it. Soon the increasingly heated protests began, all of the post-Tet Offensive and all the post-My Lai press. Certain images were a constant torment. So in 1969, Fitzgerald decided to hump it the hell away from the USA, put on a backpack during the summer of love, then travel through parts of the world he'd never got to see. Anyway, he met and married this Italian woman. He talked about her a bit, and I could see right off that theirs had been a bone-deep passion. Her name itself was gorgeous. Patricia. He pronounced her name with a hard second syllable, then a soft, sibilant "C." Her roots were Sicilian. But they met in Naples. Her father ran this chain of fruit stands. While backpacking through Italy, Robert Fitzgerald had stopped for directions, then he considerately bought a peach. Next, he bought a cellophane bag full of Italian plums. "She handed them over and looked me in the eye," Fitzgerald told me. "Straight in both irises. And that was all she wrote." He laughed again. At the time he'd been twenty-two years old. Not very long out of his tour in Vietnam. Luckily, Patricia spoke English in addition to two other languages, plus her father's island's dialect. For the next week and a half, she and Robert Fitzgerald talked a lot. She was bright, affectionate and, just like him, interested in everything. Her occasional odd phrasings, her quasi-British continental enunciations, were a cause for some light-hearted ribbing. But her accent was less of an impediment than a source of fascination. Another allure. They fell in love quite fast, then for a while their love held on tenaciously.

Some cultural differences did crop up. There were the complications occasioned by her tough-to-deal-with Sicilian father. He was a straight-forward enough guy. A wonderful businessman. Still, the less he knew the better. Her father was an old country patriarch of patriarchs who once called Patricia into the living room to hand him the TV remote, which was sitting on top of the television set. He was simply in his chair and wanted to watch the evening news. At first, Robert and his future wife saw each other secretly. Her father didn't know all the ins and outs. But there was something else—something he and Patricia's father shared. Her father was a war veteran, as well. A POW survivor of World War II.

Her father had fought for the Italian forces. But he was imprisoned because of an ironic twist of fate. In early 1941, he joined the army with several others from his childhood village, Campo Felice di Roccella, located between Palermo and Cefalu, then their battalion was stationed in Greece, sided with Mussolini and the Axis powers. Suddenly, the tables looked like they might turn, though, and Patricia's father's life was instantly transformed—all because his commander's name was General Pietro Badoglio, a leader who decided to switch sides against Hitler. General Badoglio refused to be complicit with what he saw going on in Greece. The balance of power had changed. He was going to rebel and the Nazis suspected as much. Some of the men fighting directly under General Badoglio were detained and held suspect for betrayal. Off to Baden-Baden in a train for Patricia's father and for many other young Italian soldiers from his hometown. Several of her father's closest friends were allowed to starve, freeze, or die of pneumonia. The cold was a killer in Southwest Germany during the winter of 1943. Yet her father managed to survive. On the spur of a the moment, he had told a lie, and this falsehood saved him. He told the camp directors that he was an electrician, received an inside work detail, and therefore did not freeze. For a while, her father pulled it off without a hitch. Although once he was almost shot in the back of the head after some electrical sparks starting flying for the third or fourth time. A guard witnessing the sparks accused him of sabotage. Then threatened to shoot him. But more quick explanations were made. Thus, her father made it through the winter alive, through the war, then eventually back to Rome and Naples (such a harrowing rattling home it must have been, the arrival sounding just like the prior departure and prior approach of a freezing doom). Apparently, he looked like a skeleton when he stepped off that train.

Once Patricia's family had shown Fitzgerald a single, well-preserved photo. He said the guy had looked dead. Twenty-six years old. Tubercular, hollow-eyed, half-starved. But he'd started his very first fruit stand, then built his wholesale business up from that. Fitzgerald told me that he'd liked Patricia's father quite a bit. Once he'd seen him dance a beautiful tango with Patricia's mother, a determined, set-jaw and serious, lovely human thing to behold. That husband-and-wife dance had brought water to his eyes. Whenever the old man left the mainland every August for a month in Sicily with his whole family, Nino would talk to the other men and women who worked the land, buy cheese from them and olives, bartering with what he'd grown himself. He had built a house in Campo Felice di Roccella which was very beautiful, kept a little plot of blood oranges and pomodoros, even made his own wine.

"So what happened to you and Patricia?"

Robert Fitzgerald did not smile.

"Back in those days, I was a bit more intransigent. Much more mule-headed than I am now. Than I'm in the process of becoming."

"Like me, huh?"

"Didn't say that," he replied. "All I said was that you reminded me of myself." He smiled his smile. "You know, it's not funny. What happened to us was fairly simple. I was just out of Vietnam."

Fitzgerald paused.

Waited for this to sink in.

"So we got married. But I had this great idea for a honeymoon. We were going to walk the length of Italy together. South to North. So that's what we started to do. Patricia seemed to like it. Then one day she wanted to quit. I guess you could say she gave me an ultimatum. So I gave her one right back."

"You didn't stop?"

"That's right. We got into a screaming match. Then I finished what I'd started. She went back to her family, and they were not very pleased. When the trip was over, I returned to Naples and tried to talk with Patricia. Guess you could say that we never managed to patch things back up."

. . . .

The next day at sea was gorgeous. May 20th. My sister's birthday. Just by coincidence. The weather was uncommonly warm, quite sunny, about as placid as it gets on the Pacific Ocean. We anchored off the northern edge of Channel Islands National Park, the northwest side of Santa Cruz Island. The Swan's owner also had a couple rods and reels. Fitzgerald caught some kind of small fish, then gutted it, then used the guts to catch some more. We were surrounded by lots of pelicans and gulls. Plus, we saw three sea otters swimming in the kelp beds. There were some five to six foot blue sharks. Didn't spot any pilot whales, or gray whales, but Fitzgerald assured me they could be seen in the area. He said there were plenty of mating sea elephants on San Miguel, the Channel Island farthest away from the mainland. Some other day we'd go over and take a peek.

The ocean was very cold, but around noon we took a quick dive in, then climbed back on the boat. We both took a nap late in the afternoon. Around twilight we fished for a couple more hours and I caught a nice-sized cabrillo. Seven or eight pounds. Grilled that up with lemon. Very tasty indeed. The orthopedic surgeon had a little Weber grill on his sailboat and some mesquite charcoal to do the thing just right

By the time we started home Saturday it was quickly growing dark once more. So it would be another night crossing. Heck, why not, I thought. This guy certainly knows his stuff. We waited as long as possible, kept putting off heading back to shore. We fished a little more. Quickly swam again. Didn't pull up the anchor till the sky overhead was midnight-blue, and the water beneath us returned to obsidian. Mirrorlike. Shimmering yet black. Finally, Fitzgerald got behind the wheel and started back to the coast. The wind was light, so it took a while. Around three in the morning, the lights off the coast were still clearly visible. Fitzgerald told me he was getting sleepy. Would I mind being captain while he rested down below?

"No problem," I told him. "I'll try."

So Robert Fitzgerald goes below, and I start sailing for the first time. I'd been sick before. Desperately grasping at the helm. Now I am alone. Feeling much better. There are all these gadgets in front of the wheel, and I don't understand a lot of the stuff around me. But I can tell the speed. The boat's doing four and a-half knots. The compass heading to the Ventura marina is about twenty-eight or thirty degrees magnetic.

That's not so hard, staying on the magnetic reading, just as long as you don't have to tack. Just as long as the wind stays roughly the same. Once again, this wisp-from-full moon comes out, lighting up the ocean's surface. My job basically involves watching out for other boats, not heading back out to the open sea.

Well, pretty soon, I'm starting to really like this borrowed sailboat for a weekend. When I first came to California, I'd never eaten a fresh artichoke or an avocado. Never had ceviche or prosciutto either, which I tried in this Westwood Italian restaurant once with honey-dew melon for the very first time. Didn't think I'd like melon with that raw-looking meat. It wasn't country ham—much less Smithfield ham—a couple of delicacies from the South I love so much and especially on my grandmother's biscuits. But that prosciutto sure is some tasty stuff. Unexpectedly enjoyable, kind of like this sailing trip with Robert Fitzgerald was turning out to be. This guy who has punched me in the mouth, put his hand around my gonads and my throat. Damned near crushed my windpipe. This guy who was asleep below, or who was acting like he's sleeping. He has given me two gifts already.

Now it's very quiet on the sailboat's deck.

No one else is around. Just me.

Suddenly the wind picks up. The sailboat leans over a little to the right—then a little farther to the right. Pretty soon it's clear from the sensation of movement alone that the boat is going faster and faster. So I look down at the speedometer, or whatever it is called, and the thing reads six point two. This is something, I'm thinking. Really something. I'm feeling very lucky, and I don't know what else, about this man-made object and all the stories I had just been told. The whole experience, know what I mean? Haven't you seen a particularly beautiful canyon or waterfall? Or a view from some mountaintop? It was just drop-dead gorgeous. Being on that boat. Heading toward Ventura. And before long, there was this slow-but-quick unfolding of light, this multi-colored sunrise was happening right before my eyes. The eastern sky gradually started to brighten: first purple, then violet, then rose, then tangerine. Boy oh boy. Sometimes this life on earth. Sometimes it sure is sweet.

V.

A few weeks later, I found myself having Sunday brunch at a little place called The Three Rose Café. The whole day before, Fitzgerald and I had worked on the ranch-style adobe we were currently building, racked up some overtime, earned some extra cash. It had been sweltering, miserable stucco work. We deserved a drink and a good meal that didn't consist of ham, cheese, Frisch's squeeze-bottle mustard, potato chips, and soft drinks. Of course, a good meal is what we received. Plus, another conversation I remember to this day. David Stillman and his girlfriend Jill ran the place, a little A-frame house with light-blonde pine paneling and a redwood deck overlooking the ocean. He had this make-shift bar, stocked with imported beers, Dos Equis, Jamaican Red Stripes, and Kaliks from the Bahamas. This was the first time I'd spent time with Fitzgerald while he was around another Vietnam vet. They stick togeth-er. There's no word to describe the bond. Fraternity or club doesn't do the camaraderie sufficient justice. Seeing any of your old buddies is wonderful. A beer is a beer. A backslap a backslap. But there are pro-fundities that other pairs of friends cannot imagine, unwooden interiors, brotherhood depths they've never had to plumb.

"Ready for your hots?" David Stillman asked, just as soon we walked through the door. He extended his suntanned hand, the size of a first baseman's mitt, long slender fingers which matched his six-foot-four frame.

"You bet." Fitzgerald smiled. He shook this hip-looking veteran shake. "Hots means hot food," he told me. "Anything not C-rations."

"The so-called holidays," David Stillman said.

He turned and looked directly at me and straight through me, like I was made from plexiglas, one of the bubbles on the Loach helicopters his cousin used to fly in the A Shau valley.

As for himself, David Stillman had been in the Marine Corps. Nearly one full tour. He looked like a true *ursus horribilis* of a male, espe-cially if and whenever he decided to be tough. He had a clean-shaven face, and for some reason reminded me of my father. Blood-ties. Little flashes of memory. Family resemblances, patterns of recollection and fleeting connections are everywhere. Yes, it was true. Something in David Stillman's eyes reminded me of my old man.

Only a few other customers were at The Three Rose Café that day. A waif-thin blonde with a Chinese dragon tattoo and an overweight boyfriend who looked zonked on something. Also, a party of four women sitting out on the wooden deck, middle-aged California businesswomen, judging from the two briefcases and their conservative pantsuits. Over by an upright piano, three long-haired surfers sat drinking Kliks, periodically trying to catch the owner's attention. Finally one of them came over and chatted *sotto voce* over Stillman's left shoulder as he stood cooking at the stove. David Stillman faintly nodded and shook the kid's cupped proffered hand. Then he said, "Okie-dokie. Sounds good to me." I'd heard a little bit about his unconventional way of doing business. His restaurant didn't have menus, or listed prices on a chalkboard. He served whomever he wanted and refused to serve anyone he simply did not like. To say that The Three Rose Café was kind of unconventional was like saying Miles Davis's *Kind of Blue* was kind of groundbreaking. The atmosphere and melody of the place was constantly shifting, a bit monochromatic, consistent in its subject matter, but thrilling all the same.

He'd decorated the place with wooden shrines and joss sticks, then placed some Vietnam war photographs conspicuously on the wall. There were two framed photos taken in Tay Ninh, dated November 27th, 1969, then a caption beneath the photos said: THE GARDEN OF CHARLES. The first photo showed a large python lounging in some boonie leaves, wrist thick jungle saplings, and reddish-brown cordillera dirt. The python was maybe twelve or thirteen feet long, but with this absolutely enormous bulge directly in its middle.

Now, if you're a snake that big, and there's a war going on, there's a lot of dead tender meat lying around to swallow. This guy from David Stillman's Gulf of Mexico days, some purple-heart recipient from Douglas, Georgia, had taken both pictures. His unit hadn't even been able to shoot the snake since they were in heavy NVA territory. So several of them jumped it, then cut-off its head. Someone in this guy's platoon had suggested these two before-and-after photographs because they had to see if there was maybe a dog tag, perhaps a South Vietnamese scout, or a small American soldier inside. So they cut it open, as the second photograph makes quite clear, only to find a South Asian red deer. A four-point buck. Antlers intact. Amazing that the snake could swallow and digest those. But that's precisely what the snake had tried to do. The pictures summed up certain symbolic and certain straightforward truths; you didn't know anything at all about the Vietnam war, not until you looked inside and exposed its guts.

Apparently, David Stillman was a *strack* warrior, someone who had fifty-plus kills, and in the right mood or the wrong mood, he would give you all the details you wanted. Or didn't. After standing at the stove a while longer, he put the three palmed joints the surfer had given him for payment beside his chrome chef's stove. He looked over at Robert Fitzgerald, then asked us both what we'd like to drink.

"Two beers."

"Okay. Jill's upstairs. She'll be right down."

He produced a couple of cold Bass ales from a mini fridge, then set them on the thickly polyurethaned bar. No mugs. No coasters.

He tilted his head again toward the four women on the patio.

"I can't fucking wait till those real estate bitches leave," David Stillman told us. "They're giving me bad vibes."

"Hey, they're good-looking."

Evidently, I should not have spoken.

David Stillman stared at me again. He furrowed his brow to put the FNG in his place.

Luckily, Fitzgerald interceded. He did the introductions. "This guy's from Kentucky. He works with me. I've been telling him the whole drive up here that you're the best damned cook on the West coast."

"Where in Kentucky?"

So I told him.

"Yeah, yeah, yeah," David Stillman said. "I've been through there once or twice. Going to Chicago." His tone was world-weary and bored. Unmenacing for the moment.

"That's what he says," I said. "That your food's great. I'll eat anything except olives and pimentos."

Another mistake.

"You don't like *olives?*" David Stillman wrinkled his brow again, like all of his relatives were Mediterranean olive growers and pimento connoisseurs. Like he detected a natural gas leak, or saw something metaphysically lost in what I'd just said.

"You first then," David Stillman told Fitzgerald.

He whipped up four eggs, added a splash of half and half. Oh, my goodness, another omelet. I didn't want any part of that. All of Stillman's cookware was neatly hanging from S-shaped hooks, aligned on a polished chrome semi-circle over the stove. This was a culinary one-man show. In less than five minutes, David Stillman presented Fitzgerald with a gigantic crabmeat, avocado and tomato wonder, a salad-like mixture on the side, walnuts and bananas mixed together with a fresh vinaigrette. Next, he looked at me and his olive-green eyes flashed like a neon-sign, saying: Who the fuck are you? And why are you in my restaurant? How dare you say I can't cook with pimentos or whatever the hell else I might possibly desire.

No kidding, it was intimidating. I just can't explain it any other way. This dude was *vehement.*

Soon Jill appeared on the staircase, though, breaking the tension which for me was absolutely real. She went out on the patio to let the four businesswomen pay; they might have been real estate agents, accountants or lawyers, who knows? But what they'd certainly come for was David Stillman's wonderful food, as I was about to discover myself. His secret was no secret. *Reinheitsgebot* I believe the Germans call it. He just used the best, the freshest ingredients he could possibly find. Only vegetables and fruits in season. Locals in the know understood that Tuesdays, Wednesdays, and especially Saturday nights were David Stillman's biggest nights of all. That's when he pulled out the stops: paella fiestas, bouillabaisse soirées, Apalachicola oyster deep-fries featuring an oyster shipment he had specially flown in from the Gulf of Mexico during the pertinent, consecutive eight months containing the letter "R." Evidently the bigger, fatter West coast oysters weren't ever up to snuff. And this oyster detail was telling. While Robert Fitzgerald knew the Pacific Ocean and the Atlantic around Stonington, Connecticut, his Vietnam Vet buddy had spent more time on the sunshine state's two very different coasts. Apparently, Stillman had sailed once with Jimmy Buffet. Sailed to the Grenadines. Sailed to Recife in Northern Brazil, which is where he met his girlfriend or wife, and I never did find out which one until later.

"You like steak, Paducah?"

"Love it," I replied.

"Your daddy work for the government?"

"He did once."

"Oh yeah?"

David Stillman shot me that eye once more.

"He was in the Marines a while."

"Uh-huh."

That was all.

We had just conversed.

Then once again, David Stillman began to cook. Soon Jill came in from the patio and put some money into the cash register. Five-six, dark-brown eyes. Natural blonde hair the color of our Bass ales. A little flesh on her upper arms that was soft-looking yet unyielding as she moved gracefully around the bar and restaurant. Very capable. Strong looking. Jill was wearing a tangerine sarong and her red-rimmed eyes looked tired. She set out two more cold beers and said hello to Robert Fitzgerald, hugging him tightly, then kissing him French-style. First one cheek, then the other. She explained that David had almost refused to cook for the four women outside, who had just paid and left. But she'd finally talked him into it.

"Gotta make a buck," Jill said.

"However," David told her, "I repeat." He spread out the next five words with maybe a second pause between each one.

"They...did...not...look...cool."

"Who cares?" Jill said.

In response David only shrugged at first. He flipped my filet mignon, slowly looked back at Jill, then said, "I do."

"Oh, shut up," Jill told him. "Give it a rest." She waved off this comment like it was a particularly annoying mosquito.

David Stillman grinned, then focused on the cooking task at hand. He had been searing the steak in teriyaki sauce. He poached a couple of eggs and produced some fresh Hollandaise from the mini-fridge. Once again, very quickly, as with the crabmeat omelet Fitzgerald had nearly reduced to nothing—six or seven minutes from the time he first touched the skillet—David Stillman served me my unordered, unrequested meal. Filet mignon medium rare, eggs benedict, broiled Roma tomatoes, and fresh parmesan cheese on sourdough toast.

"That look okay?" he asked.

"Better than okay."

Then I dug in.

"Lock the door, babe," David Stillman said. "That's it."

"We're closed?" Jill asked.

"Ab-so-fucking-lutely."

So the afternoon at The Three Rose Café began in earnest. After Jill received an answer to close up shop, she smiled and started gorgeously toward the entrance. A graceful samba of orange cloth. Bare ankles and calves. A really lovely woman, simply because of the way she walked and carried herself.

David Stillman took a step toward the sink. Everything was tightly organized, handy and tidy, just like in a galley. He ran some hot water in the recently used skillet. Then using a wooden match, he lit one of the joints the surfer had given him. He smoked the whole thing calmly and luxuriously, like it was a cigarette, never offering it over to a single one of us. The front door was now secured. Robert Fitzgerald nursed his beer. I ate my steak and eggs benedict, one of the better meals I'd tasted in a while. Don't ask me why. It looked just like an ordinary steak and eggs while Stillman cooked and when he put it on my plate. But hidden skills had been at work. Fresh ingredients, alchemy, devil worship.

Don't ask me. Something extra was simply *there*. Like how some guys have got a twenty-foot jumper and some don't. Like how some guys like David Stillman had apparently been very good over in Vietnam.

Yes, the war was going to be our topic eventually.

And I felt privileged to hear whatever I was going to hear.

Over the next four hours, I listened to things I'll always recall in their minuscule particulars: combat stories, sailing stories, blood and guts at Quang Tri and Dak To, tales of sublime but dangerous storms at sea. These two men seemed to want to get certain details of each other's lives straight. They were in different branches of the service, and their tours in Vietnam hadn't overlapped. But both of them had seen it. Also, they loved to sail. Once again, I heard a paired-down tale of Fitzgerald's nearest death experience a hundred and fifty miles northeast of the Great Barrier Reef. Next, how he'd wandered around the South Pacific, started that export business in Bangkok. For a while he studied at Brooks Art Institute on the GI bill. Next, he'd been an aircraft mechanic in El Segundo, California, worked on the Rockwell International tooling machines for the B-1 bomber. This part of his life was new to me. He'd apparently operated the tooling machines to construct the B-1's wing sections, designed to expand and contract, like the flaps on a single lens reflex camera. Like the petals of a flower opening with the sun, then closing at dark. Fitzgerald explained it like he was discussing last weekend's bowling score. He said the benefits were great. But it was horribly monotonous. So he had quit that job and moved to Ventura.

Well, I was glued. Amazed again. How could you do everything Robert Fitzgerald had done and still only be thirty-six, thirty-seven years old? And now he was slowly constructing the Chó-Fú-Sá, building yet another dream piece by piece.

Maybe his pared down lifestyle, that frugal sleeping arrangement and that old truck held part of the secret. These two guys, they'd experienced so much. It was hard to believe. Unless you heard them talk. They'd not only been to Vietnam, they seemingly had been most everywhere else—Europe, Brazil, New Zealand, Australia.

Much to my surprise, David Stillman was from a small town named Monticello, located in Northern Florida near Tallahassee. Heck, I thought that was the name of Thomas Jefferson's home. Didn't know there was a town named that as well. His mother and father had taught chemistry and biology at Florida State University. He liked the region where he'd grown up, and he'd spent most of his boyhood summers on Saint George Island. He was loyal to the area's world-class oysters and still loved the Emerald Coast.

Once he met Jill in Recife, though, he decided to move in with her. She already owned the little A-frame house just off Carpinteria Beach and PCH. So they started the restaurant together, thus The Three Rose Café was born. It was the kind of place you had to look for. From the outside it looked like someone's home, but David Stillman acted like it was his castle. The stories of him refusing to serve customers were absolutely true. This was his place, his rules, his gig, his goof, which included using slightly varying prices he determined on the spot, then told Jill, then she told you. Mostly, it was fair and square—unless you acted like one. Then the price increased somewhat. Stillman just kind of sized you up, then you paid after you had eaten. Sounds incredible, but that's precisely the way it worked. So if it hadn't been for Fitzgerald, my olive and pimento comment could have spelled disaster. If David Stillman ever cast his gaze your way, sized you up for a silver spoon gagged brat, or anything else he didn't like (several loud and posturing surfers didn't get to stay), if he thought you were spoiled-rotten or superfinicky (no man accustomed to C-rats wanted to hear bellyaching about his top-notch food), then you were history. You simply were not served. And woe be unto any would-be tough guy if David Stillman yelled *didi mau*, which meant hit the road in Vietnamese, or if you looked suddenly uptight because you smelled something funny coming from his kitchen. Suffice to say, if you were asked to leave, then you had better smile and scoot.

"It's really very simple," David Stillman explained. "I don't want to be fucked with by anyone. Not anyone, not once. Not ever again in my whole life."

Robert Fitzgerald nodded.

Then he started laughing.

I thought it best if I did not.

"I just want to run my business," David Stillman told me. "Whatever way I want to run it. If anyone doesn't like it—hey that's okay. They can hang out and eat anywhere else they want."

Like me, Jill opted to listen and absorb. Her sarong hung long, nearly to her brown ankles. She sat relaxed, slightly slumped down on an unvarnished Adirondack chair. She seemed to have heard the material before. This was clearly a discussion, a series of themes related to war, sailing and whatnot, which we couldn't handily compete with or add to that much. Once I saw her wink at David Stillman and smile appreciatively, then I saw her roll her eyes which told me something too. However, it was obvious and unquestionable that Jill loved him.

"Here's the lowdown," David Stillman explained. "Be nice, be nice, be nice."

He glared at me again. Wanted a response.

"Sounds good."

I wanted to keep my talking to a minimum.

"You bet it's good," David Stillman started saying. "How fucking hard is that to understand? I'm one-hundred percent serious. Be nice! Hurt no one! Leave other people alone! Just let them be! Let them take care of their own onions, and you take care of yours. It's like Rousseau says, how the great moral lesson is to remove oneself from any context whenever one's interests are in conflict with another person's. Of course that isn't always easy, but it's something you can strive for as an ideal. Here's the problem—other people must strive to do the same. Just a little cow, a wife, a boat, and a Swiss chalet. That's all you need."

He began to laugh.

Then we all joined in.

Afterwards came a long story about Stillman's tour in the Quang Tri province. This was clearly one story Jill had heard numerous times. But she remained attentive. For thirty minutes or so, she occupied herself at the cash register and a little desk, and from all the apparent signs Jill was the one who did the bookkeeping, bank-runs, food orders and so forth. She did the practical, business side of things, and David did his six-foot-four, polymorphous artistic stuff behind the stove. This arrangement seemed to work all right. Actually, Jill ingeniously ruled the entrepreneurial roost. Not to mention hearth and home. She was commonsensical, tough, telluric. David Stillman didn't seem to mind and understood what was for his own good.

Looking back now, Jill seems to have been his official C.E.O., grocer, gyroscope, level-headed muse, quotidian playful critic, his business manager, best-friend, ballast and bowsprit combined into one. Together, they did quite well. There was always a waiting list for Friday and Saturday dinner, and judging from the Nakamichi stereo, some of the furniture, and the fact they kept a small Mirage sailboat, their restaurant was a fair success.

Our host had started in on another joint. He offered it around this time. But Fitzgerald stuck to beer. I followed suit. David Stillman claimed he needed it. Especially on the weekends. He said it made him a "much calmer, much better citizen." According to him, it reduced one's testosterone level by nearly thirty percent. Overhearing this part, Jill teased him and suggested he use some of her sister's Vivelle instead. She would get him some estradiol ten millimeter patches he could stick on whenever he wanted or felt the urge. She kidded him some more and he seemed to like it.

Whenever David Stillman got around another veteran, though, Jill seemed to understand that he needed to talk. The military experience in his family was extensive. His uncle, his father's older brother, was a hero in the Battle of the Bulge, a proud soldier in General Patton's army, which made a final, freezing "nuts-to-you" push and resulted in thousands of winter casualties. In addition to his cousin who fought in the

A-Shau valley, David had a twin brother named Harry Stillman, who also served in the military late in 1969. But not in Vietnam. He spent two years stationed in Europe instead, and when the news came of David getting hit in Quang Tri, his twin brother Harry tried convincing his superiors that he wanted to go to Southeast Asia. Screw the exception he'd been given. Screw the five dead Sullivan brothers whose demise at sea had caused the rule designed to save mothers such unnatural grief.

"How did you get wounded?"

David Stillman studied my face.

"Mind if I ask?" I half-apologized as if I'd crossed some line.

But I'd never heard stuff like this before.

"All right," David Stillman said. "Here goes. I'm walking through the grass. Not far from point. This guy named Henderson is actually in the lead. Except I'm taller, much bigger, and you can guess that wasn't an advantage. All of a sudden, there's the sound of AK-47 rapid-fire. Whizzing bullets. I remember seeing the tips, blades of elephant grass flying off. Next thing I know, we're diving down and Henderson's hit in the chest. His pack blows backward toward me. There's another flash up in the trees, then this rocket propelled grenade goes off, lands maybe fifteen yards ahead, and I'm hit in my stomach and legs, my upper chest, and the left side of my face. So there it is. That's the wound."

He stopped for a minute, reached toward the white wicker coffee table, tweezered then relit the second joint. Once again, he smoked quite leisurely.

Jill had taken only a hit or two off the first one. She reached over and had a little more, as David Stillman pulled off his shirt, then showed me his scars.

"To this day what I recall, what I remember mostly, is *afterwards*. During the firefight, I kept thinking how it wasn't dramatic. Everything seemed so ordinary. Nothing whiz-bang. Nothing particularly scary. I'd been in-country for nine months. One moment I'm seeing that flash in the tree, and automatically I'm firing the twenty rounds out of my magazine. Some people say clip, but technically that's not right. Magazines are loaded from the bottom. So I sprayed out my twenty rounds, holding the M-16 at waist level, not taking aim exactly. It's not like you're shooting at a rabbit or a duck. I was just getting the bullets out of my gun, shooting toward the direction of the flash. After Henderson's pack was blown back that way, I realized he had been hit bad. Except I couldn't see anything but his pack. No blood. Not yet. The radio man is right behind me, and all the tips are being blown off the grass. So I'd fired out the magazine, fired everything. Before I could flip it over, that grenade launcher went off."

"Remember, I'm over nine months in. Three months from going home. They tell you when you get there that soldiers get killed right away, in the first couple of months. Either that or they die a couple months before they leave. Those are the statistics. The Nicky New Guys and the I've Got This Down Dumbshits. So I'm hit and bleeding from my chest. I'm thinking I'm one of the statistics. KIA with eleven weeks to go."

"When I first got to Nam, I remember getting out of the plane and thinking, 'This place stinks, it fucking stinks.' Then in the boonies it's all wet. Mildew and nitrates. So it just gets much worse. I'd been in basic for eight weeks, then Camp LeJeune for mortar training, Camp Pendleton for jungle and SERE. Once you were in Vietnam, they shipped soldiers pretty much right into the thick of it. Two or three months in the woods, then they'd bring you back and clean you up. Once in Quang Tri, I had me a little hootch. Pretty nice, too. Even a little refrigerator. But that was just horseshit, all that comfortable stuff we had. Probably hurt more if anything. Vietnam was so fucked up. But we took some of the fucked-up over there with us. I know this guy from North Carolina, this kid who survived Khe Sanh. Get this. He had his first drink there, alcohol mixed with pineapple juice from the can. Those trusty P-38s. Just when you need 'em. Pineapple juice and medicinal alcohol. His first drink at Khe Sanh. Now you tell me that's not some wild-assed shit."

Fitzgerald shook his head in agreement.

David Stillman took a sip of beer.

Me too. It tasted delicious.

"So my captain is dying. Bleeding to death. We're lying in the grass together. He's maybe two feet away. I'm trying like hell just to catch my breath. Maybe thirty or forty minutes go by. The radio guy has called in for WP, so pretty soon the column goes up, and next the AT high charges. Finally, someone came by and found me. They start yelling: 'Corpman up! Corpman up!' Some blood was coming out of my ears and mouth due to the blast. And I had to lie on my left side. So I wouldn't drown. Next, the Navy doc starts cutting off my uniform so he can see what's what. Some guys grab me under my armpits and at my knees, no stretcher, no litter, and we start boogying back to the LZ. Then I recall all of this Q and A. They asked me these questions to see how alert I was. Not very. So they gave me some oxygen. You know that saying, 'Marines don't cry. But they sweat out of their eyes sometimes.' Well, by now I was really hurting. Eventually, they get me to a field hospital. Say whatever you want about Charlie. They were tough as nails. I've read about those water-soaked ditch clinics across the border in Cambodia, places where even the mosquitoes wouldn't bite the NVA because of the sheer stink of their infected wounds.

"So anyway they take me into surgery. The tenth of September. Luckiest day of my life. Later, this guy in the recovery area tells me something. He says that my heart stopped during the procedure. I went into cardiac arrest. My surgeon was left-handed, I found out later, because when he went in my chest he cut around my belly button on the left side.

"Next, I'm there for a while in the field hospital. Then it's off to a hospital ship. Finally, we start for the Philippines, and—dig this—there was engine trouble on the C-130! But we get to the Philippines and we land okay. I'm there for two more weeks. Then after a brief layover in Alaska, it's on to Clark Naval Base and I'm in bed in Charleston, South Carolina for over a month."

This combat talk went on for some time.

But that's the gist of it.

"How did you two meet?" I asked our hosts.

"Well, at first we just sort of flirted," Jill said.

"That's right," David Stillman said. "At first we just sort of flirted. Par for the course. Then we got together on the weekends. It wasn't official. Nowadays we have what you might call an arrangement of 'limited risk' and 'broad commitment.'" He used his long fingers to give emphasis to these last two phrases.

"Ha, ha," Jill said. "Very funny."

But I didn't get the joke.

Fitzgerald seemed to think it was slightly amusing.

"Hey, this is real, honey," David Stillman said. "What's the verdict? Do I strike you as half-hearted? Do I take this relationship for granted? Or do I do my part?"

"You do," Jill told him.

"Which one?"

She thought about it.

"Your part," Jill said. "You definitely do your part."

Before we left The Three Rose Café later that evening, David Stillman pulled Robert Fitzgerald off to the side. "This guy came by the other day. I gave him your name."

"What for?" Fitzgerald asked.

David Stillman grinned.

"Something about a boat repair. Thought you might be interested. Seems he had himself a run-in with Hurricane Oscar last spring. Little island in Fiji."

VI.

After a couple work days went by, Robert Fitzgerald drove up to Santa Barbara to meet the guy in question. His name was Steven Wisham. He was sitting in the harbor having a toddy, chilling and relaxing, having fun in yet another boat. They talked for a couple of hours, discussed the repair costs and travel arrangements. Mr. Wisham showed him some pictures of the grounded sailboat. Fitzgerald told him what he'd need to do the repairs: someone to help with the heavy work, a few special new tools, a couple of plane tickets, and so forth. Mr. Wisham said no problem. He had an emotional connection to the boat. So they made this oral business deal which Fitzgerald requested that he write up. Mr. Wisham agreed with everything. Soon afterwards, Fitzgerald came to talk with me, and he had another so-called favor he wanted to ask.

"I just need someone to help," Robert Fitzgerald told me. "Come on, it'll be a blast. You can do this. You know how to work."

"Not on sailboats, I don't."

"Doesn't matter. You'll do fine. We'll clear away the debris and free-up the craft. Next, we can roll it onto the beach on palm trunks. Just come along and lend a hand. The airline ticket has already been paid for."

"Another chance of a lifetime?"

"Maybe so," Fitzgerald started to say. "So what are you thinking?"

"Just met this woman. Maybe she is, too."

"Could be. You never know."

A couple of gravid minutes passed. For a while, I didn't say yes, and I didn't dare say no. We were hanging out at the warehouse beside the Anchor's Aweigh boat yard. The Chó-Fú-Sá was slowly coming along. Once the job was finished, Fitzgerald's repair contract with Steve Wisham would give him enough money to buy more teak, better instruments, everything he needed to finish the boat the way he wanted.

"I'll ask if she wants to come with us."

"Ask away," Fitzgerald told me.

So I did just that and initially Deborah acted interested. At first, I thought she might actually make the trip. Neither of us had kids. So she could have done it. I desperately wanted her to come along. Wanted her to want to. But Deborah ultimately didn't want to do just that. She had this dog named Rasputin she loved and considered her responsibility. However many times I asked her to change her mind—or maybe join us later—she would not commit. She had this good job. This loyal dog and companion. Her own goals, desires, and dreams. Although I called her after I returned, she'd found someone else. Moved on. That's just sometimes the way it is. People's desires are often décale, staggered and out of synch, just do not match up in a given point in time.

. . . .

Soon we were flying to the South Pacific.

Just Robert Fitzgerald and me. Yet another gift.

Back in March of 1983, Steven Wisham had made a very bad decision. When the storm warning for Hurricane Oscar came through, most everybody in the islands had taken note, heeded the danger, motored their boats up various estuaries, then tied up on the mangrove roots. Most of the sailboat captains on Malololailai sought shelter on the Nandi River, not very far away, on the largest island of Fiji called Viti Levu. But not Steven Wisham. He got a lot of laughs around the harbor telling others about his plan. First, he maneuvers into fairly deep water and puts out three plow anchors. Lots of slack line. He brings plenty of food and more than enough to drink. So he waits a while. Then the gale picks up. The waves get larger. By day three, we're talking twenty-foot, twenty-five foot swells. But Mr. Wisham just cracks open another bottle of Wild Turkey and decides to ride out the hurricane, which is getting progressively worse, which eventually lifts his sailboat up around four a.m. one morning. Then slams it inland. Hurricane Oscar picked that fine forty-six-foot yacht up like it was a maple leaf—with a now-not-so-drunk Mr. Wisham on board—then threw it headlong into a nearby bamboo and pandanu hut tourist resort. A fairly nice hotel, formerly a copra plantation. Months and months had gone by now, and his damaged sailboat still had not been moved.

Considering what Hurricane Oscar did throughout the South Pacific, this guy was lucky to be alive. Didn't get much more than a scratch, though. He waited for the eye, crawled out of the boat, lived and drank on Fiji for a few more months. There was a cartoon of him afterwards, of the Ugly American variety, that ran in a number of local newspapers. Cowboy hat on. Blood shot eyes. This cartoon showed Wisham tying his sailboat up outside the hotel, using a rail where the small island's few horses are tied. Then his caricature bellies up to the bar, pulls twin fifths of whisky from a holster, and both of the whisky bottles are smoking.

Initially, we took an Air France flight to Papeete, Tahiti. This was my début in an airplane first-class and I've never flown first-class since. Money simply wasn't an object. Not to Mr. Wisham. He'd heard Robert Fitzgerald was very good and he wanted his boat fixed properly. So my old friend had been an ingenious bastard. He simply told that hubris-soaked millionaire that he wanted to drop by Tahiti first. That was part of the deal, or the deal was off. Fitzgerald insisted on making this arrangement, then Mr. Wisham would have to pay to get us on a smaller plane which would take us to Fiji's group of islands.

The flight over was interminable. Damn near half way around the globe. Less than twelve-thousand miles, though. Nothing like a flight over to Vietnam at age eighteen.

A few drinks. Wonderful food. Even David Stillman would have been impressed.

And French Polynesia? The South Pacific? Absolutely something to behold. We saw pink sand beaches, black volcanic beaches, climbed horizontal leaning palm trees and swam in turquoise-blue lagoons. Yes, it was all very beautiful, but the people there were the most incredible of all. But they too have had their history, and even Fiji Islanders have had their wars. We met this guy in Fiji who still had the very ax his great-grandfather used to kill a Methodist missionary in 1873. Violence has occurred in their culture as it has occurred everywhere else. Just like in Hawaii, where my Uncle Walter met his wife.

Of course, Hawaii isn't like it used to be. I read somewhere that the first white European child born in Hawaii was a missionary's son, named Levi Sarwell Loomis. The doctor didn't want any of the preacher's money for the delivery, so he received a copy of Milton's *Paradise Lost* instead. And this small detail, it really starts one thinking.

Only a few months ago, there was an uprising in Fiji. More contemporary politics and strife. Just this year, in 2000 AD. These kinds of things go on and on. More prejudice, more stinginess, more bitterness over who has what. Frankly, I doubt that any place is paradise on earth, if one can ever be found, much less devised by man. But while we were there, the Polynesian islands were peaceful. Utterly placid and serene. Maybe it's because they are so far away. Isolated from the rest of us. Certainly the people of Polynesia are special, as that painter Paul Gauguin knew, that artist who fled from his life as a Parisian stockbroker and scrawled three questions—Who are we? What do we want? Where are we going?—on one of his colorful canvases.

We visited Moorea while still in the Tahitian chain, then took a long boat trip out to this atoll where they culture black pearls. These oysters that make the pearls exist no where else. I wrote the name down in a journal so I wouldn't forget. *Pinctada margaritifera.* This oyster is found in no other ocean and if the sea around them is polluted, then the creature inside will not only fail to produce, it will shrivel up and die. The atoll was remote, relatively unvisited and unspoiled. While we were there, Robert Fitzgerald told me some things he liked about Polynesians. He said it was the friendly, yet penetrating way they deal with you, especially in the rural areas out in the countryside, away from bigger cities like Papeete. "They see all people initially the same. They look at you *through* your own eyes. They can see inside."

He told me Polynesians had a great storytelling reputation, a strong oral tradition and a largely perishable attitude toward things, as manifest by their simple homes, which any Pacific Ocean storm worth its salt could easily blow away. The Tahitian people are so beautiful—skinny, fat, medium. White, brown, caramel, and every hue imaginable in-between. Conspicuously gentle. So kind and friendly for the most part, with one exception.Something that nearly happened one night in a dark alley in Papeete.

"I really wish I knew the language," Robert Fitzgerald told me. "No one knows precisely where they came from. But the Tongans and Samoans, all the Polynesians immigrated from somewhere else, thousands and thousands of years ago. Look at their facial bone structure and their dark eyes. Of course, they tend to be less thin as they get older. But don't we all? And that might be the diet, you know. Many experts say Polynesians might have a genetic link to people of Southeast Asia. Sometimes, I really wonder. Perhaps somewhere near Vietnam."

Soon it was on to Fiji.

Our sailboat rescue and repair was on the island Malololailai—or Malolo Lai Lai, like those names of places in Vietnam, you see it spelled a couple of different ways. But if you break the word up it's easier to pronounce. Everything went without a hitch. But it took some time. Robert Fitzgerald really did know what he was doing. We freed up the boat, used the palm tree trunks just as he had planned. We got some local helpers, a couple of hired hands, until the heaviest part was finished. Anyway, we repaired the hull and made the yacht seaworthy. Yet when I say "we" please understand. I mostly just followed directions. Robert Fitzgerald was a better carpenter than I'll ever be, but what he could do with wooden boats was something else entirely.

The boat was an Al Mason designed ketch built in Hong Kong in 1960 out of cypress. Some guy name Pete Kring helped Fitzgerald build the coconut log rollers to skid the boat back to the normal tide line. After temporarily patching the hull with 1/4 inch plywood, Pete and Robert built a cradle of sorts and used a couple of rented D-6 Caterpillars chained in tandem to drag the boat. Here's where my "skill" came in. As the boat progressed, I'd keep moving the coconut trunk logs from under the cradle back into the path of travel toward the ocean. Eventually, we managed to haul the boat maybe two-hundred yards down to the low tide line—as far as the Caterpillar bulldozers could get. When the tide came in, the sailboat floated. Fitzgerald hopped in. He motored the boat, with the bilge running, over to the capital city of Suva, pulled it out using the marine railway. Then he began the painstaking repairs, using rowsawa wood, a long-grain, oily wood available in Fiji. Not unlike teak.

He had worked on lots of different sorts of boats before. But this Al Mason designed ketch was a real booger-bear to fix. Most wooden boats—prior to the late 1970s and "cold molded" construction—were "carvel planked," Fitzgerald explained. That means that the planks were each separated by a one-quarter inch wooden strip. Next a layer of cotton was packed deep into the gap with a chisel and mallet. Then filled with caulking. Once the boat was wet, the strips swelled. No leaks. The idea here was that when the boat was launched it absorbed water. However, if there were no gaps, no give whatsoever, the planks would swell and bust right off the frames.

Well, that's fine and good. But Steven Wisham's very fine sailboat was "strip planked," so the repairing woodworker's skill had to be quite high indeed. The strip plank method uses no gaps and a tightly painted exterior. So water absorption is minimal to none. The planks were smaller than the boards on more typical wooden designs. Each plank was edge-nailed, vertically affixed to its partner, as the hull was assembled. During this entire process, Fitzgerald couldn't remove any single plank since it was held captive by those above and below. So we had to dismantle and repair virtually the entire starboard side. But that's not all. On this particular "strip plank" design, the boards had been milled with a convex bottom edge and a concave top. This made Robert Fitzgerald cuss some. But it impressed him. The concave-convex assembly allowed each plank to lay absolutely flush against the next plank, regardless of the curvature of the hull. In other words, each board nested, spooned into its neighbor very snugly. The hull's design was absolutely fantastic, but it made for a devilishly hard repair job.

Anyway, we repaired the sailboat's hull. Of course, we had to test it afterwards. For three straight months, we worked and worked and played. Then we worked some more. And that forty-six foot sailboat? Once repaired? Definitely another beauty. When Robert Fitzgerald first saw it, though, sticking out of the hotel's hut, you should have seen the disgust on his face. "How unnecessary," he said, shaking his head. "What an utter waste." At any rate, we fixed Mr. Wisham's boat, and someone else fixed the small hotel's bamboo-and-pandanu hut. We repaired most all of the damage which that over-confident, rich guy had wrought.

Personally, I think Fitzgerald dragged things out. Just a bit perhaps. He saw to it that it took longer than initially estimated. So naturally, the cost of things went up. But Mr. Wisham didn't seem to care. Hey, he asked for it. All the guy had to do when the hurricane came through was go over to the Nandi River like everybody else. Just lay off the Wild Turkey, then tie-off from the brunt of the storm.

. . . .

All of these experiences changed me considerably. As I've said before, whenever I first moved out West I had a whole lot to learn. Of course, I still do. The learning just never stops. And why should it? This world sure is one complex place. But aren't you glad the world has changed to a degree? Yes, I'll be the first to agree that a few of the older ways were better. At this very moment, I'm looking for some land. Perhaps a small farm within driving distance of a city and an ocean. If possible, I'd like a place for my children to play, safely explore, roam to their heart's content.

Yes, private property and private enterprise. That's the American way. We can agree most definitely, and while we're on the subject, as Thomas Jefferson once said, sometimes the tree of liberty must be washed in blood. Hopefully very rarely though—using all the lessons we've gleaned from the past. So let's be fair. Even more complete. For example, what would it be like if you were a South Vietnamese farmer— not President Diem who had a cool, crisp fortune in his briefcase when he was zapped in 1963. What would it have been like to undergo indoc- trination lessons or obey The Three Nos—no intimacy, no love, no marriage—if you were young and of marriageable age in Vietnam, and if you broke those rules it was called "eating rice before the bell." Just what would it have been like to have your family farm taken away, after much sweat and loving labor, then turned into a cooperative? Yes, we get attached to our things. We get attached to places. We all have ownership flowing in our veins. Any good Florida, Maine or New Jersey home-owner, or farmer especially, still deep-down knows that yeoman ideal.

One of the things Robert Fitzgerald taught me was that you don't need to do anything but open your eyes to enjoy your life and keep from getting bored. Really interest yourself—absolutely naturally. Know what I mean? Not like that fake stuff Stephanie and Rick used that time. But sometimes when people form cliques, groups at any age, they can have poor judgement. Certain cliques can cause trouble, for example, the Klu Klux Klan. Or take those clubby whiz-kids of McNamera's and JFK's. Sometimes the ties that bind a community, or a nation, aren't always trustworthy and positive. Looking back, I just don't get it. Why did Cinnamon Taylor and I used to do what we did while snow skiing in Little Cottonwood Canyon? Oh yeah, did I forget to mention that we'd gotten caught? Cheryl caught me one time, and let me tell you she was not pleased. But can't one make a mistake or two? Perhaps take a detour to find one's way?

For as any good traveler knows, sometimes digression is the very sunshine of existence. But Cheryl told me I was "throwing my life away." Now is that really the case? Let's consider the matter like adults. In a 100% sober and proper manner. In a 100% optative mood. Then as the founding fathers and writers of the Declaration of Independence put it, let all the facts be submitted to a candid world.

. . . .

Let's rock and roll, as they said over in Vietnam when things got *very, very, very* serious. Yes, contemporary American values. Both per-sonal and political. Surely you see the connection if you pay social security or high insurance premiums, or if you don't have any medical insurance at all. Of course, these are sticky, quite kitchensinkish problems, and if they could ever be solved, then that person should have a statue erected in the nation's capital in her honor. Perhaps have a small forest, or a coral reef, declared a National Park. First, let's consider these two blue-blooded candidates running for President, one of whom will be elected before the year is over. Wonder which alleged "experimental" user avuncular William Bennett will vote for? Boy, what a choice for him, huh? What a couple of doozies—two regular Nehemia Americani—leading New Canaan into the horizon against all other heathens in the world. Okay, maybe one of them does appear more ecumenical, insofar as he visited a Buddhist temple and the other one visited Bob Jones III. But all the facts still aren't in and what *precisely* was being worshipped in that temple? That's what I'd like to know, for as Christopher Columbus himself once said, "Gold is most excellent, and whoever has it may do what he wishes in this world." Also, how about this connection between our aristocracy and the National Guard, particularly during times of war? Just what do you make of it and those champagne corps troops? Of course, these are big social and political questions. But how could you possibly discuss the Vietnam era and its aftermath, then leave contemporary politics off to the side? Therefore, let's just consider our present and potential leaders. Contemplate the things some people with lawyers-and-loot can get away with, while others have to wear bright orange suits for doing essentially the same thing. Let's turn up "Fortunate Son" by C.C.R. and celebrate this great land of ours. R-e-s-p-e-c-t. Tell me what you think of things. When Senator Henry Hyde, who led that wheelspinning impeachment extravaganza, was asked about that District of Columbia apartment—in which his wife did not eat bonbons or receive flower bouquets of any sort—he replied that the kept, uh, apartment, was a youthful indiscretion. But at the time of the lease's signing, Henry Hyde was forty-three years old. Who was it who said that the beautiful thing about the American public was that they were the American public? Twinkle, twinkle, Young Goodman Starr. Your think tank showed us what you are. Hark! Did I hear the click of an eavesdropped recording? Well, last spring I ran into an acquaintance of a South Carolina senator at Atlanta's Hartsfield Airport. Just so happens we were watching the impeachment proceedings and waiting for our planes. Then this guy tells me, "I talked to him the other day." This certain South Carolina senator on the TV screen. "He told me, 'Yeah this is all pretty silly. But hey, it's just politics.'" So I said to my new airport acquaintance that I hadn't even heard of this South Carolina senator before. But I was sure seeing a whole lot of him now. Next, the guy told me the senator was a nice guy, that he'd been his roommate in college. He said that these proceedings were "really going to put him on the map." Who knows? Maybe he was fibbing. Maybe he wasn't his college roommate at all. That's what the man said. Not me. So I move for consistency. To the eternal pit with constituency and all coat-tail riding which results in naught. Of course, this brings us to the next two questions: Aren't you fascinated by three-ring circuses? And aren't you fond of zebras?

Please pass the orange juice.

Thank you, I was parched.

Someone told me once that television reduces one's IQ by over seventy to eighty points, which is more than I can afford to lose. Darn it—almost lost my place. Let us convict all killers, of all races, if the physical evidence is absolutely 100% definitely there. Especially if they are repeat offenders who have hurt or hit people before, and there are three eyewitnesses of different creeds, colors, and faiths who saw them do it. But let's not stop there. What say we forgo all capital punishment and put all homicidal maniacs on that island where they filmed that mega-hit TV show *Survivor*. Boy oh boy, leave it to North Americans to manufacture hardship, then sit on the sofa with microwave popcorn and watch. Let's strand the killers, then forget them. Let 'em sociopathically sort things out. They can elect their own officials, make Timothy McVeigh president of the island if they so desire. You recall how he got caught? No license plate on his vehicle, because he wanted the U.S. government out of his life entirely, which doesn't handily explain that interstate on which he liked to drive his car. Say, that reminds me. When I cast my vote in the Spring 2000 primary—no I didn't vote for the Green Party candidate, although he does seem smarter on the issues than me, which is certainly what one wants. Isn't it? Have I got this all wrong? Anyway, this guy in the parking lot had a bumpersticker which said: "Charleton Heston for President." Hey, why not? He's got a buck or two. He's got an okay face. He puts on a good show for folks to swallow but, suffice to say, a wise Moses he is not. (Now just hold your horses, you NRA button totin' cowpokes. All you lovers of happy, warm guns. My father took me deer hunting several times in my youth. These are some of my best memories of my teenage years, and I'd like to go again sometime real soon). But did you see that footage of Chuck Heston holding that rifle over his head, acting like Davy Crockett, Daniel Boone, the Hatfields and McCoys all rolled into one?

Of course, this Hollywood actor's excesses do not excuse excesses from the other side, or shed light on what the government did at Ruby Ridge. Very recently, I went to visit David Stillman at his restaurant, and all he could talk about was those m. f. agents at Ruby Ridge, the m.f. government this, and the m.f. government that. You'll be happy to know that David and Jill are married. They have three daughters. But let me tell you something else. This sucker's *packing*. Surely all of his governmental distrust is part of the war's aftermath, and perhaps people do have the right to protect their homes. Yet when will we fine-tune and modernize our perceptions? Stop thinking that buying a muzzleloader and an AK-47 at a gunshow are equivalent and hunky-dory, protected by some antediluvean language, insofar as any day now the redcoats might be returning, and we all tend to eat a lot of fresh venison, buffalo, and squirrel.

Everything is perfect the way it is.

Why change anything, at any time, ever again at all?

Still, they say you know true sailors, stalwart adventurers, because they instinctively lean into a stiff breeze. This brings us to the bumpersticker centerpiece, the mother of all inane displays.

Last year riding along the highway, I saw this car going down the road and could hardly believe my eyes. On one side of the vehicle was a bumpersticker that read "Mean People Suck," then on the other side of the bumper was another sticker that said, "AIDS = The Miracle That Turns Fruits Into Vegetables." Absolutely true. This kind of thoughtlessness really occurs. So not only do we seem to manufacture moral certitude in America, we seem to manufacture moral schizophrenia as well. Hey, its storytime! Gather around! Once I knew a businesswoman from Gainesville, Florida. Her name was Sharon. She was a hemophiliac. She was married and monogamous for over thirty-seven years. Then Sharon had a minor operation and received some blood. She recovered from the surgery. Afterwards, Sharon and her husband kept loving each other, only each other, except they didn't know there was a problem with the blood she had received. Well, her husband got the virus first and died. Sharon lived a while longer, with the strange-sad-innocent guilt of it. Then eventually she died too. Ah, for the good ole days when life was simpler.

Say what? You could die of pneumonia in the good ole days.

Nix that idea.

Aren't antibiotics great? Isn't it comforting to trust your doctor? When you or a family member become sick, isn't it wonderful not to be against complex ideas? Aren't pharmaceuticals peachy keen? That's good. I'm glad we can agree. For certain sicknesses experts are required. Yes, sometimes special tools, specialized knowledge, even further research is necessary. But "soft money" and disease, these are gargantuan, very large problems. You know, I was absolutely serious about that national park or coral reef, so maybe we should solve one worry at the very least. Let's look at something more manageable—then again, perhaps not. Divorce and infidelity are a real problem in the U.S.A. Obviously, the 1960s caused it.

Shame, shame on you 1960s! But how long has it been in hours, or days, or weeks—or months, Jove forbid—since you showed the one you love that they are adored. Really showed them. Isn't it wonderful looking into her eyes, say, when she's poised lovingly above you; the small of her back, the smell of her neck, the feel of her hair lightly against your skin, her breasts touching your chest so ever softly. And what kind of a world is it where the word "breast" is considered vulgar? Make love not war—that didn't fix things. Another bumpersticker, another epistemological demise. Strive for monogamy. Stop blaming x, y, and z. Put a halt to all petty bickering. Time out. Go sit in the lonesome chair. (Hey, do you know why Baptist couples never make love standing up?) All potential divorcés and divorcées please think of your kids, then think of your kids some more. Sometime take the whole family to the coast on a moonlit night, then play Day-Glo Frisbee together on the beach. The laughter in your children's eyes. Their shouts of joy. Hooray! Ay! Whrrwhee! Read "Instincts and Their Vicissitudes." That single essay by Freud might help, might teach you to understand how complex our hearts and heads can be and how love can sometimes tragically transform. Perhaps look over the terrain, pinnacles and pitfalls of Madeleine de Scudery's *Carte de Tendre*. Commitment in tough times seems the crucial part. As for easy answers, surely you jest. My wife Grace and I are trying our very best, which is all two human individuals can possibly do. So enter the gloomy wilderness very carefully. Beware of strange figures suddenly on your path and devilish Indians behind every tree. As for the rules for any faithful husband and wife? All couples and lovers in love? You can do it in the rain, you can do it on a train. If you both get bored, you can do it standing on your head, or flip the mattress off your bed. You can do it over here, you can do it over there, the both of you can do it anywhere. But occasionally go the extra mile. You twirl her ticket and maybe she'll twirl yours. Dare to eat the peach and don't say, eeeeeewww, that's gross. Furthermore, if you're an adult female, or an adult male, please use the blank page we've perversely included at the end of this book. (It's because someone might think they're dancing). Don't look at me! This was all my Uncle Walter's idea! Kindly use our blank page to describe whatever is soothing and right up your alley.

Next, tear out the page. Have your loved one write their version on the back. Read what they've written and commit it to memory. All set?

Okay, rip the page lengthwise. Each of you take one half.

Now, chew it up.

Gobble it down, ingest it, and don't look back.

Behold a fellowtraveler with a book in his hand and a burden on his mind. Once she was here. Now they are gone. Flicker, flicker: the lace-flare of her hat in the sun. The Emperor Penguin Father. The Prairie Vole Pappa. The Water-Loving Beaver who helps fix fresh tree bark meals for his young. The Stickback. The Salmon. The Cichlid Fish. The Poison-Arrow Frog. The Nile Crocodile. Never, never the Gopher Tortoise. The Western Meadowlark. The Killdeer. The Magapode bird. The Desert Isopod. The Dwarf Mongoose. The Tamarin. The Timber Wolf. The Highland Gorilla. Moral dialecticism gonna get yo momma. Oh, that lovely manichean dress. Some black. Some white. June 30th. Your Mediterranean light blue eyes. j.s.p.d.m.p.c. Wild ducks, Kierkegaard, and I.B.M. The relations stop nowhere. Try to be the kind of person on whom nothing is wasted. The River Merchant's Wife. Jean Renoir's film and this comment on WWI and our species: "What is terrible in this world is that everyone has his reasons." Maybe learn some Chinese. Avoid Living in Your Own Private Pocatello, Idaho. Just a metaphor. Pretty place I've heard. My grandfather's green hayfield. That love letter about the dance. Always liked small towns from time to time. Quentin Compson's cuzzin. Same quandry. Always strive to see. The other. All sides count. Can't save the world. But every countenance of suffering lessens u.s. all. *Imana yirwa ahandi igataha i Rwanda.* Three months in 1994 from April to June. Over one million people killed in tropical Africa. Ask around the office. Ask your friends. Lots of folks don't know. *Urupfu rurarya ntiruhaga* in their language. Death eats and is never full. Lord Byron watching those poor men being hanged. I would have saved them if I could. Romantic. Realist. Combine them. Marjorie Garber, Martha Nussbaum, Hèlene Aylon's extended midrash on patriarchy and G-D at the Shulamith School for Girls.

http://www.malololailai.newsouth.org. All Eve's fault. Females never aggressive. Milk in their veins. Pain in birth. But men fight wars. V.F.W. Vice versa. Virginia Woolf on libraries, openmindedness, books, art, 500 quid, and the importance of couples. Who's afraid deep down? Well, Sigmund Freud before Ellis Island became a little nervous: "I'm bringing them the plague." Still to be lovey dovey. Still to be neat. She's filing her nails. They're dragging the lake. Pretty words don't mean much. There are some things one can't cover up. Not anymore. Yes, children are holier than either you or me, and personally I don't know about all this don't trust anyone over thirty business, because, if you ask me, I think we ought to drop the zero.

A tiny wee-wee infant. Post-lapsarian. Felix in the crib. Always already besploched. Battle of the sexes. All men are the same. Say what? *L'enfer c'est les autres.* Ashes to ashes and dust to dust. Show me a woman that a man can trust. There goes my gal somebody bring her back. She's got her hand in my money sack. Existence precedes cliches, but essentialism is alive and well. *Mais ne vous voyez pas? L'autre c'est toujours soi-même.* Or as Patti Smith once said: "As far as I'm concerned, being either gender is a drag."

First came the sea then the palpable lilies. Time Man of the Year 1965. That language calling the Vietnamese "piranhas" and "boiling ants." Better idea. A kaleidoscopic human space. That football field in Zagreb 1941. Only teenagers. Who is Jewish? All stepped forward. One giant leap for humankind. But those frigging hippies, they eat your food, stink up your house, drink your beer, wear that same granola uniform of a revolution thirty five years old, but at least they wore comfortable clothing. Practical sandals. Bare feet. Holy legacy. St. John of Damascus on circumincession, Theandric Activities, and divine maternity. Hale, healthy, hearty Mr. Hannity yelling at Patricia Ireland, then spouting off about the minimum wage. Proverbs 1:20. How much did your daddy make on average? Nice teeth. Nice haircut. Go to the ATM in your Lexus, but watch the bushes carefully and enjoy your nervous ride. That time when Rush Limbaugh alluded to "the new White

House dog," which his crack staff had heard about, then held up a picture of a fourteen-year-old freckled little girl. Imagine if she were yours.
Then Al Frankin shook a knot in his tail. Cherokee grandmother's saying. Golden rule! Only way to fly! Epistemological honesty! But it takes
elbowgrease, reflection, time. What Abraham Lincoln said about trying
what has not been tried before in the land of the big PX. Every human
space sacrosanct. This paragraph peacocky, circusy, wacky. Not quite
cricket. Over the big top. Skip for now. Come back. Key for many locks
soon in italics. Vietnam. War. History. Mistakes in thought. Lacunae are
one thing. Closemindness another. Always keep an open door. De
Amicitia. Kindness to strangers. Stop writing people off unless they
write people off. Because they drink whiskey or they drink milk, because
of their skin color, because of their nether regions. Hey, get this straight.
Don't blink. Ham wrote his father Noah off because he had some wine
and because he was nekkid. Oxford Companion to Religion. Entry on
the curse. Cobbled together poppycock. Still flies in some circles.
Hermeracineutics. What is terrible in this world is that everyone has a
so-called "light of reason." Unconscious too. Right there's the rub. You
don't believe it, huh? Dream away. Try to control them whenever your
nocturnal eyelids shut. Don't slip up. Cinelandia. Brazil. Virag.
Odysseus was a draft dodger and a farmer. He acted crazy to get out, but
they placed his son before his plow. Invented the first tank. His side
won. Splendid lust for knowledge, but the lover poet Dante says that
he's in Hell all because of the Trojan horse. He made a lot of sticky love
in all those skilled, loose, bold, bad witches' beds. He naughty naughty.
He big hero. He use his sword. At end as well. Make others bleed.
Whence that brand name? Because the little warrior hidden? Wonder
did he wear one? Perhaps from sheep. Overall very overall, but he was a
very selfish voyager who once proclaimed: "Neither fondness for my
son, nor reverence for my aged father, nor the due love that should have
cheered Penelope, could conquer in me the ardor that I had to gain
experience of the globe and of human vice and worth." Asymmetrical
warfare. Well-read militia groups. Yikes! Did they have overalls in

Greece? Oh that a good decent pacifist may flower to combat narrow-mindedness and a Lazy Boy view of the world. Fear + cruelty + righteousness. Sam Club warehouses = plenty to eat. That Anglican trained Irishman wrote in gasoline but, alas, the 1840s came all the same. Good tucker. What is physical is fleeting and incidental to the spiritual. Causal lust. Two lovers loving. No comparison. Zaftig. Cross-country skiing in the snow. Alone together. You great moralists, who are certainly laughing, may congratulate yourselves. But do not mock my wretchedness for I swear I feel it deeply. Rousseau's insistence about the one great moral lesson, right on that one, despite those children with Thérèse Whatzername. All those kids. His soul. What was her name? Me Croat, frog, injun. Me talkum funny. We're all of us mongrels if we just look deep enough. So you don't like the South? Guess what? There's more than one. Might as well toss out your radio right now. No jazz, blues, zydeco, devil's music all over this world. El mundo esta una pañuelo. Saying sí, sí, sí, si, si, si, si. Assenting to life up to the point of saying sayonara. Yes or no. All must decide. The mourning doves purl. The locusts hum-hum-hum. Shore do like it when my sweetie-pie has fun. *Between one being and another, there is a gulf, a discontinuity. This gulf exists, for instance, between you, listening to me, and me, speaking to you. We are attempting to communicate, but no communication between us can abolish our fundamental difference. If you die, it is not my death. You and I are discontinuous beings. But I cannot refer to this gulf which separates us without feeling that this is not the whole truth of the matter. It is a deep gulf, and I do not see how it can be done away with. Nonetheless, we can experience its dizziness together.* Now just imagine. That quote printed in the middle of this page. Printed skinny. Shaped like the Central Highlands. Like a map of Vietnam. With two broad patches of writing on the top and bottom. A slender wooden pole for carrying two plentiful sacks of rice. Skeleton key to prevent premature skeletons if you ask me. Homo ludus takes the grain. Do you know a poem, past, person? On first impression? All depends. Very rarely. Some impressionists are more sedulous, wide-awake, eye on the ball. Don't already have their minds made up. That individual who didn't like that Shillington, Pennsylvania author of fifty books. Actually hated him. Do you know him personally? Did you like the tetralogy? Say what? Had read one book. His first. Go eat your Wheaties. Desire is irrational. He was right on that. Zeus feathery swan. Pasiphae metal beast. On life's vast ocean we diversely sail. Passion the gale. To the crow's nest—look out! Some people's first impressions, and a Greyhound bus ticket, and a Hershey bar will get them to Atlanta—maybe Washington D.C. At least Judge Woolsey bothered to read and consult. N.E.A. committee hearings. Jesse Helms. Needs some Adrienne Rich. Diving into the wreck. His mind. Her mind. Are you ready to rummmmmmble? Place your bets and as poet laureate Rita Dove once said: "This book has a beginning, a middle, and an end." Must synthesize. I luv a reader with slow hand(s). I luv a tender touch. Don't you? Eric luvs Bonnie. But she luvs somebody else. You just can't win. Martha Stewart luvs Emeril Lagassee. Por favor. s.v.p. Don't put yourself above me. Love me like a human being. Leave no brushstoke, no semantic stone unturned. Freud's worst essay "Dora." Victorian. Egotistical. Titus Andronicus. Wrote an entire oeuvre. Don't baby with that bathwater. That guy Ham was wrong about his father because Nekkid Noah built an ark, loved God, saved the world, his sons and his daughters too. Family Romance. Most important thing. Character not a surface. Robert Fitzgerald was a flint-eyed Yankee who never saw a Paradise that didn't have three different species of not necessarily poisonous snakes. More honey, less vinegar in this world. Only connect the dots. Even kids should know to pull out bad weeds. The Little Prince. Dr. Seuss' stripes and polka dot machine. Brilliant stuff for adults. Some facts are facts. The paper of King James Bible. Billy Bob Shakespeare's folios. U.S. Constitution. First, Oscar Wilde's fall, then puritanical joy. Hallelujah! Let the first one among you with amnesia and a selective memory proceed. Go ahead. Throw some pebbles. Never sinned, slunk, stole? Never even once? Check your own palms. Fire Joycelyn Elders. You utter dog. You low-down scum. Beautiful sybarite. The man in the macintosh was Paul McCartney's distant relative across the waves. Never even stole a seedless grape, say, while strolling at your supermarket? That's different. Uh-huh. Yeah, but was that grape yours? A clever poem which corrects men's faults by means of agreeable lessons. Billets de confession. All my own mistakes, faults, shabbiness on display. House dirty. Bills to pay. All too human. Here as well. Fabio got some money for his novel. Dangerous. Worthless as the teats on Sir William O'Reilly or his idea of the national news. Milk from a duck. Perhaps he has three or four. Yes, some men. Some men are inclined to cynanthropy. But if you have a cross, not an arrow, on your circle, then beware of picking up pins that fall upon the floor. Skimming. Intolerance. Apathy. Frailty thy name is received idea. All of us should avoid having a soul the size of a piece of couscous and give each other some fresh air. Can't we all just get along? Because just because, every now and then, what's the alternative? A fine private place. Not particularly clean. Not well lit. Double entendre. Your hand is my happiness. Accept your happiness. Love laughs at locksmiths & lollygaggers & landlubbers. But Aunt Sally loves lagniappe or my Uncle Walt is fibbing some more. Always keep in mind the thought of Rocamadour, Oscar, Artemio, Blake's Black Boy, various chimney sweeps, and little Bérthe Bovary. Don't mess with Pixies! Pick on someone your own size! Our two children. So precious. Wild horses. That very first time with my wife Grace in the lovely southern hamlet of XXXXXXX. She warned me clearly. Kissing changes everything. So are you sure? I am. I do. Do you? Gitty up. Oh, the water. Oh, the water. Get it myself from a mountain stream.

Since this subject is bellicose, depressing and heavy, I sure hope that you're having some meta-fun. Watched a little M.A.S.H. perhaps? Well, that's sort of the idea. Except war isn't really about some kooky doctors drinking martinis, chasing nurses, and ribbing a dimwit named Frank. Perhaps try *Dr. Strangelove* sometime instead. Perhaps try some Fellini, whenever you're not perusing that multi-talent Tom Clancy, or maybe take a gander at Charlie Chaplin's last film. You believe in the "trickle-down effect" don't you? See there—we have something else in common. Now we have officially agreed on several points. We both agree that we like skilled and trained physicians, and that for certain sicknesses real expertise is required.

Of course, these days there are all kinds of training, skills, and discernment, like the intelligence of my car mechanic Mike and his wife Donna, who does their office books. They call their business "Midon Auto Repair" because they are a team. Also, the level-headedness of my electrician, Gary, because wiring spooks me, and all of the skilled-yet-still-poor migrant workers who grow most of America's food. Here's another little storyette you might like. Once upon a time, there was this veteran from WWII, a man about sixty who worked for my father. He showed me his scar and war wound, as well, since his stomach had been machine-gunned in Alsace-Lorraine. This guy without a doubt drank more than a smidge too much, but he was super-perceptive, very funny, and intelligent, with a photographic memory like you would not believe. Over a two week period, I once saw him take a Caterpillar road-grader apart into about three-thousand pieces, down to ballbearings, sheer nuts and bolts, these tiny springs which you could barely discern. Next, he put the dismantled machine into three separate buildings, then went on a bender which lasted a week. When he finally came back to work, though, he put the Caterpillar roadgrader back together. Made it run like a top. Yes, I've discovered this much, if not the world, since one can only scratch the surface, and there's always so much more to learn and do and see. All people indeed are created equal. Yet all opinions and skills are not the same. Some people are simply experts in different things, as I once learned to my chagrin after letting my roommate cut my hair.

Therefore, go find yourself an expert on novels. Someone who's read lots of different kinds. Ask them to read Tom Clancy's novel entitled *Without Remorse* and see what they think of his character named Pam. She is Jack Ryan's twenty-one year old prostitute turned main-squeeze, but, alas and alack, she's an absolutely "horrible cook." Also, ask your novel expert about Tom Clancy's fabulously strange title and that gung-ho photograph of the author on the book's jacket. Don't forget the hero,

Jack Ryan himself, who helps build up Pam's confidence as a cook and a lover. He's this extraordinary male who at one point flexes and displays "the magnificence of his body" quite unironically. Apparently, Jack Ryan just has an unconscious thing for prostitutes since he's had some "little childlike" ones over in Vietnam as well, although afterwards "the shame of it burned inside him like a torch." At another point, Jack Ryan confidently shoots an obvious bad guy in the head with a .22 pistol. Therefore, he takes the law into his own hands. But, hey, like Fawn Hall said, sometimes you have to go beyond the law. Then use the shredder to boot.

Where did I put my list of blockbuster movies and moviestars?

Hang in there. I'll go look.

In the meantime, there's this word in Venezuela, spelled p-a-v-a, which has to do with the not-to-be-toyed-with connection between bad luck and bad taste. You recall those pith helmets British colonialists used to wear? Kinda silly, huh? Those togas so fashionable chez the vomitorium? Just always remember: (1) the Ancient Greeks, (2) those war-loving Spartans, (3) the Romans, (4) the Ottomans, and (5) the British Empire on which the sun sets not. Did I forget to say abracadabra? Well, I'm saying it now.

Abracadabra.

Poof! They're gone!

Go ahead and write your local U.S. congressperson. Support the arts in America, then kick back and see what "trickles down." That is, if you're not too busy watching some purely escapist *schlock*. Some dangerously glorifying, mendacious, over-simplification of violence featuring Jean Claude Van Damme, Steven Segal, Bruce Willis, or Arnold Schwarzenegger. Some muscled-up dude. Some posturing badass who thinks he cannot be stopped. Of course, they've made one or two good films perhaps. But aren't you sick and tired of all of those fake Hollywood fights? All of these so-called "heroes" who think they're indestructible and invincible? Large-and-in-charge. Perhaps this John Wayne ideal of the silent macho man, this big man of few words myth, deserves a bit more scrutiny. Maybe this self-sufficient, irresistible cowboy business—this white-hat, good-guy obsession —this tall, handsome stranger stuff is much stranger than it first looks. Because as one philosopher of human intimacy has written, "whenever he is seated next to her on the same bench or bed, he should take her aside, explaining that he needs to talk to her privately, he should then express his love through gestures rather than words. If she is visiting him, he should keep her with him, claiming that he is about to prepare a medication which would have no effect unless she also were to have a hand in making it. When she leaves, he should urge her to come back; then, when she has become a regular visitor he should engage in long conversations with her, for, in the words of Gothakamouka, 'no matter how much a man loves a woman, he will not win her unless he talks to her.'"

Sweet fancy Moses! Where the heck did that come from? Okay, okay, I'll summarize myself. Here is my thesis. Politics and history and ideas are important, and we Americans often say they are, then act as if they're not. Here's my linchpin and it's fairly simple: WE ARE WHAT WE EAT. WE ARE WHAT WE EAT. WE ARE WHAT WE EAT. Although, I'm making this seem too easy. Haven't we agreed? There are no shortcuts. Cliff Notes won't do. Any bumpersticker philosophy doesn't go nearly far enough. Heritage not race. That doesn't explain, uplift, or heal a blessed thing, doesn't assuage the souls that have been hurt. Much less respect the minorities in one's state. Therefore, all open-minded patriots might check out James Madison, his notion of the tyranny of the majority, and the Federalist Papers on this particular point.

A red cardinal just flew by my window!

I'm telling you it was a lovely sight!

Yes, let's embrace all knowledge and information. Strive for a fuller picture and a well-rounded sense of self. Let's read the military historian and scholar H. R. McMaster's *Dereliction of Duty*, just in case you still think J.F.K was so good-looking that he and his whiz-kid staff could do no wrong. Let's read Bob Livingston's book if he ever publishes one.

Also, Henry Hyde, Milton Friedman, and Christine de Pizan just to be fair. Let's peruse Moliere's letters to the King and the "Brotherhood or Company of the Holy Sacrament" so they wouldn't give him the hot foot. Also, that war-ravaged, one-armed genius, that holyman-of-holymen named Miguel from Spain.

Furthermore, to seventeen year old Marta Monojlovic in Serbia and all members of OPTOR, which means "resistance," way to go for speaking truth to power and Slobodan Milosivic's megolomaniacal, homicidal tyranny. On behalf of my grandfather, Jovo Bubalo, I send you this one-quarter Croatian kiss-on-the-cheek from across the sea.

Another kiss and hug for that grandmother who walked across the USA for campaign finance reform, and for all the whites and blacks injured in the Freedom Rides whose lives aren't the same unto this day. Because as Reverend Fred Shuttlesworth once said, "Rattlesnakes don't commit suicide. They don't put themselves out, so you gotta take them out." And that's what Mose Wright bravely tried to do at the murder trial of Emmett Till as he pointed his long, proud finger and declared: "Dar him."

Also, Mr. Cal Thomas, you are forgiven. I embrace you as a fellow human being. A big hug for you as well, but shave off that mustache this very minute, because it makes you look like you know who. Forgiveness aside, you should pay for your half-truths and red-herring use of logos, pathos, ethos, chiefly for that silly article entitled "Hillary Wants to Nuke the Nuclear Family," concerning matters addressed by a Yale Law School graduate way out of your area of so-called expertise. Hillary's legal ideas had to do with things like should a minor child be allowed to perish, simply because a parent doesn't believe in using modern medicine. Dying kids, Cal. Why oh why, did you have to trot out the A-bomb? Just what does that say? Why not tell your readers the whole story? For all your half-versions, sir, take *that* with my white glove. For that one fustian title alone, I'll meet you at high noon on Larry King Live any single day of the week. I'll explain how to write a more complete summary, absolutely free of charge, then we'll see how you like them kumquats. Oh, this is a favor, Cal, believe me, because Hillary Clinton would eat your lunch.

By the way, has anyone seen Newt Gingrich? (Where did he go? Is he still crying back in steerage? Has he shacked-up with that pretty young schoolteacher?) Tell you what Cal, Newt, and Kenneth. Let's be bipartisan. Let's shake hands across the aisle. My Uncle Walt and I are express mailing three topaz rings, twenty seven birdnests for soup, one deluxe *fruits de mer* platter—some salt and pepper that you might dine comfortably—and may your recently acquired Pfizer stock swell and grow of its own accord.

Goodness knows how the 2000 Presidential Election will finally end up. But this much seems quite sure. The common man and common woman have been squelched. Of course, when the whole shooting match, the sickening spin, and all the partisan half-truths are over—but not the nausea—verily these resonant words of the Caribbean prophet-musicians-seers will still ring true, insofar as: "These are the big fish who always try to eat down the small fish. I said, the small fish. And they would do anything to ma-ter-ial-ize their every wish. Oh, yeah. Oh, yeah." Yes, someone will win. But something bigger has been lost. Scant hope is dashed. Our idealism has been misused. Surely what this country needs is a sharp-as-a-tack commoner who really puts his or her soul into the job. Not another pampered, self-propelled, oligarch nepotist with violet blood lineage out the ying-yang. Someone who made C's in college, or someone else who conflates the truth and loves to be a policy wonk. (As for which side is worst perhaps it's sixes. But they've got their mind on their money and their money on their minds, if I can borrow the hip-hop chiasmus). Yes, still conflates and masks the truth. Rather like in Vietnam. For example, when they gave purple handkerchiefs to the woebegone sprayers of defoliant, those brightly-colored handkerchiefs bearing the unfunny legend, "Only You Can Prevent Forests," supposedly to dignify the dangerous Operation Ranchhand task. Oh, the horror! The on-going horror of it all! Yes someone will win and they can drink their big champagne and laugh. Ha! Ha! They can drink their big champagne and laugh. Ha! Ha! But when they run to the sea, the sea will be boiling. When they run to the rock, the rock will be melting, all along, all along the way.

Yes, I sure hope you've had one laugh or two right now, because in the end my friend Robert Fitzgerald gets killed. He dies a very real death on the freeway in Los Angeles, which is the death he honestly and truly died. (Was that my alarm clock? How distracting). One thing they leave out of the Protestant work ethic is that even preachers go troutfishing. Some of the preachers I know back in Kentucky go after crappie, bluegill, or bass. Sometimes they even take a friend, because everybody needs somebody sometime, and we could all use a diversion every now and then. Piety can stand an interruption. Otherwise it would be hard to floss one's teeth. Spread this wonderful news! You can go to watermelon cuttings, ice-cream suppers, contemporary fiction and poetry readings, and still be a good person. What's more you can even embrace your faith, turn your soul inside-out, stamp your feet and sing to your heart's content, like Joe Turner, Louis Jordan, Aretha Franklin, Little Richard, Louis Armstrong, June Carter, Loretta Lynn, Otis Redding, Sam Cook, Roberta Flack, Wilson Pickett, Reverend Al Green, Jerry Lee Lewis, Howlin Wolf, Eric Clapton, Van Morrison, Reverend James Cleveland, Clara Ward, and Goody Mob. Not to mention that wildman, anti-moralist moralist Rabelais, who studied the Holy Bible in Latin and Greek (yes he was serious), then studied medicine, then wrote a joyous affirmation of all human existence. Not to mention those three blind wise men, Stevie Wonder, Ray Charles, and John Milton—who rocked the house more than once himself—particularly in *Aereopagitica* and the greatest Christian poem in the English language, as all North Carolinians who love Jessie Helms and his campaign ad style are surely aware.

Now, I'm personally not one of those people who feel that NASCAR is the downfall of western civilization, or that TV is the opiate of the masses. Personally, I like a good horse race and I've been known to watch a little colored television. Yes, TV and thoroughbred horseracing, troutfishing and bassfishing are all equally permissible. Just beware of the hooks, and ideally go after more than just one kind. Some politicians fish a whole, whole lot. Also, meretricious writers who really pump 'em out. My four-year-old son used to play a card game called "Go Fish." That's sort of akin to readers who are exclusively interested in science fiction set on planet Zaxthron, readers who are convinced that men and women are from Neptune, Pluto, or Mars. Readers only interested in "glitz-novels" by Judith Krantz. Only in vampire tales. Only in fake-blood novels. That is to say, absolutely unscary stories concerning slobbering St. Bernards, or supernatural teenage girls who—yikes, run for the hills—have telekinetic powers at their high school proms.

Surely, the whole cultural mix, the kit-and-caboodle does matter. Surely, Vietnam was our most decadent and self-indulgent war. Such activities and proclivities have helped destroy other "empires" before. So study the lists above and all lists that follow. Don't walk under any ladders, especially carrying a black cat. Check all pertinent websites and if you do a word search for the number "three" in this novella, certain patterns will emerge, or if you search for the phrase "held out his hand." Always look for patterns, the hermeneutical patterns. Discern the threads and weave. References to all sorts of food for thought. For example, here's something else I never learned in Sunday School. (Bettcha they don't teach it at Liberty University either, where, when he introduced Oliver North, Jerry Falwell once bizarrely declared to all, although apparently Fawn Hall couldn't make the speech: I will remind you that our Lord himself was once accused of being a criminal). Did you know that Karl Marx liked to take his wife and kids on picnics? They often went on sunny afternoons to have lunch together at a favorite London park. Can you imagine such a thing? Karl Marx eating tunafish! Picnicking with his children! Why not check out the recent biography. Oh, it won't turn you commie. Just to round things out, considering that capitalism's here to stay.

But reading's boring, right? Perhaps you have a point. I tried that Tom Clancy novel once myself, and you talk about one long haul. If you had time for that silliness, then you won't mind these taxonomies—or reading this *very real* list from The Book of the Dead. Here are five soldiers, randomly taken from pages 618-619, who are unfortunately with us no more:

JIMMY L. SERRILL; 2 LT Air Force; date of casualty 18 MAR 68; born Morgontown, Ky; Panel 45E, line 29.

ALVIN MARION SHIFFLETT JR.; BM3 Navy; date of casualty 26 OCT 66; born Russellville, Ky; Panel 11E, line 115.

CARL EUGENE SHIRLEY; SGT Air Force; date of casualty 18 May 1968; born Louisville, Ky; Panel 63E, line l.

KENNETH R. SHOEMAKER JR.; 1st LT Air Force; date of casualty 30 NOV 67; born Owensboro, Ky; Panel 31E, line 17.

EDWIN FRANKLIN SHOLAR; WO Air Force; date of casualty 04 June 69; born Murray, Ky; Panel 23W, line 68.

Oh, this is the real McCoy. Not gung-ho nonsense. Some lists are very important. Some truths and books help create trails of freedom for us all. You know, old Huck Finn, he sure had an imagination for blood and disaster, although Huck also said "I don't take no stock in dead people" and felt the Widow Douglass was a goody-two-shoes hypocrite, considering how much she enjoyed her snuff. Merely use your imagination. You and I could have gone. One of our children could have been drafted. But these brave young men from my homestate just happened to be in Vietnam instead. Oh yes. Some lists are very important indeed, as that geophysicist, whale connoisseur, breathtaking treehouse architect S.T. Acquabella once said. "Because the truth is a fulcrum and only children's knees move above and below it." Futhermore, there is a coffee cup to be found in Memphis, Tennessee, *a momento mori* with a saying, something Elvis Presley kept repeating in that very Southern way all his life: "Don't criticize what you don't understand son. You never walked in that man's shoes." Gunter Grass. Le Minh Khue. Salman Rushdie. Larry Levis. Jorie Graham. *Di questi artisti nessuno se ne sogna da noi.* So don't you think we need to look at this escapist "beach novel" addiction? This habit of reading whatever's in the cardboard tower at Barnes and Noble simply because it's up front and that's what you are being sold. I.S.B.N. Why not try some Mark Twain instead? Some Marilyn Nelson, Zora Neale Hurston, or watch "Regret to Inform" by Barbara Sonneborn. Put Tom Clancy in the remainder p-i-l-e which is a fairly nice way of saying that's what he writes and precisely where that novel of his belongs.

Just what is this you're reading, right now? Who is its audience? Well, audiences are like Joseph's coat of many colors. Take a wild guess, then you tell me. The first question is easier by far. This is a one-time-and-one-time-only, written-in-the-year-2000, time capsule novella on the subject of war. Friendship and sailing. Human nature and nature period. Next time around, I promise something tighter, perhaps on scrimshaw, however, this piece is called a "narrvella" and these are "sprawlagraphs" in progress. Tell you what, I'll leave the nomenclature open. But personally, I find the term metaphysico-theologico-cos-molooningology most helpful. This style is also called "centrifugal," since everything the Vietnam War was cannot be spun inward, then compacted into a neat-and-tidy nugget or tasty gumdrop.

Oh yeah, before I forget. That story I told you about the little girl and the newspapers never happened. Not to me. My cousin Leigh actually said the n-word on that distant, sweltering summer afternoon. But this is neither here nor there. It was a *parable*. Of course, you've read the New Testament and understand how these things work. Did you ever really believe that a Missouri kid named Huckleberry could float down the Mississippi River with a runaway slave in 1844? Much less all of that King and Duke business? That's good. I'm starting to like you. It's nice to be nice and to find some common ground. Only connect. Isn't it great to be on better terms, then put your arm chummily around a new friend's shoulder?

Long live competitive sports! Basketball, baseball, soccer, billiards, jai-alai, tennis and horseback riding. Long live all art and music, because who was that famous wise man who said that "life without music is a mistake?" Viva all the words on the page! Viva the writing on the wall! Yes, TEACH YOUR CHILDREN WELL, put some across-the-board, revolutionary love in their hearts. That's my very best, golden-rule advice with a little help from Crosby, Stills and Nash, and if it's didactic so be it, because I sure hope you're having some jee-haw fun. Also, for the record, Nietzsche didn't say "God is dead," he said God is dead and *we have killed him.* Isn't it great to have a fuller picture? See what happens when you're overly fond of short cuts? Smarmy fastfood, bumpersticker shibboleths, Chicken McNugget versions of the facts?

This land is great. This land is good. But we can also do great wrong, then be hypocritical as all get out, as Frederick Douglass' 1855 autobiography will make quite clear. Yes, status quo white males have caused a problem or two in history. Therefore, one more bumpersticker before we go: "All tribes, all tongues, all colors and creeds—or BUST!!!"

So as my plot moves forward, please pardon the *narrativus interruptus* for Robert Carlton Fitzgerald's death is tragic and true. Wouldn't it be nice if we could put the deaths of our loved ones off? Talk to one another longer, put on some good music, have a big meal together and stretch things out? But whatever you do, do not listen to the devil's music. Follow directions, respect your elders, do your homework, finish all the vegetables on your plate. Do not cross the color barrier—never ever jump that fence—or smudge between the lines. Of course, if you think my style or tone is "inappropriate," then I'll gladly cross the fence myself. I'll say what that great artist Jimi Hendrix once told Dick Cavett when he asked if Hendrix knew some people might consider his 1969 solo at Woodstock "unpatriotic" or "improper." You know, that concert where Jimi Hendrix played the national anthem at sunrise? Check it out again on DVD. Some kinds of technology can be quite good. Note the innovation, the skill, the sober concentration in Hendrix's face as he plays, then deftly places a few notes from "Taps" in the middle of our country's most definitive song.

By the way, you know that Jimi Hendrix was in the very prestigious 101 Airborne don't you? He trained at Fort Campbell, Kentucky, a few years before the war broke out. Anyway, re-watch that interview. Re-watch the Woodstock footage. See how Jimi Hendrix looks over at Dick

Cavett, how his expression indicates he meant that song from the heart. He says that he meant for the anthem to be lovely. He meant for it to be beautiful. Boy, I sure wish he was still around to play that amazing guitar. People are like fingerprints; everyone expresses herself or himself differently; they have different skills and make different sorts of mistakes. Jimi Hendrix made his and paid the ultimate price, but he knew that sometimes art can be oblique. Sometimes art comes at you sideways. Hey, it ain't always easy. Just like life. Therefore, here's another golden nugget for your piggybank—which is perhaps what some people really want—another doodad for the temple to Lakshmi in your heart. Surely, we can agree. Human life is complex. Sometimes confusing. Not always straightforward. So if all reading were easy and told you an overly simple story about any human complexity whatsoever—like war, aggression, or desire—then that version would essentially be a lie. And if you never had to look up a single word like "meretricious," "Lakshmi," or "schlock"—now tell the truth, did three people just leave the room—if all writers only spoonfed you kindergarten truths because they'd already learned everything in kindergarten, if they all warned against sweating the small stuff because everything was small stuff, then how could writing ever possibly help at all? So I have to go with Jimi Hendrix on this one, and perhaps you've had three or four smiles. Hopefully, you think this section is *very, very, very* serious, some well-intentioned, truth and beauty kind of stuff.

VII.

Here's how Robert Carlton Fitzgerald died. He was driving his battered Datsun pickup on the Santa Monica freeway in the summer of 1985 when he noticed a stalled car on the side of the road. The driver was standing on the freeway's shoulder, stranded there and waiting with his wife. They had the hood of their car up. Both of them looked worried. Both of them looked frantic because their car had overheated and would not start. So Robert Fitzgerald pulled over to help, since among his various skills he was also a fine mechanic. He had this if it's mine something will eventually go wrong at the worst possible time attitude. A very handy outlook to take with you out to sea. Who knows where he learned it. Perhaps his father. Anyway, Fitzgerald had gone to L. A. that day, for a bilge pump and some other things he needed. With the money he'd made in Fiji, the Chó-Fú-Sá was coming along nicely. Ever since we'd returned, Fitzgerald had been in a wonderful mood. He'd stopped to be a Good Samaritan toward the husband and wife. They stepped to the far side of the freeway. They watched as Robert Fitzgerald worked on their car.

He was fiddling under the hood, checking for a leak in one of the radiator hoses, when suddenly this semi-truck driver fumbled with a cassette tape while going seventy m.p.h. He took his eyes briefly off the road then drifted over to the right, slamming into the pint-sized Datsun pickup which slammed into the overheated car with its upraised hood. Seconds later, an Allied Van Lines driver also hit the wreckage. The Ventura County newspaper, the *Star Free Press*, even had an article which read as follows: "California Highway Patrol officers said neither of the truck-and-trailer rig drivers was badly injured. The spectacular accident blocked traffic for nearly five hours, forcing it to be rerouted onto a frontage road and so clogged the bridge that firefighters, Highway Patrol officers, and other rescue workers had to park behind the bridge and walk to the victims. A spokesman for the Highway Patrol office said he did not think citations would be issued to the truck drivers. The pickup was stopped slightly in a traffic lane. The deceased is currently unidentified, but was pronounced dead at 12:05 p.m. Reportedly a free-lance construction worker he has relatives in Connecticut, officials said, but none of his family had been located by late this morning."

Someone called for an ambulance. But there was no point. The husband and the wife were unharmed. Both truck drivers were okay. Robert Fitzgerald was crushed. Alone and dead. It happened so quickly, as it so often does, only months after we had returned from Malololailai and our extended South Pacific trip. The accident occurred very close to rush hour. On a hot Los Angeles afternoon. To think of it. His last breath on a freeway in the desert, although he loved the ocean so much, although he'd survived a war fought in a distant land with over two thousand rivers and monsoon rains.

. . . .

Consequently, a few weeks ago the past screamed loudly. Just some things I heard on the radio, you know? How the radio alarm goes off, then you lie there and listen? Well, this news report comes on the radio, and it's being broadcast live from Vietnam. And right then, I knew that I'd have to undertake something I'd put off, denied the necessity of doing despite what I felt deep-down. Right then, I knew I would have to write all this down. Record what happened. Don't ask me to explain why I have to write it. This is just the way I feel. Like a stomach full of something irksome, something too rich, too sweet or sour, something that absolutely must come out. Like that very first time I went sailing on that Swan. This story is about over—Robert Fitzgerald's story, that is— because it has to be finished. But there's so much more. So much I have left out. How he had saved money for a few acres by Mount Shasta in Siskiyou County, a real place to live when he wasn't on the Chó-Fú-Sá. How he protected me in that dark alley in Papeete. How Fitzgerald stayed calm despite his fear that night, or when our sailboat hit that thunderstorm with a waterspout and I was so scared. So terrified as the waves lifted higher, then higher still, as if imploring heaven for mercy and everlasting peace.

Once again, the past screams loudly. The past screams loudly because the Vietnam war is all over the news again. So I wonder what Robert Fitzgerald would have thought of all the coverage? I have to wonder. How could I not? It's currently mid-May in the year 2000. John McCain is out and George W. Bush, Jr. is in, the worldwide media is looking over its shoulder, fresh from covering the twenty-fifth anniversary of the fall of Saigon. Senator John McCain is definitely a hero—no doubt about it whatsoever. He even used his clout to reestablish free-trade between the USA and Vietnam. But then he goes back over, shortly after Bush has pulled ahead. He goes over and tours the Hanoi Hilton with his beloved son. Then he sums up by saying "the wrong guys won." That's all? Black hat, white hat. That's how it all boils down? Given that kind of rationale and thinking about Vietnam, just exactly who does that make right?

Yes, it's all back in the news once more and what have we learned from all we have learned? Anything at all? There are wonderful new films like *Regret to Inform*, photo-journalist exhibits, retrospectives, commemorative get-togethers of helicopter pilots, SAROs, medics and nurses and docs. A slough of new books, everything from the newest installment in Robert McNamera's sorry-about-that-fellas "Presbyterian confession," as Senator McCarthy and wheelchair-bound Senator Max Cleland put it so well—everything from that to the new scientific studies on the long term effects of Agent Orange.

On that NPR broadcast, which started me thinking of Fitzgerald, there was this sad-voiced doctor speaking in heavily-accented English from modern day Hanoi. She described the genetic effects on the offspring of parents liberally doused with dioxin. She was currently treating a twenty-four-year-old woman, mentally retarded and uncommonly hirsute, totally covered with hair and sagging tumors all over her back. "If both sides only had a second chance," I said once. "They might have decided not to fight." However, Robert Fitzgerald told me that a second chance wouldn't have mattered squat for some of the Vietnamese. "That's something we didn't understand to begin with." He showed me something to read, something that Ho Chi Minh had said shortly after World War II when he had to allow the French back in to protect against a possible threat from the north and fill the vacuum left by the ousted Japanese. He made me read this quote by Ho Chi Minh, responding to his critics well before the battle of Dien Bien Phu: "You fools! Don't you remember your history? The last time the Chinese came, they stayed for a thousand years. The French are foreigners. They are weak. Colonialism is dying. The white man is finished in Asia. But if the Chinese stay now, they will never go. As for me, I prefer to sniff French shit for five years than eat Chinese shit for the rest of my life."

Sure, historical hindsight. Piece of cake. But, as you see, this was not just a civil war. This was a country which had been screwed-with for over two millennia, whose officials were sometimes corrupt on both sides, venal and self-propelled, quite capable of lying and misleading its citizens. Sounds horrible, right? And a bit familiar? "Didn't I tell you?" Robert Fitzgerald told me. "You have only scratched the tip. Didn't I tell you that this was a can of cobras, green pit vipers, and bamboo snakes?"

Sure, war is war. But you're not saying anything particularly insightful there. Keep talking. Nothing will come of nothing—speak again. Haven't we discussed this? The problem with boiling things down too much? Just saying "war is war" points where? Perhaps to the pit of another certain hell on earth. Therefore, that comment about "the wrong guys," it just rubs wrong. Of course the times were different; the Cold War was still unthawing; and nothing historical happens exactly the same way twice. But there's always China, always the yellow horde—and there's always Taiwan. *Warning, warning, warning Will Robinson!* Yes, I'm getting scared again. This future on earth won't be easy. Some people say that a lot of life is "timing." Being in the right place at the right moment. Well, yeah, and the other way around. Too often, we leave that part out.

More people like my mother need to be in politics. That's essentially what I think. Let's try more women and mother leaders, and not Margaret Thatcher types either, who send their jets thousands of miles to Las Maldivas in Argentina, thus prolonging those naughty, naughty, British colonial habits of yore. But let's not be naïve, though, let's train them. Let's prepare our politicians beforehand, which is what they do at ENA in Europe and some other places in the world. Let's not just elect people simply because they are marinated in cash like Donald Trump, Ross Perot and Steve Forbes.

Let the wind flow through all the dorade boxes!

Throw open all the portholes!

Doesn't it feel good? That breath of fresh air!

While we're waiting for all global mothers, or women who have had good mothers, while we're waiting for more females to run things a while, just traipse over to the library and I promise I'll do the same. Read about what happened between China and Vietnam in 1978 and 1979. Maybe the Domino Theory was right to a degree, but the Domino Theory was very flawed as well. So let's not do it again. Let's not fight certain kinds of war. Not ever again. Also, we were fighting the Northern Communists, right? Well, look for a recent article published in the *American Journal of Public Health*, concerning one of the most toxic molecules ever made by man, read how the dioxin called "2,3,7,8-TCDD" contained in Agent Orange persists not only in the northern provinces but in the blood, tissue, and breast milk of many South Vietnamese women and their children, who never fired a bullet in their whole lives. Please go to the library and read this one article. Check for the photograph of the Vietnamese farmer plowing his fields with a water buffalo, in today's Quang Tri province, in the year 2000. Look at his three children well under twenty-five years old: a teenage boy who is not complaining at all, then two girls around ten or eleven and one of them wears a great big smile. They're all three crawling on the ground, beside the plow and their daddy working in the field, because they've never walked upright due to genetic deformities in their spines. Not one single bullet. Not one single bullet in their whole lives.

. . . .

Robert Carlton Fitzgerald was *there*. He faced it. He smelled it. Luckily for me, I had some time to spend with him once he made it home from the war in Vietnam. Some time to watch, absorb, and listen. This was the kind of guy you could ask, how does a television or an air-conditioner work? What's the difference between AM and FM? And he would know or find out the answer. He gave. I took. Received so much. Definitely the beneficiary by far. I wish he could meet my wife and two beautiful children because he didn't have any children of his own, not unless you count yours truly, born again in a way, thanks to his headlock in that mud puddle. So wherever his pillow and poncho liner are right now—wherever his humble berth—I hope the winds are favorable. Five knots minimum and sweetly perfumed. I hope there's a piece of grilled cabrillo being served with fantastic wine. Because he helped me. Guided the blind. I just want to say, "Thanks again Robert. I love you, man."

I'll always remember. Never, never forget.

Not even when I revisit Washington DC, and fail to find your name on that very important wall.

Perhaps another Thanksgiving service is in order. In honor of everything he was I want to offer my thanks. For his various skills and for his intelligence. For his brave service and valor and for all the other soldiers he represents. For his overall love of life and the myriad human connections he sought to make. For Robert Fitzgerald's refusal to be oblivious, I'm deeply grateful, and for those first sailing lessons upon the Pacific Ocean where, tranquil or stormy, in solitude or shared company, you feel your physical smallness and capacity for compassion, sense your inner spirit and thereby the presence of a vital and living God.

Author Acknowledgements

Hopefully, the variety of these fictions will appeal and if I can make one request it would be that readers glance at the thirteen openings to see which stories might initially strike their interest. This collection is dedicated to my parents and family and most of all to Michael and Rachel. The bulk of these short stories first appeared in *Other Voices, Florida Review, New Mexico Humanities Review, Pleiades, Kiosk, The Bilingual Review/Revista Bilingüe, South Dakota Review, The Distillery, The Journal of Kentucky Studies, Utah Holiday* and elsewhere. My special and heartfelt thanks to three individuals in particular, David Kranes, Henry Staten, Larry Levis, for their unstinting inspiration, their simultaneous commitment as teachers and writers of absolutely wonderful books. Hefel Freres of Lausanne, Switzerland for my first construction job outside of Kentucky. S.T. Acquabella for sailing, skiing, and tiger-catching in red weather lessons. Piper Cherokee N4675R. All my friends from 43 rue du Temple. Celita, Roxanne, Rosa, Carlos, Adolfo Rodriguez, and many other generous people from Buenos Aires. Thanks for sharing the city and your precious spirits. Also, to my *compañeros del alma* Mike, Josh, Al, Carole, Steve. Finally, I would be remiss not to mention a series of teachers who instilled a love of literature, beginning with my second grade teacher, Nancy Holshouser, who regularly read poetry aloud in class, my seventh grade teacher, Irma Woods, Tony, Flip, Arant, and the most stupendous high school trigonometry teacher in the world, Nancy Johnston, who absolutely knew her stuff and never went through the motions. My special thanks to Tay Fizdale, Anthony Vital,

Ann Killkelly from Transylvania University. Also, from the University of Utah: Robert Caserio, Karen Lawrence, Joel Hancock, Susan Miller, David Mickelson, Francine Prose, Marina Harris; Candace Slater from UC Berkeley for her N.E.H. seminar on Amazonia, and all the other fabulous people I've encountered along the way. A very special thanks is in order to all of the staff at Mercer University Press: Marc, Marsha, Kevin, Maggy, Divina, and to Mary Frances and Jim with Burt&Burt Studio. Last and certainly not least, I feel compelled to thank my creative writing students over the last decade, all my good friends and wonderful colleagues at Virginia Commonwealth and Valdosta State University.